A DARKER SHADE OF CRIMSON

AN IVY LEAGUE MYSTERY

PAMELA THOMAS-GRAHAM

SIMON & SCHUSTER

SIMON & SCHUSTER
ROCKEFELLER CENTER
1230 AVENUE OF THE AMERICAS
NEW YORK, NY 10020

DESIGNED BY BARBARA M. BACHMAN
MANUFACTURED IN THE UNITED STATES OF AMERICA

1   2   3   4   5   6   7   8   9   10

LIBRARY OF CONGRESS CATALOGING-IN-PUBLICATION DATA
THOMAS-GRAHAM, PAMELA.
A DARKER SHADE OF CRIMSON: AN IVY LEAGUE MYSTERY /
PAMELA THOMAS-GRAHAM.
P.   CM.
I. TITLE.
PS3570. H5923D3   1998
813'.54—DC21   97-40630   CIP
ISBN 0-684-84526-1

ACKNOWLEDGMENTS

Heartfelt thanks to my friends in the Harvard community who gave me eight wonderful years to cherish and remember;

To all my McKinsey friends for their unfailing encouragement and support, including David Acorn, Tom Woodard, Jerome Vascellero, Pete Walker, Don Waite, Jon Spector, Andrew Parsons, Norman Selby, John DeVincentis, Roger Abravanel, Stacey Rauch, John Anderson, Rob Rosiello, Roger Ferguson, Nancy Killefer, Roger Kline, Bart Robinson, John Rose, Dana Norris, Marshall Lux, Helene Enright, Celeste Molina, Emilia Diez, Liz Frank, Tim Kulick, Karen Tanner, Jill Levine, Jacalyn Walsh, Todd Juenger, Doug Moser, Ed Hall, Mike Sherman, Gervase Warner, Bernard Loyd, Luis Ubinas, Liz Webster, Kim Morgan, Varsha Rao, Lauri Kein-Kotcher, Alison Fried, Christine Bucklin, Eileen Thomas, Vivian Reifberg, Richard Foster, Ennius Bergsma, Rajat Gupta, Doug Smith, Jim Tiberg, Triss Stein, Margaret Loeb, Gene Zelazny, Judy Marcus, Carmen Pagan, Brian Hoesterey, Marc Miller, Wesley Wright, Jackie Gill, Alan Miles, and all my friends in the BCSS and from CLW "Team A";

To Jan Elstub, my assistant, sounding board and friend; to Katie George, who went out of her way to give me the "inside scoop" on life as a Harvard graduate student; to Professors James Cash and Derrick Bell, true mentors and friends; to Anne and Andrew Tisch;

To Angelo Barozzi, Ron Frasch, Marty Staff, and all my friends at GFT; to my board colleagues at the New York City Opera, the American Red Cross of Greater New York, and Girls Incorporated; to Jerry Stacy and Rosina Costantino; Bob Johnson; Debra Lee;

To Lauren Tyler, Elisabeth Radow, Barbara Thomas, Kristine Langdon, Sheri Betts, Margaret Morton, Nancy Linnerooth, Melissa James, and Rosabeth Moss Kanter, women who have inspired me by keeping numerous balls in the air with unfailing poise and humor; to Leigh Bonney, for a series of splendid "girls' nights out"; to Dauna Williams, for sharing her thoughts and her laughter with me;

To Andre Owens, Bruce Wilson, Jay Ward, Gail Busby and Marguerite Gritenas, dear friends who tolerate my infrequent phone calls and somehow agree to remain; and to Betty and Richard Graham and Richard Jr., who have always made me feel like one of the family;

To my brother, Vince; my grandmother, Mattie; my aunts, Julia, Magnolia, Bessie, Frances, and Azalia; my uncles, James and Michael; all my friends at Fort Street; and my parents, Albert and Marian Thomas, whose hard work and belief in me carried me all the way to Cambridge;

To my editors, Michael Korda and Chuck Adams, who were unfailingly brilliant, charming, and insightful; to Victoria Meyer, Pam Duevel, Lynn Grady, and the terrific team at Simon & Schuster; and to Jack Horner and John Delaney at ICM, for being patient, amiable, and responsive; to David Rosenthal; Christine Saunders;

To my agent, Esther Newberg, who made truly extraordinary things happen with the utmost grace;

And most of all, to my husband, Lawrence Otis Graham, who believed in this book from the very first; who patiently weathered my bouts of doubt and euphoria; who supplied endless pots of coffee, rambling midnight walks, and a spacious room of my own; thank you, my dearest. You made the dream come true.

FOR

MY DARLING HUSBAND,

LAWRENCE OTIS GRAHAM,

WHO MAKES THE

DREAMS COME TRUE

THEN HIT THE LINE FOR HARVARD

FOR HARVARD WINS TODAY!

WE'LL SHOW THE SONS OF ELI

THAT THE CRIMSON STILL HOLDS SWAY.

SWEEP DOWN THE FIELD AGAIN,

IT'S VICTORY OR DIE!

AND WE'LL GIVE THE GRAND OLD CHEER BOYS,

WHEN THE HARVARD TEAM GOES BY.

—*Harvard Fight Song*

I WAS IN HARVARD, NOT OF IT.

—*W. E. B. Du Bois*
Class of 1890

CHAPTER ONE

DIED AND GONE TO RED BRICK HEAVEN

Laugh at their jokes. Shout when necessary. Maintain a certain distance. Dress impeccably. Know who's who. Save your money. Look them in the eye. Count to ten. Straighten your hair. Pray for strength. Plot your revenge. Have a best friend. Call home often. Keep it real. Call them out. Work the phone. Remember where you came from. And be very, very good.

Being young and black at Harvard requires advanced survival skills. Seven generations of us have found it exhilarating, perplexing, difficult, and dangerous. For Rosezella Maynette Fisher, it was murder.

The day she died was the first day of the fall semester, and word spread quickly through the campus, eclipsing stories of summer jobs, August love affairs, and the biannual ritual of course selection. The unexpected death of a Harvard Dean, especially an outspoken black woman who had bulldozed her way up from being a level-3 part-time secretary, was worth a few moments' pause in even the most harried undergraduate's life.

Ensconced in my second-story office in the Economics Department in Littauer Center, I looked down on the lush green of the Yard and the small clusters of students making their way among its narrow paths, musing about how the semester would go on inexorably, with or without her. There would be a perfunctory ceremony at Memorial Church, at which the sages of the university would offer a few kind, well-scripted words for the next morning's edition of the *Crimson*. Then the whole episode would be forgotten by most people.

But not by me.

You see, I was the last person to see her alive.

My name is Veronica Chase, Nikki to my friends. An Assistant Professor, I have the dubious distinction of being the only black member of Harvard's Economics Department. At thirty, I often feel that the mantle lies heavily on my shoulders. For a time, Rosezella Fisher made it lie heavier still.

Ella came to Harvard by way of Tunica, Mississippi, and the Letter Perfect Secretarial School, class of '67. Born in a tin-roofed wooden bungalow, the third daughter of a black itinerant sharecropper, she escaped her probable future as a washerwoman and the mother of a brood of children by hitchhiking to Memphis, then hopping a Greyhound to Boston. The year was 1965, and she was seventeen years old. Her father said she was a fool for listening to those "high yellow Negro teachers and all their college talk," but she was in search of an education beyond the black high school in town, and more than a few teachers had told her that there were plenty of schools to pick from up in Boston.

Ella fell in love with the city, with its gaslights and cobblestones, and coffee shops where you could sit and read for hours. Having grown up in the segregated South, she had never seen blacks and whites eat in the same restaurants, stand in the same lines for movies, or sit next to each other on a downtown bus. There was a marked decrease in petty indignities, a measurable increase in the level of hopefulness on the faces she passed in the street. She wrote her mother that she had died and gone to red-brick heaven. But the city's fancy colleges cost money, and a severe lack of funds diverted her to secretarial school instead.

The counterculture of the late sixties swept Ella into a revolutionary lifestyle that extinguished any lingering chance of her returning to Mississippi. Seduced by the radical fringe of the civil rights movement, and imagining herself a local version of Kathleen Cleaver, she took up for a short time with a newly formed chapter of the Black Panthers, then lived on a commune in New Hampshire. She finally emerged from bohemia in the early seventies, along with the rest of the country, and decided that it was time to prove her father wrong, once and for all, by earning her own living.

Going mainstream with a vengeance, she received her first paycheck at a temp job in the office of Kirkland House, one of Harvard's ivy-covered residential dormitories. Endearing herself to the House Master by working late hours and by charming the frequent alumni callers, she quickly landed a permanent place on his staff and in the Rolodexes of a number of wealthy alums, who could always count on her to secure the most coveted football tickets, share the most scandalous campus gossip, and sneak their children into Kirkland via the Master's reserved list after they had been assigned to a suboptimal dormitory through the housing lottery.

The secret to Ella's success was her combination of East Coast ambition and the "bowin' and scrapin' " she had learned as a child in Jim Crow Mississippi. She instinctively understood what people wanted to hear from her and how they needed to be treated. For one thing, realizing that it made her both more memorable and less threatening, Ella never dropped her deep Southern accent. Callers loved how she greeted them with a lilting "ma'am" and "suh" and "darlin'," never realizing that she had her tongue buried firmly in her cheek as she did it. All the while, she was perusing the pages of *Town and Country* and the Social Register, absorbing the fine distinctions between the Lowells, the Cabots, the Burdens, and the other well-established WASP New England families. For when it came to stroking wealthy people, she was discovering that the cliché was true: knowledge was power.

Her eleven-year stint at Kirkland ended when Harvard Law School appointed a new Dean and the call went out that he needed a new executive assistant. Ella dropped a few discreet words to her alumni network, and the favor bank swung into action. After only two rounds of interviews and a short typing test, she got the plum assignment. Although she never achieved more than thirty-five words per minute, she had other skills—including dazzling charm and a fierce protectiveness toward her handsome, fast-tracking young boss, Leonard Barrett—that quickly earned her his undying loyalty. So it shouldn't have been a complete surprise that when Leo Barrett was named President of the entire university a year ago, Ella was swept upward in the rising tide and rewarded with a high-profile new job: Dean of Students at Harvard Law School.

It *shouldn't* have been a surprise. But it was.

In her new position, Ella was responsible for overseeing course registrations, resolving disciplinary problems, and distributing funds to student organizations. The truth was that it was basically simple administrative work with fairly low pay. But the job came with an unbeatable title, and was an important stepping-stone to higher positions in university administration. With tenure at Harvard an unattainable dream for all but the most brilliant Ph.D.s, administrative jobs were highly coveted amongst the junior faculty as a way of remaining at Harvard while saving face. Any opening would have been attractive, but this job included an almost priceless perk: direct access to the President, since he often returned to his old digs at the Law School to rub shoulders with the faculty and administrators.

Not surprisingly, several upwardly mobile Ph.D.s and assistant law professors had been anxiously waiting to be tapped for such a position, so when Ella took the job at forty-six, she immediately became one of the few truly powerful and envied women at Harvard. With only a diploma from Tunica Colored High School and a secretarial school certificate, she had leapfrogged countless ambitious Ivy League scholars in a single bound.

Not surprisingly, the losers reacted with a vengeance.

Ella's appointment became a flashpoint for the entire university. Certain members of the conservative WASP elite openly derided the decision as a case of affirmative action run amok, mocking the President as a limousine liberal clearly blinded by his quest for diversity, using Ella's promotion as evidence that "political correctness" was eroding standards. Privately, even more ungenerous rumors circulated—she had gotten her job by sleeping with the President; she was blackmailing prominent Board of Overseers members with compromising photos; she was another beneficiary of the "liberal Jewish mafia" that was taking over the university. Innuendo, crafted with the care generally devoted to the footnotes of a dissertation, placed her in darkened restaurants with Barrett, in a secret ski hideaway in Vermont, in the alley behind the Cambridge Savings Bank, in open shouting matches with Barrett's wife.

Liberals, on the other hand, celebrated the appointment as a symbol of the "new Harvard," a clear statement that hard work and smarts at last counted for more than a fancy diploma. In the early days, "You go, girl," was shouted more than once by both blacks and whites as Ella strode across the Law School Quad.

Ella ignored it all, and to further the indignity, spent her first year as Dean of Students managing her office with an overbearing demeanor that made those passed over for the job grind their teeth in rage. She made the classic mistake of an inexperienced manager: assuming that instilling fear in her subordinates was the only way to gain their respect. Of course in her case, she might have been right: it wasn't as if people in the Dean's office were lining up to have a black woman tell them what to do. In any case, in that first year she was a management nightmare: a boss with strong opinions and no facts, obsessed with the trappings of her office, with no trusted adviser to set her straight. As always, money was tight— contrary to popular belief, the Law School alumni didn't tend to- ward great wealth or generosity. Sneering at the students and administrators who looked down on her, Ella seemed to take par- ticular pleasure in denying student research grants and slashing ac- tivity budgets while demanding that fresh roses and an ample supply of Danish pastries be delivered daily to her office.

By the end of her first year as Dean, lots of people hated her. They had good reason. I, however, was uncharacteristically ambivalent.

I had quickly learned about Ella's performance as Dean through the gossip circuit that thrives among the black professors and grad students, and part of me resented her before I even met her. In addi- tion to her full-time job, she had an exhaustive agenda of extracur- ricular activities, in which she played the outspoken sister-girl on campus. A darling of the recently revived Afro-American Studies Department, she was frequently seen at student association meetings and rallies, agitating for more minority hiring and loudly criticizing the light-skinned "bourgeoisie" blacks at Harvard, who had grown up rich and gone to white schools and didn't believe in unduly upsetting white people. Since that was a fairly accurate description of me, I was immediately defensive. Her favorite targets were what she called the "English dandies": two prominent black men in the university ad- ministration, both of whom had grown up poor in black communi- ties, yet had acquired British accents—and one a white wife—after arriving at Harvard.

The words "Uncle Tom" and "handkerchief head" weren't used, but we all knew where she was heading.

Now that she was moving up the Harvard hierarchy, she seemed to be thumbing her nose at the rest of us, exaggerating her "blackness" just to prove a point. Granted, most of her criticisms were spot on—but it was still maddening. Nevertheless, I knew what it meant to be different, and to have one's credibility questioned as a result. I was no stranger to accusations that the primary reason for my rapid rise in the Economics Department was that I was a black woman, and therefore "checked two boxes," and I knew how infuriating her treatment at the hands of the white Harvard elite must be. So I kept my mouth shut until the day I could meet her and form my own opinion.

The opportunity presented itself soon enough. In the spring of his first year as President, Leo Barrett decided to appoint a university-wide commission called the Crimson Future Committee to examine how the College and the university's ten graduate schools could coordinate their fund-raising efforts into the next century. It was a volatile issue, since most of the schools were flush with money, while a few, like the School of Public Health, were struggling to meet their operating budgets. The rich schools didn't want to share their endowments, and the poor were too proud to beg. A bipartisan commission seemed to be in order to resolve their differences. Ella and I were appointed as members, along with ten others. I was ostensibly named to the committee as the representative of the Graduate School of Arts and Sciences, but the truth was that I was there to do the analytical work that the lordly tenured professors wouldn't touch. I figured Ella was only there as Barrett's spy.

I'll never forget the first time I saw her. She came striding into the President's conference room in Harvard Hall for the committee's first official meeting, two hundred pounds of woman in green leather stiletto heels, with African braids dangling down to her shoulders. She had flawless dark brown skin and huge, intelligent brown eyes, and she was wearing a purple suit with a large paisley shawl, several gold necklaces and dancing gold hoop earrings. The rest of us, chatting idly in small clusters, scattered before her the way smaller animals do when a very important lion approaches the watering hole. In that moment I was convinced that at least some of the rumors could be true: as she sauntered across the room throwing off clouds of Chanel Number Five, she radiated the kind of flamboyant sexual confidence that certain men find devastating. She looked like a woman with stories it would take all night to tell, and she could easily have been leading Leo Barrett around by something other than his nose.

Over the ensuing months, I realized that many of the other rumors about her *were* wrong. Ella was curious and sharp—there was nothing simpleminded or shallow about her. She asked good questions, and didn't tolerate faulty logic. She was the only one willing to deflate the pompous speeches of the senior professors in the group, most of whom were used to pontificating at will, and she was learning to do it with such a light touch that they were left dazzled. I watched how she handled them, how she soaked up knowledge about the way the university worked, then used it to further her own causes. I even used a couple of her tricks myself, with good results. We started meeting for coffee after the committee meetings, and she had recently opened up her Rolodex for me when I needed to interview one of her alumni friends for a paper I was writing. By the end of the summer, I had come to admire her. The woman had started at the bottom of a huge bureaucracy and over the course of twenty years had wrested from Harvard everything she had ever wanted: power, prestige, and security. It was something that I had yet to do. And she had never, ever apologized for her background, her weight, or her success. The lady had balls.

And now she was dead.

"Professor Chase?" A deep, lilting voice startled me from my reverie. "Sergeant Detective Raphael Griffin. Harvard Police."

I looked up to find a dark-skinned, heavyset black man standing in the doorway of my office. His thick black hair was salted with gray, his good-natured face creased with wrinkles. He was wearing horn-rimmed glasses, a well-worn plaid sport coat, a neatly pressed white shirt, brown tie, and brown slacks, and he flashed the badge at his waistband briefly as I looked him over. "I hate to bother you, miss, but I need to ask you some questions about Miss Rosezella Fisher." From his accent, it sounded as if he was from the Caribbean.

I remembered that I had spoken briefly to a Cambridge police officer at the hospital last night, and he had said that the Harvard cops might need to talk to me today.

"Sure, come on in." I beckoned to him. We sized each other up as he walked toward me, both of us surprised and pleased to find a fellow black in our respective lines of work. "It'll have to be brief, though. I've got a class to teach in half an hour."

The wooden joints groaned in protest as he wedged himself into one of the university-issued chairs in front of my desk. "Don't you worry, this won't take too long." He looked around my office, noticing the photographs of my parents and brothers scattered across the desk and bookcases.

"Nice family you got there," he said, settling in. "That short one, there," he said, pointing at my brother Eric. "He could be the twin of my cousin Ti-Jean."

"Yeah? Where are you from?"

"Oh, Lord, no place you ever heard of, Professor Chase."

"I've heard of a lot of places. And call me Nikki."

"Well, Nikki, I was born on the island of Anegada."

I shook my head. "You've got me there."

"You know the British Virgin Islands?"

I nodded. "Vaguely. Tortola, right?"

"Yes! Well, Anegada is the smallest, the flattest, and has the prettiest girls of them all."

"Sounds like paradise," I said dryly.

"Ah, you would love it. Bougainvillea everywhere. The best coral reefs in the BVI. But we got to get to work here." He abruptly flipped open his notebook, and was suddenly all business. "Last night, you told the officer that you were working here in your office until about half past eleven yesterday?"

"That's right. I had just gotten out of a meeting in the conference room downstairs, and I was about to start working on my lecture notes for my intro economics section this morning." I'd been teaching Ec. 10 for five years—I was now the course head—but, as usual, I hadn't finalized my lecture until the last possible minute.

"Now, what was this meetin' about? And who was there?" His hand was poised expectantly over the pad. I felt bad that I didn't have anything scandalous to offer him.

"It was a meeting of the Crimson Future Committee. Have you heard of it?"

"I think I read about it in the *Crimson*. Is it the one analyzin' the funding for the university?"

"Exactly. We're supposed to come to a consensus on how to coordinate fund-raising going forward."

"Who else is on this committee?"

"There are twelve of us all together—one representative from each of the ten graduate schools, plus an undergraduate from the College, and Ian McAllister, who's the head of the Economics Department and also the chairman of the committee. Ella Fisher is—was—the Law School representative. You may have heard some of the other names before: Rona Seidman from the Business School, Asif Zakaria from the Medical School, Bob Raines from the Kennedy School."

"Sounds like herdin' cats down the street, gettin' those kind of folks to agree on anything," Griffin muttered under his breath. He finished scribbling the names into his pad, then paused and shook his head. "Two sisters on a committee full of folks like that? That's something!"

Our eyes met. "Better late than never," I said with a shrug.

"So did you all work together closely?"

"Well, Ella Fisher and I were writing the draft of the final committee report together. President Barrett is going to hold a press conference three weeks from today on the steps of University Hall to announce his fund-raising plans for the next ten years, and he'll read from our committee's report. Ella and I had been going through the university's historical income statements, because we were trying to project Harvard's funding needs for the next ten years. I built a simple model on my PC that uses the historical data to project future needs. All Ella had to do was input the past ten years' financials, and we'd know what our funding needs would be, going forward, under different scenarios. Then the committee could recommend how we were going to meet them. She was using an old set of university financials and we were supposed to get a revised set last night." I paused. "Still with me?"

He nodded. "Was everyone on the committee at the meetin' last night?"

"Yes. President Barrett even surprised us and showed up."

"What time did the meetin' end?"

"I think we broke up around eleven. We all hung around for a bit afterward talking; then I came up here to my office."

He nodded his head approvingly. "You're a hard-workin' woman, eh?" Griffin was smiling faintly as he looked at me, wearing the same proud expression that my older relatives did whenever a young black person made good.

"I do my best."

"Did everyone else leave the building at that point?"

"No. There were a lot of people hanging around in the lobby because it was raining really hard. Most of them didn't have umbrellas, so they were waiting out the storm. President Barrett and his entourage were surrounded by students asking him questions. That always happens to him. Ella Fisher needed to get the updated financial statements from Ian McAllister for the analysis she and I were working on, so we came upstairs together, and she went into his office." I remembered resenting Ian's impatient tone with her when she asked for the information. He had acted as if it was a huge inconvenience, when all we needed were some spreadsheets.

"Was this Ian McAllister with you upstairs?"

"No, he was supposed to be coming along right behind us. He said he had to talk to Barrett about something first." Typical Ian, networking like mad, even at eleven o'clock at night.

"So when did the lights go out?"

"Well, I had just turned my computer on, so it couldn't have been more than a couple of minutes."

"Whole place just suddenly went black, eh?"

I shrugged. "The lights may have blinked a couple of times. I'm not sure. I remember that just as my computer screen was lighting up, they went out completely."

"Spooked you, huh?" He grinned.

"I'm not afraid of the dark, Officer."

"I'll bet you aren't. Then what?"

"I decided I might as well go home. With the lights out, I wasn't going to get any work done. So I grabbed my lighter from my desk drawer, and started toward the stairs."

"The main spiral stairs?"

"Right. It was totally dark. Even the outside floodlights were out. I could hear people talking and shouting in the lobby. I know this building pretty well, so I followed the noise. About halfway around the first flight of stairs, my lighter went dead, so I slowed down even more. And that's when I fell over her."

"The decedent?" he asked.

Apparently, even the most plainspoken policemen love jargon. "Yes, Ella."

"What did you notice when you found her?"

I shook my head regretfully. "Not much. It was dark. Totally dark. I couldn't even see my hand in front of my face. When I tripped over her, I thought I heard a very faint cry, but there was so much commotion in the lobby I can't even be sure of that. I real-

ized someone was sprawled on the stairs, but I couldn't see anything, so I started calling for help."

"You knew who it was at that point?"

"I suppose I had some idea. She was facedown, but I could feel
thick braids under my hand. I could tell it was a large person. But
everything was happening really fast."

He nodded that I should continue.

"I felt dampness on my hands after I touched her head, a kind of
warm, sticky dampness, and I guessed it was blood. Finally someone
showed up with a flashlight, and we saw who it was. The back of
her head was covered with blood, and she seemed to be unconscious." Remembering it now, Ella had looked defeated, vulnerable,
damaged, so far removed from her usual self that it hardly seemed
possible that it was she. "I rode with her to the hospital, but they
pronounced her dead on arrival."

I realized I was talking faster and faster as I relived the experience,
and Griffin's expression was growing concerned. He took off his glasses
to inspect me more closely, and I saw that he had very kind eyes.

"You were a friend of hers?" he asked gently.

"Yes," I said slowly, really realizing the truth of it for the first
time. "I was a friend of hers."

He asked me a few more questions, I repeated the same things I'd
said the night before, then he rose and turned toward the door.

"There's something that's been bothering me, Detective Griffin,"
I said abruptly. "I'm certain that she was bleeding from the back of
her head."

He paused in the doorway, waiting for me to continue.

"I mean, what are the chances that she would have hit the *back*
of her head so severely if she tripped on the stairs and landed face
down?"

"It's possible," he answered, a shade too quickly. "She was
halfway down the stairs when you found her. Could have hit her
head two or three times on the way down."

His eyes narrowed as he looked at me. "You got some reason to
believe that it was something other than an accident, Professor
Chase?"

I shook my head. At the time, I didn't.

CHAPTER TWO

NO VISIBLE
MEANS OF
SUPPORT

"Mr. Edelstein. Help us understand Adam Smith's 'Invisible Hand,' and how it is relevant—if at all—to the U.S. economy."

Edelstein's face turned as red as his fiery head of hair as he looked first at his textbook and then at me.

"The 'Invisible Hand,'" he recited after frantically scanning his notes, "is the mechanism, if you will, by which the private interests and the passions of men are, so to speak, led in the direction which is most agreeable to the interest of the greater society."

Scattered laughter erupted across the room. I shot the culprits a dirty look and then nodded encouragingly at the anxious freshman. At least *he* had actually completed the prereading assignment.

"That's right, strictly speaking. But would you like to give it to me in English this time?"

My Monday afternoon section of Ec. 10 was identical to the morning's—the same mix of eager-to-please freshman and bored upperclassmen who seem drawn to introductory economics every year. I had talked them through my usual introduction and posted my office hours, and now we were discussing the first of the economic philosophers covered in the class.

"Well—" he stammered.

"Let's start at the beginning," I encouraged. "What was Smith trying to explain with this theory?"

"He was trying to understand why society works with no visible means of support," Edelstein said. "Why it happens that a random group of individuals somehow produces all the goods and services that they collectively need as a society."

"Right, without the church or the government getting involved and telling them what to produce," piped up a tall blond man in the back of the room.

"Well, why *is* it?" I asked, turning to the rest of the class. "How would Smith explain the fact that in his native England there was no central planning authority, no dictatorship, yet all of the tasks necessary for survival were carried out? Was it out of the goodness of people's hearts?"

"No," the blond man called out confidently. "Smith would say that everyone in society acts in his own self-interest."

"Go on, Mr. Stafford," I prompted.

"Smith would say that if everyone *does* act in his own self-interest, then they'll end up collectively producing what society needs."

"That sounds too good to be true. How can this be?"

"Because if something's *not* being produced, then society will pay a lot to anyone who *will* produce it," an Asian man spoke up. "Any market voids will be filled by self-interested people."

I scribbled the phrase "self-interest" on the board and then turned back to the class. "So being greedy is its own reward?"

"It would take a man to think up something like this," a young woman in the front row muttered under her breath.

"So far, what you're describing makes capitalism sound like a loose federation of selfish people all out for their own ends. A bit like scorpions in a bottle. But I'm not understanding how this rampant self-interest keeps society in check. Help us out here, Ms. Collins." I gestured to the woman in the front row.

"Because the other half of the theory is competition," she said, rolling her eyes. "Smith would say that if self-interest leads people to be truly greedy—overcharging for their products, or underpaying their workers—a competitor will come along and take their business."

"So the threat of competition keeps all these selfish people honest," I said, sitting on top of my desk. "It protects both the consumer and the workforce from the worst impulses of the producers."

"Exactly," Stafford echoed. "Smith would say that competition creates social harmony by ensuring that everyone has an incentive to produce what society needs in the quantity and at the price it desires."

"So, Mr. Edelstein. Back to the original question. Whether you agree with Smith or not, what insight—if any—does all of this give us into the U.S. economy?"

"Well," he said tentatively, "it explains why we have antitrust laws to preserve competition?"

"Very good!"

Edelstein flushed with pleasure.

"What else?" I appealed to the rest of the class.

"It explains why the government should stay out of the economy as much as possible," Stafford said. "And why we'd be better off with a lot less government regulation and taxation."

"What it really explains is how fat-cat capitalists can justify their own selfishness," snapped Collins.

I decided to intervene before a class war broke out. There was plenty of time for that later in the semester, when we got to Karl Marx. "We'll continue this discussion on Wednesday, when we compare this relatively benign world view with the more cynical perspective of David Ricardo. I think you'll like Ricardo, Ms. Collins. See you then."

After class, I decided to check in with Ian McAllister to see how we were going to complete our committee's work now that Ella was gone. It was almost four-thirty when I arrived at his office. Paula, his secretary, was standing by an open file drawer.

"Where's the boss?" I asked.

"You just missed him." She looked at her watch. "If you run, you might catch him. He's on his way to the airport for a trip to Washington. He's going out the front," she called after me as I raced down the hall.

I could see McAllister at the main entrance of Littauer, just heading out the door. As I approached, I was struck, as always, by his classic good looks. At six feet four, with patrician bearing, meticulously groomed silver hair, a deep bass voice, and a complexion ruddy from weekends sailing in Edgartown, he was the *ancien régime* of Harvard personified. In his impeccably tailored dark blue suit, white shirt, and rep tie, he looked ten years younger than his impending fifty-sixth birthday would imply. Anyone who didn't know better would have thought that he was the university President, not just the head of the Economics Department.

I called out and he turned impatiently. Then his expression softened. "Hey, champ!"

"Listen, I know you've got a plane to catch," I said quickly. "Let me walk with you to your car and maybe we can spend a few minutes talking about the Crimson Future Committee and the New Century press conference."

Ian and I had a complicated relationship. I had known him since I was a sophomore in college, and through the years he had been teacher, mentor, and tormentor, usually all at once. Now, as the chairman of my department, he held my career in his well-manicured hands: I had a one-in-twenty chance of getting tenure five years hence, and his support would be critical. Ian was brilliant and moody, arrogant and urbane, and I had learned years ago that my success was going to be contingent on understanding him extremely well and behaving accordingly. That meant skipping the niceties and getting straight to the point (unless he felt like chatting, of course); laughing at his jokes and reassuring him as needed; being grateful, but not sycophantic. Managing my relationship with him felt a lot like playing the doting wife, or perhaps the consummate courtesan.

"So." He turned to me as we started down the broad stone stairs of Littauer. "How was the rest of your summer? I haven't seen you since the July committee meeting."

So we were in bantering mode today. "It was great. Spent most of it working on the new course I'll be teaching in the spring, but we made some progress on the Future Committee report, too. How was Martha's Vineyard?"

"Excellent," he said, looking highly satisfied with himself. "Connie is still out there with the girls."

"I guess you heard about Ella Fisher," I said as we approached Mass Ave.

"Yes, it was a bit of a shock, wasn't it?" he said dismissively. "But what kind of idiot tries to walk down a spiral staircase in high heels during a blackout? This is the caliber of person that our great President, Leo Barrett, foists off on us?"

I bit my tongue and let the comment pass. This was exactly the kind of thing that made me feel like a whore for devoting most of my waking hours to this man. Not only was I insulted as a black woman, *and* as a person who had also tried to come down those same stairs in the darkness in high heels of my own, but I was one of Leo Barrett's strongest supporters, and Ian knew it. I watched his expression out of the corner of my eye. Ian was always confident, but today he seemed positively *smug*, as if he had just successfully negotiated a great deal. Maybe the stock market was up this morning.

"With Ella gone, we're shorthanded on finishing our final committee report," I continued. "I've been thinking about how we can get it done in time for the New Century press conference, and the best solution could be to—"

We had reached Mass Ave, where I assumed he would either hail a cab or pick up his car from the faculty lot. Instead, we stopped in front of a sleek black stretch limousine. A uniformed driver emerged from the front seat.

"Hello, sir." The red-headed, pink-cheeked chauffeur looked all of twenty.

"Frank, you'll have to take the back roads or we won't make it," Ian warned sternly. "Next time, meet me at the door."

Frank took the overnight bag from Ian, and McAllister turned to me, smiling again. "Ride with me to the airport. Frank will bring you back, and that way we can discuss this press conference. 'New Century'—what a name," he muttered under his breath.

Certain that I would comply, he nodded at his driver to get the door. As Frank hurried to my side, I marveled that an economics professor—even one with an endowed chair—could have parlayed a Ph.D. into such a lifestyle. Since when did Harvard professors, even department heads, have stretch limos and private drivers? McAllister had just been named to the Board of the Harvard Management Corporation, which managed the university's endowment. That appointment, combined with his outside consulting work and lecture fees, must really be paying off.

With Frank at my elbow, I climbed into the limousine, and was immediately transported back to my investment banking days in New York. The dim, lush interior was dark blue, with small yellow lights near the doors and windows. A bar ran along one side of the passenger compartment, complete with crystal glasses. I could also see a television, a telephone, and what appeared to be a fax machine in the far corner. Out of habit, I slid over to one of the seats facing backward. Riding backward nauseates me, but the jump seat is where the most junior person sits. That's how it was on Wall Street, and I was certain that those rules would apply here.

Ian climbed in after me, and settled into what was clearly his rightful seat: facing forward, close to the telephone.

"Sir, shall I tune in to the news?" Frank asked.

"No, we've got work to do. Put in the Schumann CD." Frank complied, and a soft stream of music filled the space. "Let's get going," Ian commanded. "I'm not missing this flight."

Ian turned to me as the car pulled out. "Now, you were talking about the press conference."

"I think the best plan for this week is for me to work with Rona Seidman to get the draft report done." Rona was the Business School representative to the Crimson Future Committee. "She worked on and off with Ella and me over the summer, and I can bring her up to speed pretty quickly. We can present a preliminary version at our meeting next Monday, then the group can sign off on it before it goes to Leo the following week."

"Do you have the time to make sure it's accurate?"

"It's going to be tough."

The ring of the telephone interrupted him before he could reply. "McAllister," he answered. A silence ensued, and then he barked, "Fine, Paula. Put him on."

There was a brief pause, and then Ian snapped, "What's the problem now, Feldman?" He frowned into the phone for a moment, then growled, "Look. I told you, we're jamming this through. Let the SEC deal with it later." Another pause, then he huffed, "I don't give a damn what the Herfendahl index is. We both know that's just one measure of antitrust implications. That's why I'm on the Board. Because there are plenty of other ways to measure economic impact. Don't whine, Feldman! It's unbecoming. Put my secretary back on the line.

"Damn lawyers," he muttered impatiently under his breath.

Ian must be advising on another merger. He'd managed to create a lucrative sideline serving on corporate boards, particularly those who were about to stretch the limits of commercial law and needed a Harvard economist to justify their actions. I watched him closely while he ticked off a couple of brisk commands to his assistant. Something good had definitely happened to him—now that Feldman was off the line, he was practically humming under his breath.

"Now, you were saying, Nikki?" he said as he hung up the telephone.

"Just that it's going to be a bit of a scramble to get this report finished." My plan was to get him to name a new person to the committee. There was no way that I could do all this work on my own.

"Well, maybe we need to get you some help."

"That's not a bad idea," I concurred. "But how are we going to find anybody this quickly?"

"I'll take care of it."

"Will Leo need to be involved?" I asked.

"Why would we need him? *I'm* the Chair," he responded brusquely. Apparently his mood wasn't so benign that the rivalry between himself and Leo Barrett couldn't dampen it. It was no secret that McAllister aspired to be President himself, and there were those among the faculty who still held out hope that he eventually would be. There was just the small matter of what to do about Leo.

"Leave it to Leo Barrett," he continued, "and we'll end up stuck with a Native American Jew with a Spanish surname in a wheelchair, just to satisfy his itch for 'diversity.' We'll have to move quickly before the special interests start to circle their wagons."

That was a bit much, even for a handkerchief head like me. "Ian, there's nothing wrong with having a group that reflects different views," I said sharply. "Or are you afraid of a little healthy debate?"

We knew each other well enough that he immediately realized he had gone too far.

"Of course, I meant no harm, Veronica," he said gruffly. "I take your point. In the meantime, here's the information that Ella Fisher was pestering me for. I was supposed to give it to her last night." He extracted a computer disk and a small sheaf of spreadsheets from his briefcase and handed them to me. "These are the numbers we pieced together on the university's finances for the past ten years, broken out by school and by major category. I don't know why we don't have better financial systems in place, but Barrett and I had to pull these together ourselves. So now you can get to work analyzing them."

Great.

"And while I'm gone, there are a few other things I need your help on."

"Sure," I said, stifling an impatient sigh. When was I going to be senior enough to stop playing bag-carrier for this man? It had grated on my nerves when I was a doctoral candidate, and now that I was an assistant professor, it was nearly intolerable. I dug a pad of paper out of my backpack and waited expectantly.

"My speech for that conference down at Princeton has to be submitted by Friday, so you need to finish those last charts we discussed."

"Right."

"The *Times* wants me to write a piece on direct foreign investment. Why don't you try to draft something and I'll review it when I get back? And call Paula and tell her that you're coming with me to talk to Harris at Polaroid about the consulting project he mentioned. It's chump change, but every little bit helps, right?"

I scribbled furiously for a moment, then looked up to see him pouring a Diet Coke for himself. "Oh, and Davis and I have our heads together over the next meeting of the assistant professors' review committee. I'll let you know how it goes."

Lest we forget who has the power in this relationship.

"So what takes you to DC?" I asked. It seemed best to change the subject.

"I'm speaking at an RNC fund-raiser tonight—five thousand dollars a plate."

"Gearing up for next year?" I asked cheerfully. I'm a rock-solid labor-side Democrat, always have been, but I learned early in my acquaintance with McAllister to keep that part of my life under wraps. He is a stalwart member of the Republican National Committee, and extremely impatient with bleeding hearts.

"The presidency will be no contest. It's the congressional races that will be most interesting."

We discussed politics until Frank came to a screeching halt in front of the Delta terminal. I watched longingly through the back window as Ian disappeared through its glass doors, wishing I could fly away, too. The man had just managed to dump his entire workload for the week onto my shoulders.

Maybe *that* was why he was in such a good mood.

CHAPTER THREE

THE REPUBLIC
OF TEA

After Frank dropped me off at Littauer, I debated going back
to my office to put in a few more hours on a paper I was writing for
the upcoming American Economic Association meetings, but I was
still emotionally exhausted from the late hours at the hospital the
night before and decided that what I really needed was an early
night.

High fives, brotherly handshakes, and wild embraces dotted the
Yard as students reunited with each other after the summer break.
I agreed with them. Thank God it was finally over. Except for the
annual Fourth of July escape to Oak Bluffs, the summer stinks.
Swimsuits designed to fit hipless waifs. The cellulite war. Sweating
after a fifteen minute walk to my office. Multilegged insects in
places they don't belong. The campus deserted and lonely and suffused with ennui.

The summer just past had been particularly bad. Having broken
up with boyfriend number twelve over Memorial Day weekend, I
had spent the ensuing three months holed up in the library writing
materials for a new economics course that I was developing, and
moping. For six months I had been dating Roger, a black man here-
after to be known as His Highness. He was a certified member of
what Ella would have called the "light bright set": father a surgeon,
mother a professor at Georgetown, whole family with skin the color
of lightly baked bread, green eyes and straight hair. He was a sec-
ond-year student at Harvard Business School in search of a fair-
skinned black woman to parade around at parties, having himself
just split up with his longtime girlfriend. Of course I was familiar
with the word "rebound," but feeling adored and having regular sex
brightened my mood to the extent that I actually believed it would
last, and visions of marriage and an air-conditioned summer house

31

in Sag Harbor began to dance in my head. And last it did, until the night when, drunk on Dewar's and self-pity, His Highness turned to me and announced, "What the hell. Let's get married." That was when it dawned on me that perhaps this wasn't a great love affair after all, that there had to be at least one other brilliant, handsome single man in the world, and that with any luck he would turn up at Harvard sometime soon. Three months later I was fighting low-grade panic about being single the rest of my life and eagerly searching the faces of the new arrivals on campus.

The sun was just beginning to set as I turned the corner onto my block; the brilliance of the day had given way to a liquid golden light that filtered down through the weathered trees lining the narrow one-way street. A cluster of children played softball in the street under the watchful eyes of mothers scattered along the wooden porches that protruded from every house.

I live as many students and junior faculty at Harvard do: at the top of an old wood-frame house in Cambridge. The town is full of them: former single-family houses that now hold several tenants. The homes were stately when they were built in the 1920s, but the twentieth century has taken its toll, and now they are shabby and worn. The expressions that they present to passersby seem somewhat sheepish, like that of an elderly aunt who has come down in the world.

My house, which was once a brilliant blue but is now covered with shards of bluish-gray paint, has a set of crumbling stone stairs leading up to a narrow wooden porch. The dilapidated exterior belies the gracious home inside. My landlady lives on the ground floor; on the second floor there is a large, two-bedroom apartment, which until last month had been occupied by a visiting physicist and his wife. The two lower floors have been lovingly restored, with bright white walls and gleaming hardwood floors. When there's enough money in the coffer, I expect that the exterior of the house will receive its own facelift.

My apartment is the top floor, which somehow escaped renovation and retains its original somewhat seedy character. Dark, narrow stairs lead up to a small space in the eaves that holds a living room, one bedroom, a kitchen, a bath, and an impossible dampness in spring. I've covered the dark floors with brightly colored rugs and runners, and an occasional scrubbing of the windows admits sufficient light for a few plants in each room. My furniture is early American graduate student: an old sofa from home, an end table scavenged years ago from an abandoned stack on the street, a kitchen table and chairs that were left by the previous tenant, and my treat to myself, a rocking chair with a blanket to curl up in. Occasionally the place seems shabby and confining, but mostly it feels warm and safe.

I'd been wanting to live this way my whole life: in a place with character, pointed toward the future. Growing up in Detroit, I had long dreamed of escaping that dying city's burned-out buildings and abandoned storefronts. I'd spent my childhood on a tree-lined street in one of the few remaining upper-middle-class enclaves within the city limits, but all around us were the signs of a metropolis brought low by neglect and riots and despair. The color line had been dug so deeply between the city and the suburbs that it might as well have been Johannesburg. Cambridge, to me, was the promised land. With a bit of residual guilt, I skipped town for the East Coast at eighteen and have never looked back.

After I landed in the top five percent of my class, Harvard offered me a generous scholarship to pursue a Ph.D. in Economics. But I succumbed to the siren song of Commerce instead, opting for an M.B.A. from Harvard Business School and then a job in New York City at the most prestigious of the Wall Street investment banks. After two years of swigging antacid straight from the bottle to deal with the stress induced by long days, the demands of impatient clients, and the machinations of neurotic partners, I fled back to Cambridge and into the waiting arms of the Economics Department and this charming, dusty old house on Shepard Street. For the past four years, for four hundred dollars a month, I've had the alcove of my dreams and a landlady-*cum*-confidante to welcome me home every night.

"Nikki!" a smoky voice summoned as I sorted through the mail piled on the table in the entryway—bills, catalogs, a letter from my little brother. "You're early! But I've got the hot water going."

I stashed the mail in my bag and made my way through the cluttered hallway, stepping around a bicycle and over the piles of books on the floor, finally arriving in the kitchen where Magnolia Dailey held court at the end of every day.

"Now if I were to trip and break my neck in that hallway—" I grumbled, leaning over to kiss her cheek.

"I'd tell you to pick your feet up and remind you that I've got no insurance. What's it doing out there now?"

"It's nice," I said, bending over to pat Horace's sleek head. The black Labrador smiled sleepily up at me from his place at Maggie's feet. "Not as humid as it was this morning. My hair isn't doing anything goofy, is it?"

"Girl, I told you if you'd quit relaxing it and wear an Afro like the rest of us, you wouldn't be asking me such white-girl questions."

"Like the rest of us?" I felt the need to remind her that the sixties were long gone and she was about the only woman I knew still wearing an eight-inch Afro.

"So how were your kids today?"

"Same as always," I said, glancing at today's wardrobe: a kente-cloth tunic, long strings of beads, and black, wide-legged pants. African Queen all the way. "They were scared, ambitious, and probably a little surprised to see my black face. My first question was what they hoped to get out of introductory economics."

"How original. Let me guess," she said, pouring herself a cup of herbal tea from a flowered ceramic pot on the table. "Sixty percent of them are poor kids who want to go to B-School and end up rich; twenty percent are there because they want a class that meets after ten A.M.; the other ten percent are wealthy Republicans who need to learn how to hold on to their money so they can screw the rest of us."

"Aren't we bitter, Miss English Major?" I reached up for a mug from one of the well-worn white cabinets. "Just so you know, that doesn't add up to one hundred percent."

"I allowed for a ten percent absentee ratio. You have to underestimate, since it's only the first day of class."

I settled into a chair across the round kitchen table as Maggie filled my mug.

"Well, Sister Professor, I was gonna share some good news," she said, "but your face looks like you just lost your best friend. What's up?"

"I guess it didn't hit the morning papers." I filled her in on the events of last night and Ella's death, but kept to myself my doubts about whether it was really an accident. It would only worry her.

"That's a damn shame," Maggie said softly. She shook her head. "Although you know how I felt about that appointment from the get-go. The girl didn't even have a college degree. Sure bet the only reason she got that job was because that Leo Barrett had to keep her happy."

"What does *that* mean?"

"Girl, unless she had some kind of dirt on him or was sleeping with him, there is no *way* she would've gotten that job! He's so slick, there's no telling which one it was. Everybody knows that man will do anything for a piece of—"

"Maggie!" I interrupted. "What's up with you and Leo Barrett? Everytime I mention his name you go off on him."

"I'll tell you my problem with him. You seen the *Crimson* today?"

I shook my head.

"Well, have a look." She slid the paper across to me, and I saw a huge photograph of Leo underneath the caption "An A+ Freshman Year." The first line of the piece gushed that his first year as President had been highly successful, a breath of fresh air after his predecessor. The article went on to profile his personal background and recent accomplishments.

"That's some big, wet kiss," I commented, skimming the rest of the article. Maggie snorted. "So what's your problem?"

"I don't like him," she snapped.

"Well, that's obvious. But why? He's young and smart, and he's doing great things for the students." He was also extremely attractive, which wasn't hurting his popularity in certain quarters.

She sighed impatiently. "This article is going on and on about how 'diverse' his appointments have been, how he's changing the face of the university."

"Well, he has. *Four* women got tenure this year, remember?"

"Yeah? Well how come he hasn't named any female department heads? Or better yet, made a woman Dean of one of the graduate schools? And how many black folks has he advanced?"

"Come on, he promoted Ella, and he put both of us on the Crimson Future Committee."

"I've already told you what I think of him and Ella. And no offense, darlin', but it's not like the man got you *tenure* or anything!"

Diversity was clearly in the eye of the beholder. In Ian McAllister's world, advancing two blacks and four women in a single year made Leo practically a Communist.

"If he can't do something like a little committee appointment for a safe, company girl like *you*—who just happened to graduate in the top five percent of her undergraduate class—what black *is* he going to do something for?" Maggie continued. "This way, he can point to you and prove to everybody that he's—what did that article say?—a 'true progressive.' "

"What do you mean, 'company girl'?"

"No offense, darlin', but it's not like you're the type who's going to get in his face."

"Hey," I said sharply, "just because I pick my battles doesn't mean I'm a pushover. I'll get in his face if I need to. But I think you're being too hard on him. It's only his first year, Maggie."

"I don't care what you say. You mark my words. Miss Ella Fisher had to have something on Leo Barrett to get that Dean's job. Harvard has never been *that* egalitarian."

I started to defend Ella and her ability to do her job, but the look in Maggie's eyes stopped me. I knew she was remembering her own tenure review thirty years ago.

"They weren't fair to you, Maggie. They really weren't."

"Yes, my sister, I know that. I was smarter than any of those idiots. You know I had to be, getting admitted into the Harvard Graduate School of Arts and Sciences in '59."

This was a story that I had heard before, but I let her tell it again. It made both of us righteously angry, and that gave us courage to face the world outside the front door.

"I still don't know why I didn't just go to Spelman like my father told me. The President there read one of my poems and he said it made him cry. Made him *cry*, do you hear me? But no, it had to be Harvard. Had to be the best. Had to go up North where the white folks could validate my intelligence. And they kept me around so they could validate it, all right. Boy, did they ever. Kept me teaching and writing for almost twelve years so they could take credit for having a Negro faculty member. I was flying all over the world, lecturing and publishing. But all they cared about was parading me out when the press came to campus during the riots. And didn't they just make sure I was kept out of their club when it came time to making the big decision? I remember it like it was yesterday."

Maggie paused as she stood over the sink, rinsing lettuce in preparation for dinner. "That sorry little tenure review committee was all up in my face, so sweet: 'Happy to keep you on in your

Associate position. With no expectation of tenure.' And then, almost thirty years later, those S.O.B.s give somebody like *that* a Dean's job."

"It's not fair," I repeated, wishing I had the words to make her feel better. "But Ella Fisher really knew how to play their game. Girlfriend had the President of the Massachusetts National Bank calling the President to get her that job."

"No she didn't!"

I nodded. "It's true."

"Well, I never would—and never will—get ahead like that. Calling them 'ma'am' and 'sir' and saying 'may I' and 'could you.' I'll be damned if I will!"

"I hear you."

Maggie paused again, pensively patting the lettuce leaves dry. "But she sure didn't deserve to die over it. Lord have mercy."

"Do you regret it, Maggie? I mean, not playing the game?"

"I'd rather starve than kiss anybody's butt. I live the way I please, on my own terms."

"So why didn't you just leave Cambridge and go get tenure somewhere else? There must have been plenty of places that would have been thrilled to have you."

"Girl, no prestige white school was ready for a tenured black woman professor in '64. Most of 'em were just getting used to having black *students*. And I didn't want to go down South to one of our own schools, with all the mess that was going on down there then. Hell, they were still lynching us for looking at 'em too hard. You can imagine what they woulda done to *me*. Besides, I loved Cambridge. This place was my home." She paused. "Now, don't you start feeling sorry for me. Old Cambridge Rindge & Latin School starts to grow on you after a while, and those kids need me."

We sat for a moment in sisterly silence. "Hey," I interrupted the quiet, "so what's your big news, anyway?"

Maggie regarded me skeptically. "Well, it isn't diddly squat compared to yours. But I've found two new tenants for the second floor."

"That's great!" I leaned over to refill my mug. Whatever this stuff was, it actually wasn't bad if you drank it fast enough. "Who are they?"

"Two white boys. One's junior faculty at Harvard, and the other one's a lawyer at a clinic in Roxbury."

"Are they friends or lovers?" I asked. "Not that it matters."

"They're definitely not gay. One of them had a lady friend along when they came by to sign the lease. She was hangin' all over the boy. You'll be happy to have them around—neither one of them is too hard on the eyes. The dark-haired one has a nice butt."

I couldn't help laughing. "Your Wesley Snipes calendar just isn't enough anymore, eh? Do these pinups have names?"

"Down, my sister," she said with a laugh. "Let's see—the dark-haired one is Dante, and the blond one is Ted," she said. "Dante Rosario and Ted Adair."

I coughed and swallowed hard. *Good Lord. He's back.*

"What's the matter with you? I know you can't be getting indigestion from my tea." She peered more closely at my face and her tone softened. "Do you know these boys?"

Did I know these boys? Not anymore. Once I knew one of them very well indeed.

"If he's who I think he is—and I seriously doubt there are two Dante Rosarios in the world—then I went to college with him. I'm just surprised to hear his name after all this time." I checked my heart rate to see if it had slowed. It hadn't. "When are they moving in?"

"Tomorrow. But they're coming by tonight for dinner, at seven o'clock. Why don't you stay? He'll probably be glad to see a familiar face."

"Sorry," I said, quickly gathering up my bag and jacket. "I've got a ton of work to do tonight, and then I'm going to curl up with John Maynard Keynes."

"All right," she said, looking disappointed. "I'll make your apologies. Tell the furball I said 'hey.' "

Keynes is my cat, my analyst, and occasionally the bane of my existence. He graciously deigns to share my apartment with me so long as I keep it well-stocked with cat tchotchkes and tuna treats.

I climbed the stairs with a sense of impending doom. First Ella Fisher's death, and now the return of Dante Rosario.

What next—Armageddon?

CHAPTER FOUR

DOWN BY LAW

"Gwen, what did they say?"

"They have no idea where he is, and he hasn't been calling in for messages."

Damn.

Tuesday morning found me in my office cursing at my secretary and at the computer disk Ian McAllister had given me the day before. It was supposed to have all the information I needed to model out the funding streams from the various schools for the final Crimson Future report. And it was coming back with a "disk error" message. I had tried it on the laptop down the hall, and still no luck. So it wasn't my computer. Of course, I could have used the hard copy that Ian had given me. But who had time to work on paper?

"When is Paula coming back?"

Gwen looked up from her computer. "She's got the flu, and they have no idea."

"All right, I'm going to have to go to Ella Fisher's and see if she had another copy. Get her office address, will you?"

I knew that Ella had an old version of the university financials that she had gotten from one of her friends in the bowels of the Treasurer's office. He was one of her "Underground Railroad" contacts, part of the invisible network of people that helped her understand how the university really worked. I had seen the old set of financials briefly, even though she hadn't yet shared them with the rest of the committee, and I knew she kept them stored either on a disk or on her computer. If I could find the old set, it would at least be faster to compare it to the new version than to type twenty new pages of numbers into my computer.

A quick check of the Harvard directory revealed that Ella's office was on the third floor of Langdell Hall, a stately, ivy-covered sandstone building that houses the Law School library and several classrooms of the type immortalized in *The Paper Chase:* large crescent-shaped auditoriums that angle downward to a podium presided over by an alarming Harvard professor. Of course now the horrific figure was as likely to be a slim young woman as a balding old man, but the premise of Socratic questioning directed at impressionable young minds still held, at least for the first-year students. I have my own theory of jurisprudence, which is that people obey laws that make sense and break the ones that don't, which is why we all obey red, yellow, and green traffic signals, but refuse to follow the "no right turn on red" rule when there's no traffic coming anyway.

I passed several clusters of students laughing and sunning themselves in the Law School Quad as I approached Langdell's imposing bulk. It was a warm day, but the trees that lined the pathway were already faintly tinged with red and orange, and the air was full of the promise of a new semester. I still wonder sometimes if I did the right thing pursuing a Ph.D. instead of sticking it out on Wall Street. The way the market was moving, the four years I'd just spent tracking down theories of developmental economics and pinching pennies would have yielded huge dividends—the type these newly minted lawyers would be seeing soon if they played their cards right.

I walked up the shallow steps of the building's main entrance and crossed the atrium at the center of the building. The staircase to the third floor was lined with portraits of former professors and large donors, a severe and humorless group. At the top of the stairs, I turned down a darkened hallway, passing the office doors of professors that I had read about in the *Times* and the *Globe*. The interior of the building was curiously spartan, in contrast to its grand exterior. Perhaps dark carpeting, institutional beige walls, and lack of sunlight foster great legal thinking. Ella's office was at the end of the corridor. I could hear a breathy, girlish voice talking to someone as I approached.

"Yes, Mother, that *was* my boss. It's so upsetting, and so incredible! To think that someone I know, personally, is dead; I just can't believe it! No, I haven't heard from a single family member yet. What?" The voice dropped to a whisper. "Working class, certainly . . . But she was actually *quite* nice . . . From someplace in the South . . . No, I think Alabama, it was one of those really poor states . . . That's true. They *are* all over the place now."

I shook my head, mentally trying to conjure up a face that could accompany this voice and this conversation. I saw as I turned the corner into the office that the culprit was a startlingly beautiful, ethe-real blond girl with milky white skin, in her early twenties. With the aid of her large, expressive blue eyes she was emoting breathlessly into the receiver of her telephone. "Yes, it is appalling," she nodded vehemently as she adjusted the collar of the white turtleneck that peeked out of her gray-and-pink Fair Isle sweater.

Good Lord, I thought. Someone actually does still buy clothes from the Talbots.

"Mother, I meant to mention it before, but I need to borrow some money from you," she said airily. "The Jaguar broke down again, and they say it will cost big money this time. Something to do with the valves. Well, I *told* you we should have traded it in when the warranty expired, but you wouldn't listen! They say it will be at least five thousand . . . *dollars*, not *pesos*. Very funny!"

As I watched her twirl strands of shoulder-length blond hair around her finger, it occurred to me that she still hadn't noticed my presence. I cleared my throat.

"Oh my." She turned and waved me closer. "Mother? I have to go. I'll get it from you tonight. Yes. Yes, I know, you're sitting down promptly at eight. Another one?" Her voice went up another oc-tave as she rolled her eyes. "You have to stop setting me up with these men! I mean it. I'll see you tonight."

She sighed as she swiveled around in her chair to greet me. "My mother. I'm sorry. Can I help you with something?"

"I hope so. I'm Veronica Chase. I worked with Ella on the Crim-son Future Committee."

"Oh!" she exclaimed. "Sure, I recognize your name. Aren't you the one who . . . who *found* her?"

"Yes, I am."

"The only reason I know is because President Barrett came by yes-terday briefly, just to let us all know what happened. It was so won-derful of him to take the time to do it personally. Isn't it just *awful?*" Her face flushed pink and her eyes began to brim with tears.

I looked down to give her some privacy.

"Gosh, I'm being rude," she said, hastily recovering her poise. "I'm Ella's—I mean Dean Fisher's—assistant, Lindsey Wentworth." She rose and extended her hand and I realized that she was very small. I'm average height, and I felt as if I were towering over her. She *and* her pink corduroy skirt.

"This must be hard for you," I said sympathetically.

"I think we're all still in a state of shock." She sighed heavily. "I just can't believe it. I said good-bye to her Friday and now . . ." She dabbed at her eyes and turned slightly away.

"Have you been working for Ella long?"

She nodded vigorously. "A little over a year. Ever since I graduated from Wellesley. My parents think it's crazy for me to be using a degree in Romance Languages from a Seven Sisters college for something as menial as this, but it's been such a learning experience! Much better than one of those Sotheby's internships. I really needed to discover the real world, and I certainly wasn't going to do that putting price tags on Louis XIV furniture. If you know what I mean." She was talking quickly to fight back her tears. I wanted to offer her a Kleenex, but I thought it might embarrass her.

"Wellesley," I repeated lightly. How many times had a Harvard man deserted me or one of my girlfriends to go to parties there? "I hear the social life is fabulous."

That coaxed a smile from her. "Oh, you don't know the half of it. Everything about our school is fabulous. Everything. Not only was I the *chef d'équipe* of the equestrian team, but I was also President of ZA for two years. We co-sponsored the first intersociety Sadie Hawkins dance. It was magical. Truly magical. And I must say that every formal party we ever gave outclassed Tizzie. But of course, that's not why I went there."

She turned to face me and her expression took on new animation. "It was just so exciting to be in an atmosphere controlled by intelligent women. And working here with Ella just reinforced that for me. She was so strong! And so very bright."

Her voice was growing stronger, and it appeared that she might go on forever now that she had her emotions back under control. I decided it was time to get on with the business of the day before she launched into another round of Wellesley-speak.

"Lindsey, I'm hoping that you can help me with something. Ella and I were working on the final report for the Crimson Future Committee and she had some information that I need, hopefully either on her computer or saved on a disk. Mind if I look around in her office to see if I can find it?"

"I suppose that would be all right. I'll come and show you where things are. I haven't been in there since . . . you know."

Lindsey turned on the ceiling light as I surveyed the terrain. Ella's office was filled with heavy, Harvard-issued furniture. A large wooden desk was flanked by two uncomfortable-looking high-backed wooden chairs. One wall was covered with built-in book-cases. A computer was placed on a small metal table with a shelf running underneath it.

"Here's where she kept most of her disks," Lindsey said, gesturing toward the shelf underneath the computer table. "You're welcome to see if what you're looking for is there. If it's not, it may be in one of the desk drawers. As a rule, she wasn't very organized."

"And if I don't find a disk, is there a file on her computer that has the work for the Crimson Future Committee?"

"Yes. I'll get it up on the screen for you." She booted up the computer and then clicked on a file entitled "Crimson Future."

"This should be everything," she burbled, apparently in better spirits now that she was able to focus on a specific task. "I managed her computer files, so they're a lot more orderly."

"Great. Then I'll get to work." As I began to rummage through the disks on the storage shelf, Lindsey perched on top of Ella's desk.

"God, it's so strange to be here without her," she said softly. I glanced over my shoulder and saw that I had been mistaken about her brightening mood. Tears were welling up in her eyes again.

"I can imagine," I said. There were about thirty disks, but so far, none appeared to have anything to do with the Future Committee.

"So what was it like when you found her? Was she—did she—"

"Did she suffer?" I rifled quickly through the disks, pausing once to look up in sympathy. I knew I was being horribly rude, but I really needed to get to work on that report. Ian would kill me if I hadn't made progress by the time he returned. "To be honest, I really can't tell you. She seemed to be unconscious when I found her. But there was so much commotion, it was hard to be sure." Where *was* that disk?

"They said that the lights had gone out?"

"Yes," I said distractedly. "That's why she was coming down the stairs, and why there was such pandemonium. The storm blew out the electricity, and we were all trying to make our way out of the building."

"Were there really that many people? I would have thought it would be deserted at that hour."

"Well," I said, turning to survey the rest of the office, "you know we had that Crimson Future Committee meeting, and most of the members were still in the lobby, waiting out the storm. Plus, there were some students, and since Barrett and his entourage were there, none of the students would leave." Maybe in one of the desk drawers?

"Did she scream when she fell? I mean, did anyone hear it happen?"

I paused for a moment. "I don't know. I didn't hear anything, but as I said, there was a lot of noise and confusion in the lobby." But it was a good question. Why *hadn't* anyone heard her scream?

The phone on Ella's desk rang loudly, and Lindsey jumped. "I'll get that. I'll take it outside, so I won't disturb you."

With Lindsey gone, I was finally free to focus on my search. With nothing useful on the computer shelf, I tried her hard drive next. But a quick scan of the files in the Crimson Future folder brought up nothing helpful. She had a lot of memos about upcoming meetings, a few typed requests for information. But no spreadsheets of any type, which was strange, because I knew she had been working off of an old version of the financials to do some preliminary analysis. I had seen the printouts of what she had done. So where were the spreadsheets?

I turned to the top of her desk. Papers everywhere. Maybe Ella kept the analysis on a disk and it was lost in one of these piles. Lindsey had said she was disorganized, and the state of her desktop bore that out. It was covered with random stacks of files, as if she had walked away in the middle of four or five different projects. She must have been working Sunday night before the Future Committee meeting. I found one stack with old Future Committee documents. But still no sign of a disk.

I was momentarily distracted by the silver picture frames at the far corner of her desk. One held a tattered black and white photograph of a man and woman in front of what looked like an old general store. They were standing in the middle of a dirt road, squinting at the camera in a haze of fierce sunlight. They looked a lot like Ella. Must be her parents. I wondered if they were still alive. The second picture was more recent: Ella and a younger woman with strawberry blond hair smiled engagingly from the porch of what appeared to be a summer house. The other person looked strangely familiar, but I couldn't figure out why. Ella's eyes were glowing, and she seemed utterly content. The last frame held another black and white shot, this one of Eleanor Roosevelt surrounded by a group of small black children. She was bending toward them with a look of forthright compassion, and they gazed up at her with curiosity and trust. I felt the unexpected pricking of tears behind my own eyes. What did that picture mean to Ella? And why was she gone before I had the chance to ask her?

I saw her again, crumpled on the staircase. Most likely the victim of a silly, tragic accident. So why couldn't I get that head wound out of my mind? And why *hadn't* there been a loud scream as she fell? Was it because she was already unconscious?

If it wasn't an accident, then someone had wanted her dead. Wanted it badly enough to risk killing her in a building full of people. But who would do that? Ella was a middle-aged administrative dean—what could she have possibly done to inspire such enmity?

I glanced over my shoulder at the open office door. Lindsey was chattering into the phone. So I had a clear shot at poking around. It couldn't hurt, and I needed to look for that disk anyway. Impulsively, I turned to Ella's desk drawers. If Lindsey came back, I'd say I was still looking for the disk.

I wasn't sure what I was looking for, but I found nothing of interest on my first try. Ella's top right drawer was filled with yellow legal pads, pens and pencils, yellow markers, loose change, and chewed pen tops. There was a calculator and an unopened ream of computer paper in the second drawer. The bottom right drawer held two pairs of shoes, one black and one brown, an extra pair of chocolate brown pantyhose—size D—a curling iron, and a box of tampons. I'm convinced that every working woman in the world has one desk drawer like that, be she CEO or mail clerk.

The drawers on the left side were equally useless. Files from various projects and student organizations. A small tape recorder with no tape. Souvenirs of her professional and social life: matchbooks from the Faculty Club and various restaurants and dance clubs around Boston, programs from lectures and plays. Idly, I opened one, and saw a name circled: Alix Coyle. *That* was why the woman in the photograph looked so familiar. Alix was one of the members of the ART, the American Repertory Theater at Harvard's Loeb Drama Center. I've had a subscription there for the past five years, seen her perform, and even talked with her at a couple of the "meet the cast" events over the years. I'd forgotten that she and Ella were friends.

My eye fell on the phone on top of her desk and I pushed the "Last Number Dialed" button. The police had probably already beaten me to it, but I was curious to see with whom she had spoken the last time she was in her office. I scribbled down the number that appeared on the phone: 776-8139.

I was about to start on her file cabinets when I heard raised voices in the hall outside.

"Look, Wentworth, where is she? Stop covering for her and tell the old girl I'm here!" a young male voice demanded. Curious, I stepped into the reception area and was confronted by a handsome, wiry, brown-skinned black man in dark gray slacks and a heather cable-knit sweater. His large dark brown eyes, which were fringed with incredibly long lashes, were fixed angrily on Lindsey. Her face was flushed and I could see her fists clenched at her sides.

"Mr. Simms," she said hotly, "I've told you that Ella isn't here. You're going to have to take up your complaint with the Assistant Dean. And I'd rather you refer to me as *Miss* Wentworth."

"Listen, Wentworth, I'm not going through any assistant. Ella swore to me that there wasn't going to be a problem with certification, but now I get some asinine memo in my mailbox this morning rejecting our application. I want an answer and I want it from the Dean herself. When is she expected back?"

Lindsey's eyes filled with tears. Great, I thought, the floodgates are about to open again.

"Don't you read the paper or listen to the news, you idiot? She's dead! She's not coming back, ever!" She angrily pushed her chair aside and walked quickly into the hall, dabbing at her eyes again.

Mr. Simms turned to me. "What is she talking about?" he demanded, exasperated.

"I'd say she made herself pretty clear. Ella fell down a flight of stairs last night. She's dead."

"Jesus Christ," he whispered. "I slept late and came straight over here. The Hark was deserted when I checked my mailbox. I had no idea. You must think I'm the biggest asshole alive."

"Doesn't matter what I think," I said sympathetically. "But you aren't picking up any style points for subtlety. Why all the shouting?"

He sighed. "I've had plenty of unpleasant encounters with Dean Fisher in my time, and little Lindsey drives me nuts. She's determined to become a carbon copy of her mentor, right down to the screaming fits when she doesn't get her way. I just assumed she was running interference. You know, another battle over who's in charge at this school, the students or the bureaucrats."

"You mean, you have to ask? Nikki Chase," I said, proffering my hand.

"Justin Simms. President of the Law School Council. Let me guess. You're at the Business School."

I laughed. "Wrong. Economics Department. FAS. But I *am* an alum of the B-School. How'd you guess?"

"The handshake. So formal. So stiff. You could only be a card-carrying proponent of the capitalist system. Besides, if you were at the Law School, I would have found you before now." He was still holding my hand.

"No, just a starving economist. A member in good standing of the proletariat."

"Chase, this could be the beginning of a beautiful friendship." He motioned me into the sole chair in the reception area and, commandeering Lindsey's for himself, pulled it around the desk and sat in it backward. In another time and place, it would have been the occasion for serious flirting. He was clearly a master. But this was business.

"So what happened to Ella?" he asked.

I explained about my discovery of the body.

"Too bad. I argued with her a lot, but she wasn't a bad person. I see little Lindsey is taking it pretty hard."

"Do you know her well?"

"Lindsey Van Nostrand Wentworth? Ella's pedigreed watchdog. The girl hates me, and I love to remind her that she has to play nice with the tuition-paying students. She's very well connected, you know."

"How so?"

"Great-grandfather Van Nostrand owned a textile mill in Lowell, and the Wentworths had a cotton plantation, complete with slaves. Like Balzac said: 'Behind every great fortune there's a spectacular crime.' " He leaned closer. "The family's been giving away large sums of money to charity ever since, trying to expunge the stain. I think they peaked with her father's generation, and now they're attempting to stave off the inevitable decline."

I had vague memories of the Wentworth name from the society pages in the *Globe*, but I had no idea they had a daughter who doubled as a secretary.

"What's she doing here?" I asked. "She said she wanted to experience the real world, but I thought she was joking. How did a white girl with that pedigree end up working for a sister like Ella?"

"Daddy is a friend of the President's wife. Ella was a friend of the President. Lindsey needed to get something out of her system. And there you have it."

"You're very well informed, aren't you?"

"I read *Jet*. Don't you?"

"So is Lindsey very smart? She must be bored to death working here."

"Don't pity her too much. She's no rocket scientist. All she does is regurgitate what she reads and hears from other people. And wears all six of her emotions on her sleeve."

This was far too much fun. "You seem young to be so wise." I would have guessed he was no more than 20 years old.

"Skipped a couple of grades in school, took sophomore standing in college. Don't worry, I'm old enough to go out with you without getting you arrested."

Before I could reply, he rose to leave. "Got a class at noon that I haven't been to yet this semester. Thought I'd better check it out today. But look, let's do the lunch thing sometime, okay?" He took a notepad from Lindsey's desk and scribbled his number on it. "I wouldn't insult you by asking you for yours, so here's mine. I won't consider my heart broken until at least a week has gone by. See you!"

He was good.

I waited until his footsteps receded down the hall, then looked around for Lindsey. She emerged from the hallway as if on cue. "Is he gone yet?"

"Yeah. Nice guy."

"Right," she said, sharply. "Just because he's smart he thinks he can run all over everyone. No manners at all. If you only knew how many of those people Ella had to put up with. These students are so coarse! It was such a terrible thing—she could never get anything accomplished because they just swarmed around her, demanding the most outrageous things, and fighting with her when she'd already told them no."

"Sounds like it was pretty lively around here. Did she really argue with everyone?"

"Oh, of course I'm exaggerating a little. But there were definitely people that never even *tried* to get along with her. I used to hear them shouting so loudly I wondered if I should interrupt. . . ." Her voice trailed off.

"Who are you talking about?" I asked sharply. "Students, like Justin?"

"Well, yes, there were one or two others like him. But they're not so bad. The worst were the ones who wanted her job but didn't get it."

"After a year, people are still talking about that?"

"Well, you Harvard people are ambitious," Lindsey said defensively. "And everyone loves gossip. I'm sure you heard the stories that were going around about her when she got the job—you know, about her and President Barrett. No one could accept the fact that she was simply very good at what she did. They all had to invent a sinister reason why she was so successful."

I liked the fact that she was so fiercely loyal to Ella. I wouldn't have expected that from a rich white girl.

"And they wouldn't let it go!" she continued. "Christian Chung was here on Friday, arguing about something, and I know it was just to spite her."

"Christian Chung?" The name sounded vaguely familiar. "Who is he?"

"Just some know-it-all Chinese kid," Lindsey said dismissively. "You know they're everywhere—just taking over the place. He works in the Treasurer's office. I guess he thought he was next in line for Ella's job because he's such great friends with President Barrett. After she was appointed, he got his current job as a consolation prize."

"Do you know anything else about him?"

"Not really. Ella used to call him a spoiled Harvard brat. You know what they're like—really pushy. And so superior. I think he went to college here." Lindsey paused. "But he *hated* her. He really did. He used to come over and pick fights about fund-raising and budgets for student activities, just to prove that he was a financial whiz and she was just a former secretary. I can just imagine how *he* feels today."

Christian Chung. Of course! I remembered him now. He was my instructor during my junior year for a seminar on international economics. At that time he was a rising star in the department, arrogant, brilliant, and very attractive. But from what I remembered of him, Lindsey's jingoistic description didn't ring true. He wasn't the type who would still be holding a grudge over a promotion a year later. He was the type who would have been working the phone the day after the announcement and have landed a higher position than the original one by now.

I looked back at Lindsey. She still looked pale. The commotion surrounding her as the news of Ella's death got out must be taking its toll.

"Did you find what you were looking for?" she asked.

"No. You haven't deleted anything from her computer recently, have you?"

Lindsey looked down and then met my eyes again.

"No," she said slowly. "But you know, there have been so many people in and out of the office for the past couple of days . . . I hope they didn't delete anything by mistake."

She shook her head as if to clear it. "I hope I haven't been stupid in staying out of her office. The Dean would *kill* me if anything gets lost because I've been careless. I've just been letting people come and go. It's been so hard. . . ." Her voice trailed off.

She was clearly at the end of her rope. But I still needed that disk.

"Has anyone from the committee been by? Because maybe that's why I can't find what I'm looking for." Maybe Ella had already given her preliminary spreadsheet to Ian or to Rona Seidman?

"Well, Ian McAllister was here. He's on the committee, right? But I don't think he took a disk. He was looking for some papers of some kind." She furrowed her brow. "Christian Chung's not on the committee, is he? Because *he* came by. Oh, and Torie Barrett, the President's wife. But that was about something else."

We'd reached an impasse. I left Lindsey chattering into the phone with a student caller, her emotions momentarily stabilized. I knew Ella had to have that information.

So where was it?

CHAPTER FIVE

ACTING OUT

"Okay, you got me, waddaya want?" a husky female voice drawled into the telephone receiver.

"Hello, this is Nikki Chase," I stammered. This wasn't exactly the way most people answered their phones, at least not during the daylight hours.

"Nikki Chase? Do I know you?"

Alix Coyle sounded as if I had awakened her from a deep sleep, even though I was calling at three-thirty in the afternoon.

"We've met a couple of times. I have a subscription to the ART, and I've been to a few of the 'meet the cast' parties."

"Sure, sure," she said. She sounded unconvinced. "So waddaya want?"

"I'm calling because I was working with Ella Fisher on a report? And I was hoping that you might know whether she kept any of her work files at home?" I was starting to sound like my Ec. 10 student, Edelstein, but for some reason, this woman was intimidating me.

"You worked with Ella?" The line went momentarily silent.

"Hello? Are you there?"

"Yeah, I'm here," she said softly. "You worked with her, huh?"

"Yes, on the Crimson Future Committee. We were writing a report together before she—before the accident. And now I have to finish it, and I can't seem to find a computer file that I'm sure she has somewhere, and I thought it might be at her house. I know the two of you are friends, so I thought—"

"Well, I don't know anything about any computer files. But I'm going over there tomorrow night to help pack up some of her belongings and check her mail. Hang on just a minute."

"Diana! Now put that down, sugar! You know better," I heard her shouting in the background. "All right. Thank you, sweetie. Okay, I'm back," she said, sounding a bit breathless.

"Is that your daughter?" I said sympathetically.

"Lord, no! Diana's my dog. And she knows that she shouldn't behave that way. She's just acting out because I've been away for the past few days. Yes, I can see you," she shouted, presumably not at me. "You look stunning."

"So you say you'll be at her house tomorrow night?"

"Right. You're welcome to come over and look for your computer stuff then. I could use the company anyway."

"Well, thanks. I'll meet you at . . . ?"

"Eight o'clock should be good. I have a rehearsal until seven-thirty. Yes, Diana, I'm coming!" she shouted. "Will you take a pill?"

This was why I lived with a cat.

My next stop was the Littauer basement vending machine. I needed sugar, starch, or nicotine to get me through the rest of the afternoon. As I fumbled for change, a familiar voice rumbled, "Need a quarter, missy?"

I turned to find Percy Walker—Littauer's building superinten-dent—rummaging through the pockets of his green Buildings and Grounds overalls, his black skin glossy with perspiration. Percy and I go way back, all the way to my freshman year in college. When-ever I passed through Littauer on my way to the library or to a pro-fessor's office, we would exchange a smile or a nod. Pretty soon, he was corralling me in the hall to engage in conversation or feed me the latest campus gossip. Some of my friends found it strange that I was on close speaking terms with a maintenance worker, but he re-minded me a lot of my grandfather: dignified, hardworking and a wonderful storyteller. I loved listening to him tell tales about the high and mighty professors who occupied the building, and remi-nisce about his native South Carolina. Percy had four granddaugh-ters, and he wanted all of them to go to Harvard. Through the years, we had become fast friends, and I was used to sharing a bag of chips or the occasional smoke with him in the late afternoon.

"Hey," I said, accepting the change from his hand, "thanks. How's it going?"

"Oh, my back's aching a little today, but other than that I can't complain." Percy was almost seventy, and determined to go on working forever.

"You want anything?" I asked, retrieving a Diet Coke and a bag of potato chips from the machine.

"Naw, I just had a pop. So how are you doing? I heard you had a rough time of it on Sunday."

I tapped the can, then snapped the top off. "Yeah, it was lousy. A minute earlier, and it could have been me falling down those stairs. This building should have some kind of emergency lighting."

"Well"—Percy lowered his voice—"it does. But they found this problem with the wires."

"What?" I said sharply. Footsteps echoed on the stairs above us, and Percy motioned me to keep my voice down.

"*What* problem?" I whispered.

"Come on."

We started down the hall and turned off into a glass-enclosed office with the Buildings and Grounds logo stenciled on the door. A wall of keys faced us, and one side of the room was cluttered with tools and several tarpaulins. The office adjoined the boiler room, and the air was heavy, warm and oily.

I sat in my usual spot, atop his workbench, while Percy settled into his chair.

"Okay," I said, leaning forward, "give me the goods!"

"Well," Percy said expansively, "Sunday night the building was open until midnight, like always."

"Right," I said, taking a sip from my soda. I was used to his storytelling style, which required a long buildup. It was usually worth the wait.

"I made my eleven o'clock round like always, you know, locking all the doors, and checking to see who was still around." He reached into his shirt pocket and pulled out a butterscotch in a cellophane wrapper. "Candy?"

"No, thanks." I shook my head. *Give him time.* "So were there many people around in the building?"

"Not too many. Never are on Sunday. As I recollect, the second floor was deserted, but there were two or three people over in the Government wing on the first floor. A bunch of folks in the library. And your committee meeting in that conference room on the first floor."

"So what happened after you made the eleven o'clock round?"

He smiled a bit sheepishly. "I came on back down here and had a pop and some crackers."

"And?" I prompted.

"Well, I usually take a little nap right around then."

"Is that what you did Sunday?"

"Yeah, and when I woke up all hell was breaking loose upstairs."

"Right, all the lights had gone out. So what did you do?"

"Well, I found my flashlight and came on upstairs. They had just left with the lady—Fisher, I think her name was—in an ambulance." Which explained why I hadn't seen him that night. I had stayed with Ella for the ride to the hospital.

"Then what?"

"Well, I went to try and get some lights on. I came on back down here." He leaned forward confidingly. "And that's when I found out that those lights didn't go out because of the storm." He paused dramatically. "The wires were cut."

He grinned at my shocked expression. "That's right. When I was upstairs, I saw that the lights were still on in the Science Center. Now, I know this building is on the same circuit. So I checked the fuse box, and sure enough, the wires had been cut."

"Can you show me?" This was incredible.

"Sure. Come on." He rose slowly from his chair and led me through the boiler room; against one wall was a large gray metal box with black clips. Multicolored wires trailed from it in all directions.

"Now, this is the main fuse box, see," he said. "Whoever did it wasn't taking any chances." He laughed to himself. "They cut every doggone wire in the place to make sure they got the right one. Only reason we have lights now is because they spliced us into the backup feed. They're coming to fix this thing tonight after the building closes. Gonna take a few hours to straighten all this out."

"Unbelievable," I muttered under my breath.

It looked like the work of someone in a hurry. Someone in a panic.

I looked up to see Percy regarding me with concern in his dark brown eyes. "This isn't getting you upset, now, is it?"

"No, Percy." I laid my hand on his arm. "Not at all. Have you told all this to the police?"

"Oh, sure. I told 'em it was probably some kid tryin' to be funny. And see what happened."

"Is there any way to get in here other than through your office?" I asked, as we walked back to the office.

"Nope. They must have snuck by while I was asleep." He shook his head.

"Are you in trouble over this?" I said softly.

"Naw, the union will watch out for me. Not my fault if some smart aleck wants to cause trouble."

"That's great, Percy." I looked at my watch: four o'clock. "I've got to go; I've got a ton of work to do. But thanks for filling me in."

A deliberate blackout at Littauer.

Who was crazy enough to do that?

The light on my answering machine was blinking when I opened the door to my apartment much later that evening, and I flipped the playback switch before heading for the kitchen to make coffee. A strangely familiar voice filled the room as the messages played back:

"Okay. Now. You do this the right way. Okay. Get a pen. Okay, get a pen, get a piece of paper. This will take definitely no more than one minute. You write down my two phone numbers. Home is 354-6159. The Law School Council is 495-8130. Pick one of them. Immediately dial it. As soon as this message ends, dial that number. Wait till you get the answering machine and then leave your answer about whether you'll go to the Friends of the Fogg party with me on Saturday night. That's it. Hang up the phone and walk away. Boom. Done. You're a busy woman, you don't have time for things that last more than a minute. And certainly this phone call is in danger of doing so if I don't hang . . ." The machine beeped.

So much for Justin Simms waiting for *me* to call *him*. I smiled as I scribbled his phone numbers on a piece of paper, wondering idly if the older woman/younger man thing was really worth an experiment. It would be fun to be in control of my emotions for once.

Impulsively, I dialed his number at the Law School. A female voice answered "Law School Council," and after a brief pause, Justin came on the line.

"Justin, it's Nikki Chase. We met this morning in Ella Fisher's office."

A brief pause, and then, "Ah, yes. Are you asking me over for dinner, or something more special?"

"Are you reading these lines out of a book, or just free-associating?"

"I'll take this as a 'yes.' "

"Nice to know there's no shortage of hubris over at HLS. It could be a 'maybe.' Or even a polite 'no.' "

"You don't seem like the type to break a man's heart at work. Especially with all these people watching."

"Well, since you made it in just under the Wednesday deadline, it *is* a 'yes.' "

"I have great respect for the Wednesday deadline. A real lady never accepts a Saturday date after that. But is it Wednesday morning, or Wednesday evening?"

"It depends on who's asking." I twirled the phone cord around my finger. "You could sound a bit more relieved."

"If only you knew, beautiful."

"Listen, while I have you on the phone, how well did you know Ella Fisher?" Those cut wires in Littauer were no prank. I was sure that they had something to do with Ella Fisher. And this man knew her world far better than I.

"You mean you don't want to hear about my day?"

"I wouldn't mind, but I'd rather hear about why you spent so much time arguing with the late Dean."

He sighed. "Okay, okay, we have the rest of our lives to flirt. Let's get serious." He lowered his voice slightly. "I personally argued with her because of my position in the student government. I'm responsible for making sure that the administration devotes an adequate amount of money to each of the student organizations on campus. The problem was that Ella and I didn't always agree on what was adequate, or on what constitutes an official organization. I hate to criticize a sister, but frankly, the woman was an egomaniac. Adamant about everything, even things that didn't matter."

"Lindsey says that other students fought a lot with her, too."

"Yes, she could be pretty bitchy sometimes. Over everything from scheduling use of the rooms on campus to which parties could have alcohol to how much money we could spend on doughnuts for the first-year's orientation breakfast. Cheap as hell. And paranoid. I heard a rumor that she kept a recorder in her desk so that she could secretly tape all her conversations."

I remembered seeing a pocket-sized tape recorder in her office earlier that day. But there was no tape in it.

"Did anyone ever threaten her?" I asked.

"Over whether they could serve alcohol at a party? I don't think so. I used to threaten to burst into tears, but that was the extent of it."

Was he capable of being serious for more than two minutes? "What do you know about her personal life?" I asked.

"Nikki, you have a curious mind. I like that. Our children will almost certainly get into Ivy League schools."

"Is that your subtle way of avoiding my question?"

"No, I'm just intrigued by your interest in her. What's going on?"

"Nothing," I said lightly. "I'm just finding myself thinking about her. It's not every day that someone you worked with dies."

"Right. That's okay, I'll pretend to believe you for now; I hear women like men who are big and stupid and I gotta score on one of those criteria. To answer your question, I didn't know anything about her personal life. But I'd love to know more about yours."

"Ah, look at the time. I've got an article to finish." I paused. "Thank you for asking, Justin."

"You're so welcome. Dream about me tonight."

I hung up the phone and flopped backward onto my bed, staring pensively at the ceiling. Keynes jumped on my stomach, and I idly stroked his head. I was flirting like mad with a twenty-year-old. And liking it. Go figure. But Dante Rosario was back in Cambridge.

And an insurance policy seemed in order.

CHAPTER SIX

PHAT FARM

Six o'clock Wednesday morning. Socks. Shorts. Sunrise still a promise. At least no rain. T-shirt. Shoes. Tie them later. Keys. God, working out at the crack of dawn always sounded like a great idea right up until the moment the alarm went off.

"*Hello*. Frankenstein in the house," a voice drawled as I stumbled across Bennett Street toward the plaza outside the Charles Hotel. "Somebody's havin' a *real* bad hair day."

"Don't even *start*."

Jessica Lieberman is my best friend. That's the *only* reason that I subject myself to this ordeal four times a week, and sometimes even that isn't enough.

We met as freshmen at Harvard, but only became close during our senior year. She had studied at the Sorbonne during junior year, and when she returned, we became inseparable. I know it had something to do with the fact that we had both decided to start wearing better clothes and acting more sophisticated that year; that we both fancied ourselves as smart, ambitious women; and that we both started dating men we thought were far too gorgeous to be interested in us. Thus was an enduring friendship formed based on mutual admiration and shared fears.

That year, we fell into the same habits almost immediately: working on our honors theses all night, sleeping until lunchtime, taking "power naps" at four in the afternoon, smoking in our dormitory's courtyard at night under the stars, and generally pissing off all our old friends because we were so happy. I can talk to her about anything, and she has shared the best and most embarrassing times of my life since then.

She was waiting for me on a bench outside the entrance to the Wellbridge Fitness Center—a yuppie haven in the Charles Hotel. Always fashionable, she was wearing a deep purple tank top and black biker shorts, her long, curly dark-brown hair pulled into a ponytail at the top of her head.

"What gives?" she said, as I collapsed next to her. "You're always early and suddenly you actually show up at the scheduled time. Are you sick?"

"No," I said, squeezing her arm in greeting. "Just up late last night. I love that tank."

"DKNY. And yes, they had it in red."

"So how was the conference?" We nodded appreciatively as two men in shorts disappeared through the club entrance.

"Lots of Jewish doctors. The usual *mishegoss* over who was attracted to whom. But the party on Saturday night was phat!"

Jess had grown up in Hewlett Harbor, Long Island, and was now a resident in the ER at the very urban Mass General Hospital. As a result, her vocabulary was a cross between Henny Youngman and L.L. Cool J.

"Did you wear the black dress or the champagne one?"

"The black. And it looked fierce!"

"Your mom will be thrilled that there was ample husband material. What time did you get in last night?"

"Midnight, or I would have called. So gimme the 4-1-1. What'd I miss while I was gone?"

"Plenty. Come on, we're gonna be late."

The familiar scent of chlorine and sweat wafted around us as we entered the club. We chatted more about Jess's weekend while storing our bags in the crowded locker room. Women in various stages of undress swarmed around us, laughing and telling stories about diets and boyfriends and work. When I first joined the club, I was amazed at how willing the members were to parade around before each other with no camouflage, but I had since come to treasure the sisterhood of a place where no one's thighs are too big, and we can all walk around naked and proud.

"Something's up, I can tell." Jess deposited herself on the floor next to me in the aerobics studio. "What—McAllister still cracking the whip over your head?"

"Of course, but that's nothing new. The man obviously hasn't heard about the Emancipation Proclamation. The slaves is supposed to be free now."

"So why don't you pull a Sojourner Truth on him and get the hell off the plantation, girl?" She sat cross-legged on the floor and began stretching upward.

"I can handle him. That's not what's bothering me." I sank into a hamstring stretch and felt myself starting to awaken. I described the past three days' events in a low tone as the instructor came in and began fiddling with her tape.

Jess flexed her feet. "So you think someone cut those wires deliberately to hurt Ella Fisher?" she whispered.

"Maybe. I don't know, maybe I'm being paranoid." By the light of day, it seemed a bit hysterical to think that there was a murderer loose in the halls of Littauer. "I poked around in her office a bit, but I didn't see anything unusual. Certainly nothing lethal."

"Well, old girl wasn't very popular, was she? Didn't she piss off a lot of people?"

"Yeah, but enough to kill her? I don't think anyone hated her that much."

"It doesn't take much, girlfriend. We've got people coming through the ER who've been shot because they looked at someone funny on the Turnpike. You have no idea."

"Come on, Jess," I scoffed. "This is Cambridge, not South Boston."

"Well then, maybe Ella wasn't the target, Sherlock. Maybe the murderer was after someone else and got her by mistake. Didn't you say the President was there?"

"Yes, but he was on the first floor the whole time."

"So, maybe someone intended to jump him once the lights went out, and when Ella fell down the stairs, it ruined the plan."

I shook my head. "Unlikely. Leo wasn't even expected at the meeting. He turned up at the last minute."

"You don't think that man does anything on impulse, do you? I'm sure his entire staff knew well in advance that he was going."

"But who would want to hurt Leo, either? Everyone adores him. Well—I take that back. The students adore him."

"Your boss sure hates him."

"Ian's just jealous. He's been on a vendetta against Leo ever since he became President, and it seems to be getting worse. He actually asked me if I thought his wife, Connie, was prettier than Torie Barrett."

"I hope you took the Fifth on that one. You better keep your head down, girl."

"I can't. Leo has been too good to me. He put me on this high-profile Crimson Future Committee, he's been talking me up at the Economics Department faculty meetings. And remember that time he invited me over for dinner and Tom Brokaw was there?"

She nodded. "And just think. You owe it all to me."

"I know, I know, you were the one who made me call him about co-authoring that article. I can't believe it was only three years ago."

"I told you he was going places. That law professor I was dating said so. And you both have this strange interest in commercial law, which I don't understand, but whatever."

"And I've only thanked you half a million times for suggesting it, but who's counting? He really is amazing—so smart, and so charming—"

"And so sexy! The way he leans in to listen when you ask him a question, and looks deep into your eyes when he answers—"

"You need to stop. He's the President of the university, not a Ken doll."

"Gimme a break. That'll be the day, when *men* have to worry that we're not taking them seriously because they're so cute. So what's Ian's problem with him?"

"Thinks he doesn't have the proper demeanor to be a Harvard President."

"Stop."

"It's true. If I've heard it once, I've heard it a million times: 'He's an operator. A bon vivant. A media hound. A skirt-chaser. How can such a person lead this great institution?' Like it's Leo's fault he's not an uptight Puritan WASP like all his predecessors."

"What *is* he, anyway—Portuguese? He's got those haunting dark brown eyes. . . ."

I shrugged. "He calls himself a mongrel. The *Crimson* ran a profile of him a couple of days ago, and I think it said that his father moved from Ireland to Brazil, where he met Leo's mother, and they emigrated to the United States before Leo was born. I think he grew up in Philadelphia. All I know for sure is that he worked his way through City College in New York, was admitted to Harvard Law School, and fifteen years later, he's the President of the university. It's inspiring. Ian's just pissed because he wants the job himself."

"Huh," she snorted. "How badly does he want it?"

The aerobics instructor finally arrived in the front of the room, abruptly ending our conversation by ordering us to our feet. It was a great workout—she actually made us laugh in the middle of push-ups, which is no small feat—and by the end, I felt relaxed and happily exhausted.

"That's it," the instructor cooed, as the cool-down music washed over us. "Breathe, and stretch."

"Where are you going?" I called as Jess made an unsuccessful attempt to head back to the locker room. "We have to do our weights."

"Girl, I've got to be at the hospital in forty-five minutes. I don't have time!" she groaned.

"We agreed we would *make* the time. Remember, weight-lifting is the ultimate feminist act," I scolded as we headed for the Cybex machines.

"I know, I know, we'll never need a man for anything, not even to open a jar." She rolled her eyes.

"Speaking of which—you won't believe who's moving in downstairs."

"I give up. Who?"

"Dante Rosario."

"Get out!"

"I wish I could, but—"

"No, really, get out of here, I can't believe it, that's great!" She was laughing with pleasure. I was incredulous.

"Did you hear what I said? He's going to be living downstairs. In my house."

"So what's the problem? He's a *mensch*. When did he get back from California?"

"How should I know? I haven't spoken to him for eight years."

She fell silent for a moment, watching me, then an evil smile spread over her face. "Oh my God. You're worried about this."

"No, I'm not."

"You're wondering what he's looking like these days."

"Of course I am. Aren't you? But that doesn't mean I'm *worried*."

"You're in for it all over again. I can feel it."

"No, I'm not. Stop it. He's probably bald and paunchy. Anyway, I've met a great new guy. He's a gorgeous black Law School student, and he flirts like a dream."

"What? I leave town for three days and it starts raining men?" She settled in at the chest press machine. "Are we talking 24–7?"

"Well, there is one small catch."

"Married?" She shook her head sympathetically.

"No! Are you nuts? No, he's twenty years old."

"Girl, you are completely *meshugga* when it comes to men. Haven't you learned *anything* from me?"

Apparently not.

My morning section of Ec. 10 was starting to take on its own personality, as sections inevitably do. The class was neatly divided between liberals, moderates, and conservatives, and we had an impassioned discussion about Ricardo's theories of worker exploitation. It reminded me why I loved to teach in the first place.

Feeling energized from a brisk walk across the Yard, I took the broad stone stairs outside Littauer two at a time, pushed through the tall glass doors, and started across the lobby. That was when I saw Dante Rosario, and the sight of him stopped me dead in my tracks.

He was coming down the spiral staircase—the same one that Ella had fallen down—looking like Michelangelo's David in motion. His shiny dark brown hair was now flecked at the temples with silver, but his face was still the same: large, intelligent, dark brown eyes; a strong jaw and a soft mouth. The Dante uniform was intact: faded jeans, a black turtleneck, and a well-worn black leather jacket.

For a son of a bitch, he was extraordinarily attractive.

I had been given fair warning that a reunion was in the offing, but now that it was here, I felt woefully unprepared. Before I could retreat, he had spotted me.

"Nik? I thought that was you!"

This was not how our first sighting after so many years was supposed to take place. After the breakup, I had nursed the fantasy that we would meet again someday, but that we would be in Manhattan. I would be stepping out of a limousine on Park Avenue, wearing a Chanel suit and black stiletto heels, carrying the prospectus for my latest deal. He would be standing on the sidewalk, a patently pathetic, balding perpetual graduate student with a paunch. Our eyes would meet and his expression would be full of regret and lust. I, unmoved, would turn away, ducking into the Four Seasons for lunch. Instead, my lunch was tucked in plastic sandwich wrap in my shoulder bag, I was wearing a two-year-old dress from Urban Outfitters, and Dante was looking far from pathetic.

"So, the investment banker returns to her roots," he said, smiling wickedly. I hardened myself against the unwelcome onslaught of memories brought back by the sound of his voice. "I'd heard you moved back to Cambridge," he continued.

"Yes, the offer to join the Harvard Fellows program was just too good to reject. And you're back from—where was it?—Berkeley?" I asked, knowing full well that it had been Stanford.

"Actually, Stanford," he responded easily, apparently confident in the knowledge that his résumé was, in fact, engraved upon my brain. "I know all those California schools tend to sound the same after a while."

"Right. UCLA, SMU, Cal Tech, whatever."

"SMU is Texas," he said, smiling. He actually seemed to be enjoying this. "You don't get out much, do you?" He touched the lapel of my jacket and pulled me ever so slightly toward him. "Still wearing your funky clothes, I see."

"Well, it's a timeless look." I hated him. So why was my heart beating so fast?

"I hear we're neighbors," he said. "At Littauer and at home." He slowly released his hold on my jacket.

I met his gaze squarely. "Yes, of all the houses on all the streets in all of Cambridge, you had to move into mine."

"Well, with the schedule I'll be keeping, I doubt we'll see much of each other anyway," he said lightly.

Good.

I glanced at my watch. "Well, it's been fun. I've got to see someone before he leaves for the day—"

"Wait." He lightly touched my arm. "Before you run, let's set a time to catch up a little bit. We can grab a cup of coffee."

"Hmmm." I stalled for time. "When?"

"How about tonight?"

"Sorry. I've got a date tonight." Another point for me; I knew Alix Coyle would prove useful for something.

"Then what about tomorrow? We can go to Cafe Algiers."

Cafe Algiers? A return to the scene of the crime?

"Thursday would be fine," I said lightly.

"Great. I'll meet you at Algiers at eight-thirty. I've got a seminar that gets out at eight."

Then he was gone, and I could breathe normally again. An evening out with an old flame was the last thing I needed right now.

But Dante Rosario had been carrying around a piece of me for eight years. And it was time I got it back.

I arrived at Ella Fisher's apartment shortly after eight o'clock that evening. She had lived on Francis Street, a few blocks north of the Divinity School. I knew the neighborhood from my frequent walks; the houses there were antique and beautifully preserved, and I liked to roam there, particularly in autumn, dreaming of the day when I might live in my very own Victorian. Ella had lived in an old three-story townhouse that had been renovated as part of a new condominium development. I crunched through the russet leaves just beginning to cover her front walk and rang the doorbell, but there was no sign of life.

"Hey. How's it going?" A throaty voice with a hint of Texas twang echoed through the night air, and I turned to find a willowy strawberry blonde with hazel eyes regarding me curiously. Alix Coyle. She wore brown cowboy boots, a red flannel shirt over a white T-shirt, and skinny faded jeans. Smoke from a cigarette trailed through her fingers. If the Marlboro Man could assume female form, this would be it.

At her side was an oversized Siberian husky with bright, intelligent eyes.

"I recognize you now," she said, walking toward me. "Orchestra, aisle H, right?"

"That's me," I laughed. "And I assume this is Diana." At the sound of her name, the dog barked loudly.

"That's right," Alix said, patting her head. "You're the Goddess of the Hunt, aren't you?" she said to the dog. "Say hello. It's alright."

"Can I pet her?" I asked. It seemed wise to ask first, since Diana was easily one hundred pounds of muscle.

"What do you think, Miss D?" Alix asked seriously. After a pause, Diana barked again.

"She's had a hard way to go, so we're takin' it step by step. I found her at an abused-animal shelter, and she's still learning that she can decide who touches her." As Alix turned to reassure Diana, I saw that her T-shirt had a quote from Euripides on it: "Woman is woman's natural ally." Apparently so.

Having established that I, too, was an ally, I patted Diana's massive head, and then the three of us proceeded into Ella's apartment.

I was surprised and a bit disappointed when I saw how it was furnished. The entry foyer and living room were tasteful but very bland, so harmonious that I suspected that Ella had gone to a furniture store and bought an entire floor display rather than risk revealing any of her own taste. The walls were ivory, and there was a pale pink sofa and matching love seat and chairs; a contemporary wooden coffee table and a wall unit holding a few books, pictures, several record albums and an old stereo and tape player. A woven cotton rug completed the decor. Where were the traces of her personality? Had she snuffed them out completely? The place looked like a photo shoot for the Door Store.

"So how did you meet Ella, anyway?" I asked, as we crossed into the kitchen.

"She was a regular at the ART. She used to stick around after the performances to talk to the cast, and we hit it off."

The kitchen was long and narrow, but large enough to accommodate a small table and four chairs.

"You want somethin' to eat? I'm starved." She opened the refrigerator door.

"Sure."

"Shouldn't have spoken so soon, I guess," she muttered, rummaging around. "There's not a damn thing in here."

I looked over her shoulder. The fridge held a bottle of apple juice, a six pack of diet soda, a bottle of champagne, three lowfat yogurts, some wilted spinach, and a jar of wheat germ.

"I forgot she was on some macrobiotic diet or something."

"Check the freezer," I said hopefully.

The freezer had three Lean Cuisine dinners, a half pint of fat-free raspberry sorbet, and a bag of ice. The cupboards were equally spartan: coffee, oatmeal, unsalted saltines, and packets of Equal. We did discover one hidden vice among all the virtue, though: a package of Double-Stuff Oreo cookies that was three-quarters empty.

"Let's polish these off, then we'll grab dinner when we're done, okay?"

I nodded in agreement.

"You want a pop, too? At least she's got Diet Coke. Although I prefer RC."

"Sure, I'll have one."

"I can't believe we're in Rosezella Fisher's house, and starvin'," Alix groused. "That girl could *cook*, and she used to have all kinds of stuff—" Her voice caught, and I looked up in time to see her brushing a tear away.

"I miss her," she said simply. She shook her head. "You must be thinkin,' 'What the hell am I doin' here, holdin' up a weepy ol' gal when all I wanted is some work information?'"

"Not at all—"

"Come on, her computer's upstairs," Alix said, suddenly brusque. "Cryin' won't bring her back."

The second level of the condominium had a small family room with a television set, an older sofa and matching chairs, and a computer. A vase filled with wilting red roses sat on a side table. Dominating the room was a rather large painting of a thin, unclothed black woman stretched across a bed, the sheets pulled carelessly up to her waist. Behind her, looking pensively out a window, was a naked black man. The woman's expression was at once languid and piercing, an indictment of the entire idea of men and romance.

"And I thought *I* was bitter," I said, hoping to coax a smile from Alix.

"Yeah, she bought that after her divorce. The thing always reminds me of my ex-husband, Bud," she said, squinting up at it as she took a swig from her Diet Coke.

"How nice."

"That man has the same look about him. The type that talks loud but with no real guts. A chickenshit."

"Where is Bud now?" I asked, settling into the chair in front of the computer.

"He's back in Muleshoe, Texas, where I left him. Last I heard his gas station had gone belly-up and he was working at a refinery on the night shift. Saving up to buy a circle of cotton."

"Muleshoe?"

"A sweet little place in the heart of west Texas. My hometown."

"Sounds delightful."

"Don't get haughty with me, Miss Harvard. Muleshoe's a fine place if you like riding horses and driving trucks and going to church. The backbone of America."

"So then why did you leave, Marlboro Girl?"

Alix barked a laugh. " 'Cause a future of either working the cash register at Allsup's like my mother or staying home all day like my Aunt Fay just wasn't what I had in mind. Fay used to say that if I played my cards right, I could marry some rancher and live the good life. That was enough to get me on a Greyhound out of there. And I'll be out of here, too, as soon as my agent gets off her ass and finds me some steady work in New York."

"So what is Ella's ex-husband like?"

"Isaiah Fisher? An asshole."

"Why do you say that?"

"Ike's still livin' in Cambridge, runnin' some used book store and art gallery. Art, my butt. Just like a Capricorn not to know when to pack it up and call it quits. You can't tell 'em anything!" She paused, and looked momentarily chagrined. "You're not a Capricorn, are you?"

"No. Gemini."

She breathed an audible sigh of relief. "Yeah. That would make sense. I kept telling Ella to change back to her maiden name, but she wouldn't. She was too quote-unquote 'professionally established' using Fisher."

"So was Ella seeing anyone when she died?"

She shook her head. "We used to spend hours bitching about our ex-husbands and figuring out how to get laid. Despite what people said about her and Barrett."

"People did talk about the two of them a lot."

"That really pissed me off. She worked her ass off for that man and made him a big success. So he rewarded her. But the stories she would repeat that were going around about the two of them—as if the only possible way that she could've made it into that job was by sleeping with him. Men are such pigs sometimes."

I started to point out that my female acquaintances were as willing to spread those rumors as anyone, but what would that prove? That women can be porcine, too?

Alix shook her head and stood up. "Hey, you better get crackin' on her computer. And I've got a bunch of packing to do. I don't know how to turn this thing on, though," she said, standing over Ella's PC.

"Don't worry. I'll figure it out."

Alix left me alone upstairs, and I flipped the switch on the back of the PC. While it booted up, I quickly examined the drawers underneath the computer table, and was immediately rewarded with a pile of disks. The third one was labeled "Crimson Future."

I loaded the disk into the a: drive and opened it up. And lo and behold, there were the spreadsheets I'd been looking for. There were a few other letters and memos on the disk, too. I was about to copy the spreadsheets onto a blank disk when it dawned on me that I could take her only copy. It wasn't as if Ella would be needing it anymore.

Since Alix was occupied downstairs, I took the opportunity to snoop around in Ella's bedroom, which was a half-flight up from the den. Clothes were strewn across the room in small piles, and the bed was unmade. The scent of bath powder or perfume still lingered in the air. I began with the place where I keep all my secrets: the nightstand beside the bed. It held a dozen matchbooks from restaurants around town, a diaphragm that looked like it hadn't been used for a while, and a small key that looked like it could belong to a safe deposit box. I pocketed it, just in case. Under the bed, two pairs of slippers lay jumbled together amid the dust bunnies. The bathroom yielded the usual assortment of lotions, cold cream, perfume, and makeup that burden every professional woman.

There were two toothbrushes, both bone dry.

Did she keep a spare, or did she have a recurring overnight visitor? Alix had said Ella didn't have a lover. But would she really know, if Leo Barrett was the lover in question?

Lost in thought, I headed back downstairs before Alix could get suspicious. I found her at the kitchen table, sorting through the mail and chatting amicably with Diana.

"I found the disk!" I announced.

"That's great, sugar."

"What can I do to help you here?"

"Stack up those magazines and newspapers and put them in the recyclin' bin."

"So did Ella ever talk about the Crimson Future Committee?" I asked as I straightened up stray issues of *Essence*, *Ebony*, and *Working Woman*.

"Just to insult y'all. Not you, really. But she hated that guy, what's his name—McAllister?"

"Hated? Ian McAllister?"

"Yeah, evidently he knew just which buttons to push to make her feel completely useless on that committee. To hear her tell it, that guy definitely had it in for her."

"He's got a sharp tongue. But Ella always gave it right back. She seemed to enjoy it."

"Enjoy it? You obviously didn't know her." Alix looked up from the pile of mail. "She was really unsure of herself, especially around you Harvard types. She wanted to be one of you, you know, but didn't quite know how. That's why she let Barrett foist that high-society secretary off on her."

"Lindsey Wentworth?"

"Yeah, Princess Lindsey."

"I met her yesterday. She's pretty torn up about Ella's death."

Alix shrugged. "She's a good kid. She hero-worshiped Ella, and that was good for Ella's ego. Ella used to tell her stories about growing up in the South, and Lindsey's eyes would get as big as saucers. I used to tell Ella she was working her too hard, but Ella said she liked it."

"Ella liked giving people shit, didn't she?"

Alix laughed. "Yeah, she did. It was her way of protecting herself. You know what turtles are like? Hard ol' shell and nothin' but mush inside? That was Ella. I just wish she'd enjoyed herself more."

"I always thought she did."

"She used to. But something was botherin' her before she died."

"Really?" I tried to sound nonchalant.

"I don't know exactly what. But I think it had to do with money."

"Did she talk about it?"

"Not really. But look at this." Alix burrowed into a pile of papers on top of the kitchen table and produced a checkbook with a blue vinyl cover.

I flipped through to the end of the check registry and saw the withdrawals.

Ella had written three large checks to cash in the last two months: two for $3,000 and the last for $3,500. What was she doing spending cash like that? It was big money for an academic, even a high-flying one. The registry went back a little over a year, and there were no other entries for amounts of that size. She must have been pretty disciplined with her credit cards, unless she had another account, because this one had a steady stream of payments to one Visa issuer and a few stray payments to Filene's Department Store. The deposit ledger was also pretty consistent; a paycheck every two weeks, and a few random deposits that said "expense reimbursement."

So in the last two months of her life, cash had been flowing out at an unusually high rate.

"What do you think those withdrawals were?" I said, looking up at Alix. Could Ella have started taking drugs?

"You're the professor, gal. I don't have the slightest."

Neither did I. But I was planning to find out.

An hour later, desperate for food, we set out for Young and Yee, Alix's favorite Chinese restaurant in Harvard Square. Diana had been fed and was sleeping peacefully on Ella's kitchen floor, so Alix decided to leave her be. Francis Street was deserted and hushed at that hour, and we walked in companionable silence. The only sounds were the wind rustling in the trees overhead, the leaves crunching underfoot.

And the sharp report of footsteps behind us.

Suddenly, I felt a hand brush by me and fasten on Alix's arm.

"Okay, bitch, we can do this the easy way or the hard way." A fat, swarthy white face flashed by me, as a man who had to be over six feet tall swung Alix around until she was facing him.

"What do you want?" I said quickly.

He ignored me, gripping Alix's arm even tighter.

"Hey, why don't you just take my purse and get it over with?" I said lightly. For once, being broke was doing me some good.

Alix said nothing, just fastened those eyes on him.

"How about you, showgirl? What are you offering me?"

Showgirl? Did they know each other?

The man leaned closer to her face. Just close enough so that she could land a wad of saliva right in his eye.

"That enough, asshole? Or do you want more?" she hissed.

"Now you've screwed up," he snarled. His hand went for his jacket pocket. Was he reaching for a weapon?

Alix wasn't waiting to find out. She landed a knee in his groin and twisted away from his grasp. He doubled over, still fumbling in his pocket.

"Alix, come on!" I shouted, turning to make a run for it.

But she wasn't finished. The toe of her boot met his lip, drawing blood, and the mugger gave up looking for a weapon and decided to use his hands. One backhand sent her staggering, and then he was on her, hands fastening around her throat.

"Help! Get off her!" I yelled. I tugged on his heavy brown leather jacket, then tried going for his throat, but found myself nine inches too short to reach it. Alix was still giving him the devil with the toe of her boot, so I figured he didn't have a choke hold on her yet.

It was at that point that the cop showed up.

"Hey, what's going on here?" he shouted. Tall, redheaded, and very young. For a moment, I wondered who he thought was attacking whom.

The policeman pried our attacker off Alix, who promptly delivered a final kick that sent him staggering to the ground. As the cop bent to help him sit up, Alix leaned over and whispered something in the mugger's ear. His face went blood red, and she grinned at him before she turned to me.

"Ready?" she said.

"Yeah," I mumbled, willing my hands to stop shaking. "But I think this guy is going to want a statement."

"I'm sure the nice officer wouldn't keep two thirsty women from a bar at a time like this," she said, smiling. "Am I right?"

The cop was smiling and nodding in sympathy, his face beginning to match his hair color. Dazzled by her eyes and this whole scene, no doubt. "Here's my number," she said, scribbling on a piece of paper from her bag. "Call me when you need me." I was sure he would. We set off down Francis Street.

"What did you say to that guy when you whispered in his ear?" I asked.

"I told him to suck my dick."

"Oh."

That pretty much said it all.

I arrived home from dinner with Alix around eleven that night; in the end, we had eaten at Bartley's Burger Cottage in the

Square so that I could calm my nerves with a cheeseburger and onion rings. After hanging up my jacket, I discovered Maggie and my new housemate Ted Adair in the kitchen. Busily swapping stories, they were already on their third pot of tea. It turned out that Ted worked at a legal clinic in Roxbury, and Maggie knew some of the lawyers on staff. I reluctantly turned down Maggie's invitation to join them for peaches and pound cake, since I need to get started on my report for the Crimson Future Committee now that I finally had the financials. I resisted the urge to ask where Dante Rosario was. Hadn't Maggie said that he or Ted had a woman hanging on him when they signed the lease?

Spreading out the hard copy Ian had supplied on the table next to me, I quickly got the contents of the disk up on the screen. It held copies of the budgets of each of the ten graduate schools and the College. I quickly looked to see if Ella had done any major analysis on them. To my surprise, it looked as if she had already done a lot of what we had agreed would be required. She had calculated historical compound annual growth rates for each line item, and had already begun the forward projections.

Since Ella had already done so much work, I *really* didn't want to have to redo it. So I spread Ian's hard copy out in front of me, and began scanning the rows of numbers. Unless there were wild differences between Ian's and Ella's versions, I was going to keep working off her version.

The first five graduate schools were identical in both versions, and I was congratulating myself for having gone to the trouble of finding Ella's disk rather than working off Ian's hard copy. Then I got to the Faculty of Arts and Sciences, and realized that there was a discrepancy of about $2 million in its total budget between the two versions.

I groaned aloud. Of all the budgets, FAS was the most complicated to analyze. Unlike the Law School, for example, which was one cohesive unit with one master budget, the FAS budget was comprised of individual reports from each of its over thirty-five departments. To find the discrepancy, I'd have to go back line by line and compare the spreadsheets for all of them. It was 1:45 A.M. Whatever the discrepancy was, it could keep for the night. Our forward projections were being done at a very high level, and $2 million plus or minus wasn't going to make that much of a difference when the most recent FAS operating budget was $521 million.

Before turning in, I looked to see what else was on Ella's disk. Apparently, she composed most of her memos on her computer, because there were about fifteen short letters on the disk. No wonder Lindsey had so much time to talk on the phone. From the file names, they appeared to be letters announcing meetings, minutes of previous meetings, and requests for data. I read a few of them, just being nosy. Ella's writing style was tediously correct, with little flair or emotion, as if she were afraid of giving anything away.

One file was marked Lindsey Wentworth. Up on the screen came a performance review. It praised Lindsey's work attitude but chided her for spending too much time on the phone. Then came a termination letter.

A termination letter.

The date was Friday, September 17. Two days before Ella died. Key phrases jumped off the page: *"Lindsey Wentworth will be leaving my employ effective immediately," "this termination is for cause," "call me directly for further information."*

So why was Lindsey Wentworth still beavering away in Ella's office if she had just been fired? And why the river of tears over Ella's death?

Girl Friday had some explaining to do.

CHAPTER SEVEN

TILL DEATH
DO US PART

The Harvard Police headquarters on Garden Street is easily the happiest office on campus. Renovated five years ago to make it more accessible to the public, the building seems more like a day-care center than a police station. Bright yellow walls, lime green carpeting, and cheerful signs directing visitors to the bicycle registration and parking desks seem wildly incongruous with campus crime.

Thursday afternoon found me at Sergeant Detective Raphael Griffin's desk near the back of the building. When I approached, he had his back to me and was talking animatedly with a group of four middle-aged white men, all wearing police uniforms.

"So I said, I think you got the wrong fellow, mon!" he exclaimed, playfully punching the man standing next to him in the chest. One of the other men saw me waiting and beckoned me into their circle.

"Detective Griffin," I said as he turned around, "I'm Nikki Chase. We spoke on Monday?"

"Of course, Professor Chase," he said, his face brightening even more. "Do you think I could forget a woman such as you? This lady is a professor in the Economics Department, gentlemen. Show some respect. Sit down now, sit down. What can I do for you, Professor Chase?"

"First of all, you can call me Nikki," I said, settling into a chair. The rest of the men dispersed, grinning.

"Done! What else can I do for you, Nikki?"

"Are you still handling the file on Ella Fisher's death?"

"Yes." His expression quickly turned sober. "How can I help you?"

"It may be nothing," I said. I paused, wondering whether I was about to waste this cop's precious time with what could be just a random string of coincidences.

"What is it, Nikki?"

"It's just that—look, I'm beginning to think that Ella Fisher's fall down those stairs wasn't an accident."

"Really?" He watched me quietly, waiting.

"Well, first, there's her head wound. I still think it's strange that it was so severe. I mean, she was bleeding very heavily from the *back* of her head, as if she had received a direct hit there. But how likely is it that you'd hit the back of your head if you fell down a flight of stairs and landed face first? I'm positive that she was lying facedown when I found her."

"You mentioned that Monday mornin'. So there must be somethin' else." His expression was inscrutable.

"Yes. It may have been a prank, but the wires were deliberately cut at Littauer to cause a blackout just before she fell."

"How do you know that?" he asked sharply.

I couldn't drag my source, Percy, into the middle of this. "Come on, Officer, I work in the building. I've seen the maintenance guys hauling around bales of wire and mumbling about tampering for the past three days. It doesn't take a genius to put two and two together."

"Go on."

"I also found out some information about her secretary, Lindsey Wentworth. You know that Ella and I were working on this Crimson Future report together?"

"Yes." He took off his glasses and slowly cleaned them with a white handkerchief.

"Well, I had to track down some data, and it's a long story, but it came to my attention that she fired Lindsey two days before she died. But Lindsey's still working in Ella's office."

He regarded me closely for moment. "You say it came to your attention? How was that?"

I explained about the computer disk and the letter.

"So the letter may not have been sent?" he asked.

"Right. I couldn't tell."

"Anything else?" He looked at me expectantly as he put his glasses back on.

I told him about my visit to Ella's apartment, her checkbook, and the series of withdrawals.

He took a few notes as I spoke, and when I was finished, he leaned back in his chair and looked at me gravely.

"You've been busy. It's not everyone who would spend so much time on something like this."

"I told you. She was very good to me when she was alive." I felt I knew her better now than I did then. And liked her even more.

"Well, we appreciate your giving us this information. You let me know if you come across anything else that doesn't make sense to you, all right?" He nodded dismissively.

"That's it?" I asked, exasperated.

"Is there a problem?"

"Aren't you at least going to tell me if any of this makes sense? Am I right? Was she murdered?"

Griffin leaned toward me, a faint smile on his face. "Child, you must know that I can't discuss a pendin' case with you."

"Come on, throw me a little crumb to tide me over," I cajoled.

"Afraid not," he said, grinning. "But you keep in touch with me now." He stood up.

Clearly, if I was going to get any further information out of this man, it was going to take time and charm. So as I rose to leave, I paused to look at the photographs on his desk. One looked like a family portrait, with five kids that all looked related. The other was a faded color photograph of a beautiful young woman, her head swathed in a brightly colored cloth. "Is this your family?"

"Oh, now, if you're gone to be askin' me personal questions, you need to call me by my first name. Rafe."

"Okay, Rafe," I said, testing it out. "Who are the people in the pictures?"

"Well," he said, beaming, "these are my brother and sisters. That's Theodora. She's a schoolteacher in St. Thomas. And Esperance. She lives in Queens, in New York, now. And the little one, Prince. He's a fisherman, still livin' in our house in Anegada. And that's my cousin Ti-Jean. He runs the best bar on Virgin Gorda!"

"And the fifth one is you, isn't it?"

"Yeah, that's me, back when I was a little ol' dog."

"Who's this woman? She's beautiful."

"That's my Esmerelda."

I knew the answer immediately, but I asked anyway. "Is she your wife?"

"She was. Long ago, on Anegada, I was married to the prettiest little girl on the island. She was a smart one, too. Ran our own charter business."

"What happened to her?"

"Oh, the Lord took her from me. Fishin' accident."

"I'm so sorry," I said softly.

"These crazy folk, runnin' around divorcin'," he muttered. "Don't know what they got. Till death do us part. That's what the good book says."

"You still miss her."

"Oh, sure, child. But Essie and I talk all the time, never you fear," he said, the smile returning to his eyes. "That woman was always a big talker, doncha know."

He made me repeat my promise to keep in touch, and I said my good-byes with an idea germinating.

He was handsome, hard-working, and charming.

Just what Maggie Dailey needed.

I rambled across the Cambridge Commons, musing about Ella's death. Thinking about the cut wires at Littauer, Lindsey's termination letter, the checks Ella had written shortly before she died. And hadn't Lindsey said that there were a lot of people milling around the day after Ella died, retrieving papers from her office? Images of Vincent Foster danced in my head.

This was ridiculous. As much as I cared about Ella, there was another reason I was so anxious to pursue the cause of her death. To my intense annoyance, Dante Rosario had been my every third thought since I had seen him the day before. I was determined to find something to occupy the part of my brain that refused to surrender the image of him standing near me, touching my sleeve, drawing me ever so slightly toward him.

I was crazy to be wasting thought time on this. I was a tenure-track professor with course materials, several of my own articles and working papers, Ian McAllister's *Times* piece, his Princeton speech, *and* the Crimson Future report hanging over me. I had time for neither violent murder nor violent romance.

Nevertheless, my feet took me toward Ella Fisher's office as I passed the Law School. I just wanted to see if Lindsey's termination letter had caught up with her. And if things had calmed down any.

But Lindsey was still hard at work when I arrived. And true to form, she was on the telephone.

"Yes, Mother, I told you, the class is going to cost about thirty-five hundred dollars. They want it up front. Well, you said that you wanted me to continue my education! He's supposed to be the best."

I caught her eye and she waved at me. "Mother, I've got to go. I told you, I'm staying home tonight. Please don't call him. Promise me you won't, because if you do, I'll tell him I have herpes. Yes, I will. I've got to *go*."

She sighed noisily as she turned to greet me. "Hello, Professor Chase. What can I do for you?"

I smiled despite myself. "You can start by remembering to call me Nikki. You're making me feel old." Maybe that letter had never been sent. She seemed far too guileless to have retrieved it from the mail. If she even knew it had been written.

"Sorry," she said breathlessly. "Do you want some cake? I brought one of Baby Watson's chocolate fudges in for the girls today, and we have plenty left."

"Sure, a small piece would be great." Fat and sugar were just what I needed to put me back on an even keel.

"By the way," I said, as she passed me a paper plate with a hulking piece of cake on it, "I managed to find those financial statements I was looking for."

Her face brightened. "That's great. Where were they?"

"At Ella's house," I said, settling into the chair next to hers. "It was just as I hoped. She had them on a disk. I've got it now, and it's saving me a lot of time not having to work off the hard copy."

"Her house? That's great. I should have thought of that. She spent so much time agonizing over those numbers, she must have been working on them in her sleep. But how did you get in?"

"A mutual friend. Alix Coyle." I took a bite of cake. "What do you mean, she was agonizing over those numbers?"

"Are you kidding? It was all she would think about for a while this summer. She was pretty sure that there was something wrong with some of them. You want some coffee with that?"

I shook my head, putting down my plate. "What do you mean, something wrong with them?"

"Well, she frequently worked late on the committee report, you know. One night I was here with her catching up on my filing, and she started telling me about some of the expenditures being high, or something. I'm not sure." Lindsey broke off, looking confused.

"It's funny, she never mentioned that to me."

"Well, she wouldn't have. She told me she wasn't sure if she was misinterpreting something, and she was going to do more research first. You know how she couldn't stand to be wrong, so she wanted to be sure."

I thought back to what was on the disk that she had been working on. Financial statements from each of the schools. What had she found that was worth spending that much time on?

"Did she say what kind of expenditures?"

"I really don't know, I think it was outside contractors, something like that. She didn't say." Lindsey looked at me, frowning. "I really should know, shouldn't I? But she could be very secretive sometimes. She wasn't the easiest person to work for."

"Sounds like it."

Lindsey smiled wryly. "She was such a control freak. She even used to tell me that one of these days she was going to fire me, just to keep me in line."

"You're kidding." Did that explain the letter I'd found?

"Yes, she used to write termination letters. She'd show them to me and everything. She'd do it just to remind me who was in charge."

I watched Lindsey closely as she spoke. It seemed a bit too coincidental that this subject had come up. But she seemed sincere.

"That must have really pissed you off," I prodded.

"Well, yes. But I knew it was because of the type of childhood she had. I mean, really, who could blame her for a harmless power trip every now and then? Poor people are always living under constant threat."

"You're a better woman than I am, Lindsey."

"Well, thank you," she said primly. Just then, a loud male voice emanated from Ella's office.

"Who's that?"

"Isaiah Fisher. Ella's ex-husband. He says he's got to pick up some mementos from her office. I think he just wants the use of a free phone." She rolled her eyes. "He's been in there for an hour! Freeloader."

"Fine, Rufus, be like that," I heard the voice shout in an exasperated tone. "Twenty dollars a box. Yeah, man, it's been a pleasure doing business with you, too."

Ten seconds later, he emerged from the office, still talking loudly. "Damn. I can't get a break from this brother. There's no better businessman than a lapsed Marxist. That dialectical materialism makes 'em more hardheaded than the rest of us." He paused and looked at me. "What are you staring at?"

He was 180 degrees different from what I was expecting. Given Ella's frequent criticism of haughty, light-skinned blacks, I would have envisioned her ex-husband as dark-skinned and curly-haired, with rounded African features. But Isaiah Fisher was a very fair-skinned black man, tall and slender, with a neatly trimmed goatee, wavy brown hair and a rather sharp nose and jawline. He looked as if he was pushing fifty, even in his youthful loose-fitting beige pants and tunic. On his head was a triangular hat made of kente cloth. An African crown.

"I guess the sister has never seen a real black man before," he drawled.

Was he kidding?

"I didn't mean to be rude," I said slowly, still incredulous that he was Mr. Ella Fisher. "I-I'm Nikki Chase."

"I-I'm pleased to meet you," he said, the merest hint of mockery glinting in his eyes. "So who are you?"

"She's a professor at Harvard who worked with Ella on a committee," Lindsey said briskly. "Are you finished in there?"

"Yes, I have what I came for," he said, turning to Lindsey. "Although I don't know how much good this bourgeois literature she's got on her shelf is going to be for my store. *Before the Mayflower. Up From Slavery. Letter from a Birmingham Jail. Member of the Club. Reflections of an Affirmative Action Baby.* The collected writings of William Junius Wilson. That office is like a pharmacy stocked with the opiates of the black middle class."

"What are you talking about?" I said sharply. I had all of those works on my own bookshelf.

"My customers at Liberation Books are not interested in reading some accommodationist Oreo's ramblings about how to make the white folks less afraid of them," he said, facing me again. "I should have known my integrationist ex-wife wasn't going to own anything I could use. A room full of self-help books for confused wanna-bes."

"Liberation Books. Is that the place on Mount Auburn?" I had a vague recollection of a small basement storefront on the outskirts of Harvard Square near the post office, its front window papered with posters of Malcolm X, Haile Selassie, Bobby Seale, and Huey Newton. It never seemed to be open when I passed by, but Maggie shopped there sometimes.

"Yes, that's my establishment. How kind of you to notice us. We specialize in the literature of the African diaspora. But I don't think I've ever seen you there. I assume you don't get around to reading black authors, your being at Harvard and all." He dragged out the name Harvard so long that it began to sound like an obscenity.

"Now why would you assume that?"

"You must live around here. You've never been in my store. You've got this *Friends*-looking hairstyle going. What am I supposed to think?"

"If you treat all your potential customers this way, it's no wonder your store's been empty every time I've gone by it," I snapped. "Lindsey, thanks for your help. I've got to get going."

"Is there anything more I can help you with?" Lindsey asked.

"No," I said, glaring at Fisher. So Ella was once married to this self-righteous Eldridge Cleaver wanna-be. No wonder she couldn't stand light-skinned black people. Probably brought back too many memories of him. I was amazed that she had married an asshole like this in the first place, given how strong she was. She must have been totally color-struck: fooled into believing that as a dark-skinned woman, she was so lucky to have a light-skinned man interested in her that she should ignore the fact that he was a complete idiot.

"I'll walk out with you," Fisher said. Despite the fact that I was vibrating with annoyance, his eyes were roaming over me as if we were in a dive bar and it was fifteen minutes to closing time. Not exactly the grieving widower.

"So what department do you teach in?" he asked, as we started down the stairs.

"Economics."

"I see, one of those Ward-Connerly-capitalism-forever types, huh? Let me guess. Gingrich supporter."

"All right, that's it." I stopped and faced him. "I don't know what your problem is, but you don't know *jack-shit* about me, and I don't have to justify myself to you." I've been called a lot of dirty names, but Republican has never been one of them.

"Girl," he mocked, "you need to read some Shaharazad Ali. Learn how the black woman is supposed to talk to the black man."

"Let me give it a try," I said sweetly. "Forgive me for speaking harshly to you, my African prince. Please, let me carry that load the white man has placed on your shoulders, since my own life has been so easy and carefree, and I have no burdens of my own."

To my surprise, he grinned at me. "Damn, you're just like her, aren't you?"

"Like who?" We started back down the stairs.

"Ella."

I looked over at him, and saw a wry smile flicker across his face. "Weren't you divorced?" I asked.

"Well, sure, but she was still my running buddy," he said, surprise in his voice. "She was still down."

"So it was an amicable divorce?" I said, a bit more interested now. After all, he could certainly educate me about Ella. "I thought that was an oxymoron." We passed through the entrance of Langdell Hall and out into the sunshine.

"Well, we married young, and I guess we shouldn't have been surprised when it didn't work out."

"Had you known her long before you married?"

He shrugged. "Six months, maybe. It seemed longer, though."

For the first time, he sounded sincere. Without discussing it, we paused near the stone steps of Langdell.

"So where did you meet?"

"In Harvard Yard, believe it or not. I was the President of the Boston University SDS chapter, and I was in the Yard for a candle-light vigil in the spring of '69. We were marching through on our way to Mass Ave. and I caught a glimpse of her at the top of the stairs of Lehman Hall—you know that red brick building at the corner of the Yard?"

I nodded.

"I found out later that she was just getting out of an Extension School course and was on her way home. I saw her and stopped dead in my tracks." He shook his head and sat down on the steps. "Burned my hand on the candle wax and didn't even notice." A new tone had come into his voice, and I sensed that he was drifting away into his memories. "She had the largest, sweetest brown eyes I had ever seen. The girl looked so intense. So hungry."

That sounded like the Ella I knew.

"So you followed her home?" I prodded, sitting down next to him. He had probably picked a fight with her first.

"Not quite." He laughed softly. "I got her to join the march, *then* I followed her home. And it was the beginning of the best time of my life. Old girl didn't have enough money for school, so she was taking secretarial classes during the day and attending a free class at the Extension School in the evening. She moved into my apartment in Central Square after I'd known her for a week, and we'd sit up for hours into the night, discussing the war, the Panthers, Malcolm X."

He focused his attention on me with an intensity that startled me. "Those were wonderful days, Harvard. Days that someone your age can only imagine. My God, back then I could walk through Harvard Square shouting that I needed ten people to get on a bus to Mississippi to help with voter registration, and I'd get 'em within ten minutes."

That did seem less likely, now that the Square was choked with tourists, yuppies, and Young Republicans. But not impossible.

"People in my generation really *believed* in economic justice," he continued. "It was a way of living, a way of being that was noble and beautiful and proud."

I shifted restlessly in the face of a rising wave of sanctimoniousness.

"You don't get it, do you?" he said, annoyed that he was losing me. "A good-looking, smart black sister like you, working for a big white institution like this. You probably don't have any idea what it feels like to believe in something so deeply that it changes your life."

That got my attention. "If there's one thing I can't stand, Mr. Fisher, it's people being condescending to me about how the sixties were the last decade that anyone felt anything or fought for anything. Just because the issues aren't as clear-cut now doesn't mean that my entire generation is lazy and complacent. You think it's easy being the only black person in the entire Economics Department? The way I see it, you're hiding out in that bookstore and I'm out here fighting on the front lines."

He stared at me in shock. "You're very eloquent, Harvard."

"You were telling me about Ella."

He looked as if he were going to resist my changing the subject, but then sighed and continued. "There's nothing more to tell. I loved her almost from the moment I met her; when she looked at me with those big brown eyes, I would've swum to Africa and back for her." He sat quietly for a moment and then laughed sharply. "Sorry. I haven't been down that road for a while."

"So why did you divorce?" What snake crawled into your Central Square Eden?

"Blame it on Harvard. This damn place brought us together and then split us up. We had ten great years just hanging out on the East Coast, moving from Cambridge to Harlem, going to meetings in Chicago. Just living like gypsies, but we loved it; even joined a commune for a while."

"It must have been tough, being away from your families, moving around so much."

He leaned toward me. "Are you kidding? It was great! Shoot, we never had any problems until Ella started working for Harvard."

"Why was that a problem?"

"Her ambition. She decided it was time to settle down, and make a mark, and she went after it with a vengeance. She spent all her passion and energy fighting her way into the middle class. She started acting like some white girl, like she was an ice person."

"What?"

"When I met her she was passionate about the same things I was: racism, socialism, the war, the ridiculous lifestyle of the bourgeoisie—"

"But Harvard took that away," I said skeptically.

"Damn straight!" he replied defensively. "They treated her like shit when she started working here. Like she was their maid or their Mammy. But instead of telling them where to stuff it, she starts reading self-improvement books, management books, *diction* books, for God's sake. *Dress for Success, Looking Out for Number One* and shit like that. Anything to make her feel more qualified to be working with whitey. I tried to understand, I really did. We'd been trying for years to have kids, and she'd miscarried three times. I know that she was bitter about that, and she was looking for an escape. But she went too far. She decided that she was going to make it big at Harvard, and she wouldn't stop at anything to do it. Like the time I wrote that speech—" He stopped abruptly.

"What speech?" I prodded.

"She needed some speech for that House Master she worked for. Isn't that just like those rich white assholes? Calling themselves 'House Masters'? Like the rest of us are still their slaves. Well, I wrote this speech for her. And she got all the credit. Brilliant, he called her. Hah! Would it have killed her to share the spotlight with me?"

"How did that make you feel?" I could guess.

"Her ambition for money and power? It made me sick. She betrayed the cause. She betrayed everything I stood for." His voice hardened, and for a moment I found it quite easy to believe that he could have sent her flying down a flight of stairs.

"So you divorced," I prompted him.

"We were separated for a couple of years, but then she decided to make it official." He laughed bitterly.

"But you said it was an amicable divorce?" Let's keep our stories straight.

"Well, after a while, yeah," he said softly. "At the beginning, it was hell. I was pissed off and totally strung out about it. I dragged around town, hanging out at the places we used to go."

"So why did you stay in Cambridge if it had so many bad memories?"

"Because I love this town!" His voice regained its earlier animation. "The whole country has gone crazy. Cambridge, Berkeley, Madison, Ann Arbor, and the West Village are the only safe places left. I had a good life here, and my store was just getting established. I couldn't let her run me out of town. A town I'd been in long before her."

"So you kept in touch with Ella after the divorce?"

"After a year went by, I started to call her, just to shoot the breeze. She seemed to want to talk to me, too, and we just got to calling each other every now and then. I don't expect you to understand, since I see you're single, but there's a bond that gets formed during a long marriage that lasts, somehow. I didn't talk to her all the time, I hadn't spoken to her for over a month before she died. But in the end, she was still one of my best buddies."

The words were right, but I was beginning to feel that something was missing. Nostalgia, anger, and resignation over her death had been blended so expertly into this conversation that it didn't quite ring true. Could he have recovered from his shock and surprise in the space of three days?

"Did you ever talk about work with her?" I asked.

"Sometimes. Not usually. She liked to keep that to herself. You can understand why, given the scene when we divorced."

"Did she ever talk about working with President Barrett?"

"Ah, so you've heard the stories, too. They were real tight, you know." His smile was the merest bit louche.

"Are you implying that they were lovers?" I asked sharply.

"You don't need a weatherman to know which way the wind is blowing, Harvard."

"President Barrett is married, isn't he?"

Fisher's lips twisted into a smile. "He has a wife. I'm not sure that he still has a marriage."

I glanced at my watch and realized that I was about to be late for my afternoon lecture.

"Will I see you again, Harvard?" he asked as I stood up.

"Not unless you change your mind about the university and enroll in one of my courses." I heard him laugh as I started for Littauer.

I walked through the back door of the building feeling that I had returned to the present after an unplanned trip to the sixties. SDS, the war, Malcolm X: acronyms and names that seemed quaint and a little dusty from being stored on the shelf were still central to this man's life.

I wondered if somehow they had been to Ella's, too.

CHAPTER EIGHT

IT'S ALL COMING BACK TO ME

Harvard Square at dusk is a carnival, a fashion show, an attitude, a breath of indigo air. I had come home from the library Thursday night earlier than I had originally planned because I couldn't concentrate on my work: remembered conversations with Dante Rosario came between me and the capital investment theorists, so I reluctantly surrendered. I spent the early evening staring moodily into my closet, trying to determine what one wears to a casual conversation with one's old obsession and current housemate. It wasn't a date. I had no desire for it to be a date. But revenge required that I be absolutely stunning.

After a half hour of internal whining about the state of my wardrobe, I settled on a red wool sweater that Jess says makes me look buxom; black jeans and black leather boots to remind myself that I was in charge; and a pendant on a silver chain so that I'd have something to play with when the conversation got awkward, as I was certain that it would. I pulled on my black suede jacket, wound a silk scarf around my neck, and surveyed the overall effect in my mirror. A little too contrived, but at least I didn't look like a *Glamour* Don't.

I passed the usual assortment of Cantabrigians on my way to the Square: a solemn, bearded thirty-something man walked by with a boom box playing Bach and a tortoiseshell cat on his shoulder; a trio of broad-shouldered blond men wearing Harvard Varsity Crew sweatshirts crossed my path at the Johnson Gate, loudly discussing the upcoming Head of the Charles regatta; a young woman dressed entirely in black read the *Paris Review* beside a bounteous stack of pumpkins and Indian corn at the Out of Town Newsstand; and at

the corner of Church and Brattle Streets, an elegant black man
played the saxophone as passersby dropped coins in the case at his
feet. I contributed a dollar and then crossed the street and made my
way toward Cafe Algiers. It was the first official night of autumn,
and stray orange leaves swirled under my feet as I pulled the door
open.

Cambridge has always been famous for its coffeehouses, where
people gathered to drink cafe latte and eat Sacher tortes long before Seattle made it safe for the rest of the country. Cafe Algiers is
my favorite, nestled into the basement of a small wooden building
in the heart of the Square. The dim, subterranean space is filled
with brass-topped tables, tapestries, woven baskets, and African
masks—the air heavy with cigarette smoke, the smell of dark coffee, and the sound of intellectuals pontificating.

Dante Rosario was there when I arrived. The clock on the wall
informed me that dithering over my outfit had made me ten minutes late. He was leaning against the doorjamb, coolly watching the
crowd. I remembered other nights we had spent here, arguing,
laughing, signaling to each other. As I walked toward him, I considered what message to send tonight. We spent an awkward moment tacitly considering the etiquette of greeting: to kiss, shake
hands, hug, or just wave? The choices seemed limitless and time
was short. We settled on a light kiss on the cheek. We were going
to play nice.

Dante surveyed the room with an amused expression as I slipped
into my chair. "It's been a while. The last time we were here, the
Germans wore gray and you wore blue."

As I slipped off my jacket, smiling despite my firm intention to
be difficult, I found him watching me. He was wearing an expression that seemed almost . . . appreciative.

"But I see that some things do change," he said, eyes twinkling.
For a moment, I entertained the idle fantasy that he would actually
compliment my appearance.

"You used to be on time for everything," he said smoothly.

Fine. We were already playing the game. It was all coming back
to me.

"My years in New York taught me the importance of making an
entrance," I returned. "So what brings you back East?"

"Well, with my dissertation being published by Farrar, Straus and

Giroux in January, it seemed to make sense to be closer to New York," he said casually.

I swallowed hard. "I guess that would make sense." *Shit. His dissertation was being published? By a commercial press?* "But that doesn't explain why you're in Cambridge."

"Columbia made me a great offer. But my family's still in South Boston. Besides, I missed Harvard. I had some great times here." His eyes challenged me to figure out if he was including our relationship in the category of "great times."

Sadist.

"I'm surprised you didn't stay on at Stanford, preaching to the heathen," I said archly. It was high time I reminded myself of why this man was no good. For one thing, he came from a long line of immigrant Republicans and remained unapologetically conservative, like his father and grandfather before him. And he was smart enough to know better.

"I gave it my best shot for eight years, but it's a lost cause," he said ruefully. "I was starting to feel like Joshua in the wilderness."

"You think it'll be any different here? Demon political correctness is running amok on campus. We don't even call the women 'girls' anymore."

"Damn. Not even socially?" A waiter brought us two tall goblets of water and promptly disappeared without taking our order.

"I wish you luck," I said blithely, studiously avoiding his eyes. "From what I hear, the liberal eggheads that run the Government Department are fairly unforgiving of heretics, free spirits, and malcontents among the faculty." To my horror, my hand brushed against my glass as I finished talking, and water promptly spilled everywhere.

"Here, let me get that." Dante was on his feet instantly. "Did it spill on you?"

"No." I pulled my arm from under his hand as if I had been singed. "No, it's just on the table. Thanks." I dabbed at the spreading pool of water, praying that a chasm would open up in the floor below me and swallow me whole. So much for New York sophistication.

"Excuse me." Dante touched the arm of a passing waitress who turned impatiently and then softened as the full effect of his eyes took hold. "Could you help clean this up and bring us another glass of water? And we're ready to order."

The waitress smiled at me as she mopped up the table. Her expression said, *Honey, we've all been there.* "So, what'll you have?"

"I'll have a double espresso," I said, telegraphing my thanks.

"Afraid I'm going to put you to sleep?" Dante interjected, grinning.

"Hardly. And the gentleman will have?"

"A cafe latte. And biscotti. Bring enough for two, okay?"

It was definitely time to change the subject before I completely derailed. "So have they given you an office yet?" I said briskly.

"Yes, it's on the ground floor of Littauer." He seemed to sense my change in mood, because he, too, straightened up in his chair. "My first night was pretty eventful."

A bus boy came by with a fresh glass of water, and I cautiously slid it to the center of the table, well out of harm's way.

"Eventful? How so?"

"A woman died in the building right after I left."

"You were in Littauer on Sunday night?"

"Yeah, I was unpacking boxes all afternoon, and I decided to stay late and finish it off, since I had to teach first thing the following morning."

The waitress returned with our coffee and a plate of biscotti and chocolate-dipped strawberries. I gingerly sipped my espresso.

"So did you miss the blackout Sunday night?" I prompted.

"Yeah, I must have left right before it happened. Although I had a small adventure of my own. I found an earring in the hall outside my door when I was leaving."

"Really?"

"At the time I thought it belonged to my secretary. But it's not hers, and she says that no one has claimed it, even though it seems to be quite expensive."

"Expensive?" I reached for a strawberry.

"It's a diamond earring. As my secretary, Angie, says, a whopper of a diamond surrounded by sapphires."

"Which office are you in, anyway?"

"The one just off the main lobby. Someone named George Brille used to have it."

"And you're sure this earring wasn't there when you came in earlier that day?"

"You couldn't miss this thing. It's huge. It definitely wasn't there when I went out to grab dinner."

An earring dropped on the floor just off the main lobby. Right before the blackout.

"Look at those eyes," Dante murmured under his breath. "Like stars." For a moment, I was puzzled about whom he was referring to. Then he looked at me, smiling, and I felt my heart turn over. "What's going on, Nik? You're glowing."

"Nothing. I'm not glowing," I said, shaking my head adamantly. "I just think it's fascinating."

"Hey, this is me, okay? I know you."

"Not anymore," I said lightly. "So where is the earring now?"

"In my office somewhere. I think in my desk drawer," he said softly. His eyes were searching mine intently, but I was still on the earring trail.

"Did you notice whether it was a clip-on or a post?"

"Come back to my office with me and we'll find out," he said quietly.

I choked on my last sip of coffee, caught off guard by the electricity that shot through me at the tone in his voice and the expression in his eyes.

Oh my God. It's happening again.

"Let's not go there, Dante," I said. We both knew what was likely to happen if I found myself alone in a dimly lit office with him, and I knew from experience that I'd be the one who'd be sorry later.

"Where? To my office?" he said, disingenuous to the end.

"Right," I said dryly. "Look at the time. I've got to go," I said, looking around for the waitress. *And fast.*

"Are you sure?" he said, not withdrawing an inch. "You seem a little . . . flustered."

I *was* flustered.

"I've missed you, Nik," he said softly. He used to be able to play me like a violin when he looked at me like that.

"You are *so* arrogant," I muttered, stifling the urge to scream it at the top of my lungs.

"I'm showering you with compliments and I'm arrogant. Interesting theory. Care to explain?" he said, laughing.

This was clearly just a game to him.

"Cut the bullshit," I snapped. "If you think you can buy me an espresso, tell me you missed me, and then get laid, think again."

"Oh, but it worked so well before," he said sharply, leaning back in his chair and frowning at me. "Why not now? I mean, that's all it was, right? Never did care about you as a person. Never could handle your formidable intelligence. Is that about it?"

"I never said that."

"That's *exactly* what you said the last time we talked. Maybe I was indecisive then. But I never deliberately set out to hurt you."

"You got exactly what you wanted from me, which was a roll in the hay with a black girl whom you'd never have the nerve to bring back home to Southie to meet the folks. And then you took off. Eight years went by, and I didn't hear from you again until you happened to move into my house. But you've really missed me. *Please.*"

"That's completely unfair, Nik." The volume of our conversation was rising, and our waitress shook her head sympathetically as she tossed the check on the table.

"There were a lot of things going on then that you didn't know about. And it had nothing to do with race."

"Come on, Rosario. How stupid do you think I am?"

"Look, I couldn't be with *anyone* then. You were as close—closer—to me than any other woman."

I shook my head emphatically. This was humiliating. "You know what? I really don't want to talk about it." I stood up and pulled on my jacket. "We've both got better things to do with our time than muck around in ancient history." I tossed five dollars on the table.

"Not so ancient that it still doesn't get to you," he mocked, pulling on his coat and depositing another five on the table.

"You know, you are the same arrogant jackass that you were eight years ago," I hissed as we left the table.

"And you're as self-righteous and argumentative as ever."

"Then why don't you find another apartment? That way you'll escape ever having to deal with me again."

"Now, there's an idea." He followed me out into the street and gripped my arm as I turned and started to walk away. "You know what? Your problem is that you want your life to run just like one of your economic models, with all the data points in nice logical clusters with a neat theorem to explain it all."

"And you have a problem with that?" I snapped.

"No. Just as long as you consider me the outlier. The one data point that you just can't explain."

"Great," I retorted. It was just like him to try to one-up me with a statistics metaphor. "Then I can do with you what I do with all the other outliers in my databases. Throw them out."

Stick to your own academic discipline, asshole.

Ten seconds after we parted, I was blaming myself for having agreed to see him. Hoping to walk off my frustration, I headed for the river. The night air cooled my flushed face as I walked along Memorial Drive. If I had any hope of getting work done that evening, I had to shake off my memories of the housemate and think about something more intellectual than the curve of his lips when he smiled.

The Charles River was sparkling in the moonlight as I reached the Weeks Bridge. I paused at the top of its span, contemplating the row of stately red brick Houses curving along the bend in the river. Dunster House is my old dorm, named after Henry Dunster, the school's first president. The donor who funded construction of the original Houses had intended that each be named for one of the first seven Harvard presidents. The university had balked, however, at designating one for the seventh President, Dr. Leonard Hoar.

I could hear wisps of laughter from the Dunster courtyard, and a small flickering light indicated that the cool night air hadn't chased everyone indoors. I could make out a group sitting at one of the wrought-iron tables scattered across the courtyard, the light streaming from the library's large French windows supplementing a candle.

It was an autumn night exactly like this the first time that I saw Dante Rosario. It was sophomore year, and I was climbing the stairs to my room. He was spraying acrylic spiderwebs out of a metal can onto the stairwell for the annual Halloween party. I stared as I walked by, fascinated that artificial spiderwebs existed and that someone who looked like that had found his way into my stairwell.

It turned out he was a Government major who lived two floors below me. So I saw him again, quite a lot, in the following years: in the dining room, on the stairwell, at parties, and occasionally in my dreams. I would have dated him in a New York minute if he had asked. But he didn't, for quite some time, despite my best efforts to the contrary. It wasn't until the autumn of our senior year that we began what could be called, if the definition were stretched to the limit, our relationship. Even now, I don't know why he turned to me then. Even now, I'm not exactly sure why we couldn't make it work.

The first time he kissed me, I was holding a book in my hands, and while the symbolism of it was lost on me then, I later realized how appropriate it had been. For books we could talk about, endlessly it seemed. We spent long nights closeted away in his room, chewing over texts from classes and recent articles on politics. And even though we disagreed about almost every idea that came up in conversation, the talk was rich, dense with political theories and reform proposals and heated arguments about policy. But as for feelings? Well, those we couldn't seem to talk about at all. I knew I was never enough for him, but I never knew exactly why. Was it my race? Was it his fears? Was I too smart for him? Or not smart enough? Whatever the cause, in the end, all the wit in the world couldn't hold him with me, and when he left, I felt as if a piece of my vocabulary went with him. He is the only person that I have ever known who is interested in conducting everyday conversations that require words like justice and equity and honor. The only person I've ever known who seemed capable of talking the stars right down out of the sky.

I started back up JFK Street for home. Astounding that he would be there when I arrived. I was passing the Charles Hotel when I saw Lindsey Wentworth and Isaiah Fisher just ahead of me.

The sight of them brought me forcibly back to the present. What was wrong with this picture? What could they possibly have in common? The two of them looked as if they were having quite a night. Arm in arm, they were laughing and flirting as if they were mid-way through a very successful date. So much for being all broken up about Ella's death.

I remained a few feet behind them and followed them through the Square. I could hear Fisher describing the economic challenge of trying to run a bookstore and how much more he could accomplish with more funding. Lindsey seemed sympathetic, and I wondered how long it would be before Daddy Wentworth would be writing a check. Fisher managed to mention said father and his money twice in the five minutes that it took them to reach their destination, the Wursthaus Restaurant. They disappeared inside the German eatery and I debated trying to eavesdrop on their conversation. They looked drunk enough so that it was conceivable that they wouldn't notice me. And what harm could come of it, even if they did?

I plunged into the darkened entrance and followed them up the stairs.

The second-story bar at the Wursthaus can seem either very romantic or very seedy, depending upon your mood. It was almost completely dark, except for the streetlight making patterns on the tables as it shone through the venetian blinds. Lindsey and Fisher were ensconced in a booth on the left side of the room, so I slipped into the booth directly behind them and quietly asked for a glass of white wine.

This proved to be my fatal mistake, as the Wursthaus is justly famous for its lengthy list of domestic and imported beers. My waitress seemed particularly amused that a solo drinker would bother with this particular bar unless it was to partake of the house specialty, and became increasingly louder and more insistent that I sample something on tap. The ever-cordial Lindsey stuck her head around the corner of the booth to recommend what she was having, and I was cold busted. Thus does a priss make for a bad detective.

"Professor Chase! It's you!" she cried. "What are you doing here?"

"Yes, Harvard, what brings you to the Wursthaus?" Fisher echoed, his eyes openly mocking me as I stood up and came around to their table.

"I'm meeting a friend, and he seems to be late," I said smoothly. "I'd better go down and check on him."

"Well, it was nice to see you," Lindsey called after me.

I started rapidly down the stairs, angry at myself for having tried such an obvious stunt. I'd utterly failed in my attempt to figure out what was going on between them.

And if Ella really *had* been murdered, and one of them was involved, I had just put them on notice that I was watching.

CHAPTER NINE

PUBLISH OR PERISH

"Look, fly the damned book up from the Library of Congress if you have to. Just get it on my desk by the end of the day today." I had one nerve left, and this research librarian was standing right on it.

It was Friday morning. Ian McAllister was back in Cambridge, and had called at seven-thirty that morning, insisting that I help him complete an article for the *American Economic Review* that had to be on the editor's desk in seventy-two hours. This chore was in addition to my two Ec. 10 lectures that day; Ian's article on direct foreign investment for the *Times*, which was now overdue; my paper for the American Economic Association conference in January; and the Crimson Future report.

"I can do a rush retrieval from storage, but it's going to cost a lot of money. We're very short-staffed right now, with the students not working yet."

Before I could answer, my secretary, Gwen, buzzed me over the intercom.

"Look, do whatever you need to!" I snapped at the librarian. "I already told you we'll pay whatever the cost." It was supposed to be publish *or* perish, but I seemed to be doing both.

I hung up and pressed the intercom button. "What?"

"Sergeant Detective Griffin. Harvard Police. Returning your call. Again."

"I'll have to call him back." My second phone line began ringing. "Didn't you tell him when he called the last time that I'd get back to him later?"

"Hello?" I said briskly, silencing the insistent phone.

"It's me," said Ian McAllister. "Did you call the library?"

I stifled a screech of frustration. What did he think I was doing, sitting in my office polishing my fingernails? "Widener can retrieve Marshall's book by the end of the day, and I'm getting the rest of the data on-line."

102 • P A M E L A T H O M A S - G R A H A M

"Fine, fine. The Princeton speech draft looks quite good, champ."

"Thanks."

"By the way, how's that Crimson Future report coming?"

"I started to tell you this morning. I had a slow start because—"

"What is it, Paula?" Ian's secretary must be hovering over him. A pause, and then he barked: "Tell him two minutes."

"The report is coming along fine," I said quickly. "But the disk that you gave me didn't work, and I didn't have the time to work off of the hard copy."

"Paula's got another copy of the disk!" he snapped. "Why didn't you get it from her?"

"She was out sick most of the week, so I—"

"Well, she's back now," he cut me off. "Come over and get another copy right away. How could you let this much time go by, Veronica? This report has to be first-rate. The press will devour it."

"Look, Ian, I'm doing my best. I even went to—"

"My next meeting is starting. Get on it right now."

My muttered expletive was stifled by an indifferent dial tone.

Seconds later, Gwen buzzed. "This cop insisted on holding for you. Said to tell you that he needs to know why you were calling."

Groaning, I picked up the line.

"Rafe?" I said rapidly. "Listen, thanks for calling back, but it's really crazy here right now. Can I call you this afternoon?"

"Listen, Professor Chase, if you were callin' about Ella Fisher, I need to know sooner rather than later."

His tone was all business. It jolted me right out of my paper chase.

"Yes, I *was* calling about Ella," I said more slowly. "And call me Nikki, will you?"

"What did you want to tell me, Nikki?" I had failed to get even a small chuckle out of him.

"You remember that Crimson Future report Ella and I were working on? A couple of days ago, I found a slight discrepancy in the financial statements we were working with." I reminded him of my odyssey to come up with a disk with the financials, and told him how I had discovered that there was a difference between Ian's and Ella's version of the numbers.

"How big is the difference?" he asked.

"About two million dollars. It's actually not very much, given the total FAS budget. And I'm fairly certain that it's because some administrative costs were reclassified. But apparently Ella was troubled by something in the financials. She even mentioned it to her secretary, Lindsey."

"Yes, we've spoken with her," he muttered.

I leaned back in my chair. He was worried, although he wouldn't say it.

"Come on, Rafe," I coaxed. "We both know something's not right. What's going on?"

There was a pause, and then he spoke softly into the phone. "I'm not supposed to be talking about this, now. But you've been a good child, bringin' me everything you know. So you deserve to know somethin'."

He paused again. "We think it may not have been an accident."

Hearing him confirm my suspicion sent an electric charge through me. My hunch had been right all along.

"Holy shit," I whispered. "She *was* murdered."

"Now, I didn't say that, child," he growled. "We don't know that."

"But you're running a criminal investigation, aren't you?"

"I'm not sayin' another thing. And you'd best not, either."

"Listen, how can I help?" My adrenaline was soaring.

"You can't, Nikki. Other than keepin' your eyes open, just like you've been. And I want to see those financial statements."

There had to be something more I could do. Who had wanted Ella Fisher dead?

"Listen," I said impulsively. "We're having a dinner party tomorrow night. We have two new tenants in my house, and my landlady is having a welcome bash. Why don't you come, and I'll show you the financials while you're there?"

For the first time that day, I heard a smile in his voice.

"That's mighty nice of you. You sure you got enough?"

"Are you kidding? When Maggie cooks, we have enough food for the entire block. My best friend, Jess, is coming, too. Besides, I've been wanting you to meet my landlady."

"Really, now?"

"Yes. Say you'll come."

"Okay, then. If I can bring one of my pecan pies."

"Sold."

The rest of the day sped by in a haze of hurried lectures, irate phone calls to Widener Library, and fits of writing documents. By five-thirty I was frazzled, and wondering why I had ever left New York to come here and be paid a tenth as much for the same amount of work and even more stress.

The mood lifted when I crossed through the Canaday Gate and entered the Yard. It was the magic hour, and the sun was dappling the red brick buildings with gold. The anticipation on the faces of the students rushing by was contagious; it was the first Friday night of their college lives, and I wished them luck. The Freshman Mixer might just be the start of something big.

I completed my usual Friday errands in an increasingly cheerful mood, soothed by the amiable jostling of the early-evening crowds: Cambridge Savings Bank for cash, the Coop for a pair of socks, CVS for cold cream and toothpaste, and then a quick stop at the Harvard Bookstore for weekend reading material. Afterward, it would be back to my office to finish Ian's article for the *American Economic Review*, assuming that the Widener librarians had gotten off their collective butts and retrieved my book.

The aisles of the bookstore were crowded, and I shouldered my way through to fiction, stepping over people sitting on the floor, leaning against the shelves, and perched on step stools, all with their noses buried in books. I adore bookstores, and I've always been incredibly greedy about owning books. Even with signing privileges in one of the world's great library systems, I still buy three or four a week. Someday I'll open the Penultimate Bookstore, where the second-to-last copy of everything will be on sale, but the final ones will always be mine.

That evening I spent a cursory amount of time browsing the shelves. Ntozake Shange's new novel, a book of short stories by Alice Munro, and a new biography of Adam Clayton Powell and I was on my way. As I headed toward the cashier, a high-pitched squeal stopped me in my tracks.

"Nikki!"

I turned to find Jennifer Blum standing behind me, a formidable stack of magazines in her arms. Jennifer was the undergraduate representative to the Crimson Future Committee, and stood for almost everything that I'm against. But somehow, I couldn't quite give up on her. Despite her retro political views and sex-kitten wardrobe, she was a lot of fun.

She stood before me today dressed in her usual uniform: black micromini and form-fitting sweater, black tights, and army boots. Her brown hair hung straight and shiny to her shoulders, and a coquettish expression flitted across her face.

"What are you up to tonight?" she cried, putting her hand on my shoulder and turning me smartly toward the cash register.

"Nothing fun. I've got to finish an article over the weekend, so I'll be in my office all night," I said, sucking in my stomach. The girl always made me feel ten pounds overweight.

"Great. Then you can come with me to the President's Open House. I need a gal pal to check out the male flesh with me."

"Where is your usual coterie that you need an aging professor for this duty?"

"Cut that out, Nikki. You're the best. By the way, I love your sweater! If you must know, Sarah and Mitzi are in New York this weekend. Will you come?"

The President's annual Autumn Open House. Decent appetizers, terrible sherry, cynical upperclassmen, and potentially interesting conversation. Or my office, with Ian's article and a greasy pizza to keep me company. It was a close call. I shrugged. "What the heck. For male flesh, why not?"

We ambled down Plympton Street on our way to the President's residence. The sidewalk was well worn, its red bricks having been trodden on by generations of upperclassmen racing back and forth between the River Houses and the Yard.

"Hurry up—this is the Fly," Jennifer muttered as we crossed Mount Auburn Street and passed a low red brick building with a discreet crest over the door. "I just broke up with someone there."

She *would* be dating a finals club boy. When I was in college, it was only the arrogant, the rich, and the WASP wanna-bes who were "punched" to join the all-male finals clubs. I knew a couple of guys on whom this honor was bestowed, and ever after they averted their gazes when we passed on campus, their eyes obviously cast on a higher plane. My feeling was that they didn't call the Porcellian Club "The Pig" for nothing.

We arrived at the door of the President's house on Channing

Place as a nearby church bell was chiming seven o'clock. The three-story red brick house was framed by a low white picket fence, the front lawn arrayed with weeping willows and flaming orange maple trees suffused with the last few rays of sunlight. We made our way through the crowd of students at the front door, Jennifer calling out to friends real and imaginary, and entered an oak-paneled living room dense with the fog of cigars.

As I crossed the threshold, I was greeted with a long-forgotten sight: Christian Chung, my old economics tutor and the alleged bane of Ella Fisher's existence. He was standing near the fireplace, engaged in animated conversation with an older, silver-haired man. From where I stood, he looked exactly the same as he had years ago: muscled physique, narrow waist, shiny jet black hair, and the demeanor of a caged tiger. He was wearing a snow-white shirt and gray wool pants, and as he leaned in to make a point to his companion, I took in his tie, which was deep red with a subtle gold inlay, and his left cufflink, which was shaped like a miniature white porcelain faucet reading "Hot."

Did the right one read "Cold"?

And was it just me, or did he really look good enough to eat?

Despite her plea for a companion, I knew that Jennifer would operate better without me trailing around after her, so when I heard Christian ending his conversation, I walked toward him, smiling.

"Christian, I don't know if you remember me, but I was in your economics tutorial almost nine years ago. I'm an Assistant Professor now. Nikki Chase."

He shook my outstretched hand a bit distractedly. "What brings you to the President's House?" he asked with a proprietary air. The man acted like he was hosting this party.

"Hello, Scott," he nodded to a passing silver-haired man in a tweed blazer. "Head of the Biochemistry Department," he murmured.

"Wonderful dinner last week, Christian," another aged personage said as he brushed by me, squeezing Christian's arm. "Audrey still wants that recipe."

I was unfazed by the extent of his social connections. What could a biochem professor do for my career?

"You seem to have a lot of friends here," I commented.

"Well, I've been a member of the Lowell House Senior Common Room for the past four years. And of course as the university comptroller, I tend to strike fear in the hearts of every department head at least once a year at budget time."

I nodded, unimpressed. "I usually don't attend these Open Houses, but one of my fellow Crimson Future Committee members invited me."

At the mention of the committee, I felt his eyes fully focus on me for the first time.

"That's it!" He snapped his fingers. "I thought your name sounded familiar. It was in one of the weekly Barrett Reports discussing the Crimson Future Committee." He looked me over again, thoroughly this time. "Nice work. Very high profile. That appointment was hard to get."

I murmured something about how the committee needed at least one assistant professor just to crunch the numbers. Suddenly, I had his full attention.

"You're almost finished, aren't you?" he said, moving closer to me. "The press conference is in three weeks, isn't it?"

"Well, we may have to postpone it now," I replied. "There's been a terrible accident that could prevent us from finishing. I'm sure you've heard about Dean Fisher."

"The woman who died earlier this week? That's right, she was on the committee, wasn't she?"

Why was he acting as if he didn't know Ella? Lindsey had said that they argued constantly. "Yes," I answered slowly. "In fact, the two of us were responsible for drafting the final report. Now that this has happened, I'll have to take it over myself."

"That'll be a lot of work. We'd better get you some sustenance. May I fetch you some hors d'oeuvres?" he purred. "Even with that perfect figure, you do eat, don't you?"

I felt his hand slide slowly across my back. Apparently, even in the thick of the social climb, he had the energy to make random passes. Instinctively, I pulled away from his touch. Since when did Asian men make passes at black women? I was a veteran flirt, and this was a first.

I reconsidered my recoil as he firmly drew me back toward him. He clearly wanted something from me. Why not play along and see what it was? I relaxed and shot him a smile. "I'd love something to eat."

"Around that corner behind the French doors is the President's study. Why don't you wait there? It'll be a little more private."

As I waited for Christian in the study, I browsed through the mahogany bookshelves that lined the room floor to ceiling. Just to the right of the fireplace, there were two shelves of old periodicals—*The New Republic, Commentary, The Nation.* As I idly leafed through a 1967 issue of *Partisan Review,* I noticed that it contained an article written by Leo Barrett, entitled "Why Negroes Should Support Bobby Kennedy." He must have been eighteen or nineteen years old at the time. But what drew my attention to the article wasn't Leo's name. It was the fact that the bottom of the first page of the article had been altered. The space where there would have been a contributor's note briefly describing the author's background had been cut out. The edges were so smooth that it was as if it had been done with a razor.

Just then, Christian returned, bearing a plate of food.

"What are you reading?" he asked, rapidly crossing the floor.

"Just an old article of the President's."

"Come, sit down. I'll put it away for you." He set the plate down and steered me firmly toward a crimson leather wing chair with one hand, while deftly removing the magazine from me with the other.

A minute later he was sprawled at my feet. "So," he said, passing me a plate daintily arrayed with caviar, chopped egg, and sour cream on toast points, "how have you enjoyed working on the Crimson Future Committee?"

"I'm sure you can imagine what it's been like. Outsize egos on parade. Ian McAllister, Bob Raines, Ella Fisher. But I guess you know firsthand about her."

"What's that supposed to mean?" he said, signaling a waiter passing in the hall. "Champagne?"

I nodded assent. "My mistake, perhaps, but for some reason, I was under the impression that the two of you didn't get along."

Christian snorted. "She and her stupid Barbie doll of a secretary utilized that fiction from time to time to explain legitimate problems that I had with her operation. If you can call it an operation. They were fond of telling people that I wanted her job." He sipped from his glass and then continued. "My feeling is that the President saw fit to give her the position. I didn't agree with his choice, but it was a done deal for some time, and I could live with it. I generally don't dignify their accusations of jealousy with a response, but when intelligent people start to believe it, I get concerned."

Thank you so much for classing me with the intelligentsia.

"Leo!" he suddenly cried out, scrambling to his feet. I looked up to see Leo Barrett, Harvard's twenty-sixth President, striding through the doorway of the study. Close on his heels were two older men whom I recognized as the Dean of the Faculty and the Master of Eliot House.

Christian was on his feet and halfway across the room before I had fully processed what was happening.

"I've been looking all over for you, sport. We've got to discuss that meeting tomorrow." As always, Leo was in perpetual motion. He swiped a toast point from the plate Christian and I had been sharing while quickly surveying the room. His eyes lingered momentarily on me.

"Professor Chase!" he summoned, while simultaneously motioning for a waiter to bring him a drink.

I'd been in the same room with Leo Barrett many times, but I always felt the same nervous thrill when his full attention was bestowed on me. It wasn't just that he was the President. He was also an extremely attractive man. On first impression, he appeared to be vaguely foreign, but in a dashing, matinee-idol way: he had a delicate nose, full mouth, and an aristocrat's high cheekbones, which were balanced by piercing brown eyes and lush black eyebrows. At fifty, his hair was still jet black, and he always wore it cropped very close to his head, which made his eyes seem even larger. That night he was wearing a navy suit perfectly tailored for his tall, lithe physique. His yellow patterned tie and subtly striped white shirt provided a brilliant contrast to his smooth, tanned olive skin.

It felt as if his smile was just for me as I crossed the floor.

He took me by the elbows as he kissed both my cheeks in greeting. "I was thinking of you just yesterday, Nikki. I was reading Frantz Fanon, and remembering that discussion we had with Duncan Kennedy. Christian, have you met one of our most brilliant up-and-coming economists?" One of his hands was on my back, the other on Christian's shoulder.

"Of course," Christian muttered. My easy access to Leo clearly annoyed him.

"Christian used to be my economics instructor way back when."

"Yes, we were just talking about how hard Veronica has been working on the Crimson Future Committee," Christian interjected. "She's taking over Ella Fisher's responsibilities."

Leo's smile dimmed. "Terrible accident, wasn't it?"

"Yes," I said, my eyes still on his face. "We're all going to miss her." Now that I was closer, I realized that he actually looked tired, which was very unlike him. Faint dark circles ringed his eyes. His shoulders were stooped, and his whole demeanor seemed a bit subdued, in sharp contrast to his usual assurance. I knew he was about to launch a major capital campaign at our upcoming New Century press conference; knowing his usual compulsion to become personally involved with even minor decisions, he was probably spending too many hours reviewing budgets and press releases.

"Hello?" a strangely familiar voice called out. A moment later, Lindsey Wentworth appeared in the doorway, her arm linked through that of an imperious middle-aged blond woman with a page-boy haircut.

"See, Torie, I told you he'd be hiding out in here."

Victoria Wolcott Barrett, Harvard's First Lady, did *not* look pleased to find her husband holed up with us. She was wearing a tailored dove-gray suit with a snowy white blouse that revealed a tiny waist and narrow hips; a black headband graced her hair. At forty-something, she was the very picture of a well-heeled doyenne of Boston society. Justin Simms had told me that Lindsey Wentworth's parents were old friends of Victoria's. That was how Lindsey had gotten her job with Ella. It certainly showed tonight. Standing there in the doorway, Lindsey and Victoria looked like sister debutantes. Blond and blonder.

"Leo," Victoria said, releasing Lindsey and striding toward her husband. "I've been looking all over for you! Al Williamson is here, and I told him that the two of you should discuss that trip to Los Angeles."

"In a moment, Torie," Barrett said. "Say hello to Christian. And you remember Nikki Chase."

"Hello, Dr. Barrett," I murmured, extending my hand. Victoria had a Ph.D. in philosophy, although she hadn't published or taught for many years. I'd been to her house for dinner twice in the past three years, but she still never seemed to remember anything about me.

"Nice to see you," she said, briefly grasping my fingers in an ersatz handshake. Her attention wandered as she pulled a stray blue thread from Leo's suit. "Leo, you really should get your tailor to take care of these things."

"Victoria, please," he said sharply, shaking off her hand.

"Now, now, Torie's just looking out for you, Mr. President," Lindsey chirped. She and Leo exchanged a smile while Victoria withdrew her hand.

"Do you know everyone here, Lindsey?" Leo said, placing a paternal arm around Lindsey's shoulders. That was one of the reasons that people, especially women, responded so well to Leo. He frequently touched people, which, if done in the wrong way, would be annoying and inappropriate. But somehow his touch felt appreciative, and gentle, and strong.

"Yes," she burbled, "Christian and I met at one of your dinner parties last year. And I know Professor Chase because she was working on a committee with Dean Fisher. I'm just so glad you found Ella's disk with those financials on it. I know Ella was really concerned about that."

"I appreciate your help finding the disk," I said, resisting the urge to roll my eyes. I glanced at Christian to share my amusement, but he was watching Leo.

"Sir, you wanted to talk about our meeting with Bryce tomorrow," Christian interrupted.

The two men turned away and I heard Christian begin, "He wants to do the deal, so you can afford to play hardball." Was it really worth it? I wondered. The pinnacle of power, and Leo's work hours were as bad as mine. Victoria frowned as she watched her husband drift off with Christian.

"Torie, you were right to urge him to see Mr. Williamson," Lindsey chattered. "Daddy told me that the trip to LA could be a great start for the capital campaign."

Looking past Lindsey, I saw Leo's hand tremble as a waiter offered him a glass of sherry.

"So, have you had any luck with Ella's disk?" Lindsey asked.

"Really, Lindsey, I'm sure she doesn't want to talk about Ella Fisher now." Victoria sounded exasperated. "We've all had quite enough of that."

"Did you know her well?" I asked. Why was she suddenly in such a pissy mood?

Victoria smiled briefly and focused her full attention on me for the merest second. "Not really. I never had the pleasure. If you girls will excuse me, I must speak with someone. Bob!" she exclaimed, taking the arm of a man who had just wandered into the study. "I haven't seen you since the Cancer Society benefit last spring. How is Judy?"

Christian and Leo were still deep in conversation, Leo's brow deeply furrowed. As Lindsey turned to accept a glass of champagne, I saw Christian slip his hand into his left pocket and emerge with a small round red object. It looked like a pill. Leo surreptitiously accepted it from Christian's hand and slipped it into his mouth, then quickly nodded his thanks as Christian smiled.

Maybe Leo wasn't just tired. Maybe he was sick.

Seven forty-five already. I had to get moving. I excused myself to find Jennifer Blum. Ten minutes later, I finally discovered her in the entry foyer, surrounded by four men with adoring expressions. I gave her the high sign that I was leaving, and she nodded a blissful good-bye.

As I was heading for the front door, a shout went up from the study.

"Help!" a female voice cried. "The President has collapsed!" It sounded like Lindsey Wentworth. Collapsed? Leo Barrett was one of the most energetic people I knew.

A loud murmur went up, and a crush of people flooded toward the narrow doorway, blocking my path.

"Stay back, folks, please." One of the waiters barred the door with his arm. "He needs air. Is there a doctor in here?"

"Move back, please," an authoritative voice rang out. "I'm a physician." A dark-haired man elbowed his way through the crowd and disappeared into the study. Christian Chung emerged from the living room.

"Hey." I grabbed his arm as he started toward the study. "They're not going to let you in."

"You don't understand," he barked. "There's something they need to know."

I watched Christian disappear into the study behind the doctor. What the hell was going on between him and Leo?

I started back for my office with a sick feeling in the pit of my stomach.

Had Ella Fisher's death been just the beginning?

CHAPTER TEN

BIBLIOMANIA

Eight forty-five Friday evening found me racing through the Yard toward Widener Library. In honor of the weekend, I was carrying the Prada backpack that Jess had given me for my birthday last year. But I was still working. The book that I needed for Ian's *American Economic Review* article had finally been retrieved from storage, three hours later than expected. The library was closing at nine, and my dear friend the librarian had made it clear that if I didn't retrieve it by closing time, I'd have to wait until Monday morning. A full moon beamed down through the trees, lighting the pathways and creating inviting shadowy enclaves in the stairwells and entries of the dormitories. In a few hours, they would be the site of fledgling romantic encounters and the occasional bout of nausea. For now, they waited expectantly.

Widener's imposing bulk emerged regally from the shadows, its fifty shallow granite steps leading upward to ten stately columns. The stairs are a popular meeting place and observation spot, particularly on balmy afternoons. That night they were deserted except for a young couple, probably freshmen, already smooching in the shadows. I sprinted up the stairs two at a time, trying not to think about what Dante Rosario might be doing that evening.

It was ten minutes before nine when I arrived, and the librarians had already posted signs saying that the circulation desk was closed. I had a spirited argument with one of them that sent her in search of my book, her eyes shooting daggers at me as she went.

Two minutes later, she returned with her hands empty.

"I'm sorry. Your book's not here."

"What do you mean?"

"It seems that we retrieved it from storage—"

"Right."

"And then someone reshelved it."

"What do you mean, reshelved it?"

"They seem to have placed it in the stacks."

"Listen, I have to have this for an article that I'm writing with the chairman of the Economics Department. An article that's due first thing Monday morning. You're going to have to go get it."

She shook her head, glancing at her watch. "Oh no. We close in seven minutes. I'm here by myself and I can't leave, so—"

"Just give me the citation. I'll get it myself."

Snatching the slip of paper from her reluctant fingers, I waved my ID card at the lone student manning the entrance and plunged headlong into the darkness that is the Widener Library stacks.

Entering the stacks is like descending into the dungeon of a castle, or perhaps a medieval monastery. The first time I toured them, I was filled with wonder: this was genuine Harvard, and the grandest paean to the hardship of research that I had ever seen. The cinderblock walls of the six-story-deep stacks are dark brown and covered with dust, as are the floors, except for the faint markings guiding the lost soul to the nearest exit or to a neighboring library. The only light is provided by naked incandescent bulbs hanging from the ceiling by dust-encrusted cords. An eerie silence pervades the space, punctured only by the occasional sighing of students reading in the study carrels and the clicking footsteps of passersby. The primeval odor of aging paper and ripening leather permeates the air. Only a serious scholar would dare brave this territory—only the best would make it out alive.

I made my way quickly down the rickety metal stairs, the pressure of my foot wringing a groan of protest from each step. My book was on Level C, four floors below the ground. Several students had passed me on the way out, and I was reminded that I had five minutes to find the book and get out of there, or I could end up spending the night, something one of my friends boasted about having done with his girlfriend in search of sexual adventure, but clearly nothing one would want to do solo.

I turned a few corners and hit area C South. The cite read "PL D0589 S134.5." I pulled the cord to turn on the lightbulb dangling above the nearest row of shelves. It had notations starting with PL A1000. So D0589 would be a few rows down. I walked over a few more rows and turned on another light. This was my row. As I walked deeper into the column of books, I heard a passing guard's warning, "Two minutes to lights out. Please exit the library. Two minutes."

I followed the notations down. D0589 was, of course, on the bottom shelf. On my hands and knees now, I peered intently at the row of books. Finally: K. T. Marshall's *Capitalism in Third World Economies*. I opened it and read the first sentence:

> Any Western economist attempting to explore the markets of the Third World does so at his peril.

Just then, the lights went out.

I looked up quickly, fear flowing through me like a surge of electricity.

Fumbling around for my backpack, I tucked the book under my arm, and then felt my way slowly down the row of shelves. It was pitch black, the darkness velvety thick on my eyelids, and I murmured softly to myself to keep my spirits up. "Just the guard. The jerk is probably around here somewhere."

"It's not the guard, bitch." The words echoed evilly behind me.

I froze for a fatal second, and an arm came from behind me and locked around my neck. Instinctively, I jammed my elbow back into his chest but got no reaction.

Oh shit. He's strong.

I started to scream. But his hand clamped over my mouth. I bit down hard and was rewarded with a mouthful of leather glove.

This can't be happening.

I twisted violently, but his arms were like iron bars, squeezing tighter and tighter. I could smell his breath, or maybe it was his cologne; something was giving off the strong scent of cloves and I was sickened by the strange intimacy of being so close to him that I could feel his heart beating.

Before he could get a firmer grip around my throat, I brought my heel down hard on his instep. That loosened his grip, and I twisted away. I ran down the pitch-black narrow corridor, stumbling between the bookshelves, as if the devil himself were after me.

I could hear him close behind me. He had the advantage, because I was the one running into things; he could tell where I was by all the noise I was making. Blindly, I began pulling books off the shelf, sweeping them, along with the bookends, into his path to try to slow him down. I knew I had been successful when I heard him fall. He growled like a wild animal, and I picked up speed. Maybe I could pull this off.

I had to find the stairwell. "Help!" I screeched. "Help me!" I was answered by silence. Silence, then the sound of his advancing footsteps behind me.

Finally, the main corridor. A few lights still burned, and I started sprinting, not knowing which direction to go, praying that I was headed toward the stairs. I darted around a corner and ran smack into the tiny library elevator. I had forgotten it existed. I didn't have time to wait for it to arrive, but I pushed the button anyway. Maybe it would distract him.

I forced myself to slow down, to silently move around the corner so that he couldn't hear the click of my boots on the floor. He reached the elevator and stopped. I sidled further away, and then started running again. It was a small lead, but I had bought myself a little time.

As I flew down the corridor, I passed a fire-alarm box, and instinctively pulled the red handle down. I thought it would help get the guards' attention. But I knew right away it had been a mistake. The clanging bell was deafening, and now no one could hear my screams. And now I couldn't hear his footsteps, so I had to look back to see where he was. I glanced behind me and saw him clearly for the first time, and the sight made my blood freeze: he was tall, and muscular, and he was wearing what looked like a black wetsuit, dark gloves, and a black ski mask with a slash of red for the mouth opening. So this encounter wasn't spontaneous.

It had been planned.

The noise and the realization that he was getting closer and closer brought me to the edge of hysteria. It felt like the world was ending.

I rounded another corner and saw the dimly lit stairwell at the end of the corridor. I sprinted for the stairs, clambering down as noiselessly as possible. With any luck, he would assume I went up. I knew there were other ways out of this labyrinth, and I headed down to the lowest level of the stacks. There was a tunnel there that would get me out.

When I reached the bottom of the stairs, I listened for footsteps. Nothing. The clanging of the alarm had stopped, and it was dead quiet. Maybe he'd given up. I leaned against the wall, panting, and considered my options. Maybe he was gone, or maybe he was headed upstairs.

Just then, the elevator arrived on the bottom floor. As the doors opened, I squeezed myself under the desk in one of the carrels that lined the wall, drawing my legs up under me. *Please, be a security guard.* Instead, the black ski mask emerged. My skin tingled as if I'd received an electric shock, and I crouched lower under the desk.

He stood silently in front of the elevator, listening. Whoever it was must know this library very well: he had realized that I would try to get out through the tunnel. The light from the elevator spilled over him, and I peered out, trying to memorize his height and build. When it was over, I was going to have to figure out who the hell this guy was. Unfortunately, the wetsuit and mask covered every inch of skin. He was tall, almost six feet from what I could tell. And muscular. The stillness of the place was oppressive. Could he hear my heart hammering in my chest?

The figure moved away from the elevator and let the door close. An inky blackness filled the room. Suddenly, a wide beam of light sliced through the darkness and I realized that he had a flashlight. He swung it in large arcs, then began methodically illuminating the shelves and carrels on the opposite side of the floor. It was only a matter of time before he found me, and then what? My heart was pounding so hard that it made my whole neck pulse. My hand started to shake with fear, stress, and the unbearable urge to move, and I realized that I was still holding the Marshall book. I set it down quietly and reached behind me for my backpack as I watched the flashlight slowly moving across the other side of the room. The only thing in there that could be remotely useful was my keys; if he got too close, at least I could try scratching his eyes with them. Slowly, I slipped them out of my bag, clenching the key ring in my fist to keep it from jingling.

I had to get out from under the desk, fast. He had turned his flashlight to my side of the floor and was headed straight for me. I shifted my weight to try to get the blood flowing in my numbed legs, and bumped against the Marshall book again. It was large, and I debated whether it would serve better as a weapon or a distraction. I wasn't keen on the idea of his getting close enough for me to hit him over the head with it, so I took a deep breath, and then heaved the volume into the air.

At the sound of the book falling, the figure darted for the far corner. I burst out from under the desk, and plunged into the tunnel leading to neighboring Lamont Library. The lights were still on here, and I raced through the white tunnel, yelling for help.

"Somebody—please help me!" I screamed.

Where the hell were the guards?

I would have made it but for my boots. Halfway through the passageway, I sprawled headlong on the floor, tripped up by my own shoelace. I stuffed the laces into my boot and scrambled to my feet. But it was too late. He emerged from the end of the tunnel and started sprinting for me.

I started running again, screaming as I went. I was halfway up the stairs to Lamont when he caught me.

He clamped my wrist in an iron grip, and then my rib cage collapsed as he slammed me face first into the wall. I pulled away, screaming, kicking and scratching. Then I lunged for him, scratching with my key chain, aiming for his eyes. His mask shielded him, so I tried driving a knee into his groin, but I was getting weaker from the punishing blows he was driving into my rib cage. I doubled over in pain, feeling dizzy and nauseated, and felt myself being yanked up by the hair and slammed again into the wall.

This was no rapist or mugger. The son of a bitch was trying to kill me.

His flashlight rolled across the floor, and I dived for it as he grabbed my shoulder. I brought it crashing down on his forearm, and he howled in pain for the first time. Lying on my back, I found the strength to land a kick in his stomach as he leaned over me that sent him sprawling on the floor. I crawled to my knees and tried to get up but he was on me again and I felt him fastening his hands around my neck. My windpipe was constricting, and it was almost impossible to breathe. Frantically scratching and gasping, I struggled, but I was losing consciousness. Faintly, I heard footsteps over our heads on the stairs.

"Hello?" a querulous voice called out.

The attacker shoved me hard to the floor. He grabbed my backpack and then raced down the stairs, back toward Widener. I struggled to sit up as the face of an elderly security guard appeared at the top of the stairs.

"Ma'am? You know, the library's closing soon. Better get a move on."

They took me to the University Health Services to clean me up and make sure that I hadn't been seriously injured. I was lying on a hospital bed, propped up by four pillows, when Rafe Griffin arrived. He lingered at the foot of my bed until I waved at him to come closer.

"Child, you had a rough night, eh?"

I nodded weakly and smiled. "And I thought my students were animals." My throat was sore from screaming, the skin on my right cheek had been rubbed raw from being slammed into the wall, and my neck was sporting the beginnings of a dull purple bruise. At least the attacker hadn't managed to break any ribs. "That son of a bitch took my Prada backpack."

"They told me you fought the mon off all by yourself," he said softly.

I shrugged nonchalantly, although my hands were still shaking. "Just a few bruises. I'm fine."

"Bad luck seems to be following you these days."

"Yeah, I think someone is trying to send me to meet Ella for coffee."

"Now, why do you think that, child?"

I told him about the attacker's ski mask. About how it had all seemed planned.

"They may not have been tryin' to hurt you. More likely they were tryin' to scare you."

"Well, if they were, they succeeded." I couldn't shake the memory of those hands around my throat. Or that mask. "But why do you think they weren't trying to kill me?"

"Because if they had wanted you dead, you would be," Rafe said quietly. "No gun and no knife, right?"

"All I saw was a flashlight and two big hands."

"See, if they wanted you dead, he would've had a knife. Simplest thing in the world."

"Are you trying to make me feel better or worse?"

He leaned forward and looked at me earnestly. "I'm tryin' to get you to see that you need to be careful."

"Fine. Message received. But Rafe, who are 'they'?"

"We're workin' on that." He patted my shoulder. "But I shouldn'ta gone gettin' you all worked up, child. After all, it still could'a been a robber after that fancy backpack of yours. Or a rapist. My boys are workin' the stacks with the Cambridge police, looking for him. We may hear somethin' later tonight."

"You'll let me know what you learn, won't you?"

"Yes, Nikki, I will."

"By the way, Rafe. Did you hear that President Barrett collapsed tonight at his Open House?"

"Yep. Why?"

"So what happened after the medics showed up?"

"They took him to Mass General. They'll probably keep him overnight for observation."

"So is he really ill?"

"You ask a lot of questions, don't you?" He smiled down at me.

"Come on, Rafe. I'm not going to tell anyone else. But I'm a little worried about him."

Rafe lowered his voice. "I heard on the Q.T. that the mon is suffering from exhaustion."

"Exhaustion? What does that mean?" That word was an accepted euphemism for any number of more serious celebrity ailments, including drug use and AIDS. Was that why Leo had taken that pill from Christian?

"That's all I know, child. If you want more, you'll have to ask the mon yourself." He stood up and leaned over me. "They keepin' you overnight?"

"No. As long as I promise to go straight to bed when I get home, the doc said I could go whenever I'm ready."

"Then I'll give you a ride. And since you've been such a good child, I'll even let you work the siren."

As I eased stiffly into my jacket, I vowed that tomorrow I would take my first Boxercise lesson at the gym.

Because the next time I crossed paths with this guy, I was planning to kick his ass.

CHAPTER ELEVEN

CHEMICAL REACTION

I slept late the next morning, and lingered under the covers after I awoke, luxuriating in the warmth of the Saturday morning sun streaming through the windows, secure in the soft cocoon of my bed. No black-gloved hands at my neck, just Keynes curled up on my head and the faint smell of coffee wafting up from Ted and Dante's apartment. Nice to be alive.

Reality intruded with the jangling of the telephone.

"Did I wake you, beautiful?" a voice demanded.

Now I was definitely awake. "Who is this?"

"Justin Simms. You mean you still don't recognize my voice? I'm bummed."

"Can I help you with something, or did you just call to practice your pickup lines before the weekend rush?"

"Oh, the rejection of a Harvard woman is like none other—hang on, I have to grab a scarf and some gloves. It's freezing over here!"

"Stop!" I started laughing. "I'm half awake and defenseless against your charms. What's up?"

"Actually, I did call for a reason other than to hear you laugh. We have to make arrangements for the big date."

"Big date?"

"Ouch! You do remember that you agreed to go out with me tonight, thank you very much? Friends of the Fogg Museum black-tie gala? Cute answering machine message?"

"God, I am so sorry!" I said. "You would not believe how busy I've been. Of course I remember. I'm looking forward to it."

"That's okay. I've been blown off by better women than you," he said lightly.

"Now it's my turn to say 'thank you very much.' Are we square now?"

"Yes. I'll pick you up at your place tonight at nine-thirty. And be prepared to start taking me seriously."

"Stop it," I said. "I do take you seriously. We've been having a great time, haven't we?"

"Sure, but I detect a certain tone of voice. A tone of voice that says, 'You're funny and cute, but no thanks.' What is it, Nikki? My lack of yuppie accoutrements?"

"Please."

"Then what? It's my age, right? So I'm only 20. Everyone is dating younger men now."

"Everyone?" I laughed, hoping it wouldn't offend him more.

"Well, there's Mary McFadden. And Melanie Griffith. And Whitney Houston."

"Oh well, if Whitney is doing it, I'm there." I paused. "It's not your age." I had briefly considered lying, but it seemed unfair. "It's that I seem to be having a chemical reaction with a man I used to date."

"I knew it! I knew there was something. But you're still going to this party with me tonight?"

"Absolutely."

"Then prepare to change your mind about me."

I should be so lucky.

After a quick shower, I turned my attention to Ella's financial statements. Maybe I had missed something that would lead me to her killer. In any case, I had to make sense of them for the Future Committee report.

I retrieved her disk from the top drawer of the desk in my living room, and loaded it into my laptop. The spreadsheets materialized in front of me.

The first order of business was reconciling Ella's version of the numbers with Ian's. After forty-five minutes of work, it became clear that the only discrepancy between the two versions was in the budget for FAS. So I began methodically plowing through each of the thirty-five departments, first just checking the totals and the large items. It took almost two hours, but I finally detected a pattern. In each of the schools, the line item for outside services was higher in Ella's budget than in Ian's. Not by much, usually less than $150,000. If it was only in a couple of places, I would've sworn that it was a typo. But it was a fairly consistent pattern, and the difference was sufficient to generate a $2 million discrepancy between the two.

"Outside services," I muttered aloud. "What gets accounted for in outside services?"

I checked Ian's hard copy, and found a footnote in the executive summary of the FAS budget. Outside services included a wide range of outside contractors, everything from accountants and consultants to temp secretaries and maintenance workers.

What had Lindsey said that Ella was worried about? That some expenses were too high? Now that I knew what to focus on, I looked at the growth rates just for the outside services items. And they were growing very rapidly in Ella's version: in some cases, they were up twenty percent over the course of two years.

I leaned back in my chair. There was a simple explanation for why Ella's version could be different from Ian's. The outside service expenses could have been reclassified in the later version of the budget. If they had moved out of FAS and into the central overhead budget, it would explain the difference. I quickly sorted through Ian's hard copy, but it didn't include a budget for the President's and the Treasurer's offices, which is where the missing dollars would be.

But if it was that simple, why was Ella Fisher so distressed?

I realized that I had never called the last number dialed on Ella's office phone. It might be important to know who she had called that very last time. I rummaged through the pockets of the pants I was wearing the day I searched her office and found the scrap of paper I had scribbled the number on. Expecting to interrupt some Law School student in the middle of a study session, I quickly dialed it.

The answering machine at Christian Chung's apartment picked up on the third ring.

Early afternoon found me surrounded by string beans. Maggie had roped me into helping her prepare for the welcome dinner for Ted and Dante that night. At Ted's request, she was cooking one of her down-home Southern extravaganzas: fried chicken, ham, rice, sweet potatoes, collard greens—the works.

I'd met her in the kitchen at two o'clock, dressed to work, wearing sweats, a naked face, and my tortoiseshell glasses. My Saturday rule is no makeup and no contact lenses. Let the world accept me as is at least once a week.

"Well, look who decided to grace us with her presence," Maggie drawled. "Sleeping Beauty."

She had been cooking all morning, and the fruits of her labor perfumed the room, the smell of fresh-baked bread mingling with roasting ham and peach cobbler. She was wearing an oversized apron that read "Kiss the Cook," and was fussing over a pot of greens on the stove. A yellow chicken waited on the counter to be cut up and fried, and a cheerful stack of red and yellow floral dishes perched on the round kitchen table, awaiting the feast.

I dutifully kissed her cheek and then pushed up my sleeves. "What should I do first, ma'am?"

"String beans. In the bottom drawer of the icebox. Wash 'em and then snap the ends and put them in that bowl, there," she said, waving her hands in my general direction.

I pulled open the refrigerator door and was greeted with more bounty: a large Jell-O mold quivering on a plastic plate, coleslaw in a glass bowl, a huge chocolate cake, and a carton of heavy cream waiting to be whipped.

"My Lord, Maggie! Who else are you expecting?"

"Well, you're bringing Jessica, aren't you?"

"Yeah, and she'll eat her usual two mouthfuls and then announce that she's on a diet."

"And you're bringing that cop, too."

"Oh," I said slowly, peering at her over the refrigerator door. "*That's* what this is all about."

"I don't know what you're talkin' about," she snapped. "Now get moving on those strings. I don't have that much space on this stove, and they're scheduled to go next. Got to keep moving."

"You're really going to like him," I said with a grin, burying my head in the fridge to retrieve a plastic supermarket bag stuffed with string beans. "He's really handsome. And smart."

"I doubt that, Miss Lady. A black cop? In my day, black folks were getting our butts kicked by the police. We weren't trying to *be* the police. Probably some Uncle-Tom-Clarence-Thomas-supporting-Stepin Fetchit."

"Mark my words. You'll be thanking me by the end of the evening."

"And he's West Indian, isn't he?" she continued, ignoring me. "Those folks are always acting like they're the *good* blacks, and it's the rest of us that are the problem. Using those fake British accents to make the white folks trust 'em. 'If those hardworking island folk can make it in this country, why can't you all?' " she mocked. "Because you're standing on my neck, that's why!"

While Maggie grumbled to herself, I got to work snapping string beans.

By three o'clock I was up to my elbows in apple cores. Despite the chocolate cake, a peach cobbler, and Rafe's promised pecan pie, Maggie had insisted that I make an apple pie. As she put it, there was no telling what kind of store-bought, too-sweet, not-enough-nuts kind of pecan pie a West Indian cop would bring, and we couldn't have people leaving the table hungry. I was surrounded by Granny Smith apple peels and lost in thought about Dante when Maggie's laugh penetrated my thoughts.

"Girl, you look like a passage from the Song of Solomon: '*Stay me, oh comfort me with apples, for I am sick of love.*' What's stuck in your craw?"

"We can't go there right now," I shook my head. "This is at least two teapots worth of conversation."

"Then we'll save it for tonight. Meanwhile, I'm going to the cellar for the sweet potatoes. And you better move faster, Miss Thing," Maggie called over her shoulder. "I want that pie in the stove by the time I get back."

I had tossed the apples by hand with sugar and cinnamon and was standing on a step stool pulling a tin of nutmeg down from the top cabinet when I heard the front door open. Within seconds, Dante Rosario strode into the kitchen, black leather jacket thrown over his shoulder.

Yes, I would be wearing glasses, no makeup, a shapeless gray sweatshirt, and apple gore up to my elbows at our first meeting since our argument Thursday night. *Perfect.*

"So," he said, grinning up at me as I turned to face him. "Still on your high horse, I see."

At this, the nutmeg jumped out of my hand and clattered to the floor, seemingly of its own volition. Clearly, this man had been sent back to me as punishment for some particularly vile sin.

"The better to avoid the bullshit piling up on the ground below,"

I snapped, carefully stepping down. The way things were going, I'd trip and end up in a heap at his feet. I avoided his eyes as he scooped up the nutmeg tin and placed it on the table.

"So does this mean you've been domesticated?" he said, gesturing at the mess of apple peels, kitchen implements, and flour that littered the kitchen table.

"Not even close. Just lending Maggie a hand."

"Nice to know that some things never change." He tasted one of the sliced apples for the pie filling. "This could use cloves. And a little lemon. In addition to that nutmeg."

"Thank you, Paul Prudhomme. I'll keep that in mind."

"I really like those glasses," he said softly. For a moment, I thought he was talking about Maggie's juice glasses, which were drying next to the sink. But he appeared to be talking about mine.

"These?" I touched the rims carefully. "They're old."

"They look like the kind of glasses beautiful girls wear to keep the wolves at bay. The kind that they only remove when they let down their guard."

Well, if that wasn't a mind game, what was? Complimenting my *glasses? What did that mean?*

"Do you still have that earring that you told me about? The one you found last Sunday?" I asked sharply. I realized that I'd never mentioned it to Rafe. But then, I wanted to see it first myself. It might shed some light on what really happened Sunday night.

"Sure. It's still in my office. Angie says someone is going to steal it if I'm not careful."

"She's right." With any luck, I'd be that person.

"What happened to your neck?" he asked, coming closer. I had completely forgotten about that souvenir from last night. Maggie hadn't even noticed it.

"Are you finished?" Maggie called out, her footsteps echoing on the basement stairs.

Am I ever.

"Hey," she said cheerfully to Dante as she reached the top of the stairs. "Hang around here and I'll put you to work slicing sweet potatoes."

"Sorry, my publisher is screaming for the final draft of my manuscript, and I need to put in a couple more hours before dinner," he said, laughing. "But one of these nights, I'll make you my grandma's famous wild mushroom risotto." He turned to me as he started out the door. "It requires a lot of tending, but it's well worth the wait."

"I'll take you up on that, darlin'," Maggie said, as he started up the stairs. "As long as there's no meat!" She turned back to me. "It's gonna take a month for my system to get over the cholesterol from this dinner, girl. What's wrong with you?"

I was frozen in place, looking at the doorway through which Dante had disappeared.

He liked my *glasses?* What was that about?

The doorbell rang promptly at six-thirty that night, and I opened the door to find Rafe Griffin standing under the porch light, wearing a gray suit and holding a pie in one hand and a floral bouquet erupting with birds of paradise in the other.

"This the Chase residence?" he said, grinning.

"I hardly recognize you without your uniform, Detective. Come in and meet the family."

"Don't you look nice, now," he said as I ushered him into the hall and relieved him of the pie. I had upgraded my appearance from the afternoon, and was wearing a cropped red wool sweater and a black miniskirt. And my contact lenses.

"Maggie," I called, "our guest is here."

Maggie emerged from the kitchen, a dripping spoon in her hand, wearing a burnt-orange sweater and a long paisley skirt. She had wound a purple scarf through her thick black hair, and looked absolutely beautiful to me.

Apparently, Rafe agreed. "These are for you, Mrs. Dailey," he said, gallantly proffering her the bouquet. "Birds of paradise for a bird of paradise."

For the first time since I'd known her, I believe that Magnolia Dailey was actually left speechless. She accepted the flowers with a shy smile, and the two of them stood frozen in the hallway, looking at each other.

"Maggie," I said gently, "say thank you."

"Oh yes," she said, shaking herself. "Thank you. Very lovely."

"Look, he's brought his famous pecan pie," I teased. "It looks delicious."

Maggie's usual skepticism reemerged as she took the pie from me and started back toward the kitchen. "We'll just see about that."

We convened around the table shortly after I introduced Rafe to Dante, Ted, and Jess. Maggie had created a centerpiece out of miniature pumpkins, gourds, and rust-colored mums, and she ordered us to our seats while lighting a pair of thick orange candles. A firm believer in boy-girl seating charts, she placed Dante and Jess on one side of the table, while Rafe and I were seated on the other. Ted presided at the head of the table, with Jess and me on either side, and Maggie sat at the foot between Rafe and Dante. I was told in no uncertain terms that as my chair was closest to the kitchen, I was to see to it that everyone had more than enough food on their plates at all times. Then Maggie said grace and we tucked into our dinner.

"My date and I rented a fantastic movie last night," Jess announced. "It was about an Italian postman on a tiny island who falls madly in love. It reminded me of you, Dante. He was a hopeless romantic."

I glared at her, but she continued. "He doesn't even know how to read until the poet Pablo Neruda teaches him. And then Neruda becomes his yenta."

"Ah, Neruda," Rafe said. "He was Chilean. Most folks remember him for his political writing, but I prefer the *sonetos de amor*."

"You know Neruda's work?" Maggie asked incredulously.

"What, you think a policeman has no soul?" Rafe smiled at her. "Magnolia, *nombre de planta o piedra o vino, de lo que nace de la tierra y dura.* Magnolia: the name of a plant, or a rock, or a wine, of things that begin in the earth, and last: word in whose growth the dawn first opens, in whose summer the light of the lemons bursts."

His voice was lilting and deep, and I could almost hear the ocean and the wind and the rustling of wildflowers in the silence after his words ceased. I looked up to find Dante's eyes on my face.

"Her name was actually Matilde. He wrote that for his wife." Maggie broke the silence, blushing furiously.

"Yeah, I suppose you're right," Rafe replied gently.

"Rafe, how do you know his work so well?" I asked to give us all a moment to recover.

"On Anegada, we used to have a little ol' library. Only about a hundred books. So we all grew up reading 'em, over and over. And most of them were poetry, because Miss Esperanza, the lady who bought the books, had a very soft heart."

"Maggie is a poet, you know," I said. "Her work is really beautiful. It always makes me cry."

"I'd surely love to read some of your poems, if you would allow it, Mrs. Dailey," Rafe said kindly.

"Perhaps," Maggie said, with a smile that made her look like a schoolgirl again. "And please call me Maggie."

"So does the *postino* get the girl in the end?" Dante asked.

"Of course. He woos her with his newly-discovered words," Jess sighed. "As if."

"You sound skeptical," Ted said. From what I could tell, he hadn't taken his eyes off Jess since she first started talking.

"That never happens in real life," Jess declared. "You know what my date said? That it just showed why reading books was a great way to get laid. *Putz*."

"Sounds like you've been dating the wrong man," Ted said.

"Could be," she returned.

They were actually flirting with each other. Already. My eyes involuntarily strayed toward Dante's. From his amused expression, I could tell he was thinking the same thing. Ted had no idea what he was in for.

Impulsively, I turned to Rafe. "More sweet potatoes?"

"Thank you, child," he said. "I'll have more of everythin'. It's delicious." He was looking at Maggie as he said this. Was it my imagination, or was the whole table collectively smitten?

The phone rang, and as at least two couples seemed mesmerized by each other, I rose to answer it.

"Pink or red?" a voice demanded.

"What?" I said, before I realized it was Justin Simms.

"Do you prefer pink or red roses? This nice lady at the Brattle Street Florist says either would do, but I want this to be perfect."

"Well, I'm wearing black, so I guess red."

"Done. I'll see you soon, beautiful."

I stood staring at the phone receiver after he hung up. How had he known that this would be a good time to remind me that I had options?

I returned to the table. Five faces looked up expectantly at me. I smiled. "Just my date, calling to make sure that I haven't changed my mind about tonight."

"Just wrapping the mon around your little finger, eh?" Rafe teased.

I felt Dante's eyes on my face again and glared at him. *Yes, I do have a date, thank you very much. What's it to you?*

"Jess, you're going to the Fogg party, right?" I said evilly. "Tell us about your date."

She smiled coyly in Ted's direction. "It's a blind date. The former roommate of someone on my rotation, teaches Finance at the B-School. I'm told he's an excellent piece of merchandise."

Maggie raised her eyebrows. "What constitutes excellence these days?"

"Oh, you know, handsome, and smart, and funny, and sensitive."

"Your basic Denzel Washington. Sounds too good to be true. What are the chances of those things being present in one male form in this day and age?" I piped in.

"What are the chances that you'd recognize it even if they were?" Dante said sharply.

"There they go again," Jess laughed. "No fighting at the dinner table, children. Ted, what are we going to do with them?" I could have killed her at that moment with my bare hands.

"What do you suggest?" Ted replied, clearly besotted.

I could tell where this was headed, and I quickly excused myself to start serving dessert. Maggie followed me into the kitchen, looking suddenly somber.

"Isn't he great?" I whispered, squeezing her arm.

"Oh, he's a fine man," she said quietly. "But what I want to know is, what's going on between the two of you?"

"What are you talking about? You know Rafe and I are just friends," I said, digging in the drawer for the pie server.

"I'm not talking about Mr. Griffin. I'm talking about you and that Dante." She planted herself at the kitchen table.

"Nothing, Maggie! Why are you asking it like that?" I stopped fiddling with the drawer and looked at her. She was deadly serious.

"He keeps looking at you, and you keep looking at him, and I know what that means."

"What does it mean?" I sighed heavily.

"It means *he's* the one you've been doing all this daydreaming over. And that you'll be with him soon. And I don't like it," she said firmly.

"Hold it right there! I won't 'be with him soon'; we hate each other."

"I know you, my sister. You're like my own child, you know. And you do not need to be falling in love with some Italian man with a strange name."

Well. There it was, out in the open.

"I'm sure you think he's very nice," she continued, "but he'll never take you seriously. He wants one thing from you, and once he gets it, he'll be gone again. That's all they ever want from us."

"Well, maybe that's all I want from him, too," I snapped.

"You can't fool me. I see the way you look at him. You should cut it off right now, before somebody gets hurt."

Well, it was far too late for that. Somebody had been hurt already, but I took her point.

"Look, if I were in love with him, which I'm not, there'd be nothing we could do, would there?" I said with a shrug. "It just happens."

"No, it doesn't just *happen*. I never allowed myself to get close enough to a white man to fall in love with him. You don't just look across a room, you know. You have to spend time with the person. And you can pick who you spend time with."

"Sometimes it does happen that way, Maggie," I said quietly.

"Girl, black people, especially educated ones, do not have the luxury of romance. We are in a state of siege, families falling apart, children dying. You and the rest of these middle-class integrated black kids have an obligation to stop playing around with these whites. Find yourself a good black man and settle down." She took a pie in each hand. "You think about what I said. I know you understand what I mean."

I remained in my chair, lost in thought. She hadn't said anything that I hadn't heard before, hadn't thought about before. I knew she was right. That was the whole reason I had stayed with Prince Roger for so long. But heaven help me, part of me couldn't help wondering what she saw in Dante's eyes when he looked at me that was so powerful that it triggered a sermon.

When I returned to the dining room table, the conversation had circled back to Jess's blind date.

"So what course does he teach?"

"First-year Finance," Jess answered. "If it doesn't work out between us, maybe I'll pass him to you, Nikki. Between the two of you, you might make a major academic breakthrough."

"Well, if it's a breakthrough in economics, at least it can't be dangerous," Ted said, laughing. "Not like a breakthrough in genetic engineering or foreign relations."

"Thank you so much for taking my life's work seriously," I said lightly.

The conversation turned to politics, as it inevitably did in our house. In the good old days, this would have resulted in Dante and me insulting each other in public and kissing wildly in private. But under Maggie's watchful eyes, I kept quiet, weighing the import of her words.

Perhaps she was right.

With a murder to solve, and a life to build, I probably couldn't afford the luxury of romance.

CHAPTER TWELVE

A Fête
Worse than
Death

Maggie corralled Dante and Ted into helping her with the dishes after dinner. Meanwhile, I quietly pulled Rafe aside and showed him the financial statements on Ella Fisher's disk. He took copies of the printouts of her version and Ian's, then joined the cleanup party in the kitchen. Jess and I were excused to primp for the Friends of the Fogg Museum Gala.

My wardrobe choices for a black-tie event are limited, and I had already decided to wear my favorite evening dress, which is short, black, and sequined. I retrieved my killer patent leather stiletto heels from the back of my closet, wrapped a long black chiffon scarf around my neck to hide my bruise, and stole a spray of Maggie's Opium. She had bought it because of the name, but I actually liked it.

Justin arrived at our door promptly at nine-thirty with a bouquet of a dozen red roses and a tuxedo with a crimson cummerbund and bow tie.

"Wow," he said, slowly circling me. "Bow-wow-wow."

"Thanks!" I laughed. "You, too, look good enough to howl at."

"Don't laugh at me," he said. "This is a last-minute Keezer's special. I was going to rent, but everyone said that I should buy a tux to prove that I really did attend an Ivy League institution."

"How bourgeois," I teased. "Beware the slippery slope. Before you know it, you'll be shopping for a Range Rover and a house in Weston."

"Let's go before I change my mind."

We grabbed a taxi on Mass Ave and in ten minutes we were climbing the slate stairs of the Fogg Museum. The internationally renowned museum was the jewel in the crown of Harvard's archives, and had been lavishly renovated only two years ago, the red brick facade scoured free of years of Cambridge soot and the entire interior remodeled. As a result, the grand hall looked fabulous, but was rented out almost every Saturday night to help pay for the building's multimillion-dollar facelift.

It wasn't until we crossed the marble threshold and the light hit us fully that I realized Justin was wearing red high-top sneakers with his tux. What we used to call "Chucks" when I was growing up.

"Nice shoes," I said, stifling the urge to roll my eyes. *This is what I get for dating a twenty-year-old.*

"Oh, loosen up, Chase," he murmured, putting an arm around my shoulder. "The style police aren't issuing tickets tonight. And you'll thank me after I step on your toes on the dance floor."

As we moved further into the museum, it became clear that the party was already in full swing. The strains of "Night and Day" were spilling from the main exhibition room into the foyer, which was crowded with chattering undergraduates, swells from various graduate schools, and the cool doyennes of Harvard society, the faculty wives.

Justin went to check our coats, calling out greetings to two of his friends from the Law School, and I ventured into the two-story Italianate main hall just beyond a pair of towering granite sculptures. The dance floor was ablaze, lit by a series of crystal chandeliers and the whirling brilliance of men in tuxedos and women in glittering gowns. An arched stone balcony encircled the room, and already couples were perched on the railings overlooking the scene, waving at friends below. A twelve-piece swing band was stationed in the far corner, and waiters in black tie proffered glasses of champagne from sparkling silver trays. An unexpected *frisson* of excitement passed through me. It felt like a night for romance.

Just then Ian McAllister, who had been holding court with a group of students on the edge of the dance floor, caught my eye. He looked splendid in his tuxedo, and I smiled as our eyes met. This was the perfect chance to find out more about the discrepancy in those financial statements.

"Veronica." The professor kissed my cheek in greeting. He promptly turned me away from the group. "How's that *AER* article coming?"

"Pretty well. I'll definitely have a draft for you to send out Monday morning. But you're going to have to live without the Marshall material."

"But you said you were getting the book—"

"Look, it's a long story, but I had the book, then I lost it." The last time I'd seen it, the volume was flying through the air in the Widener stacks. "Trust me," I interjected as he started to protest, "the article will be fine."

"If you say so." He sounded doubtful. "What about the Crimson Future report?"

"I got another copy of the disk from Paula, and I'll be meeting with Rona Seidman tomorrow to create a document for our committee meeting Monday. But I have a question for you. Have there been any recent reclassifications of overhead expenses between the Treasurer's office and the individual schools?"

"What kind of overheads?" He signaled the waiter for a glass of champagne.

"You know, administrative support, office supplies, outside contractors, that sort of thing."

Ian's eyes narrowed slightly in concentration. "Yes, I believe there was. Why do you ask?"

I shrugged as we both accepted champagne from the waiter. "I found a discrepancy between an older version of the university financials that Ella Fisher had and the set that you gave me. The overhead expenditures in FAS were a bit off, and I just wanted to understand why."

"Ella Fisher had an older version of the university financials? That can't be," he scoffed. "Where would she have gotten them? The comptroller keeps all those records."

"Apparently she had a friend in the accounting department who got them for her. I think she decided to start analyzing them while we were waiting to get the latest version from you."

"That woman." He shook his head irritably. "Wasting time working on old numbers when the new ones were coming in a matter of days. I hope *you* didn't spend a lot of time on it."

"No. None at all, actually. I knew Ella had the information, but I had no idea she had been working so hard on it. That's what I started to tell you yesterday. When your disk didn't work, I got one from Ella's house with the older version on it, to speed up my analysis."

"So she'd worked on it a lot, had she?"

"Yes. She'd already done a lot of the baseline analysis, compound annual growth rates, things like that. It was a nice piece of work."

"Well, you're going to have to redo it," he barked, looking increasingly annoyed. "I'm not trusting our entire committee's recommendation to the work of a glorified secretary. You've got the new disk now, and I wouldn't waste any more time on those old financial statements. They're completely out of date. And we've got too much ground to cover to lose any more time, Nikki."

"I know, Ian." I sighed impatiently.

"Are you alone tonight?" he asked, mollified. I could tell that he was already scanning the room for someone more important to talk with. "Hello, David," he said, nodding to one of the tenured professors in the Government Department.

"No, I actually have a date, but he seems to have wandered off. Where's Connie tonight?"

"Headache," he said, and turned to greet a gray-haired man approaching us from the dance floor whom I recognized as one of the university's newest trustees. Happy to be dismissed, I turned away. I knew the source of Connie's headache: more often than not, when she did come to social events with him, Ian ignored his wife completely and spent the whole evening schmoozing the trustees and influential alums in his eternal quest to climb higher in the Harvard food chain. Who needed to primp for hours just to play mannequin all night?

I walked the length of the dance floor watching the couples twirling, some smoothly, and others simply with wild abandon, to "Take the A Train," and hummed the melody under my breath while scanning the crowd for Justin. I needed to find my date, sneakers notwithstanding, and hit the dance floor.

I found him a few minutes later in animated conversation with Lindsey Wentworth, the bookseller manqué Isaiah Fisher close at her side. As I approached, I did a double take. Lindsey had dyed her hair.

It was jet black, and much shorter, and it made her look incredibly sophisticated. Almost powerful. I'd never seen a natural blonde go brunette before, but it was working for her. She was sporting a sleek red dress with a cropped jacket that I recognized from the September *Vogue* as a Thierry Mugler. There was only one nod to tradition: she was still wearing those preppy pearls.

Fisher was wearing a tuxedo with a kente-cloth cummerbund and bow tie. What on earth were they doing together? I'd heard of radical chic, but this was ridiculous.

"Lindsey!" I said. "Long time no speak. Great haircut."

"Nikki, I didn't know you were going to be here!" she gushed. "I can't believe how much I've seen of you lately."

"Yes, it's an awfully small world, isn't it, Harvard?" Fisher chimed in.

"How true," I returned, shooting him a look. "I would never have expected to see you here."

"Not expect to see *me?*" Lindsey interjected. Had she deliberately misunderstood me, or was she really that self-absorbed? "You must be joking. Benefits are my life. My family has given hundreds of them at this place, what with my great-grandfather—you know, the Commodore—having been one of the founding members of the Fogg Museum board of trustees."

I was watching Isaiah Fisher's face during this soliloquy, and it was clear that he wasn't with Lindsey for her sparkling conversation. His eyes were practically crossed in exasperation.

"I see you've met my date, Justin."

"Yes," Fisher answered. "Apparently he and Lindsey have known each other for a while."

"Yeah, we go way back, right Lins?" Justin said mockingly, putting his arm around Lindsey's shoulders. "We're homies. Love the new 'do."

Lindsey frowned and shook off Justin's embrace. "Mother hates it. She says it makes me look common. But Isaiah loves it, don't you darling?"

Fisher nodded and smiled expansively. *Darling?*

"I was asking brother Fisher about his bookstore's monthly newsletter," Justin continued. "I've been thinking about starting one of my own at the Law School. I'm going to call it *This Just In.* Get it? Got any tips for me?"

The two men turned away to continue their conversation, and I took the opportunity to pull Lindsey aside.

"Listen, I know it's none of my business, but what's the story with you two? Don't tell me you're a couple now."

"No! Of course not!" she said, looking mortified. "Mother would be horrified if she knew I was spending time in public with someone of his background. I mean, he was *arrested* once."

"So what are you doing with him?"

"Well"—she dropped her voice to a whisper—"it's important that someone stay close to him."

"What does *that* mean?"

"I can't talk about it right now," she muttered as Fisher turned back toward us. "Did I tell you I'm taking a course at the Extension School?" she said loudly. "I think it's going to help me a lot."

"That's great," I said, playing along. "What is it?"

"It's called practical philosophy."

"What is that, Benjamin Franklin?"

"No, it's spiritual," she began, when Fisher interrupted us.

"Get you a drink, baby?" Fisher put his arm around Lindsey and smiled jovially. Clearly, he wasn't a man to let a little thing like Afrocentrism get in the way of a good time.

"I'll come with you," she purred, her arm encircling his waist.

As they disappeared into the crowd, Justin led me out onto the dance floor. "Watch your toes, ma'am," he said. "No warranty of danceability with this package, just an honest effort to avoid maiming you for life."

"The trick is to just hold me close and sway," I said, laughing.

"That's the best offer I've had all night, woman!" I grimaced slightly as his arm went around my waist. My battered rib cage was still sore from the night before.

"Nice party," I offered.

"Yes, you've been quite the little butterfly. Not avoiding me, are you?"

"No, I just happen to know a few people here, and I haven't seen most of them since the summer. You won't be hurt if I circulate just a little tonight, will you?" I teased.

He squeezed my hand. "As long as you leave with the man that brung you." The song ended and he looked down at me, smiling. I dodged the look in his eyes and asked for a glass of champagne.

"Veronica." Christian Chung glided up to me as Justin disappeared into the crowd. He was wearing a black tuxedo with a deep blue vest and bow tie, and looked as if he had stepped straight out of the window at Louis, Boston. "You're looking recherché this evening," he said.

As he had done last night at the President's Open House, he immediately crossed into my personal space, standing so close that I could smell his aftershave. *What did recherché mean?*

"Are you here alone?" he asked, his eyes traveling slowly up my body. "Because it would be a shame to waste that dress."

In a split second, I decided to go ahead with my plan to get closer to him. So what if he was a bit predatory? He knew things about Leo and Ella that I needed to know. Ella had called him, *at home,* just before she died. And he clearly wanted something from me. So I tossed my hair and shot him my most dazzling party-girl smile. "I do have a date, but the dress may be going to waste, anyway. He's definitely junior varsity. How about you?"

"I'm bach-ing it tonight," he said, grinning. "I generally enjoy myself more that way. And I'm feeling that tonight will be no exception. Dance with me."

I straightened his tie ever so slightly, lingering just long enough to get his attention, and then took his hand as he led me onto the floor. The orchestra was playing a waltz, and he clearly knew his way around a dance floor; he was graceful and strong, one of those partners that makes you look like a better dancer than you really are.

"So how is your committee work going?" he whispered in my ear.

"Very well. We have a report due Monday."

"So you've gotten stuck plowing through all of those financial reports?"

"Yes, I have new appreciation for your department. I don't envy you at budget time."

"But I have a large staff. Are you doing this all on your own?"

"Yes, all on my own—note the dark circles under my eyes."

He tipped my head back slightly for a feigned inspection. "Deep, dark eyes, yes. But no circles."

"Nice of you to say. Listen, I have a question for you. Do you know if there's been a reclassification of overhead expenses from the FAS budget to some other department? I'm talking about items like temp secretaries, florists, that sort of thing."

"As a matter of fact, there has," he replied, twirling me expertly. "The university has been consolidating those types of expenditures in the budget for my office for the past couple of years. It's a cost-control measure. We have a central purchasing manager now, whose job it is to achieve volume discounts from an approved list of vendors."

That would explain the difference between Ella's and Ian's versions of the financials, which meant that I didn't need to spend any more time reconciling the two. I breathed a heavy sigh of relief. "You just saved me *hours* of work. Bless you."

"So what do I get in return for this extraordinary level of service?" he murmured.

"What did you have in mind, Mr. Chung?" *What* did *he have in mind?*

"You're not the prim little economist I had you pegged for, are you?" he said, sliding his hand slowly across my back.

"No," I whispered, "I'm all grown up now."

The things I would do for Ella.

"And you like to play with fire," he said, smiling assuredly.

"It has its rewards."

"Pardon me," Justin Simms's voice interrupted. "I'd like to cut in, if you don't mind."

He was standing behind Christian, looking extremely annoyed. Christian gave him the briefest glance, and then looked back at me. "Do you want to ask the kid to leave, or should I?"

"Kid? What's that supposed to mean?" Justin said, sounding surprised. "This is my date, and I'm cutting in."

"Let's not make a scene," I said, looking at Justin. "I'll join you as soon as this dance is over, okay?"

"Or maybe the one after that," Christian said with a grin. "We'll let you know, kid." He turned back toward me with a wink.

"Listen, buddy, I don't like your attitude," Justin said angrily. "What gives?"

People were beginning to stare at us, and I was starting to feel horrible. I hadn't been thinking about Justin when I started this. My investigation would have to wait. I took Justin's arm and turned to Christian. "Thanks for the dance, Christian. I'll see you later, okay?"

The expression in my eyes, with its promise of future access, was sufficient to calm him down, and I walked with Justin to the edge of the dance floor.

"Nice Neanderthal act," I said lightly. "What do you do for an encore? Throw me over your shoulder and run bellowing from the room?"

"Is that him?" he demanded.

"Who?"

"Him. The man of the emotional baggage. The one you're still not over."

"No, it's not."

"Great. So you just look like that at any guy who comes along?"

"What are you implying?" It came out more sharply than I had intended.

"I saw the way you were looking at him. That wasn't just a dance, that was a prelude."

"Justin!" A black woman in a green bugle-beaded dress popped up suddenly behind us. "You owe me a dance, baby!"

"I'm sure you'll excuse me, Nikki," he said gravely. Then he was gone.

I swallowed the lump of guilt in my throat as he turned away. He was a sweet man, and I was completely mucking this up. In search of solitude, I slipped upstairs to the balcony overlooking the dance floor. From the darkness, I looked down on the crowd below, and just watching for a few moments began to restore my good humor. It was the quintessential formal evening. The men in their tuxes were gorgeous without even trying, which always infuriated me, because the women were obviously trying very hard indeed: there were elaborate hairdos and rivers of makeup, dresses that pinched or were too short to sit down in. And as usual, most of the women were wearing black; between their dresses and the men's tuxedos, the crowd could have been attending a wake rather than a soiree.

Despite my cynicism, I was still susceptible to the night's magic, and in short order my annoyance had dissipated. Perhaps it was the smell of the perfume, or the witty conversation, or most probably the music, but I always felt ridiculously hopeful at these dances. Who wouldn't, when a soulful tenor crooned that love was here to stay; that night and day, you were the one; that it had to be you, while a pair of strong arms whirled you around amidst a dazzling crowd. It did seem, just for one night, that anything was possible, and love really could just walk through the door.

Jess and her date finally had arrived; I could see them crossing the dance floor. She was wearing a sparkling emerald green dress that set off her hair, and she looked wonderful. Mr. Business School was definitely attractive; I wondered if he fit the rest of the description. Jess looked happy, which meant nothing, because she has smiled her way through dates from hell many times before. I knew I'd get the full report the next morning.

That's when I saw Dante, laughing as he slipped a dark brown mink stole from the shoulders of a tall blond woman. Yes, love really can walk in the door on a night like this. But he'll have someone else on his arm. I watched them for a few moments, and then sank to the floor and regarded a Henry Moore sculpture through a furious haze. What was he doing here? He hadn't said a word about it at dinner. I could hear Maggie's voice ringing in my ear. *He'll never take you seriously.*

Footsteps clattered on the stone floor and then Jess's face appeared above me.

"Hey, I saw you leaning over the railing. Taking a foot break?"

"No, I'm throwing a temper tantrum."

She joined me on the floor. "Yeah, I saw them when we came in. Who is she?"

"How the hell should I know? Some white girl with a mink stole. What's to know?"

"Look, you kicked him to the curb Thursday night. What did you expect?"

"Damn it, I expected him to mope around for at least a week, that's what."

"Girl, either make him come correct, or tell him to step off. But don't sit up here sulking."

"Okay, I can handle this, thank you very much," I snapped. "How's your date?"

"Too early to be sure, but I get the feeling he's a dim bulb."

"You're kidding! I thought he was on the B-School faculty."

"Get this. In the cab on the way over, I told him about an article I had just read in the *New Republic,* and you know what he said?"

"What?" I said, beginning to regain my good humor.

"He said, 'Wow, I figured you were a Democrat.' "

"What, did he think you should be reading the *Nation?*"

"No, he thought the *New Republic* was a magazine for *new Republicans.*"

"Well, it might as well be, given the editorials they've been running for the past five years," I said, laughing. "Give the man some credit—maybe he actually reads it." I shook my head. "Dating sucks, doesn't it?"

"Now, I didn't say all that. Take that housemate of yours, Ted. Cute. And a lawyer. He's all that and a bag of chips."

"Jess, he's a *poverty* lawyer, remember?"

"We'll see," she said mischievously. "Never hurts to have a couple of lines in the water when you're after a big fish."

"Well, I'm pulling in my rod."

"Now, now—no whining. Come on, let's bust a move."

On our way down the stairs, I was intercepted by one of my Ec. 10 students. We chatted about the course for a while, and then I set him free to rejoin his date; life was too short to waste it talking to professors at parties. Fisher danced by with Lindsey, and I overheard him say, "I never wear jewelry of any kind. Every time I do, something bad happens." Like what, I wondered. Theft? Allergic reaction? A public display of bad taste?

A hand touched my elbow and I turned to find Rafe Griffin behind me, turned out in a tuxedo.

"Rafe, what are you doing here?"

"We got the call that the President was comin' to the party, and two of my officers called in sick tonight. So here I am."

"Too bad you couldn't bring Maggie."

"Now, I would never ask a woman to a party where I had to work," he remonstrated. "It wouldn't be right."

"But you two did get along, right?"

His smile was bright enough to light up the entire room. "Yes, child, we got along."

"Here's the man now." Rafe nodded. I followed his gaze to the foyer as a collective gasp went up from the group. The President had arrived. Victoria Barrett preceded him, her head held imperiously high as she cut a swath through the crowd. Leo followed behind, shaking hands, waving at friends, bending to listen to a whispered comment or two, and generally basking in the adulation. A flock of students, mostly women, immediately surrounded them, and Leo smiled confidently as he fielded their questions.

I was happy to see how well he looked, considering that he had spent last night in the hospital. Victoria, relegated by the masses to a spot somewhere behind Leo's left shoulder, rolled her eyes as a tall redhead asked how Barrett could justify cuts in student aid to fund building renovations.

"Leo," she said peremptorily, "we're needed up at the podium. I'm sure you all understand that the President isn't here to discuss policy this evening," she said, dismissing the assembled horde. "You really must excuse us." With surprising force, Victoria plunged into the crowd. After a long pause, Leo turned and followed her.

"That woman is trouble," Rafe muttered under his breath.

Just then, a shout went up from the dance floor. Rafe and I arrived at the edge of a quickly-forming crowd in time to see Justin Simms getting up from the floor, blood trickling from the corner of his lip as Christian Chung stood over him.

"Was that enough, or do you want another?" Christian said sharply. *Jesus. He really was a predator.*

"You're a real asshole, you know that?" Justin shouted, hurling himself at Christian, fists flailing.

I grabbed Rafe's arm hard as he started to wade into the fray. "Get rid of the bigger one for the night, will you?" I whispered. "I'll explain later, but I need him to be gone." I clearly needed to rethink my strategy. Maybe I *couldn't* handle Christian alone. Either way, I wasn't going to accomplish what I wanted with Justin hovering over me; better to deal with them one at a time.

"All right, now, that's enough," Rafe barked. Christian had given Justin another punishing blow to the jaw and was standing over him with a murderous expression. "You," Rafe said, jerking his head in Christian's direction. "Out. Now."

"What?" Christian exploded. "You've got to be kidding."

"Look, mon," Rafe said, "I'm a Sergeant Detective with the university police. You've got ten seconds to clear out of here or you'll be spending the night in a holding pen."

"Look, Officer," Christian barked, "you probably don't know who I am—"

"I'm pressing charges," Justin called from the safety of the other side of the floor. "You hit the wrong man, bully boy."

"Fine," Christian said, quickly recovering his composure as the crowd grew larger and filled with more prominent faces. "But I'd do it again to preserve a lady's reputation," he proclaimed. "You were way out of line." Then he disappeared into the crowd.

I joined Justin as someone offered him a napkin to clean the blood off his face.

"What happened?" I whispered, as we stumbled toward a row of chairs.

"I told him I didn't appreciate the way he was running his hands all over you, and he slugged me," Justin mumbled. "Asshole."

Rafe sauntered over to us and looked down at Justin. "Am I gone to have to ask you to leave, too?" he said gruffly.

"No, sir," Justin said quietly.

"Silly children," Rafe muttered. "Have me in the middle of a race riot before you know it. You're lookin' a little green around the gills, mon," he said to Justin. "You gone to be all right?"

"Actually, I think I'm going to be sick," Justin said, faintly.

"Come on, boy," Rafe said gently, taking him by the elbow.

"So you know that cop, eh?" I turned to find Isaiah Fisher standing behind me, smiling knowingly.

"Yes, I do. He's dating my landlady. Why?"

"The brother's been hassling me, that's all."

"Really? About what?"

"He went all circus on me, asking me questions about Ella, about when I last saw her."

"It's just his job. I wouldn't worry," I said easily. "Let's dance." I was dying to know why Lindsey had said that someone needed to stay close to him.

The orchestra was playing a foxtrot, and Fisher whirled me around the floor in surprisingly smooth circles without any apparent effort.

"You're pretty good," I commented.

"Back in the day, my folks trotted me off to dance school. Busy tryin' to hang with the white folks."

"Like Lindsey Wentworth? Somehow, I wouldn't have placed you with an 'ice person.' And she tells me that Mother really wouldn't approve."

He laughed easily. "See, it's sarcastic black sisters like you that are drivin' us to the white girls."

"Seriously, how did the two of you hook up?"

"Seriously, Harvard, that's none of your business."

Refusing to be baited, he spent the rest of the dance regaling me with predictions of the financial success of his newest newsletter, for which he planned to charge $1.00 a copy, even though according to the numbers he was throwing around, it sounded to me as if it would cost almost $2.50 an issue to produce and mail. Great, I thought. We're losing money on each issue, but we're planning to make it up on volume.

At the song's end, he bowed slightly and disappeared into the crowd.

I looked around for Justin and found him hovering by the bar like a Bedouin at an oasis, clutching a glass of champagne. As I approached, I could hear him trying to provoke an argument with anyone who would stand still long enough to listen, going on and on about the need for more African art in the university collection. He appeared to be completely drunk.

"Hey, date of mine, you look like you're having some evening," I said, steering him toward the chairs that lined the perimeter of the room. "Are you feeling all right?"

"I'm fine!" he roared jovially. He seemed to be completely out of control. When had he found the time to drink so much? "But you women," he said, flopping down into one of the chairs, "you women—I'll never understand you!"

"That's very likely true," I said lightly. His face was flushed, and he was talking very quickly.

His voice dropped to a whisper. "I've been watching tonight. I've been watching very carefully. And I don't get it."

"What do you mean?" I said, signaling a waiter to bring some water.

"Why do women carry so much junk in their purses?"

"Because male designers never put pockets in our clothing. Justin, seriously. Are you feeling all right?"

"I told you, I'm fine. And why do they share everything? Huh?"

"I guess we're just naturally generous spirits," I said, holding his arm as he tried to stand.

"I actually saw a woman letting another woman wear her earrings!" he whispered. "Can you believe it?" Maybe he really was just drunk. But how could it have happened so quickly?

"Depends on whether they were clips or posts," I said, accepting a glass of water from a sympathetic waiter. "Here, drink this."

His brow wrinkled as he took a gulp from the glass and swallowed hard. "Sapphires."

"What did you say?"

"Sapphires are the blue ones, right?" He took another sip of water.

"Justin, what exactly did you see?" It couldn't be a complete coincidence that he was babbling about sapphires and earrings after my conversation with Dante.

"Oh no," he muttered suddenly. He was starting to look green again. "Would you excuse me?"

"Justin!" Before I could stop him, he had bolted for the hallway. What the hell was going on?

I was in desultory conversation with a fellow professor, impatiently waiting for Justin to return, when the orchestra launched into a sultry rendition of "More Than You Know" and a warm hand caressed my arm.

"Nice dress, Nik," came a familiar voice low in my ear. "No wonder you set off a riot. If you keep this up, they'll have to call the fire department, too."

I turned and found myself nearly in the arms of Dante Rosario. I made the mistake of meeting his gaze directly and was rewarded by having my knees go weak.

"Nice tux," I said coolly, pulling away from him. If my heartbeat didn't slow, I was going to need an emergency vehicle myself.

"You used to like to rest your cheek right about here on the slow songs," Dante smiled, fingering his lapel.

"Really?" I said, meeting his gaze squarely. "I don't even remember."

"Whatever you say, lady."

"At any rate, now a new cheek graces the site. Where'd you find her?"

"She found me. In the library tonight. Convinced me that I could catch up on my Hobbes another night."

"And offered to help you return to the state of nature, no doubt."

"She's a biochemist," he said, ignoring me. "Working with Professor Childs on the Human Genome Project."

"A biochemist with her very own mink stole. What serendipity that you were being a wonk this evening. How's the apartment hunt going?"

"Very well. Danielle, my date, is looking for a roommate."

"Well, there you go; you'll avoid that awkward issue of how soon to call tomorrow morning."

"Good point. I'll also be in a very good negotiating position with her shortly."

This man was pure evil.

"Dante!" a voice called. I turned, expecting to find the intended victim, and was instead greeted with the sight of Victoria Barrett smiling delightedly in our direction. She was wearing a floor-length navy taffeta gown with dazzling diamond earrings, and swept regally across the floor as the music faded.

"What are you doing here?" She smiled up at Dante, ignoring me completely. "I thought you were in California."

"I was, until last week. I'm back in the Government Department now as an assistant professor. It's great to see you, Torie."

He called her Torie?

"This is absolutely wonderful," she said, beaming. She was actually batting her eyelashes at him. She took his arm and turned him away from me, toward the dance floor. "We'll have to have you over for dinner very soon. Leo will be thrilled to see you again."

Stung, but unwilling to lose track of their conversation, I remained behind them as the conductor announced that President Leo Barrett had a few remarks to make.

As Leo walked toward the microphone, I heard Victoria murmur to Dante, "I hope he realizes how important this is." She sighed. "I keep trying to get him to understand that these types of functions are critical to his success, and that he needs to rehearse, but he just walks in cold—"

"Good evening, fellow revelers!" Leo said smoothly. He seemed to have fully recovered from whatever had hit him last night. His face had regained its color, and he looked his usual dashing self. "I want to personally thank you for attending what has become an important annual event, the Fogg Museum Gala."

Victoria was shaking her head adamantly. "I *knew* he would get the name wrong. I kept telling him—the Friends of the Fogg Museum Annual Gala. How hard is that to remember?"

Dante took her hand and raised it to his lips. "Torie, give the man a break," he said, smiling as he kissed her hand. "We can't all be as conscientious as you."

"Well, if I don't stay on top of it, who will?" Her voice dropped to a whisper. "The vultures are circling, and he doesn't even realize it."

"Calm down, Torie."

She patted his arm and subsided into a series of whispered questions about Dante's return while Leo finished his speech.

"Come, I want to introduce you around," Torie said to Dante as the orchestra struck up another song. "I suppose you're on your own this evening?"

A voice interrupted my assessment of the practicality of trailing around after them all night. "Who's the hunk you were eavesdropping on?" I turned to find Alix Coyle beside me, wearing a gauze fuchsia slip dress with silver lamé sandals.

"What are you doing here?" I exclaimed. She looked like a flamingo in a flock of penguins. As she turned to take a glass of champagne off a passing tray, I noticed that she had a large tattoo on her left shoulder: a red heart with green chain links wrapped around it.

"Brustein likes us to get out at these things; helps us raise money if you high-class types feel that you have a relationship with us," she said, sipping from her glass. "What's wrong, you never seen a tattoo before?"

"Not this close up, no," I said. "That a souvenir of Bud?"

"How'd you guess?" Alix frowned at her champagne glass. "I don't suppose there's any hard liquor at this party?"

I laughed, feeling happy to be with someone who had actually sought out my company. Screw Victoria Barrett. And Dante. "Right this way. I love your dress," I said as we started toward the bar on the far side of the room. "It's not just outrageous, it's *outré*."

"Thank you, dahling."

She looked a little unsteady, and I wondered what demon was chasing her tonight.

"Are you okay?" I asked.

"I'm fine, I'm fine." She waved her hand dismissively. "I just hate this music. Makes me feel like I'm trapped in a Coward play and I'll be shot if I'm not witty on cue. How can you stand those shoes?"

"What can I say? I'm a sucker for high heels. Come on, let's sit down." I took a white wine and she a bourbon from the bartender and then we found two chairs on the perimeter of the dance floor.

Victoria Barrett sailed back into my line of vision, *sans* Dante. This time she was with a tall blond middle-aged man, but the tableau was otherwise much the same. She was smiling up at him as they talked with a gaggle of older women who looked to be faculty wives. I recognized the face from the latest issue of the *Harvard Gazette*: the new head of the Alumni Association. He whispered something in her ear, and I heard her laugh ring out across the room. "You Exeter men are all the same," she squealed. His arm strayed to her waist momentarily, and then they drifted off to the dance floor.

Leo Barrett walked by, talking animatedly with the black woman in the green bugle-beaded dress who had asked Justin for a dance earlier. Something about them made a very appealing couple; they looked as if they belonged together, somehow. I realized what it was as Leo leaned toward her, laughing, to answer a question. Their features were very similar, their animated faces mirroring large round eyes, full lips, and a soft jawline.

"So what are you doing after the ball?" Alix asked abruptly.

"I'm not sure. I'm here with a date." Which reminded me that I needed to find him. "I'm considering trying to palm him off on someone else, but so far, I'm still obligated to 'leave with the one that brung me,' as he so eloquently stated it."

"You're trying to get rid of that gorgeous guy? Do you have my home number?"

"That wasn't my date," I said, shaking my head. "That was Dante Rosario. My housemate and ex-obsession. My date picked a fight with someone twice his size, lost the battle, and has now disappeared. And he's twenty years old. Still interested?"

"Thanks, but no. Too bad you're not on your own. There's a party in Central Square that I was going to invite you to. No Harvard types, so it might actually be fun."

"And I made the cut? Gee, thanks."

"What the hell, bring your date, too."

"Well, it does sound a lot better than playing 'dodge the tongue' on my front porch."

"Been there," she drawled. "You better come with me."

I took the address of the party from her, and set out to find Justin. It was after midnight, and I realized that almost an hour had gone by since I'd seen him. The crowd was beginning to thin out, and I said my good-byes to Jess. Dante and his date had left even earlier; I was determined not to think about that. I circled the museum, looking for Justin. Could he actually have left without me?

I heard voices in one of the darkened rooms off the corridor, and started toward the sound. As I drew nearer, I realized that it was Leo Barrett, deep in conversation with Lindsey Wentworth. He was facing her, his hands gripping her shoulders. I couldn't hear what they were saying, but Leo was shaking his head adamantly, and Lindsey looked as if she were about to burst into tears. She was probably trying to get a better job in the Harvard hierarchy now that Ella was gone, and having no luck.

I was starting to get worried when I noticed a red sneaker protruding from one of the darkened galleries that lined the main hall.

It was Justin, sprawled on his back. I saw Rafe standing near the foyer and beckoned frantically to him.

"Can you give me a hand? He must have passed out from drinking too much." My days of raiding the nursery for dates were officially over.

Rafe bent over Justin, and then put a hand to his neck.

Then he looked straight at me.

"What's the matter?" I asked anxiously. The sadness in his expression was frightening me.

Rafe shook his head soberly. "I'm sorry, Nikki. I think the boy is dead."

CHAPTER THIRTEEN

NOTHIN' GOOD
EVER HAPPENS
AFTER MIDNIGHT

"I sure do hate to leave you alone like this."

Rafe Griffin was looking down at me with a deeply furrowed brow.

It was 3:00 A.M. Sunday and we had just returned home from Mass General Hospital. Justin Simms had slipped into a coma near the end of the party at the Fogg Museum. Initial tests indicated that it was the result of excess ethyl alcohol in his bloodstream. The doctor said he had drunk himself nearly to death.

I had stayed at the hospital until Rafe and the nurses forced me to go home, and now a persistent feeling of unreality was hanging over me. This whole thing was like a nightmare.

"You sure nothin' is missin'?"

"Yes, Rafe, I'm sure," I repeated numbly. "You don't have to fuss over me."

The door to my apartment had been ajar when Rafe and I arrived ten minutes earlier. I knew I had probably just forgotten to lock it in my rush to be out the door with Justin earlier that evening, but after the attack at Widener last night, it was nice to have an overly protective cop search the place to be sure I hadn't been burglarized on top of everything else. But there were no masked intruders hiding in the shower, my few valuables were still in place, and Keynes was sprawled on my bed sound asleep.

"You should go," I said distractedly. "You must be exhausted."

"My gran' used to always say, 'nothin' good ever happens after midnight,' " he muttered. "I've got a bad feelin' about this. You sure you don't want me to stay awhile?"

"Yes." I laid my hand on his arm. "I'll be asleep before you hit the front door, okay? But thanks for asking. Really."

The sound of his footsteps echoed on the stairs, and then an oppressive silence descended.

Who was I kidding? I turned out the lights in case Rafe was watching from the street, but there was no way I was going to sleep now.

Pacing restlessly, I stopped to peer out at the darkened street below. The moon beamed incongruously bright through the window, outlining the panes in shadow on the floor. I didn't know Justin Simms all that well. And he *had* been drinking a bit, particularly after Christian Chung humiliated him. But when could he possibly have drunk enough to nearly kill himself? It just didn't add up.

Pulling my dress over my head, I quickly changed back into the skirt and sweater I'd worn at dinner, then regarded the telephone. I was desperate to call Jess, but for all I knew, her date with Mr. Business School was still in progress. And it was far too late to wake Maggie up. Still, I was too wound up to sit around the apartment; if I couldn't talk to anyone, at least I could go for a walk, get some fresh air and do some thinking. I'd bring Maggie's dog, Horace, along for protection.

Cambridge is a city that does sleep, at least lightly, and when Horace and I reached Harvard Square, most of the neon signs over the restaurants, banks, and bookstores had been extinguished, leaving only a lone counterman in Store 24. We entered the hushed Yard through Johnson Gate, and the cool, damp air wrapped me in its clammy embrace. The only sounds were the occasional bird, Horace's heavy breathing, and the muffled conversation of a passing group of students making their way home.

We crossed the Yard and came to rest on the broad stone steps of Weld Hall, a red brick freshman dormitory near Widener Library. Horace promptly curled up and went to sleep, and my thoughts returned to Justin. I could still see him lying in that antiseptic hospital room, his face looking young and vulnerable and damaged against the white sheets. I should have stayed closer to him. Maybe then he would have been all right. Slowly, tears started to sting my eyes. It was so unfair. Why had two of the few successful black people at Harvard been struck down in the space of a week? What was going so terribly wrong?

Finally alone, I buried my face in my hands and began to sob. For Justin, for the loss of Ella, for my nightmarish trip through Widener—it really hadn't been a good week.

"That must have been some lousy date, Juliet," a disturbingly familiar voice said. Dante Rosario.

Before I could move, he was beside me on the steps, and as I raised my head, I could feel his arms tighten around me. *God, he smelled like heaven.* I pulled away abruptly and dabbed fiercely at my eyes.

"No worse than the ones we used to have," I said brusquely.

Dante produced a wad of Kleenex from his jacket pocket and silently proffered one. "Want to talk about it, Nik?"

"What are you doing here?"

"I was up reading and I heard a pair of footsteps coming down from your apartment. I figured that was your date. But then when I heard a second pair, I knew it had to be you. Thought at this hour you might need more protection than old Horace here, so I followed you."

"Well, I'm fine," I said, burying the crumpled Kleenex in my pocket. *Up reading? Then where was Danielle?* "But thanks for checking. I was just taking Horace for a walk and got all weepy thinking about how much work I have to do tomorrow."

"You never have been a good liar, Nik. I like that in a woman."

The truth was, I desperately needed someone to talk to. I had to clear my head if I was going to figure this thing out, and all of my confidants were sound asleep or otherwise engaged. And once upon a time, he had been a very good listener. So I took a deep breath, and told him everything. About stumbling over Ella, the cut wires at Littauer, the attack at Widener, Justin's coma, my apartment door ajar that evening, everything.

He let me talk without interrupting. By the time I finished, he was looking at me with a troubled expression.

"You could be in real danger," he said slowly. "I knew there was a story behind that bruise on your neck."

"Damn. I knew you'd figure out that it wasn't a love bite."

"Look, Juliet, this could be really serious, so save it. How do you know your apartment wasn't just broken into?"

"It wasn't, believe me. Nothing was missing."

"What the hell are the cops doing while all this is going on?"

"They know about everything. Rafe—the cop you met at dinner—escorted me home tonight. And he's already delivered the lecture about being careful."

"And you ignored him, genius," he said impatiently. "You're out here *alone* at this hour after all that. You want some advice?"

"What? Stay home with the door locked until next spring?"

"Get some protection."

"What did you have in mind? A guard dog? A can of Mace?"

"How about staying with Jess for a few nights?"

"No way. I've got a truckload of research for my AEA paper stashed in my living room."

"You need protection, Nik. Don't be stupid about this."

"I'll be careful," I said impatiently, "but I'm not going to be chased out of my own apartment."

He muttered something unintelligible and then said, "We'll talk about this after you've gotten some sleep."

"Don't get me wrong. I know it looks bad, Dante." I swallowed hard. "It's starting to scare me."

"Good. You'll be safer that way."

A husky voice slowly infiltrated the ensuing silence between us—a black woman's voice, smoky and low and filled with longing.

"If only you knew how much I love you, if only you knew," the voice sang. *"You still haunt my dreams, as strange as that seems, if only you knew."*

I realized that the song was coming from a stereo in one of the rooms above us, probably a fresh onslaught in a particularly sophisticated freshman seduction. But it felt as if it was being spun from the very air itself.

"I hide it so well I know you can't tell, but deep in my heart it's true," the voice crooned. *"I still can't resist the lure of your kiss, my love. If only you knew."*

"So when was the last time you cried like that, Juliet?"

"That's none of your business." I refused to look at him.

"If you say so." He rose to his feet and faced me from the pavement at the foot of the stairs. "I don't believe we ever shared a dance this evening," he said simply.

He extended his hand, and I clasped it, utterly captivated, as he drew me toward him. Perhaps it was incurable, this malady of mine. If only it were contagious.

We danced together then, until death retreated into the shadows for the night, and all that was left was the fatherly countenance of John Harvard beaming down on us in the moonlight, and the velvety autumn air, and the ever-widening spirals that were Dante and me.

Sunday afternoon I set out for the Business School to work on the Crimson Future Committee report with Rona Seidman. We had agreed that she would help me generate a draft report for Monday's committee meeting, and I was grateful to be getting far away from my usual haunts.

That morning I had awakened to the sound of rain on my roof, bleary-eyed and hoping that the night before had been a bad dream. By the time I was showered and dressed, it had stopped raining, and I walked to services under a gun-metal-gray sky. The church I attend in Porter Square is a Protestant anomaly: a down-at-the-heels Episcopal parish. But the minister and the congregation are like family to me, and that day I really needed spiritual comfort. Rafe had called before I left to say that Justin was still in a coma.

I crossed the Anderson Bridge, feeling cold in my very bones. There was menace in the air, and I was dreading what might happen next.

The manicured lawns of the Business School momentarily soothed my anxiety; the school spent an inordinate amount of money on its physical plant, and today the pristine grounds sported a profusion of orange- and rust-colored chrysanthemums, bittersweet, and ash berries, glowing embers in an otherwise gray landscape. The red brick Georgian buildings that held faculty offices, student dormitories, and classrooms stood in well-mannered rows. The future captains of industry are inculcated early to the good life.

Rona's office was in the highly-coveted Morgan Hall. The building was the hub of B-School faculty machinations, and her office on the second floor was a sign of the status that she had attained as the first tenured woman on the faculty. I found her elbow-deep in papers as she looked up to greet me.

"Nikki," she said warmly, "come in. I was just finishing this up." She scribbled furiously on a pad while I cleared a space at the round table in the center of her office. Rona sat back, sighing.

"The publisher wants this manuscript by the end of next week, but it just isn't going to happen."

"Well, I can't offer you any solace. I've brought another pile of paper to add to your collection."

I settled in at the table and started unpacking my homespun Lands' End backpack. Every time I unzipped it, I remembered my stolen Prada and swore revenge. "I've brought hard copies of the historical university financials in case you want to see them." I deposited a stack of spreadsheets on the table. "But I have the data on disk and I brought my PC. I've finished building the model of the financials, so we can change assumptions and look at how they affect the university's funding needs for the next ten years. This way, we can discuss what assumptions we want to make on the forward projections, and I can run the model in real time so we can see the results."

"I'm impressed," she said, joining me at the table. "But remind me again, why is it that it's only the *women* on this committee who ever get asked to do any real work? And why do we have this much work left with only three weeks to go?"

I grimaced. "You don't need me to answer your first question. This is Harvard, remember? As to the second, believe it or not, these financials took forever to track down. Every school has its own procedures, and most didn't want to cooperate. In the end, Leo Barrett and Ian McAllister had to personally get involved to make sure that the numbers were right."

I didn't tell her about Ella's bootlegged version of the financials, as Ian had ordered me to press on with the new numbers. Since Christian had confirmed that Ian was right about the reclassification of the overhead costs, there was no point in dwelling on the discrepancies in Ella's version, and we were working off of the disk I had been given by Ian's secretary.

We reviewed the financials on my computer, and I highlighted the areas that I thought we would want to share with the committee tomorrow. The revenue line had been growing a bit ahead of inflation at some of the schools, and well in excess of it at a handful. What surprised me was how the costs had risen even faster at some schools. If it weren't for the endowment funds, a couple of the grad schools would have been in big trouble.

"So basically, we need more money," Rona mumbled to herself as she looked over my shoulder at the computer screen.

"Yeah. I don't envy Barrett having to tell the alums that."

"Let's see just how much more," she said, sliding over to the computer keyboard. "Do you mind?"

"Be my guest." She was great. Most full professors I knew wouldn't be caught dead running simple projections on an Excel spreadsheet, but she seemed to be enjoying herself.

"So if we assume tuition increases an average of eight percent a year, we still need to raise almost fifty million dollars," she said, tapping away at the computer.

"Right," I said. "And if you look here"—I pointed at the screen—"you see that most schools have achieved only five percent historically."

"What if we cut costs by fifteen percent?"

We waited a moment for the model to run. "Why, look"—Rona grinned—"we'd have a surplus."

"It won't happen, though," I said, reclining in my chair. "The two biggest expense items are wages and capital improvements. The operations staff says the capital improvements won't wait, and the unions aren't going to tolerate any more headcount or salary reductions."

"Unions," she snorted. "What are we, General Motors?"

"You know what Yale goes through every four years," I reminded her gently. Was I the only one on the planet who was pro-labor? "Harvard's been spared a major strike because we've played it straight with the locals."

"Sure, sure," she muttered.

Throughout the afternoon we played with various scenarios for growth in revenues and costs, finally settling on three that seemed to bound the spectrum of realistic future outcomes for the university. Under the most optimistic of the three scenarios, Barrett would still need to raise $75 million over the next five years. Under the worst case, it was over $130 million. I looked at my watch and realized that three hours had gone by.

"Want some coffee?" Rona asked, as we both stretched and rubbed our shoulders.

"No, thanks," I said, smiling wearily. "I'd better get home and get this analysis charted up. We still need a presentation pack before tomorrow's meeting."

"Know what?" she said impulsively. "You look completely beat. I'll do it."

"Really?" I was incredulous.

"Sure." She waved her hand. "The kids are at my mother's all afternoon, and my husband's at a conference. It'll take me an hour."

"Bless you, Rona!"

"Hey, we girls have to stick together."

Freed from preparing for the Crimson Future meeting, I headed for the library to finish Ian's article for the *AER*. It was almost ten o'clock by the time I arrived back home, and I had an urgent message on my answering machine from Rafe Griffin.

I reached him at the Harvard police station, and I could tell by the tone of his voice that he didn't have good news.

"Is it Justin?" I demanded.

"Well, yes, child," he said soberly.

"He's not—"

"No, child, the boy's not dead."

"Then what is it?"

"I probably shouldn't be tellin' you this—"

"Rafe, stop it! You're obviously going to tell me, so go ahead!"

"All right, child. Calm down. They got the lab tests back."

"And?"

"And it looks like he was poisoned," he said quietly.

"Poisoned?"

"They said they found a mix of ethyl alcohol and tranquilizers in him when they pumped his stomach."

"Tranquilizers?"

I had to stop dumbly repeating everything he said and think.

"The boy wasn't suicidal, was he?"

"No," I said distractedly. "No way. He was extremely upbeat."

"That's what I figured."

"So someone slipped the pills to him?"

"That's what we think. Someone handed him a drink with sleepin' pills already in it."

That would explain Justin's irrational behavior toward the end of the party. He hadn't been drunk at all. He'd been drugged. "But who would do that?"

"That's why I'm callin' you."

Slowly, I sank into one of my kitchen chairs.

"Did you find any fingerprints on his glass?" I asked.

"Child, all the glasses in that room, there's no way we could figure out which one he drank from."

"I can't think of anyone who would want to hurt Justin. He seemed very popular, very happy-go-lucky." I paused. "Unless—"

"Unless what?" Rafe demanded.

"The last time I talked to him, he said that he had seen something at the party. Something about sapphire earrings."

"So?"

I told him the story about the earring that Dante had found outside his door at Littauer the night Ella died.

"Huh. We interviewed all the folks in Littauer the day after Ella died, but that never came up," Rafe said. "I'll send somebody over there to talk to the boy about it in the morning."

Well, I knew a faster way than that to get the information.

"Justin has some protection, right?" I asked. "I mean, now that you know what really happened last night, somebody could try again."

"Don't worry, child, we've got a twenty-four-hour watch on his room. And his family arrived earlier this evening."

"Good." Not that I was going to worry any less. "Do you think whoever went after Justin is the same person who killed Ella?"

"It could be," he said flatly. "Could be."

So somebody could have targeted two black people for death in less than a week.

"I'll talk to you later, Rafe," I said abruptly.

I had work to do. And it was going to start that night.

Littauer was almost deserted by the time I arrived; the library had closed at ten, and while I could see a few lights on in various offices, the lobby was hushed and still. Dante Rosario's office was on the first floor, just off the lobby, and I could see as I approached it that the lights were out. Perfect. On Saturday afternoon, he had said that the sapphire earring was in his office. With any luck, it would still be there. And I didn't need a search warrant and a police badge to go and get it.

I entered his office quietly, and pulled the door shut behind me. Crossing quickly through the anteroom that held his secretary's desk and rows of filing cabinets, I turned on the light in his office and walked toward his desk. If I remembered correctly, he had said that the earring was in one of its drawers.

I pulled the middle desk drawer open and was rewarded with a neat row of pens and pencils and a couple of pads of paper. I ran my hand all the way to the back of the drawer, but found nothing, not even dust. I guess he hadn't been here long enough to create much clutter.

The right bottom drawer was full of hanging file folders holding materials labeled "Stanford": teaching notes from previous courses, recommendations for students, his dissertation, copies of articles that he had written. I resisted the urge to read them and stacked them neatly on the floor so that I could see if there was anything underneath them in the drawer. Nothing. I was on my hands and knees underneath the desk looking to see if he had taped the earring to the bottom of a drawer when I heard the office door open and footsteps start toward me. I considered hiding under the desk, but the light had already betrayed me.

"Can I help you?" Dante's voice wafted over the top of the desk toward me. I backed out from under the desk and stood up to find him looking at me with an amused expression.

"Juliet. What a surprise."

"What are you doing here?" I snapped, determined to wipe the grin off his face.

"Funny, I was going to ask you the same thing. Last time I checked, this was *my* office." He leaned casually against the doorjamb.

"Fine." I shrugged. "Call the cops and report me for trespassing."

"I don't think that will be necessary." His eyes glittered at me. "If punishment is required, I'd prefer to administer it myself."

"I suppose you're looking for this," he continued, reaching into his pocket and producing a large diamond-and-sapphire earring which he placed on top of his desk. It lay there between us, taunting me.

Damn. "Okay, that *is* what I was looking for. What are you planning to do with it?"

"Well, now that I know who owns it, I'll be returning it."

That made me look at him.

He grinned and settled into one of the chairs facing the desk.

"Have a seat," he said, gesturing to his leather desk chair, "and I'll fill you in on my evening."

Warily, I sank back into the chair.

"I decided to take Torie up on her offer to have dinner after the story you told me last night," he said, pulling a pack of cigarettes out of his pocket. "Want one?"

"Sure," I said distractedly.

He put two cigarettes in his mouth and lit them, then passed one to me, his fingers lingering ever so lightly over mine.

"So you went to dinner with her," I prompted firmly.

"Yes, she insisted that I join her and Leo at their house."

"How lovely. An intimate dinner among friends."

"If you consider eight intimate."

"Desirée must have enjoyed that," I said nonchalantly.

"It's *Danielle*, and yes, I believe she did have a nice evening." *You asked for it*, his eyes told me.

"So who does the earring belong to?" I snapped, furious with myself.

"It's Torie's," he said, his eyes searching mine.

"How can you be so sure?"

He shrugged. "I told her how beautiful her dress had looked last night and she said that she wished she had been able to wear another pair of earrings with it."

"Her dress *was* sapphire blue, wasn't it?" I said, remembering the sight of her dragging Leo through the crowd. "But why would she own up to having lost this earring, given everything that happened last Sunday night? And what was she doing in Littauer?"

"She hasn't owned up to having lost this specific earring," he said, taking a drag on his cigarette. "And she definitely hasn't admitted to being in the building last week. But when she said she lost an earring that matched a blue dress, my gut said it could be this one."

"And—" I prompted.

"Well, it wouldn't have been smart to ask her straight out if it was this one. Too easy for her to deny it. So I had a look at her jewelry box while dinner was still going on."

I couldn't help smiling. "Nice."

"And I found the twin in there. That's what this is," he said, nodding toward the desk. "The one I found originally is stowed for safekeeping with the Harvard cops as of this evening."

"Not bad, Inspector," I said, grudgingly. "Not bad. But we still don't know what she was doing here."

"Somehow I think I can spend as much time with her as I want figuring that out." I didn't doubt that, given her behavior the night before.

"Well, my work here is done," I said, rising from the chair. "Thanks for filling me in." I crushed out my half-consumed cigarette in the ashtray on his desk and sidled past him toward the door.

"Let me walk you home," he said, standing up. "You shouldn't be out alone."

"I'll be fine. Besides, I'm sure Dominique is waiting for you."

I pulled his outer office door firmly shut behind me and walked quickly across the lobby, willing myself to think about Ella and Justin. If it really was Victoria Barrett's earring, then she could have been at Littauer that night. And she really disliked Ella. But enough to kill her?

It was going to take me the better part of the night to get over the expression in Dante's eyes when he offered me that cigarette. But there was clearly something even more dangerous than that afoot at Harvard.

CHAPTER FOURTEEN

MONDAY
WITHOUT FAIL

I arrived at the top of the staircase at Littauer at twenty past two on Monday afternoon, cursing under my breath in Spanish. It was a habit I had picked up from Maggie, who had adopted it when she got a temp job at an elementary school and needed a way to blow off steam when the kids were within earshot. I was twenty minutes late for a meeting with my former dissertation adviser, Kenneth Irvin. My backpack seemed to have tripled in weight on the trip over, heavy with the unfinished AEA conference paper that we were writing together, and I was wearing the wrong jacket for such a warm day, so I felt like a wet rag. My misery was completed by a headache and bloodshot eyes from having pulled an all-nighter to get at least part of the draft completed.

Irvin's secretary, Stephanie, stared coldly as I approached her desk. We hadn't liked each other since the first time I arrived for a meeting with Irvin and she immediately assumed that I was the *secretary* of an assistant professor, and not the professor herself. Shouting had ensued, and bad feelings endured. I could have cheerfully eaten her for lunch that day, bones and all.

"So nice of you to show up, Professor Chase," she purred.

"So nice of you to have me," I returned. "Is the great man in?"

"This way," she snapped. I resisted the urge to mimic her mincing walk as I followed her down the hall.

"Veronica. It's been a while." Irvin rose from behind his large mahogany desk and motioned me into an oversized red leather chair.

He was a large man with snow white hair, piercing blue eyes, and skin ruddy from weekends spent sailing on the Cape. Ken Irvin and Ian McAllister were best friends—which was one of the reasons that he had been my doctoral thesis adviser—and they were cut from the same cloth. But Irvin's reputation for arrogance was even worse than Ian's; it was no secret that he enjoyed reducing his teaching staff to cowering mice in his presence. The two of us had wildly different personal styles, and the disparity frequently grated on my nerves; writing a paper for a prestigious conference like the AEA feels a lot like giving birth, and I had been assigned William F. Buckley as my Lamaze partner.

"Terrible tragedy about Rosezella Fisher, isn't it?" Irvin said as we settled into our seats.

"Yes. You probably heard that I discovered the body."

He leaned forward. "Yes, I did hear that. Really, quite awful. Of course, it was an accident, but to have happened here makes it quite disturbing. Quite disturbing."

I was getting a little disturbed myself. Were we just chatting?

"Well, enough about your unpleasant experience. Before we discuss your latest draft of our paper, I want to speak with you about your teaching workload. I hear that you're doing your usual excellent job as the course head of Ec. 10."

In spite of myself, I preened a little. *An influential professor like Irvin passing out compliments?* My headache receded slightly.

"However," he continued, "we're thinking that perhaps you've overextended yourself and that you should consider dropping your International Economics commitment."

"What?" I looked at him incredulously. It would be unprecedented to take a class away from an instructor once the semester had started unless the person had committed a serious violation. "Why would you say that?"

Lips pursed, Irvin regarded me critically. "Well, I've been told that you've been spending your time on so many other projects that your students may be suffering. The early reports back on your lectures haven't been very favorable."

Early reports? Since when was I being monitored on a daily basis? "What do you mean?"

"Well, for a Danforth Prize winner, your first two lectures this semester have been woefully inadequate." He arched his eyebrows, an affectation that made me want to fly at his throat. The Danforth Prize was given to the best lecturer in the Economics Department, and he knew that it was my most prized accomplishment. "I've been told that you seem very distracted. That you seem to have other things on your mind. Also that you've been asking questions about Rosezella Fisher. Of course, these may only be rumors."

Where could this be coming from? Who had I talked to recently about Ella? "What exactly are you trying to say?" I tried to ignore the feeling that someone was tightening a vise on my temples.

"Let me be frank, Veronica. I understand that you have taken a deep and sudden interest in Ella Fisher's affairs."

Victoria Barrett. Or Christian Chung. It had to be one of them who had started this. No one else would have access to Irvin.

"As a friend, I have to advise you that you should be spending your time on your work, not on someone as unimportant as the late Dean." He paused. "I tell you this as a friend."

"As a friend to whom? Me, or someone else?"

"Why, to you, of course," he said mildly. "Your prospects here are very bright, you know. It would be a shame if a momentary lack of judgment took you off track."

On another day, I might have taken the warning and let it go at that, but I was in a pissy mood and running on two hours of sleep, so I got in his face. "Excuse me for being so blunt, but are you threatening me, Professor? Because I'd be happy to discuss this with you, and with Ian McAllister in his capacity as the head of the department. And perhaps we should invite my accusers, as well."

Irvin blanched. "I beg your pardon, Veronica. Of course I'm not threatening you. I'm just concerned about your academic development. There's no need for you to overreact."

"I appreciate your concern, but I'm quite capable of handling my teaching load. I've got a very full plate with this Crimson Future report, but that will be completed very soon."

Now, how far are you willing to take this, old man?

We regarded each other coldly and then he turned away. "I'll trust your judgment on this matter. For now. Shall we discuss this draft?"

We conferred over the half-finished document for forty-five minutes. He was unusually distant, and by the time we were finished I was pretty sure that I could smell the ashes of my career smoldering in his office. My fury with Irvin was subsiding into a numbing awareness of what he could do to me if he chose. Maybe it wasn't Victoria or Christian who had set him off. Perhaps it was someone higher up in the university, someone who didn't even know me personally. Harvard certainly had no incentive for anyone to know that a murder had occurred in the heart of its campus. I made my way to the Crimson Future Committee meeting longing for a swig of extra-strength antacid.

The meeting was being held upstairs at the Faculty Club, another Georgian building constructed of the ubiquitous red brick. A fire burned in the fireplace in the entry hall in defiance of the 75-degree temperature outdoors, but the room still drew a complement of faculty members and guests who valued the Ivy League ambience more than they did a comfortable place to chat.

By the time I arrived, the other committee members were already milling around. Jennifer Blum, today in a brown micro-mini, was talking animatedly with Leo Barrett. Bob Raines, Asif Zakaria, and Rona Seidman were clustered together discussing the latest faculty meeting, and the younger members of the group were laughing over a joke being told by Michael Treger, a rabbi at the Divinity School. Ian McAllister was sitting alone at the oval table in the center of the room, reading a thick document.

I scanned the room eagerly to see who the new face would be on the committee. I was hoping that McAllister's choice might tell me something about Ella's death, although it seemed unlikely that someone had killed her just to get a place on this committee. So far there was no one in the room who wasn't already a member. Had Ian changed his mind about replacing her?

"Veronica," Ian growled, "you're late."

Seeing McAllister scowling at me sent a bolt of fear through my heart—it was terrifying to see someone with that much control over my career displeased with me, especially after my conversation with Irvin.

"Can we get started, please?" he barked at the rest of the group. I relaxed. He wasn't upset with me. He was upset with the world, which happened occasionally.

The group assembled around the long oval table, Ian at its head and Leo next to him. The two of them seemed to have reached an uneasy truce about how these meetings would be conducted: Ian led the discussions, while Leo actively participated. I still remembered the first meeting, at which they'd almost come to blows over who should call the group to order.

I started to distribute the draft report that Rona and I had worked on, but Ian held up his hand to stop me. "Just a minute, Veronica. Before we begin, I'd like to inform you all that President

Barrett has appointed a replacement for Rosezella Fisher on the committee for the duration of our work."

I looked up and caught the barely concealed contempt on McAllister's face as he said the President's name. *Barrett* had named a replacement? I thought this was *Ian's* show. Maybe this was what had him so worked up. Barrett had deprived him of the opportunity to bestow the prize on one of his protégées.

"President Barrett felt that we could use another representative from the Graduate School of Arts and Sciences," McAllister continued gruffly, "since it is the largest school." So it wasn't Christian Chung. That was a surprise. I assumed that Barrett would want a highly trusted pair of eyes and ears on the committee, now that Ella was gone, and Christian was clearly his closest aide-de-camp. "He also agreed that another assistant professor would not be taken amiss, given our deadline pressure, and so we have selected one of the rising stars in the Government Department." My mind rifled through the names. Wasserman? Burke? Lee? Whoever it was, Barrett must trust him implicitly. "He recently joined us from Stanford University. Mr. Dante Rosario." Ian walked to the door and beckoned, and a few seconds later, Dante strode into the room, nodded at the group, and took the empty chair beside me. While the other committee members introduced themselves, I leaned over to Rona Seidman. "Do you have any aspirin?"

I swallowed two tablets dry before acknowledging the newest member of our committee. Why hadn't he told me about this last night?

"Veronica, the reports," Ian prodded impatiently. Rona began taking the group through the document.

The meeting lasted three hours, and it didn't go well. Rona and I had covered a lot of ground, but Raines didn't agree with our assumptions, and Leo was demanding a greater level of detail in the scenarios. Ian didn't speak much, but looked increasingly annoyed. By the end, his face was like a storm cloud, and he called an abrupt halt to the conversation.

"It's clear to me that we need to do some intensive work before we can present these results at the New Century press conference, which as you know is only two weeks away," he said coldly. "And it is also clear that some members of this group have been working harder than others." He glared at Asif Zakaria, who glared back. "I have a proposal that I strongly suggest we adopt. I am making plans to have all of you meet at my house in Martha's Vineyard for an intensive working session this weekend. Mr. President, you're welcome to join us as well. We'll begin Friday afternoon and work until Sunday morning. We must create a document of which we can be proud."

Silence reigned for a fraction of a second, and then the excuses rolled in.

"Really, Ian, this is impossibly late notice," Zakaria began. "Barbara and I have already made plans for the weekend."

"Steve and I have, too, Ian," said Rona briskly. "Besides, I have a board meeting Friday and a piece due at my publisher's next Monday."

Ian rose to his full six feet four inches and raked the room with his gaze. "Before the rest of you start conjuring up excuses, let me remind you that this group is charged with ensuring the university's financial health for the next ten years. And all of your names will appear prominently on the final report, no matter how mediocre the end product. Are we in complete understanding on that?"

Raines sighed noisily, and then looked up at Ian. "Very well. I'll be there."

"And the rest of you?" Ian demanded.

"Okay, okay," Rona snapped. "Let's just do it."

"Splendid," Ian said, looking satisfied for the first time that day. "My secretary will be in touch about the details."

The group began to disperse. Jennifer Blum brushed by me and squeezed my arm.

"A weekend on the Vineyard! Yes!" she whispered. "Love the new guy."

I noticed Christian Chung entering the room and handing Leo a sheaf of papers as Dante strolled over to me.

"Why didn't you tell me about this last night?" I snapped.

"It didn't become official until this morning, and I—"

"This is just like you!" I said impatiently. I lowered my voice as Ian McAllister glanced over at us. "I tell you about what I've been doing, and suddenly this is your show. You're the big hero. Well, forget it!"

"Let's get something straight, Juliet," Dante whispered, looking amused. "I'm doing this to *help* you, not to steal your thunder."

"Oh sure, that's why you're off schmoozing the President, wheedling your way onto this very high-profile committee. Because you want to help *me*. You're such a Neanderthal."

Christian Chung shook hands with Ian, and then turned back toward Leo Barrett, who was in animated conversation right behind me with Michael Treger.

"Nik," Dante said softly, glancing over his shoulder, "you need air cover. We don't even know what we're dealing with here."

"Air cover," I muttered. "Why do men always resort to military metaphors when they're trying to take control?"

Leo's arm went around Christian's shoulders and they started walking away, immediately locked in deep conversation. They passed by so closely that we could hear Christian murmuring in Leo's ear.

"She's done . . ." I heard him say. "Wouldn't want it coming out . . . talk *now*."

"Fine," Leo said quietly. "We'll discuss it in the john. Give me a minute." He paused to confer with Ian McAllister on a page in the document.

"See, this is exactly the kind of thing I'm talking about," Dante breathed in my ear. "There are times when even *you* need a man, Juliet."

"Wanna bet?"

Before I had time to fully reflect on what I was doing, I disappeared down the hall and ducked into the nearest men's room. I had to find out if what was going on between those two had anything to do with Ella and Justin, and this could be my only chance.

The bathroom was small and much the worse for wear: the walls were painted a jaundiced yellow, the white porcelain urinals were cracked and rust-stained, and the floor tiles were mildewed and grey. At least the air smelled heavily of Lysol. Apparently, our Faculty Club membership dues were going for the gourmet cuisine and not for upkeep of the facilities.

"You'll do *anything* to prove a point, won't you?"

Dante Rosario was right behind me.

"Just grab a paper towel, will you?"

He handed me a sheet from the dispenser on the wall, and I quickly scribbled "Out of Order" on it.

"After you," he said, opening the door of one of the two stalls. He wedged the sign in the hinge, locked the door, and then perched behind me on top of the cracked toilet.

That was when the bathroom's outer door opened.

Footsteps cracked a sharp report against the tiled floor, and then I heard nothing but silence.

A moment later, the door opened again, and I heard Christian Chung's sharp voice. "We've got to talk."

"What's going on now?" Leo sounded on edge.

"The cops called me again this morning, asking me all the same questions again about Ella Fisher." Christian exhaled noisily.

"We knew that might happen. We talked about it, remember? What did you tell them?"

"The truth, Leo, always the truth," Christian returned. If only I could see his face. It actually sounded as if he was baiting the President.

"Don't mess around with me," Leo barked. "What did you tell them?"

"I told them again that I knew her in a professional context. That I was responsible for reviewing her budgets. That I hadn't heard from her for a week or so before she died." Why was he lying? I knew that the last call Ella had made from her office was to his home phone. Unless she hadn't reached him and hadn't left a message.

"Fine. Then that's the end of it." I heard footsteps crossing the floor. Leo was leaning against the doorjamb of the other stall. Dante silently put his hand on my shoulder.

"Like hell it is," Christian snapped, still sounding agitated.

There was a distinct pause in the conversation. "I told you, that's the end of it," Leo growled. "They're not going to figure it out."

"Well, you'd better pull yourself together, Leo, or they will. You look like shit." Christian was being far more belligerent than I would have dreamed he could be with the President. I heard shoes clattering on the floor; Christian must have been pacing back and forth.

"I'm fine. Dammit! How did this get so far out of control?"

I shook my head in disbelief. This couldn't be happening. Leo Barrett a killer?

"I told you she was going to be a problem. I told you right from the start. But you had to have her, anyway. When are you going to stop thinking with your dick?" Christian demanded.

"That's enough! Don't forget who you're talking to, boy."

"So what if they find out?"

"They won't."

My calf was developing a major cramp, and I stifled the urge to shift positions.

"Don't get cocky, Leo. It'll only take a couple of phone calls to Philadelphia. All they need is someone to point them in the right direction."

"Are you threatening me?" Leo said, sounding furious. "Because if you are, you're being really stupid."

Christian had much more power here than I had realized.

The creaking of the bathroom door hinges shattered the angry silence between them.

"Leo," a voice boomed out. It was Ian McAllister. "And Christian. I thought I heard shouting in here. Not interrupting anything, am I?" I hadn't known until that moment that Christian and Ian were on a first-name basis.

"Of course not," Leo said smoothly. "Just hashing out the latest round of budgeting. It's that time of the year, you know, McAllister. Christian, we're going to be late for that meeting."

"Right, Mr. President," Christian replied, smoothly returning to his usual deference.

We waited silently until Ian washed his hands and we could hear his footsteps echoing down the hall.

"So what do we do now?" Dante asked soberly as we unfolded ourselves.

"*We* don't do anything." My mind was racing. Torie Barrett may have been in Littauer Sunday night, and now her husband and his closest confidant were in a frenzy. So what the hell was in Philadelphia?

"You're awfully afraid to let me get involved in this investigation." Dante held the door open as we slipped into the hallway. "What are you worried about? Think I'll show you up?"

"You've got to be kidding me! Not going to happen."

"Then you won't mind if I check out a few leads of my own?"

"Be my guest." I started down the hall.

"Then I'll see you at the finish line, Atalanta."

I paused in the hallway without looking back. "English, please?"

"In the Greek myth, Atalanta will only marry the man who runs a footrace with her and wins. Anyone who loses to her dies."

I glanced over my shoulder as I walked away. "Well then, you'd best pick up the pace, *paisano.*"

After a call to the hospital to check on Justin Simms' progress, I went home to put in some more time on my AEA paper, hoping that it would help clear my head. There was no change in Justin's condition, and still no visitors allowed. Maybe work would help me stop fretting over him, at least for a while. I shuffled through the disks on my desk, looking for the one with the AEA draft on it.

I stopped and went through the pile of disks again, this time more slowly.

The disk with Ella's version of the university financials was missing.

I looked through my shoulder bag, and through the pockets of my computer carrying case. Not there. I had used it on Saturday afternoon, when I compared Ella's version to Ian's and realized that the source of the discrepancy in the disks was the outside services expenditures. But I was sure that I had put it back in the drawer early that afternoon. I hadn't looked for it when I was packing up to work with Rona Seidman on Sunday afternoon, since Christian had said on Saturday night that a change in university accounting procedures for outside services explained the discrepancy, and Ian had said to use his disk instead.

So where was it?

I pawed through the piles of papers on the top of my desk, and scanned the kitchen and the living room for good measure. No sign of it.

That was when I remembered that my door was ajar when I came home Saturday evening.

Could that *disk* be what someone had come for?

I felt my blood run cold, and tried to shake off the feeling. *She was really worried about the financials*, I heard Lindsey say.

As a matter of course, I had saved a copy of Ella's file on the hard drive of my laptop. The computer had been in my apartment in full view Saturday night, and as far as I knew, it hadn't been touched. Would a thief figure out that I was too anal to keep only one copy of a file that important? As soon as the laptop booted up, I checked the record of log-ins.

Someone had logged onto my laptop on Saturday night at 11:48. While I was still at the Friends of the Fogg Museum Gala.

Finally, it all made sense.

I could see the mugger in Widener Library Friday night, snatching my backpack and disappearing down the tunnel. Rafe had been right. He hadn't been trying to kill me. He had been after that disk all along.

I quickly opened the file with the spreadsheets from Ella's disk, fully expecting it to be empty. But it was intact. Whoever had searched my laptop hadn't known exactly what they were looking for. I had saved Ella's spreadsheets in the same file as Ian's version, and the burglar had overlooked them in his haste. *Terribly sloppy, you son of a bitch.*

Poring through Ella's version again, this time I scrutinized the outside services lines of each of the departments in FAS. It took three times before the pattern began to emerge. The expense line had started to grow in the Economics Department exactly three years ago. Before then, these types of expenses had grown at about four percent a year. That was the inflation rate, and what you would've expected for something as predictable as temp secretaries, florists, and computer charges. But three years ago, it had jumped twenty-five percent in one year. And the year after, another twenty percent. It had started to level off at the new level last year, but was still up ten percent. The Government Department showed a similar increase, but it had started two years ago. And last year, it had spread to five other departments within FAS, although not at the same high level.

Christian Chung had said that these expenses had been reclassified, and that these increases would show up in the central purchasing budget. But he could have been lying.

Whatever was going on, it had started in the Economics Department. A trip to Littauer seemed to be in order.

It was nine-thirty P.M. when I arrived outside Ian McAllister's office, and the corridors on the second floor of Littauer were empty and still. If I needed to know more about outside service expenditures in the department, this was the place to start. Of course, I could've asked Ian directly. But whatever I was looking for may have gotten Ella Fisher killed—it had certainly gotten me beaten up at Widener—and I wasn't taking any chances.

The wooden outer door to Ian's office suite was locked, the knob icy and rigid in my hand. I rummaged through my backpack and pulled out my American Express card. Glancing over my shoulder down the darkened hallway, I slipped the card through the latch and jiggled it against the lock. Within seconds, the door slid soundlessly open. It was astounding that a trick every Detroit schoolkid knows was all it took to commit a misdemeanor, but then, this was a trusting community with ancient locks on its doors.

Once inside, I headed straight for the file cabinets in the anteroom that held Paula's desk. I pulled on the first drawer and got nowhere. I moved down the line, growing increasingly frustrated. All of her file drawers were locked.

So where would Paula hide her keys?

I scanned the top of her desk, and then plunged in, shaking out her pencil cup, rifling through her notepad, running my fingers under the drawers. I found a key in a small box filled with binder clips. That key unlocked her drawer, which held a ring with about fifteen keys. I was in.

Fifteen minutes of searching got me nowhere. Paula was extremely organized, but I needed to find the invoices that the Economics Department was responsible for paying, and so far there was nothing. I did find out more than I should have known about my fellow assistant professors and their tenure prospects, which at least made me feel that the search wasn't wholly useless.

Clearly, I was going to have to enter the inner sanctum and look at the files in Ian's office. They were locked, too, but Paula's ring had the key.

I pulled out the file drawer on the left side of Ian's desk, and was rewarded with the sight of a folder marked "Accounts Payable." *Bingo*.

The file contained a sheaf of almost thirty unpaid invoices, covering things like office supplies, computer access charges, temporary secretarial agencies, florists, and maintenance workers. A few companies had more than one invoice: a company called Paralogic had four clipped together, and All Write Secretarial Services, The Consulting Group, and Arcadia Floral each had three.

I slipped the invoices into my bag, then quietly crept down the hall to the copy room. At that hour, it was deserted, and I paced impatiently as the copier noisily warmed up. Not wanting to risk shredding any of the invoices in the automatic feeder, I hurriedly placed each one by hand on the glass and copied it, keeping an ear cocked for approaching footsteps. Ten minutes later, I returned to Ian's office and slipped the invoices back into his file drawer.

That's when I heard the footsteps, and a current of fear flowed through me. Someone had just opened the door to Ian's office.

I had just enough time to straighten up and kick the drawer to make sure it was shut before Ian strode into his office, flipping on the light switch. He stiffened as his eyes lit on me.

"Veronica!"

"Hey, this is perfect!" I said, swallowing hard. "I was just about to leave you a note. I need to talk to you."

"How did you get in?"

"The door was open," I lied casually. "I knocked first, but I guess Paula had already left for the day." I made a mental note to sneak her keys back into the office before she arrived the next morning.

He looked wary as he waved me into a chair. "I thought you'd be holed up in a library somewhere after what Irvin told me about your discussion today."

"I see good news travels fast." I felt another career panic attack looming, but suppressed it. Screw it. There'd be time enough to worry after I ran Ella's murderer and Justin's attacker to ground.

"So what's the problem between you and Irvin?"

"He thinks the draft of the paper we're writing together is weak," I replied soberly. "And he's right. I was rushing, and the arguments are somewhat unpolished."

"The word 'sloppy' was used."

I resisted the urge to roll my eyes. That *poseur* had called my writing sloppy? Please!

"He also mentioned that your international economics students were complaining about your lectures."

"So he says. I don't understand why he's making a federal case out of this," I said calmly. "I probably was a bit off on Tuesday, and Thursday the material I had to cover was just deadly dull, and I defy *anyone* to make it sing. But I hear what he's saying, and it won't happen again."

"He also said you were asking questions about Rosezella Fisher's death. Why would you be doing that?" His tone was light, but my vertebrae stood at attention.

"Simple curiosity," I said, shrugging. "I found her body, you know, and I felt some need to understand how she arrived at the foot of those stairs. It's no big deal. I have far too much work to do to worry about it."

"Want some advice, Veronica?" McAllister's face was inscrutable. "Stick to doing excellent work on this committee, and on your course work, get those papers done, and don't bring her name up again."

"I hear you," I said with an adamant nod.

I didn't want to believe it, but something definitely wasn't right here.

"It's not as if we were that close," I continued, searching his face. "As I said, the only reason I asked any questions at all is because I was the one who found her. Too bad *you* didn't fall over her."

"Fortunately, I was still in the conference room when the lights went out," he said easily. "I could've killed myself on those stairs. So is there anything else?"

"No, I just wanted to discuss Irvin with you. By the way, I read an article in the *Wall Street Journal* that might interest you. A great piece on the IMF in Zambia. I'll bring it by tomorrow."

Ian leaned forward in his chair and regarded me earnestly. "Veronica, you've got a great future in front of you as long as you keep your head down and work. As long as you do that, I'll see to it that Irvin doesn't cause you any trouble."

"I appreciate your taking the time, Ian," I said, standing up. Maybe he was just watching out for me. Wasn't that why I liked him so much? Because, despite the bullshit, he actually seemed to have my best interests at heart? "I'm back on the straight and narrow path."

We said our good-byes and I continued on what was beginning to feel like the road to ruin. Because the financial discrepancy had started in my department. So how could Ian McAllister *not* be involved?

"Nikki? Hi! Uh, he's not here right now."
"I'm not looking for him. I'm looking for you."

I needed a lawyer. And with Justin in the hospital, I had only one alternative. So ten minutes after I left Littauer, I was knocking on Dante's apartment door, looking for his roommate, Ted.

He ushered me in, and I surveyed their living room, very different now from when the physicist and his wife had lived there. It was lined from floor to ceiling with books; an overstuffed sofa and a love seat nested in the center of the room, and a cheerful flame crackled in the fireplace, filling the air with the welcoming scent of wood smoke.

"Can I get you something to drink?"

"A diet anything would be great."

As he disappeared into the kitchen, I glanced at my watch. I was giving myself ten minutes. I had no desire to be here when Dante came home. My eyes traveled around the room, taking in the stacks of leather-bound textbooks, the sweaters tossed casually over chairs, the half-filled coffee cups, and the copies of *Corriere della Sera* and the *Paris Review*. It was all maddeningly familiar, the predictable Rosario detritus. And of course, Francesca was still there.

That was the name I had given to a painting that Dante had hung over his fireplace when we were in college, and that occupied the same place of honor now. It was a portrait of a willowy, dark-haired young white woman. She was sitting in a wing chair, wearing a gauzy pale pink dress and staring longingly into the middle distance, a book cradled in her lap. The dream girl. She didn't exist, of course. But she might someday. In the meantime, Dante could sit in front of the fire and brood, and dream, and wait for her. Impossible competition for anyone trying to capture his heart in the here and now. I wondered what Danielle made of it.

"Here you go. One diet something or other."

"Thanks." I flashed Ted a smile as he settled into the sofa.

He regarded me quizzically as I perched on the arm of the chair next to him. "You look like a woman with a mission," he prompted.

"I need some free legal advice," I said with a laugh. "But I don't want to be rude. Shall we chitchat for five minutes before I hit you up for a favor?"

"Nah. Go for it."

I retrieved the photocopies of the invoices I had found in Ian's office. "I need some information about some local companies, and I don't know exactly where to start."

"What do you want to know?"

"Basic stuff. Who owns them, where they're located, how long they've been in business."

"Are they Massachusetts-based?"

"I think so." I passed him the sheaf of papers. "These are invoices from the companies."

He glanced at the first couple, and then laid the stack down on the coffee table. "Consider it done."

"Really?"

"This is a couple of hours' work for one of my law students at the clinic. It'll be good practice. All they have to do is look up the companies' Massachusetts business licenses, and you'll get all that information and more. It's easy."

"You're a doll!" I beamed at him.

"Well, there *is* a quid pro quo," he returned, grinning at me.

"Really? What's that?"

"You have to fill me in on how Jessica's date went Saturday night."

I laughed as I rolled off the armrest and into the chair. "This is great! What do you want to know?"

We passed a highly enjoyable ten minutes discussing how Jess's date was no good for her, a pretty boy from the Business School who didn't even read books, and how she deserved much better.

It was exactly the kind of dish I like best, but the specter of Dante returning to find me in his living room drove me to the door.

"Why don't you wait?" Ted protested as I gulped the last of my soda. "Rosario will be back soon."

"That's the whole point. I'll keep you posted on Jess."

"You oughtta stay, Nikki," he cajoled. "The night's young."

That was true. But the sight of Francesca was really old.

CHAPTER FIFTEEN

THE
PHILADELPHIA
STORY

"**I**'m worried about you, darlin'."

"Well, you need to stop. I'm fine. Damn! Where is that paper?"

Maggie was regarding me warily over the rim of her morning cup of tea. It was seven o'clock Tuesday, and I was ransacking the recycling bin in her kitchen, looking for the *Crimson* article on Leo Barrett that had run the day after Ella was murdered.

"It don't make me no nevermind if you want to run around acting all mysterious, Miss Thing. But don't come sashaying in here making a mess of my kitchen!"

"Stop fussing, Maggie! I told you, I'll clean it up." There were over 25 newspapers in the pile, old issues of the *Globe*, the *Crimson*, and the *Bay State Banner*, and I was in the process of scattering them all over the floor.

"What are you looking for, anyway?"

"That article on Leo Barrett. I think it had some information about his childhood, and I need to see if he had any ties to Philadelphia."

"Philadelphia? You know, my sister and her husband live there. In Mount Airy. What's up?"

"Finally!" I crowed. I held up the article, which had been buried two-thirds of the way down the stack. My eye fell on the byline, and I drew in a deep breath of satisfaction. Amy Collins had written the article. Cynical, razor-sharp, darling Amy Collins, a senior who was one of the best students in my two o'clock Ec. 10 section. This was going to work out *perfectly*.

"Gotta go," I said, kissing Maggie's cheek.

"Hold up, girlfriend. What about these newspapers?"

"I'll clean them up later, Maggie, I *promise*. But I've got to make a phone call."

Forty minutes later, I was sitting in the mahogany-paneled subterranean Adams House dining room, drinking a cup of surprisingly strong black coffee while Amy Collins lit up her first cigarette of the day. When I was in college, Adams was the funkiest of the upperclass dorms—the House of choice for Manhattan natives and wanna-bes, where black clothing was *de rigueur*. Its urbane air had persisted through the years, despite the new random housing lottery, and that morning, Amy looked quintessentially Adams: her ebony hair was shaved close to her skull, and she was wearing a black turtleneck, black miniskirt, ripped black tights, and black army boots. Only a green Army fatigue jacket relieved the gloom.

"This is going to be a short conversation," she announced, inhaling slowly on her cigarette.

"What do you mean?"

"Maybe it's just a fluke that you called asking about my interview with Leo Barrett today of all days, but you're shit out of luck."

"I'm not following you."

She leaned forward and shot me a bitter grin. "My reporter's notebook, where I keep all of my interview notes and backup, disappeared yesterday. I've turned the *Crimson* office and my room upside down, and it's gone."

"I can't believe this!" I threw up my hands in frustration. No matter what I did, I was always one step behind. Amy regarded me quizzically.

"Hey, Prof, don't get too crazy. It'll probably still turn up. Besides"—she leaned back in her chair—"a good reporter keeps all the *really* important stuff up here." She tapped her forehead. "So what do you want to know? And more important, *why* do you want to know?"

"The 'why' I can't talk about."

"Come on, Prof. We've gotta have a quid pro quo here. You can't expect me to share all my info without getting *something* back."

"Give me a break, Amy. It's not like you're working for the *New York Times*."

"Not yet." She blew out a puff of smoke and looked me square in the eye.

I set down my coffee cup and leaned forward, amused and impressed by her cool self-possession. The *Times* would be lucky to have her. "Fine. I can't tell you any details right now. But when this thing I'm working on is over, I'll give you an exclusive."

"To the whole story?"

"Blow by blow."

She grinned at me and took a drag on her cigarette. "Deal. How can I help you?"

I pulled the article out of my bag and laid it on the table between us. "In the article, you wrote about Leo Barrett's background. But I got the impression that you weren't telling the whole story."

Amy shook her head adamantly. "Believe it or not, I put in everything that I had: his parents were from Ireland and Brazil, the family moved to Philadelphia when he was very small, and he has no brothers and sisters."

Philadelphia. That was what I wanted to know more about. Christian had said, *"All it will take is a couple of calls to Philadelphia."*

"Anyone as smart as you would have gotten more than that, Amy," I prodded. "You must be sitting on something."

"Hey, this man is very secretive when it comes to his family," she said defensively. "I tried six ways to Sunday to get him talking, but he kept putting me off. The most he would say is that his parents were very folksy. 'Colorful' was the word I think he used. I got the feeling that he was embarrassed about having grown up poor. He definitely wasn't Main Line Philadelphia."

"What did his parents do for a living?"

"Well, that's the funny thing. He said his father, Stephen, was a minister, and his mother was a housewife."

"So what's the problem?"

"Well, I asked him where his father went to school, and he said he attended college in the United Kingdom, but that he had graduated from Union Theological Seminary after he moved to the United States. But when the fact-checker called, the school had no record of a Stephen Barrett ever having been enrolled."

Bingo. "Amy, I think that's what's called burying the lead. He *lied* about his father's background?"

"Well, at the time I thought maybe I wrote down the wrong school or something."

"Did you call him back and ask him about it?"

"Of course I called! I got some 'information officer' telling me that Barrett would call me back. But he never did. So we had to leave it out of the article."

"Did you talk to anyone else about his childhood? Even if Leo wouldn't talk, there's always *someone* willing to dish the dirt, isn't there?"

She shook her head. "Not around here. I called a couple of the Deans that he brought in when he was named President, but they wouldn't give me anything. It was like they were all reading from the same script: '*He has a multicultural heritage. Born of working-class parents, his hard work and intelligence got him into City College and then into Harvard, and that's what makes him such an inspiration to us all.*' The only variation was that one guy said the President's heritage was truly multi-culti, and that Barrett had a great-grandfather on his mother's side who was black, which explains his sensitivity to matters of race and ethnicity." She rolled her eyes. "If you call appointing one black woman to a Dean's role 'sensitive to matters of race.'"

"Hey, you were the one who called him a true progressive in your article."

"That was my editor, not me. *I* think he's whatever these rich alumni want him to be."

"Leo must have cousins, aunts, uncles—*some* kind of extended family," I mused. "Did you try tracking them down?"

"I spent two days trying to access his records from City College in New York, but they wouldn't release them to the press. So we let it go. Remember, the point of the article was to report on his performance since becoming President, not to expose his private life."

"So what *else* did you leave out of this article?"

"Well, we had to leave the affairs out." She stubbed out her cigarette.

"The affairs?"

"Come on, Prof, everyone knows the man can't keep his pants zipped. But it's never with students, and it doesn't seem to keep him from doing his job well. He's just an all-American boy," she said dryly.

"So, is he having an affair right now?"

She nodded. "We think so. But he's learning to be more discreet. One of my contacts in University Hall says that Barrett disappears

midday twice a week or so, and that there were two or three weekends over the summer when no one could account for his where-
abouts. But no one can figure out who the woman is."

I wondered if the woman had been Ella Fisher. And if Torie Barrett had known about it.

"How does his wife feel about all this?"

She shrugged. "Who knows? I couldn't get an interview with her.
Her office said we should focus on *his* performance as President and
leave *her* out of it." She leaned forward. "So what's going on, Prof?"

"I told you, I can't tell you yet." I shook my head.

"Well, I'm going to follow up on this thing with Barrett's father.
It should be easy enough to find out if there's a Rev. Stephen Bar-
rett in Philadelphia. I think he said his father's church was called
St. Thomas—I'm sure he said it was Episcopal."

"You can't do that. Absolutely not," I said sharply.

"Why not?"

"Because it's way too dangerous. If Leo Barrett does have some
family secret, he isn't going to take kindly to having it dug up."

"Well, that's *his* problem, not mine."

"You want the exclusive, Amy?" I demanded.

She nodded reluctantly, sighing.

"Then let me handle it. I promise you'll be among the first to
know what I find out. But only if you stay out of it for now."

I lingered at the table after she left, thinking about the *Partisan
Review* article that I had seen in Leo's study Friday night. The one
with the contributor's note removed. As much as I hated the
thought of another trip to Widener Library, that was going to be my
next stop. It was time I found out what someone's careful razor had
tried to excise from Leo Barrett's past.

Twelve noon found me navigating a set of crumbling concrete
stairs that led down to the narrow front entrance of Liberation
Books on Mount Auburn Street. I'd put in a request at Widener
Library for a copy of the March 1967 *Partisan Review*, as well as for
two other articles that Leo had written in the late sixties. In the university library system, periodicals of that vintage weren't accessible
to the common people—only a trained library scientist could
retrieve them from storage. My friend the librarian had promised to

surface them in no more than twenty-four hours, and in the meantime I was on Isaiah Fisher's trail. He had called out of the blue late the night before, insisting that he had to see me, and I was dying of curiosity to hear what he had to say.

As my eyes adjusted to the bookstore's dim interior, I surveyed its decor. A street sign reading "Yusef Hawkins Blvd." hung on the wall, flanked by a large poster of Al Sharpton. A bookcase near the front door was prominently labeled "Know Your Enemies," and featured multiple copies of a book entitled *How the FBI Destroyed Black America*. A stack of copies of *Muhammad Speaks* sat near the cash register, where a young black man was making a purchase. From his Harvard sweatshirt and spotlessly clean backpack, I deduced he was a freshman. I glanced at the titles as they were rung up. *The Miseducation of the Negro. The Spook Who Sat by the Door. How Capitalism Underdeveloped Black America.* It was only a week into the semester. A bit early for the black suburbanites to be rediscovering their heritage.

"And can I have a receipt, please?" the student was saying.

"A receipt? You hear that? Mr. Man over here wants a *receipt*," the woman at the cash register said flatly to Isaiah, who was sitting on a stool next to her.

Isaiah shook his head pityingly.

"You don't trust us?" the woman said sharply. "You need it for your taxes or something?"

"Sorry," the student said meekly.

"Harvard!" Isaiah greeted me. "Can I interest you in a tape of Minister Farrakhan's speech in Brooklyn last spring?" It was his usual rap, but his heart didn't appear to be in it today. For the first time since I'd met him, he actually seemed pensive.

"What's with you?" I asked, as he came around the counter.

"Nothing." He shook his head impatiently. "Last night was just whack, that's all. I'm out with Lindsey Wentworth, and we're at this club in Inman Square, and I'm trying to talk to her about the summer of '68."

Ah, the great romance. "Let me guess," I responded, watching him play idly with the rope bracelet on his wrist. "She wasn't interested."

"Not interested would have been cool. I was talking about King's assassination, and she said, 'Rodney King was shot?'"

"You're making that up." I suppressed a laugh. The guy was a complete bullshit artist, but he did have his charms.

"Okay, so I'm shitting you a little, but I'm serious. Everyone isn't as cool as you, Harvard."

"Gee, thanks."

Somewhat benign feelings hung in the air between us, despite my best efforts to the contrary, and Fisher said impulsively, "Have you eaten lunch yet?"

"No, but—"

"Cool, neither have I. Let's go."

Twenty minutes later we were sitting on a blanket near the banks of the Charles River, basking in the sunlight and contentedly pawing through the paper bags that held our lunches. I had a double cheeseburger and a root beer from Charlie's Kitchen, and he had a grilled tofu patty and two bottles of papaya juice from Cafe Paradiso.

Fisher sighed and surveyed the sparkling river, the red brick buildings of the Business School reposing in the distance. "It's times like these that make me realize why I stayed in this town."

It was hard for me to argue with that. We were perched on a grassy knoll near the footpath that ran along the riverbank, and a meandering stream of joggers, cyclists, couples holding hands, high school kids on skateboards, and solitary walkers lost in thought passed before us. The air was tinged with the earthy smell of the soil, the river, and the scent of wood burning in a fireplace in nearby Winthrop House.

To my surprise, I felt perfectly at peace. If I got any more comfortable, I'd let my guard down. And that would be foolish.

"So what did you want to talk to me about?" I asked abruptly.

"So soon to business? I thought we could chew the fat a while about politics. Okay, okay," he said, reading my expression. He fumbled in his pocket for a piece of paper and handed it to me, leaning toward me. "Check this out."

The paper was grimy and looked as if it had been folded and refolded repeatedly. On it was a typed note:

Fishman,

I'm back and in need of cash. Remember the underground. I'll be in touch, but get ready. I need it fast.

I looked up at him, puzzled. "What does this mean?"

He leaned back on his elbows and sighed. "Some stuff from my past seems to have caught up with me, and I think it may have caught Ella too."

"Go on," I prodded, laying the note aside and biting into my cheeseburger.

"Ever heard of the Weathermen?"

"I know they were one of the radical groups that operated in the late sixties. I know they threatened violence. Don't know if they ever carried it out."

"Well, let me educate you, then," he said, sitting up and facing me. "The Weathermen were originally part of SDS—Students for a Democratic Society. But in 1969, we split off because we were tired of waiting. And yes, we did believe in violence. Because it works.

"Don't think we were a bunch of unshaven losers, either," he said, warming to his tale. "The founders were rich white kids: the son of a utility executive, the daughters of bankers and Republican legislators. I fell in with them because I made friends with Bill Ayers in New York in '62. I believed in what they were doing, and they had a lot of dough."

He took a swig of juice. "We were totally anti-establishment. *Hated* the middle class." He chuckled to himself. "We were into LSD, beautiful women, the Panthers, Kim Il Sung . . ."

I raised my eyebrows quizzically. Kim Il Sung?

"The President of North Korea. Communist. So anyway, we went around getting high school students to speak out against their teachers, even went after Mother Harvard in the fall of '69: we attacked the Center for International Affairs because it was engaged in research on suppressing revolutions in Third World countries. Tore out the phones, broke some glass, pissed in the hall—that kind of shit. The whole idea was to create chaos. It all started with the occupation."

The occupation? I wanted to interrupt to ask where he was headed with this story, but he was too far gone, his eyes ablaze with righteousness.

"In the spring of '69 SDS was getting desperate for action," he continued. "Harvard was sitting on its ass, doing nothing about the war, nothing about racism, just a bunch of rich, fat-cat white boys trying to keep the rest of us down. So we decided to take over University Hall. Make 'em see we were serious. Girl, you shoulda seen the expressions of those fat old Deans when we came through the door!" His smile faded. "But those cops damn near killed me when they raided the building. All the white boys got was a little pushing and shoving. But the black brothers? They cracked our skulls open. Even the folks that were just standing around outside. You see this scar?" His finger traced a thin line across his right temple. "Nightstick. I was bleeding like the devil, and they threw me on the floor of some cop car and took me to the station. They wouldn't call a doctor, even after I passed out. I think they were hoping I'd die."

"Where was Ella when all this was happening?"

"She was outside the building, trying not to get killed herself. She went crazy at the police station when she saw what they'd done to me."

He took a deep breath. "That's when I decided it was time to teach whitey a lesson. Take some real action. SDS wouldn't support it, so I joined the Weathermen. See, there was a bank that was accessible to us—I'm not saying where or how, because you don't need to know. But we had an inside connection. So three of my buddies and me decided to rob it. At night, after closing time. We weren't looking to hurt anybody. But it was time for the white man to give up some of his blood money. We got in the place fine. But somehow the cops showed up halfway through. And they killed one of my boys. Damn pig shot him in the back. Things were real hot for a while, so the rest of us went underground up in Canada for a year until our tracks were cool. Then we split up. One of those guys got himself killed about a month later—LSD overdose. The other one is the brother who wrote this note."

"And where is he now?" I asked. I was starting to see where we were headed.

"For a while, he was working in a used record store in the Haight in San Francisco. Now, he's a mack."

"A what?"

"You know, a mack daddy. A pimp. He's in the life. He calls me every couple of years, asking for money. I'm not sure if he's strung out or losing his mind, or what, but sometimes he gets real aggressive. Sometimes he called Ella and said things."

"Called Ella? Why?"

"Because compared to me, she was rich. And she had plenty of reasons for wanting this guy to keep his mouth shut about our past, now that she was Ms. Member of the Establishment." There it was again. That malevolent sneer when he referred to her.

"But was she involved in the robbery?"

"She wasn't *with* us, if that's what you mean. She was *supposed* to be driving the car. But she got all uptight at the last minute. She was always too old school, thanks to those down-home parents of hers. At the last minute, she decided that robbing whitey was morally wrong, and she refused to come. If she had been there, maybe it would have all gone down differently. Our timing was all off, 'cause we thought she would be there helpin' us. Hell," he muttered under his breath, "for all I know, she was the one who called the police."

I watched him, thinking about his story. It would explain the recent cash withdrawals from Ella's checking account, which fit the pattern of blackmail. But it all seemed too convenient.

"So why are you telling me this, Fisher?" I prodded.

"Because the police are really hassling me. And you're tight with that black cop, right? I tried to get him to support a fellow brother, but he is straight-up whiter than the whitest white boy. But he'll believe it if *you* tell him that this is something that they need to know about. Ella had a past. Maybe it caught up with her."

I considered that for a moment. It was possible that his story was true. But did he really think that anyone would believe Ella was killed by a renegade pimp for a few thousand dollars? Somehow, I thought the true motive was closer to home. And that Fisher was more involved than he was letting on.

"I still don't understand why you don't just go to the police with this yourself."

"Can't," he said, shaking his head. "If I do, they'll figure out the rest of the story, and I'm not about to spend my golden years stuck in some filthy jail."

"How do you know that I won't tell them the whole story?"

" 'Cause I trust you, Harvard." The look in his eyes surprised me. It actually seemed genuine.

"Why would you trust *me*?"

"Your eyes," he said, softly. "The first time I met you, I said to myself, 'A lady with eyes like that can be trusted.' "

I looked away, feeling guilty, touched, and wary in equal measure. No wonder he'd been able to lead Ella astray. He was good.

"So was it worth it?" I asked abruptly.

He looked at me, startled. "Was *what* worth it?"

"The protests, the years on the run, was it worth it?"

He relaxed visibly. "Yeah, Harvard. It was worth it. Doing what you believe is always worth it."

I took that as permission from him to do what needed to be done.

Leaving Isaiah Fisher by the banks of the Charles contentedly smoking a joint, I arrived at Sever Hall just in time to teach my afternoon International Economics lecture. I couldn't afford to be late after my conversation with Irvin yesterday. After class, I called my secretary to check messages. She reported that Ian McAllister had called twice, and that Dante Rosario had stopped by. I called Ian back immediately, only to be told that he wanted me to present a paper at the department seminar to be held the following week, and that I should stop by his office to discuss it as soon as possible. I tried protesting that I had too much work on my plate already to prepare adequately, but Ian was having none of it. The Economics department seminars, at which junior faculty members present their recent work to the senior professors, are a particularly humiliating aspect of academic life. Under the guise of keeping up to date on the latest economic research, the Assistant and Associate Professors in attendance are expected to tear apart the presenter's work in the vain hope of impressing the tenured faculty members with their keen insights. Cockfights are far more civilized.

Sighing heavily, I phoned Rafe to tell him about Isaiah Fisher's blackmail note from the mystery man. I wasn't planning to call Dante at all.

"I *told* that Cambridge city cop, this Fisher has somethin' goin' on." Rafe sounded pleased. "I've seen the type before. And his alibi is weaker than the drinks at me brother's bar."

"What's his alibi?"

"He says he was at a bar up in Somerville. Finn McCoy's. A couple of barflies up there said they recognized his picture, but put 'em on the stand and they'd crumble."

"So what are you going to do?"

"We'll have to wait on him, collect some more evidence. The mon will make a mistake. They always do."

"What about the payments from Ella's checkbook? Can you trace them?"

"Already on it. Only thing is, if she were payin' him, why would he kill the goose that was layin' the golden eggs?"

He had a point there. I hung up the phone, completely ambivalent. It was possible that Fisher was the murderer. Maybe *he* was the one blackmailing Ella over this bank robbery, and when she threatened to stop paying, he killed her. But he seemed too lazy to go to that much trouble. And there were too many other things, like the stolen computer disk, that couldn't be explained if he had killed Ella. Besides, I couldn't believe that a man so vehemently Afrocentric would try to kill not one, but two black people. On impulse, I called Alix Coyle. I could check out Fisher's alibi for myself, and she would be the perfect companion. Guys at a dive bar in Somerville might lie to a middle-aged black cop. But they'd find it difficult to lie to her.

Alix arrived on my doorstep promptly at nine P.M. wearing a cotton shirt with a huge American flag printed on it, tight black jeans, and black and red cowboy boots. Nice to be effortlessly interesting. I had rummaged through my closet and come up with a purple lace-up bustier from freshman year in college and paired it with a black leather miniskirt, black stockings, and tall black suede boots. I grabbed my leather jacket, and we were off.

Since it wasn't far from our house, I had passed Finn McCoy's any number of times, but I'd never given it a second thought. It was a typical neighborhood bar: dark, smoky windows lit with neon lights advertising Michelob and Bud. As we stepped out of the cab and walked toward the entrance, I could see a crowd of middle-aged white men lounging outside the door, smoking and talking in the unexpectedly warm night air. A large bouncer leaned against the door, laughing with one of the waitresses. He nodded at us as we passed through the entrance, and gave Alix an approving smile.

The interior was dark and smoky, a little larger than I had expected, with a few small tables scattered around the tiny dance floor and two pool tables in the back. One wall was lined with pinball machines. I could definitely see the attraction of the place for Fisher. Even though there were no blacks in the crowd, the combination of languid drinking, hazy smoke, and women in tight skirts would have proved irresistible.

"Let's split up," Alix suggested, ordering herself a beer. She was smiling to herself in anticipation.

"You've got the photograph, right?"

"Yeah, I've got the mug shot," she said, tossing a couple of dollars at the bartender. "I feel like a game of pool. See you 'round."

She sauntered off to the back of the club, and I perched on a stool at the bar. I shot the bartender a look and asked for a Bud. I watched him quietly for a while after he brought me my beer, fascinated at his smooth motions: measuring the hard liquor, topping the glass with a mixer and a straw, adding a lemon or lime if he felt like it. I always feel a rush of pleasure watching someone perform a task exceptionally well. I finished my beer and asked for another, which I drank quickly. The air was warm and heavy, perhaps deliberately so, because it was making me thirsty. It certainly seemed to be good for business. The bar was filling up with patrons: workmen still in caps, sweaty blue shirts, and soiled jeans; groups of women all dolled up for the evening; and the occasional student type, all seeking the comfort of a half-empty glass.

The bartender had noticed my approval of his technique, and when the demand temporarily slowed, he strolled over to me.

"Can I get the pretty lady something—on the house?" I put his age at fifty something.

I downed the last of my beer and nodded.

"So what's a nice piece of brown sugar like you doing in a place like this?" he said. *Nice piece of brown sugar?* Suddenly, I felt like I was guest-starring in an episode of *Get Christy Love*.

"Just lookin' for a place to relax," I said, crossing my legs and leaning forward. "I'm new in town."

"I thought so," he said, as he poured my beer. "I knew I'd never seen you in here before."

"Yeah, I just moved here from Philly. I heard this was a good place to hang out."

"Depends on what you're looking for, sweetheart. Although I can guess." His eyes dipped to my cleavage.

I giggled with what I hoped appeared to be genuine feeling. "I came with a guy. But it never hurts to look, right?"

"Be careful, sister. That kinda thing can get you into big trouble.

Most of the fights we have here start over sweet little things like you."

Most?

"You got a lot of people in here for a Tuesday night. Can't wait to see what it's like on the weekend."

He grinned at me. "Yeah, we do okay. The guys in the neighborhood stop by on their way home most nights, and sometimes we even get the college kids in here."

I lit up a cigarette and inhaled deeply, feeling quite the girl of the moment. Blowing out the smoke, I said casually, "Say, maybe you can help me with something. My old man's best friend lives in Somerville somewhere, but I can't find his address anywhere. I don't think he's even got a phone. You ever seen this guy in here?"

I pulled a newspaper page out of my purse and slid it across the bar. It was an editorial that Fisher had written for the *Cambridge Tab* with a grainy photograph above the text. The bartender squinted at it, then snorted.

"Is that Ike Fisher?"

"Yeah. Me and my family ain't seen him in years, but the old man wants me to look him up."

"He in some kind of trouble?"

Be very careful. I shrugged. "Who knows? Ma says he's always running some scam."

" 'Cause some cop was in here flashing his picture a couple a nights ago."

I smirked. "That sounds like Uncle Ike."

The barkeep looked at me closely and weighed me in the balance. I adopted a vacant stare until he breathed out and leaned closer.

"He used to come in here pretty regular. But I ain't seen him for a couple months."

How interesting. Since his alibi was that he was here a little over a week ago.

"Well, you ain't here every night, are you?" I said, sipping my beer.

"Nah, I work Tuesday to Saturday. And he ain't been in any of those nights for a while."

I shrugged and tried to look bored. "Whatever. I'll tell Mama I tried."

"Try back on a Wednesday night sometime," the bartender called over his shoulder as he went to take the next order. "That was his usual night."

I stubbed out my cigarette and went in search of Alix. She was playing pool with three large men, two of whom were wearing greasy bandannas and earrings. I watched them silently, realizing how naturally Alix fit in. Her eyes were flashing as she circled the table, and her two companions were already calling her "darlin' " and ferrying drinks to her.

"Hey, Nikki, come on over here," she called. "Meet my new friends. This is Ed, Billy, and Mack."

I nodded a greeting and coolly accepted the offer of another beer.

"I was just asking them about your Uncle Isaiah, but they ain't seen him in a dog's life."

I suppressed a laugh, assuming that a dog's life was more than two weeks, and shrugged nonchalantly. "I don't think he wants to be found, that's what I think," I said, reaching for a pool stick. "Mind if I join you all?"

By the time we finished our first game, the bar was in full swing, with people drinking, dancing, and generally whooping it up. Ed, Billy, and Mack were regulars during the week, but they didn't visit the bar on Sunday, it being a holy day and all, so they couldn't help us with the night in question.

So Alix and I lured a stream of potential alibis to our pool table, and let them think they were winning until we got sufficient information out of them. There was Pete, who came here all the time, and remembered seeing Isaiah most Wednesdays, but never on a Sunday. And Chuck, a Ph.D. candidate in sociology doing a dissertation on nightlife in urban areas. I would have happily talked with him for the rest of the night, but he knew nothing of Fisher, and Alix insisted that we dump him and move on. It was after midnight—and I was well past buzzed and on my way to being really drunk—when we met Little Bob.

Bob wasn't that little, he was actually a huge blond man with a long ponytail and a blue bandanna, but they called him that because his father was also named Bob. He recognized Fisher's picture immediately.

"Y'all are friends of Ike's, y'all are friends of mine," he said expansively as we racked up the balls. "I just talked to him the other day."

196 • PAMELA THOMAS-GRAHAM

Alix took a drag on her Marlboro and sized him up.

"Yeah, when was that?" she drawled. Her accent was becoming more pronounced as the night wore on. "You break, Li'l Bob."

"Would've been, let's see, week ago Sunday. I remember, 'cause the Pats were playin' the Lions. Great game. Lost a lot of money on it, though. Most of it to him." The pool balls cracked loudly under the force of Little Bob's stick, and the fourteen ball sank. "Looks like y'all are solids," he said, lining up his next shot.

"So were you and Uncle Ike here?" I prompted.

"Yeah, we watched the game here. He had to leave as soon as it was over, though." Bob scratched his shot and grinned as he passed his stick to Alix. "Your shot, darlin'."

I looked at Alix. When did football games end?

"So that would've been around seven, huh?" she said. "Right when *The Simpsons* was coming on."

"Right." Little Bob nodded, chuckling. "I love that show."

"Did he come back later?" I asked. In the meantime, Alix had sunk two shots.

"You know, if I didn't know better, I'd think y'all were cops, the way you keep askin' questions." He winked at Alix.

"Li'l Bob, you don't know shit from Shinola if you think the police around here look like us," Alix drawled. She lined up her next shot. "They ain't exactly into no affirmative action"—she dragged the words out—"if you know what I mean." She banked the five ball and it obediently rolled into the side pocket.

He grinned. "I hear you, darlin'. Nah, Ike didn't come back. I was here all evening, tryin' to forget my losses, and he never showed. Out spending my money, probably."

So Fisher didn't have an alibi, at least not one placing him at this bar when the murder occurred. It looked like Rafe was right. Isaiah Fisher *did* have something going on.

CHAPTER SIXTEEN

DEARLY BELOVED

Wednesday, the day of Ella's funeral, dawned inappropriately bright. Rafe had told me that they couldn't hold the funeral any sooner because of the autopsy ordered by the police. The public had been told that it was because Ella's family needed time to travel up from Mississippi and make all the arrangements. As I walked over to Memorial Church from my office, I wondered whether it was pure coincidence that every funeral I have ever attended has been on a sunny day.

Memorial Church is a striking rendition of a traditional New England chapel: built of red brick on a knoll in the Yard, its spiraling white steeple can be seen throughout the campus as a reminder of the spiritual life that the university's founders originally intended to counterbalance the intellectual pursuits of the campus. Its interior is snow white, with dark red carpet and simple wooden pews.

As I entered, I saw that a small group of mourners had already assembled. Lindsey Wentworth was sitting alone near the front of the sanctuary, her head deeply bowed. Even in her grief, she was sartorially splendid, wearing a large broad-brimmed black hat adorned with tiny black silk bows and a demure black wool dress. A group of young women in dark suits sat together toward the middle of the church; I recognized a couple of the faces from my visits to Ella's office, and deduced that these were the various denizens of the Dean's office. A few pews behind them, I saw Isaiah Fisher sitting alone. He was slouching casually and appeared to be surreptitiously reading a newspaper; he looked at his watch as I passed by. I was surprised to see that he and Lindsey were sitting apart, given how inseparable they had seemed for the past week.

At the front of the sanctuary was a simple white casket with a spray of pink and white orchids; the filtered rays of morning sun suffused the coffin and the sanctuary with an autumnal glow. I approached the casket, fairly certain that this serene Memorial

Church service was the last kind of funeral Ella would've wanted. When it was my time, I wanted total gloom: gray skies, loud wailing, and mournful gospel music. Let folks know I was gone.

I peered gingerly into the coffin. It was Ella, all right: folds of fleshy dark brown skin, black braids forming a nimbus around her face. They had dressed her in her favorite color combination: a vivid purple dress and a green silk scarf. I closed my eyes for a moment, standing by her side.

The members of the Crimson Future Committee filed in shortly after I sat down and joined me, assiduously avoiding a tour of the open casket. Rona Seidman and Jennifer Blum sat next to me, flanked by Bob Raines, a tenured professor at the Kennedy School, and Asif Zakaria, a senior Med School professor. Ian McAllister appeared and strode purposefully down the aisle a few seconds later. He sat in the pew behind us, immediately launching into an animated, though *sotto voce*, conversation with Raines and Zakaria. I was surprised that the august members of the committee had deigned to come, but at least the sanctuary now seemed respectably full.

McAllister slid down his pew and leaned between Rona and me, whispering that he was calling a special Crimson Future Committee meeting that afternoon to discuss the agenda for the retreat that weekend, and indicated that we should let everyone else know.

"Committee meeting at two-fifteen today. Pass it on," were his exact words.

Within thirty seconds, a small commotion erupted in our pew.

"Ian, I haven't got time for this shit!" Bob Raines had lost his usual cool composure and was hissing angrily. "You're the chairman. Just set the damn agenda! You can do that yourself."

Rona turned around, shaking her head emphatically while pointing to her brown crocodile datebook. "There's no way I can make it today. I've got a luncheon at the *Business Review* at one o'clock, I teach Power and Influence at two-thirty, my therapist is at three-forty-five, and then I pick up the kids at five-thirty." She paused, and then muttered, "I shouldn't even be here now—I canceled two meetings for this funeral."

Jennifer nodded in agreement. "Tell me about it," she murmured. "I have a thesis to write."

McAllister sighed impatiently. "Fine. Veronica and I will do it.

But I expect all of you to be in attendance this weekend. The President has said that he'll be coming."

Atta boy, Ian. Dangling a Presidential appearance in front of this group not only ensured attendance, it would even get some of them to do real work before the meeting.

Glancing around the sanctuary, I looked for some sign of family members or close friends, but almost everyone appeared to be faculty or Ella's former employees. There were a couple of clusters of black students who had turned out in a show of solidarity. But the two front pews, usually reserved for family, remained conspicuously empty. I chatted in a desultory manner with Rona, wondering if Leo Barrett would show up. A few minutes before eleven o'clock, Alix Coyle—outfitted in a black miniskirt, tights, a black fringed shawl, and cowboy boots—made her way to the front of the church and sat in the second pew. Two minutes later, an elderly black couple walked slowly forward and sat in the front row. As they passed, I realized why they looked familiar. It was the couple from the photograph on Ella's desk.

The minister stepped to the large podium promptly at eleven o'-clock, and, in solemn tones, pronounced a prayer. As he finished, and we rose to sing a hymn, I saw Leo Barrett slip into a pew across the aisle and slightly ahead of us, Victoria at his side. She removed what appeared to be a small piece of lint from the lapel of his gray suit as they settled into the pew. Christian Chung followed just behind them, and sat on the other side of Leo. Barrett looked almost jaundiced; his shoulders were stooped and black circles rimmed his eyes. He was clearly under incredible stress. How much of it had to do with Ella? I wondered.

The service was brief and civilized. The minister read a couple of scriptures and then the Dean of the Law School spoke for less than two minutes about Ella's contributions to the Harvard community. The reverend pronounced another prayer, and then the pallbearers came forward. One of them was a student from my intro economics course; they must have recruited outsiders because there was no one else to do it. No wonder Ella had kept her concerns about the university financials to herself. There didn't appear to be anyone else for her to turn to. The lid of the coffin slammed loudly, the result of a lack of care on the part of the hired hands, and Ella was borne unceremoniously out of the church.

As the mourners filed out of the pews, I timed my exit so that I hit the main aisle at the same time as Victoria Barrett. She was talking with a woman who appeared to be a fellow faculty wife; wisps of their conversation drifted back to me as I trailed them down the aisle.

". . . Yes, finally . . ." the friend was saying emphatically.

". . . in this church, with an Episcopalian minister, no less . . ." Victoria murmured, shaking her head. "No regard for . . ."

". . . just a low class . . . up from . . ." whispered the friend. They both laughed.

I caught Victoria's eye and smiled broadly as she kissed her friend good-bye. How dare she mock Ella at her own funeral? If this witch *had* set Professor Irvin on me, I wanted her to know that it hadn't worked. "Hello, Dr. Barrett," I murmured, extending my hand.

"Hello, nice to see you," she said. Her eyes immediately began roaming the crowd in search of faces more important than mine, but I wasn't finished with her.

"Such a shame about Ella. I guess you'll really miss her."

Victoria focused her full attention on me for the merest second. "Actually, I never had the pleasure of getting to know her."

"Oh, forgive me. I shouldn't have presumed. She and Leo were just such good friends, I naturally assumed that the two of you were, as well."

Her eyes narrowed slightly. "As I said, Veronica, I never had the pleasure. Now if you'll excuse me. Bob!" she exclaimed insistently, taking Raines's arm. "What did you make of that dinner last night? Horrible, wasn't it?"

They started rapidly down the aisle, arm in arm; I watched them disappear. She clearly hadn't liked Ella. And her earring had been found on the floor of Littauer the night of Ella's death. It might not be enough to convict her, but it damn sure was an interesting co-incidence.

I turned back to the rapidly emptying sanctuary. Lindsey Wentworth and Alix Coyle were standing near the front of the church with the elderly black couple. Their heads were almost touching as they talked quietly. The tableau was striking: they were the only ones in the entire church dressed in black, shoulders bowed in bereavement and expressions strained. The only true mourners in attendance. I approached them in time to hear Lindsey say, ". . . wish I had told her the last time I saw her."

"Nikki." Lindsey turned to me, her large blue pupils misty with tears. Dark circles smudged the skin under her eyes. "I'm so glad you came. Ella would have been happy to know that you were here, I'm sure." As she gestured, I noticed that she was wearing black silk gloves with bows at the wrists—the finishing touch. "I was just telling Miss Coyle how happy I was with the way the ceremony turned out." She dabbed at her eyes with a snow-white handkerchief.

"I told you, call me by my first name," Alix said brusquely, the mood of empathy with Lindsey apparently broken. She rolled her eyes at me behind Lindsey's head. "Nikki, have you met the Harveys?"

"No." I extended my hand to the woman and softly introduced myself.

"Hello," she said, taking my hand. "I'm Bertie Jean Harvey. This is my husband Eulas. We're Ella's godparents."

"I'm so sorry," I said.

"Will you excuse me, please?" Lindsey said. "I have to have a word with President Barrett. I think this was *perfect*, don't you?" she murmured to Mrs. Harvey. "I'm so glad to have been able to make all the arrangements for you."

"Well, I don't know about y'all, but this would'a been no kind of funeral where I come from," Mrs. Harvey whispered to me as Lindsey disappeared down the aisle. "Over so quick! And hardly any singin' or prayin'. Her secretary said that Ella would have wanted a real Harvard funeral, so we went along, but I hardly feel like it was a service at all."

"Did you see that man was here?" Mr. Harvey rumbled.

"Yes, Lord, she can't get away from that Isaiah, even in death," Mrs. Harvey murmured, shaking her head. "She was such a good child, so trusting, and he just took advantage of her. Pulled her into things a girl like her couldn't possibly understand. That man just about ruined her life."

"I'm sure that she did the right thing in the end, Mrs. Harvey," I said, squeezing her arm. I remembered Isaiah's suspicions that it was Ella who had called the police and foiled his attempted robbery. Now I could understand the strong pull she would have felt against him.

"You're a nice child to say that. I pray that you're right," she said quietly. Her eyes began to tear up. "And please call me Aunt Bert. All her friends did."

202 • PAMELA THOMAS-GRAHAM

"Are you coming to the cemetery, Nikki?" Alix asked softly.

"No, I've got a class to teach, and I really can't miss it." Not with Irvin breathing down my neck. I'd already had to postpone my morning Ec. 10 section to attend the funeral.

"Well, I hope you'll stop by the house afterward, then," Aunt Bert interjected. "We've got plenty of food. We brought a ham and a chicken with us, and last night Eulas made some macaroni and cheese."

"I'll try," I said softly. Fighting back death with down-home cooking was as good a remedy as any I knew. As I followed them down the aisle and into the narthex, I saw that a few people remained, clustered into small groups. Christian Chung was deep in conversation with Ian McAllister. After parting with the Harveys, I realized that I had left my program in my pew, and walked quietly back to the chapel.

That was when I saw him.

Leo Barrett was kneeling in one of the pews on the far side of the sanctuary. It was so still that I could hear the ragged sound of his weeping from where I stood.

A moment later, Victoria Barrett appeared in the adjacent aisle and walked toward him, not even noticing me.

"Leo, for goodness' sake!" she hissed. "You've got to stop this! You're making a spectacle of yourself."

He shook her hand off, and kept his head bowed. His shoulders continued to heave in his grief.

"Don't you care what this is doing to me?" she asked plaintively. "Don't you care about me at all?"

He ignored her. "Leo, get up before someone sees you," she muttered, taking his arm. "And get hold of yourself."

I backed away, wanting to respect his privacy. It was then that I heard him cry, "Leave me be, Torie! For God's sake, just leave me alone."

It was clear that at least some people viewed the passing of Rosezella Fisher as more than just an inconvenience.

I called Widener Library from the pay telephone in the basement of Memorial Church to see if the three magazines I was looking for had been retrieved from the stacks. In short order, my favorite librarian came on the line.

"I know you won't believe this, Professor Chase," she began.

"What is it now?" I exploded. Ella's funeral had put me more on edge than I had realized. "You didn't have time to look for them? You lost the request? You left them at home? What is it this time?"

"Professor Chase, I did everything I could for you," she said indignantly. "It's just that—"

"What? It's just that what?"

"Every one of the periodicals that you requested is missing from the stacks. It's quite"—she paused—"unusual. Extraordinary, really. That all three would be gone."

I hung up the phone quietly.

Really, it wasn't so extraordinary that they were gone. Considering that it was the President himself who had reason to make them disappear. What could Leo Barrett possibly be hiding that was so potentially explosive? Had he been in prison? Was he secretly gay?

Whatever his secret was, I wondered if he would kill to keep it buried.

I forced myself to teach my afternoon section of Ec. 10 with the care that the students deserved, and after class quietly reminded Amy Collins to keep our conversation to herself. This could get dangerous quickly, and I wanted her well out of it. Then I went to Lamont Library and tracked down the address of *Partisan Review*. I'd asked for copies of three different magazines with articles written by Leo in the mid-sixties, just in case, but all I really needed was an unadulterated copy of the issue of *Partisan Review* from Leo's study. And there was more than one way to get a back issue of a magazine. I'd lay my hands on a complete version of Leo's article if I had to drive to New York and get it from their offices myself.

When I finally got back to Littauer, Gwen informed me that Dante Rosario had stopped by again that morning while I was at the funeral. This time, he had left a message: *I'm gaining on you, Atalanta.* Ignoring the message, I set to work figuring out what to present at the upcoming department seminar. I could've killed Ian for dumping this on me, now of all times.

Early that evening, I finally got the news I'd been waiting for: I'd been calling Mass General Hospital a couple of times a day since Justin had collapsed, and the hospital was now permitting visitors.

I jumped on the "T" immediately, paperwork be damned. I couldn't bring Ella back, but maybe I could give Justin some encouragement to stick around.

After passing through two different hospital security checks, I found his room. It was being guarded by a slender, middle-aged black woman dressed in a red suit and an Hermès scarf. She sat at the door leafing through a copy of *The Atlantic*, her demeanor an unmistakable mix of exhaustion and protectiveness. She had to be Justin's mother.

"May I help you?" she said, quickly standing up as I approached.

"I'm a friend of Justin's. Nikki Chase."

Her face, which was lined with worry, brightened a bit. "Nikki! Of course. We've heard all about you."

"You have?"

"Howard?" she called softly. A handsome silver-haired black man in a gray suit turned away from the nurses' station and walked toward us. "This is Nikki Chase. The girl Justin told us about."

A smile twinkled briefly in his eyes as he shook my hand. "A pleasure."

"It's nice to meet you. You must be Justin's parents."

"Oh, my Lord." The woman laughed softly and shook her head. "You must think we're completely crazy. I'm Vivian Simms. This is my husband, Dr. Howard Simms."

I squeezed her arm gently. "You have every right to be distracted. It really is nice to meet you. How is he?"

"He's still unresponsive," Dr. Simms said, his smile fading. "There's been no change since we arrived."

"Has someone been . . . watching him?" I looked around for the guard, assuming that they knew everything I did about the cause of the coma.

"Yes, for all the good it's done," Mrs. Simms muttered.

"What do you mean?"

"I guess we can tell you," Dr. Simms said quietly, "since Justin thought so highly of you. Someone tried to get into his room last night."

"What?"

"The guard turned his back for a moment to talk to one of the nurses—I guess this was at one or so in the morning—and someone snuck in and unplugged his respirator."

"My God! Is he all right?"

"Yes, thankfully the nurse on duty had her wits about her and noticed it immediately. She saved his life."

"Did they catch the person who did it?"

"No," Dr. Simms said angrily. "They said they tried, but the person got away. These Boston policemen are totally incompetent. Too busy eating doughnuts to effectively guard my boy."

"They say they'll have a twenty-four-hour guard here. But we're staying here ourselves from now on," Mrs. Simms said firmly. "I stayed up all night with him when he was a baby, and I can certainly do it now."

"I have a friend in the Harvard Police Department who can get you some better help. He's black," I said, watching their expressions, "and he's met Justin. You can trust him. Really."

"We'll see," Dr. Simms said. I knew in the end they'd never leave him alone with any guard, no matter who he was. If it were my son, I wouldn't either.

"Can I see him?" I asked. "They said he was allowed visitors."

"Yes, he is, but only for a minute or two." Mrs. Simms put her arm around my shoulder. "They said we should talk to him. Encourage him. They say he can hear us, even if he can't respond."

Justin's room was darkened and still, save for the blinking lights and intermittent beeps of the electronic monitors at his bedside. He was lying peacefully with his eyes closed, his long lashes fringing his cheeks.

"Hey, there," I said softly, sitting on the edge of his bed. "Nice Sleeping Beauty act."

His hand felt warm and dry as I held it in mine.

"Isn't this a lot of trouble to go to just to get a girl to kiss you?" I touched his cheek softly. "Justin, we need you to come back. See, I know that whatever you saw Saturday night was really important. Ella and I need you to come back and tell us what it was. A whole group of us are working on this thing. But we really need your help."

No response. I talked quietly to him, telling him everything that I had been up to for the past three days, until I heard a gentle knock on the door.

"That's my cue. I've got to go. But I'll be back." I kissed his forehead softly. "Stay safe."

I talked quietly with the Simmses for a few moments, and then started resolutely down the empty hospital corridor. Wonderful black man, lovely black family. Whoever was trying to hurt him had vastly underestimated all of us.

It was almost nine o'clock by the time I got home. I heard Maggie's laugh as I opened the front door and made my way back to the kitchen, where she and Ted were sitting at the table. Maggie's white lace tablecloth was barely visible beneath half a yellow layer cake with white coconut frosting, two dirty dessert plates, a pot of tea, a jar of honey, and two full mugs.

"Sit down, Sister Professor," she called as I came through the door. "This coconut cake'll be gone if you don't move fast."

I kissed her cheek and turned to Ted, smiling. "You're a bad influence on her. She used to eat fruit for dessert before you got here."

"Don't make the boy feel bad," Maggie ordered, sliding her chair over so I could get to the cupboard for a mug. "I like having a man around the house again."

"I'm not taking the blame for this cake, woman," Ted grumbled. "Your boyfriend is the one with the sweet tooth."

"Boyfriend!" I exclaimed, almost dropping my mug.

"You've got a big mouth for a lawyer," Maggie groused.

"Rafe was over here tonight," Ted whispered loudly.

"Tell me more," I said, sitting next to Maggie.

"You keep your mouth shut, or there'll be no more home cookin' for you, understand?" She wagged her finger at Ted. "I'll be right back."

Her footsteps faded down the hall as I poured myself a cup of tea.

"Listen, I've got your information," he whispered. "I assume you don't want her to know."

"Definitely not," I murmured. "She'll get worried if she knows what's going on. So give. What did you find out?"

"I'll get you the details from upstairs later. But the main thing is that while twenty-nine of your companies checked out, one of them didn't."

"What did you find?"

"Well, it doesn't exist."

"Doesn't exist? What do you mean?" I demanded, almost choking on my tea.

"One of the companies, All Write Secretarial Services, isn't licensed to do business in the state of Massachusetts. It's not even listed in the phone book. We're checking to see if it's illegally operating in the state and is headquartered elsewhere. But it could be a phantom company."

I heard Maggie coming back down the hallway and quickly picked up my bag.

"Thank you so much, Ted!" I whispered. "This is exactly what I needed."

"Now, you all better cut it with the whispering," Maggie declared as she swung through the kitchen doors. "I want in on the gossip, too."

"I've got to run, Maggie," I said, halfway out the door. "Save me some cake!"

"All this galivanting around, acting all mysterious. And now she looks as happy as a mule eatin' briers. What did you say to her?"

I missed Ted's answer as I flew up the stairs to call Rafe. This was the break we had been waiting for.

"I've got it!" I cried as he picked up his home phone.

"Nikki?" he mumbled. I must have awakened him.

"Listen, I've figured out what was going on with those financials."

"What?"

"Just listen. You know how I told you that the outside service expenses were rising at the university on Ella's spreadsheet, but not on Ian's? Well, it's *not* because the numbers were reclassified. It's because someone is embezzling money from the university. Are you with me?"

"Yes, yes, child. Go on."

"They've been using a company called All Write Secretarial Services to bill Harvard for temporary secretaries. But the company doesn't exist. I'm guessing that they make up names of people and hours worked and bill the university for it."

"Slow down, now. Where are you gettin' this from?"

"I photocopied some invoices from the economics department, and had a friend track down the companies. He says that one of them is a fake."

208 • PAMELA THOMAS-GRAHAM

"But you haven't got any other proof?"

"No, not yet. But if I'm right, then someone is filing timesheets for work that was never done. And they must be leaving a paper trail somewhere."

"There would have to be names and Social Security numbers. And someone would have to be cashin' the checks. Launderin' them through some bank account."

"We'll find that stuff. I know we will. It all adds up."

"Maybe, child. But how would Ella Fisher have figured any of this out?"

"It makes perfect sense, Rafe. She was a temporary secretary herself once, right? That's how she got her start at Harvard, and I'm sure she used them herself as Dean of Students. So she knew how much these places charge, and she knew the names of the agencies. She saw the expenses going up in the budgets she was given, did some sniffing around, and she discovered this agency that she'd never heard of. And then she put the rest together. Then whoever was behind it found out that she was onto them."

"So if you've got it all figured out, then who is this person who's doin' this embezzlin'?"

"Well, Rafe," I said, putting my feet up on the sofa, "that's what we've got to figure out next."

CHAPTER SEVENTEEN

VICTORIA'S SECRET

"Right on time, Ms. Chase. Come right this way," said a silky voice. "I managed to sneak you into Marianna's book for a manicure. And we've got a wonderful masseuse who still has openings today. Interested?"

Being high maintenance definitely has its advantages.

Thursday afternoon found me at the beauty salon at the Charles Hotel for a haircut and an opportunity to vent with my stylist and confessor, François. The appointment had come just in the nick of time. I had just escaped from Littauer after a lengthy conversation with Ian McAllister that had left me even more overloaded with work. If you can call it a conversation, when one party is doing all the talking. I had to keep moving on my investigation of Ella's murder, and I had no idea where I'd find the time.

I'd already spent two hours calling Philadelphia that morning, trying to track down Rev. Stephen Barrett. His name was in the directory, but his home number was unlisted. There was a St. Thomas's Episcopal Church in Philadelphia, but no one there knew anything about a Rev. Barrett. So either Amy had the name of the church wrong, or Leo had deliberately lied to mislead her. My best hope now was Maggie—her sister lived in Philly, and I was hoping she could do some legwork for me. At least I was going to be able to get the back issue of *Partisan Review* without driving to New York. I had called the magazine's headquarters, and the archivist there had promised to send a photocopy of the article via overnight mail within the next two days. So I'd have my answer by the weekend.

The salon at the Charles is decorated in a spare, soothing style, with white, taupe, and black the colors of choice. Upon entry, each customer is swathed in a fluffy white terrycloth robe and given a cup of herbal tea or lemon-flavored ice water, the official welcome to the garden of earthly delights. My escort led me to the back of the salon, where Frankie was holding court, his ubiquitous black beret at a particularly jaunty angle.

His real name is William Brown, a moniker he abandoned along with the rest of his childhood in small-town Tennessee when he decided to escape to the big city to become a hairdresser. Until I found him, I had gone through hairstylists as fast as I had boyfriends.

"What's the problem, girl?" Frankie asked as I settled into the black leather chair at his station. Before me was an oversized round mirror that reflected back my annoyance, and behind the mirror was a row of stylists and their customers.

"You look like your old flame, His Highness, just called you up asking for money," he declared as he combed his fingers through my hair.

"Worse," I sighed. "Much worse. But I don't want to talk about it."

"I hear you. Some of these men aren't even worth the breath it takes to say their names. So what are we doing today? A cut or a relaxer? It's getting long, girl."

I briefly considered pulling a Lindsey, cutting all my hair off and dyeing whatever was left blond, but I knew Frankie would never permit it. "Just a trim," I said with a shrug.

"I see I'm going to have to leave you looking really sexy today to break that mood. Come on, let's get you shampooed."

The feel of his strong fingers on my scalp was so relaxing that I was almost back to normal by the time we returned from the shampoo bowl. So when I heard Victoria Barrett's voice, at first I thought I was hallucinating.

"Yes, it's been quite a week," she was saying. "I hope to never see another one like it." Her voice was subdued, almost defeated. Clearly, it was Victoria, but she didn't sound herself at all.

"Sit up straight," Frankie commanded. "And uncross your legs. Unless you're going for asymmetrical, I can't work my magic with you slouching."

Obediently, I followed his instructions and held still while he starting snipping. Although I couldn't see her, I figured Victoria must be sitting at the station right behind the mirror. Which would mean that she also couldn't see me.

I heard her stylist making clucking noises of comfort, and then Victoria said, "I don't know . . . be able to work it out . . . may be getting a divorce."

Getting a divorce?

I leaned forward, and Frankie's hand was immediately on my shoulder. "Will you sit still?" he ordered. "You'll be screaming at me if this doesn't look right."

I quickly subsided in my chair. ". . . think you know someone, but you really don't," Victoria was saying. " . . . after all I've done for him . . . nothing I wouldn't do . . ."

"Girl, what are you doing?" Frankie whispered in my ear. I motioned at the mirror and held my finger to my lips to shush him. "I need to hear this," I muttered.

". . . no telling what may happen," the stylist was saying. "Sometimes you say something in an argument that you don't mean, you know that."

". . . don't think that I can ever forgive him . . . claimed that he would end it months ago, but I know he hasn't."

". . . feel better," the stylist clucked. "Come on, let's get your hair washed."

I heard the creak of a chair, and immediately dropped my head. Not that Victoria would be likely to recognize me, given that I was constantly introducing myself but still seemed to be invisible to her. She moved past me to the shampoo area, and I breathed again. *Claimed that he would end it months ago?* Was she talking about Ella and Leo?

"Who's that?" Frankie asked, combing through my hair and checking his work.

"Victoria Barrett. The Harvard President's wife."

"Old girl needs to touch up her roots if she's that important," he sniffed. "It's not like that blond hair is natural. Why are you eavesdropping?"

"It's a really long story. But you have to help me with something. When they get back, help me hear what they say."

Unfortunately, the shampoo bowl seemed to have lightened Victoria's mood, because when she returned to the stylist's chair, she was discussing an upcoming benefit for the Schlesinger Library and what dress she should wear. I had abandoned hope and given Frankie the go-ahead to turn on the blow-dryer when a new voice floated over the mirror from Victoria's side.

"Torie. I had to see you," said a male voice. It sounded strangely familiar.

"What are you doing here?" she cried. Her voice dropped to a whisper, and I lost the next sentence. I strained to catch the man's voice, but it eluded me. Who was she talking to? Leo? Frantically, I motioned to Frankie to walk over to the other side and see what was happening.

All I could hear on my side was muffled whispering, and then footsteps clicking off in the opposite direction. Frankie returned grinning.

"Girlfriend was happy to see her man," he whispered. "I hope that was her husband."

"What were they doing?" I demanded, *sotto voce*.

"She was stroking his arm like it was a mink coat."

"Stop! *She* was being affectionate in public?"

"Yes, ma'am. Told him that he shouldn't have come, and that she would meet him later. And by the way she was looking at him, there'll be some sinnin' going on when they get together, mark my words."

Was it Leo? I thought she just said they were getting a divorce. "Frankie, what did he look like?"

"White. Short hair. Business suit. Nice-lookin', actually."

"How tall?"

"Girl, he was leanin' over her the whole time. I couldn't tell."

The description *could* fit Leo. It could also fit about a thousand other people in Victoria's social circle. This could have been Leo's dramatic gesture toward reconciliation. But then why would Victoria have caved in so quickly?

"Thanks, honey. I owe you."

"If you would just sit still so I can dry all this hair, it would be thanks enough," he growled.

I relaxed into the chair and smiled up at Frankie.

It must have been Leo. The man's voice was definitely familiar. Besides, who else could it have been?

Dried and fluffed and released from Frankie's chair, my next stop was my office, to start plowing through the new assignments Ian had dumped on me. When the phone rang around eight-thirty that evening, I was in no mood to talk.

"Yes," I snapped.

"Hello, I'm trying to reach Veronica Chase," said a vaguely familiar female voice.

"You've got her."

"This is Vivian Simms. It sounds like I'm interrupting you."

"Mrs. Simms!" I said, leaning back in my chair. "How is Justin?"

"I have some wonderful news," she began. "About an hour ago, he opened his eyes."

"Oh, thank God! How is he feeling?"

"He's not conscious yet. But they said that this is a very important step."

"I'm so happy for you! When can I come and see him?"

"We were hoping you would come as soon as possible. The doctors said that hearing familiar voices will speed his recovery."

"I'm on my way."

It was almost midnight when I finally arrived home from the hospital. I had stopped by my apartment to change before going to Mass General in the foolish hope that a short red dress and black suede high heels would lure Justin back to consciousness. Unfortunately, it hadn't worked. But he did look much better, and the doctors were permitting themselves to smile for the first time since he had arrived.

As I let myself in the front door, I could hear Maggie laughing coquettishly in the kitchen. She and Ted must be at it again.

"Maggie!" I called out, shrugging off my jacket. "I've got some terrific news! Justin opened his eyes!"

I was halfway through the kitchen door before I realized that her late-night companion wasn't Ted. It was Dante. The two of them were eating Rocky Road ice cream. Out of the same container.

"That's great!" he said, clearly enjoying my shock. "Who can blame him, given that outfit?"

"What are you two—doing up so late?" I shot a look at Maggie, ignoring him completely. What happened to her firm opposition to flirting with white men with strange Italian names?

"Dante made dinner for Ted and me tonight, and we just got to talking," she said, looking sheepishly down into the ice cream carton. At least she was willing to show some shame. "He was telling me about his grandmother Juliana. Did you know she was a partisan in Tuscany during the second World War? Her house was used as an escape route for the Jews during the occupation."

"Really?" I said flatly. "Who knew that the Rosarios had such a progressive streak?"

"And he spent some time working with the kids in the Oakland school district while he was in California. He knows my friend Delores Spann."

"Want some ice cream, Nik?" Dante said innocently. "We've got plenty left. Although Maggie has already picked out all the chocolate chips."

I shot her another look. Was she actually allowing him to charm her?

"You know, I was on my way up to bed. Thanks anyway." I started out of the kitchen. "You all have fun."

"Would you excuse me, Maggie?" I heard him say as I cleared the doorway.

He caught up with me at the foot of the stairs.

"So how long are you planning to wage this war of attrition, Juliet?"

"I have no idea what you're talking about." I paused on the first stair, which put us almost at eye level.

"I'm talking about your avoiding me. Refusing to return my phone calls. Leaving the room if I'm there. Asking Ted for help on your investigation after refusing mine. That war." His foot was on my step.

"Oh, is that what this is about?" I said, moving up a stair. "You're upset because your roommate did a little research for me?"

"When I offered my help, you bit my head off! The word Neanderthal was used."

"You didn't offer your help, you bulldozed your way into my investigation." I retreated up the stairs. "At least Teddy waited to be asked."

"Oh, it's *Teddy* now, is it?" He advanced after me.

"Yes, do you have a problem with that?"

"Maybe." He cornered me on the landing.

"You're actually acting jealous! Let it go, Rosario. You've charmed the pants off every other woman in sight, including our landlady. Isn't that enough?"

He grinned down at me. "Are you kidding? Those were just warm-ups for the main event."

"You're such a pig—"

"Come on, Nik," he interjected. "Not the 'P' word again." He motioned toward his apartment door. "Let me buy you a drink. I'll fill you in on *my* investigation."

I hesitated for half a second and then crossed the threshold, taunted by his smile into entering enemy territory.

He led me quickly through the living room and into his bedroom. I raised my eyebrows as he waved me toward his desk chair and closed the door.

"Relax. Ted's desk is in the living room, and he's got a big trial tomorrow. Your virtue is safe with me."

Safety wasn't exactly the path we seemed to be on, but I let it pass. His windows were open and I could smell wood smoke and hear voices floating up from the street below.

"So why have you been calling me so incessantly?" I reclined in his chair and put my feet up on his desk as he settled at the edge of his bed.

"Because while you and Ted have been chasing down business licenses, I've been pursuing a different angle."

"You men tell each other *everything*, don't you? What other angle could there be after what Teddy and I discovered?" Okay, I was exaggerating Ted's involvement, and using his name in vain. But it was getting under Dante's skin, which was just too delicious.

"So the two of you have got it all figured out?" He actually sounded miffed. I could feel his eyes roaming the length of my legs, taking in the high heels and the abbreviated dress, and I let them linger for a moment. If we were going to power flirt, it was time I started playing to win.

"Look, it seems pretty clear," I said assuredly. "Ella uncovers an embezzlement scheme that's netted someone two million dollars, and then she turns up dead. Someone chases me through Widener and then breaks into my apartment to steal the evidence before I can piece it together."

"Whoa!" His eyes were back on my face. "How do you figure that? I know you said that you were mugged in Widener, but what does that have to do with Ella Fisher?"

I explained the missing disk and the burglar's search of my hard drive.

"So it's all about money. Isn't that just like an investment banker cum economist?" He leaned toward me as he mocked me.

"Come on, Rosario," I scoffed. "Even a philosopher king like you must be aware that in the real world, people actually care about money, and some will even kill for it."

"So whodunnit, Agatha Christie? Ian McAllister?"

I shook my head, swinging my feet off the desk. "I don't think so. Much as I'd like to see him locked up somewhere with no access to a phone, it's not his style. Besides, he has a lot of family money from Connie. He'd never risk his standing in the community to get more."

"But didn't Ted say that the embezzlement started in the Economics Department?"

"Sure, but it spread pretty fast to the rest of FAS. And Ian's reach doesn't extend that far. I'm pretty sure that he's an innocent dupe, like the other department heads."

"So who's your main suspect, then?"

I leaned toward him confidingly. "Christian Chung. The university comptroller. He's got access to funds across the entire university, he had frequent arguments with Ella Fisher just before she died, he's got big strong arms for pushing someone down a flight of stairs, and I'm pretty sure that he was at Littauer Sunday night. I remember Barrett being surrounded by his aides at the end of the meeting. Means, motive, and opportunity."

"Aren't you forgetting someone, Nik?"

Leo Barrett's name hung unspoken in the air between us.

"He's not capable of that," I said quickly.

"You sure?"

Well, of course I wasn't sure, given everything I had seen and heard in the last week. I wasn't sure about anything anymore. But I was keeping my investigation of Leo's secret to myself.

"He was at Littauer that night. Then there's that conversation we were privy to—no pun intended," Dante continued. "And Torie's riding him really hard over finances. That's one of the things I've been trying to tell you. I've seen a lot of her this week, and she's obsessed with money. Leo's got to be having trouble keeping up."

I shook my head. "He wouldn't do it. He's not that kind of man."

"I don't know that your judgment is all that reliable when it comes to men, Juliet. But let's assume for the moment you're right. You're still missing the whole point."

"Really? Then please enlighten me, O Wise One."

"This is not a crime of greed. And it wasn't about money. It was about passion." His foot had strayed to the bottom of my chair, and I felt him roll me ever so slightly toward him.

"Give me a break, Rosario."

"Listen, Juliet. While you've been chasing around chatting up anyone who'll talk to you, I've been observing. And do you know what I see?"

"What?" I challenged. By then, he had maneuvered my chair well within arm's reach.

"I see a woman who hasn't been kissed passionately for months." His hands were on either side of my chair now, and he leaned toward me. "Who has every hair in place, every nail perfectly groomed, but who's actually longing to be tousled. Who wears her clothes like armor, but who's really aching to be touched."

Our eyes locked for a long moment.

"Get your hands off my seat, Rosario," I said flatly. "I'm not aching for anything."

"If you say so." He grinned at me as I slid away. "But actually, I was referring to Torie."

"You think Victoria Barrett killed her?"

"There's the sapphire earring I found at Littauer. Her serious dislike of Ella. And she has no alibi for Sunday night."

"How do you know that?"

"She told me she was at home catching up on her correspondence. Alone."

"But what's her motive?" I asked.

"Perhaps to stop Ella's affair with Leo. Torie's convinced he had a lover, and it's making her crazy."

I rolled my eyes. Of course, I suspected Victoria myself, but there was no way I was going to agree with him. "It's just like a man to assume that this is a cat-fight run amok. What makes you think Torie's so desperate to hold on to Leo that she would kill for it? She's a Harvard Ph.D. with an independent family fortune. If he were cheating, why wouldn't she just divorce him?"

"Come on, haven't you ever been desperately, madly in love, Juliet? So much that for a moment, anything seems justified?"

"Of course I have. But I got over it," I said flatly. "So—greed or passion? Which makes a more compelling motive for murder?"

"Only an *economist* would even have to ask that question."

I ignored his amused expression. "Of course, we could both be wrong. There's always revenge as a motive."

"Who would that be?"

"Ella's ex-husband, Isaiah Fisher. He told me a cock-and-bull story about a crime he and Ella committed in the sixties that they're being blackmailed over, and hinted that the blackmailer could have killed Ella because she wouldn't keep paying. But Rafe and I think *he* could have been the one blackmailing her, perhaps for revenge because she ruined one of his schemes by calling the police. And last night I helped break his alibi." I told him the story about Alix and me at Finn McCoy's.

"Juliet goes slumming. Sorry to have missed that."

Given the expression in his eyes, and the fact that somehow we seemed to be mere inches away from each other, it was clear that we were quickly closing in on the point of no return. Amazing the effect that fifteen minutes alone in a room together could still have. I stood up abruptly and started for the door, while a graceful exit was still a possibility. "I've got to figure out what to do next."

"If I were you, I'd sit tight until the retreat on Martha's Vineyard. Leo and Torie will both be there."

That stopped me in my tracks. "*Torie* will be there?"

"She told me today that she's coming. Wants to spend as much time with Leo as possible."

"That's perfect!" I exclaimed. With both of them in the same house as me for an entire weekend, I could eavesdrop to my heart's content.

"Lord, you're beautiful when you get excited," he murmured under his breath. "That smile lights up the whole room."

I looked up to find him smiling at me with the same beguiling expression as the one in his office earlier that week. And this time, I was in his bedroom. And the door was closed. And suddenly I felt so liquid that I could have melted into a puddle at his feet.

"So what were you doing tonight, anyway?" he asked, his eyes traveling over me again, at an even more leisurely pace.

"I was attempting a resuscitation."

He stood up resolutely and moved toward me. "Mouth to mouth, presumably."

Indecisive, I backed away and felt the smooth chill of the doorknob beneath my fingers. Stay or go? He was so close that I could smell his cologne. Or maybe his skin. Whatever it was, it was intoxicating.

"He'll never take you seriously," Maggie's voice said in my ear.

Who cares if he takes me seriously? As long as he takes me.

Just then, fate intervened in the form of a fist pounding on the bedroom door. If that wasn't divine guidance, what was? I jumped and turned to open the door.

Dante sighed heavily.

Ted was standing on the other side. As the door opened and he saw first me and then Dante, his smile broadened.

"What do you want?" Dante snapped.

"Hi, guys," Ted replied cheerfully. "I'm really sorry. But I really need that book back for a brief I'm writing."

Dante grabbed a book off his desk and hurled it at Ted. "So, do I sense a rapprochement?" Ted asked, catching the book.

"I'd say it's early to be breaking out the Montblancs for the signing ceremony," I replied smoothly, refusing to look at Dante. That was *way* too close a call. "I've got to get going."

I clearly wasn't in true fighting form, because I'd actually had Dante on the ropes at the beginning of the evening, and now his maddening confidence had returned. As I strode through the living room, his voice echoed after me.

"You can run, Atalanta, but you can't hide."

CHAPTER EIGHTEEN

STRANGE
BEDFELLOWS

"Jennifer, Veronica, Rona, Bob, Roberta, Tony, David, and Malcolm, you'll all be staying in the main house."

It was four-thirty Friday afternoon, and Ian McAllister was standing in the broad gravel driveway of his compound on Martha's Vineyard, reading from a list his housekeeper had just handed him. "Dante, Michael, and Asif are in the guest house. And the Barretts get the pool house when they arrive."

It had taken almost four hours for the Crimson Future Committee to reach McAllister's house in Edgartown. First we took a van from Cambridge to Woods Hole on Cape Cod. Then a ferry to the island. After the ferry docked at Oak Bluffs, there was a twenty-minute ride to the house. Ian lived nearly two miles down a dirt road from the nearest main thoroughfare.

But the compound, when we finally reached it, was well worth the odyssey. A curving gravel road swept through a massive stone gate and past a wide expanse of green lawn, ending in a circular driveway before the main house. The three-story structure was made of weathered gray cedar shingles and its many windows were framed with white shutters. The landscaping in the front was beautifully arrayed and lush: a profusion of azaleas, mountain laurel, rhododendrons, and smaller flowers was complemented by sculptures, urns, and a flagstone walkway. Behind the house, the ocean shimmered in the late-afternoon sun. Indian summer had made an early appearance, and the day was as balmy as mid-August.

The guest house that Ian was gesturing toward was a miniature version of the main house with a wraparound porch, set near the tennis courts. Of course, "miniature" was a relative term: I later discovered that it had four bedrooms, two baths, its own laundry room and kitchen, as well as an expansive living room and dining area.

But for the moment, I was preoccupied with getting settled into the main house, which was a jewel box of antiques and artwork. As we started up its main staircase to the second floor, a huge chocolate brown dog with a thick neck flew down the stairs and blocked our path.

"What the—" I blurted out as the dog snarled at me.

"Maxwell," Ian cooed, instantly down on his knees patting the dog. "Missed me, eh?"

This was not a dog that looked as if he would miss anyone. It looked to me like one of those crazy dogs that ate small children and old people.

"Is he yours?" I asked, as Ian rubbed the thick skin under the dog's neck.

"Of course. Meet Maxwell Friend the Third, our mascot."

Jennifer Blum and I eyed each other and then the dog. Maxwell Friend? He looked anything but.

The dog's bloodshot eyes roamed over me and a deep rumbling noise issued from its throat.

"He's very shy at first," Ian said jovially. "But then he warms up. That's the way mastiffs are."

Maxwell chose that moment to snap at my hand. I couldn't wait to see him after the shyness wore off.

"Don't mind him," Ian said, as he led us up the stairs. "He puts on a good show, but he's a complete pushover." He deposited Jennifer and me in two bedrooms covered in Laura Ashley chintz and facing the sea. We were to share a bath, while Rona Seidman and Roberta Williams, the Education School professor, shared one further down the hall. The master bedroom and the McAllister daughters' bedrooms were in a separate wing, which would be deserted for the weekend, as Connie and the girls had decided to stay in Cambridge. Bob, David, Malcolm, and Tony were escorted to the third floor, where they each had a room overlooking the ocean.

As I was unpacking, I heard a plane fly overhead, the drone of the engine growing louder and louder. I looked out the window in time to see a small private jet land not far from the main house. Ian, or one of his neighbors, had a private airstrip. He must be making more from his Harvard Management board position than I had realized if he was able to pay for all this splendor, plus his own aviation operation. Connie's family money couldn't possibly be covering it all.

We held a meeting for two hours around Ian's dining room table, and afterward assembled for dinner on the back lawn of the main house, facing the ocean. The meal was a New England supper: lobster, corn on the cob, new potatoes, and pearl onions all cooked in the same pot. The metaphor wasn't lost on me as I surveyed the group scattered across the terrace and the lawn in the setting sun. An economist, a government professor, a businesswoman, a doctor, a dentist, a public health professor, a rabbi, an architect, a teacher, a city planner, and a college student all bound to the same institution. Engaged in light banter for the moment, but mortal enemies in the funding battle. If it was like this at Harvard, how were smaller universities surviving?

The wind started to pick up as the caterers completed their final preparations for dinner. I noticed the waves on the ocean growing larger and the tree branches beginning to thrash.

Fasten your seat belts. It's going to be a bumpy night.

We were all clustered around the buffet table when Leo and Victoria Barrett finally arrived. Leo looked debonair as always, wearing a hunter green windbreaker over a taupe cotton sweater and khaki pants. Despite the rising winds and chill in the air, Victoria was turned out in what she obviously felt was Edgartown "resort wear": a turquoise shirt with a halter neckline and a brightly patterned skirt tied like a sarong around her waist. Ian greeted them stiffly, and promptly turned away. Victoria spotted Dante standing in line with Tony and Malcolm.

"Can I join you boys?" she burbled. She seemed to be in unusually good spirits. Maybe she really had reconciled with Leo that day at the beauty parlor.

That was when Christian Chung sauntered casually out of the back door of the main house and crossed the lawn toward me.

"Christian! What are you doing here?" I asked. I swallowed hard to contain my excitement. The situation was growing more and more promising.

"I just flew in to drop off some papers that the President needed urgently." That explained the plane I saw landing earlier. "Too important for a messenger. And McAllister invited me to stay. I was just getting a tour of the compound." He was giving me the usual once-over. In spite of my brown wool shorts, ivory cotton sweater, brown tights, and Timberlands, I suddenly felt underdressed.

"Come with me while I say hello to Leo," I coaxed. I wanted to see the two of them together. We walked toward Barrett in time to hear him muttering to Bob Raines, ". . . I'm the damn President and I can't afford to live this well, as Torie reminds me every time we get dragged out here. And of course we missed the ferry, had to wait an hour and a half until the next one."

"Leo," I exclaimed. "Nice to see you!"

His annoyed expression lifted, and he smiled as he kissed both my cheeks. "That's it, Raines. No more business talk now that we have such a lovely companion. Join us for dinner, Nikki."

"Actually, President Barrett, I need a word with you in private," Christian said abruptly. "If you don't mind."

Leo frowned. "This better be important, sport." He winked at me over his shoulder as they walked away. "Save me a spot."

I hung back from the crowd, surreptitiously watching the two of them as they moved quickly through the buffet line and then put their heads together in a secluded corner of the terrace. What was so urgent that it couldn't wait until after dinner?

I felt a strong pair of hands on my shoulder and turned to find Ian McAllister standing behind me. "Come, Veronica, let's get something to eat. I was talking with Kennedy about you today, and he's *still* talking about that paper you delivered at the last department seminar," he said companionably as we started down the buffet line. Kevin Kennedy was another senior economics professor, so this news was welcome. "Send him a note mentioning the new paper you're working on. Something short and friendly, on your letterhead."

"Will do," I said and smiled. Despite my nagging suspicions, Ian was still my navigator on this perilous journey called a career, and I had always followed his advice unfailingly. We joined the growing crowd at a large metal and glass table on the flagstone terrace, and began discussing the reaction to Ian's article in the *Times,* which had finally run on Thursday morning.

A few minutes later, I realized that Dante had settled into the chair right across from us, and was carrying on an animated conversation with Jennifer Blum. Performing her usual routine of hair tossing and breast-displaying yawns, Jennifer was squeezed into one of her famous microminis, which I was sure must have settled somewhere near her waist now that she was sitting down. Dante's grin was appropriately appreciative.

"I don't agree with these p.c. mouthpieces who believe it's a political betrayal to be reading Homer," Jennifer was saying. "The *Iliad* glorifies war. So what? Sometimes war is what's required. But you're a smart man, you already know that."

She was preaching to the choir, but I knew that was the whole point. Dante nodded thoughtfully. "Even if you're a pacifist," he remarked, "the work has something to say about human nature that an open-minded person ought to want to hear. I know it makes me sound like a fascist to some people," he said as he glanced over at me, "but I do believe that there are certain great minds that any educated person should be exposed to: Plato, Virgil, Goethe, Kant."

"This sounds interesting," Leo Barrett interjected as he placed his plate on the table next to mine. Ian looked visibly annoyed as we all slid closer to accommodate him.

I knew I was crazy to be joining battle with Dante in front of not one but two of my most important mentors, but I couldn't restrain myself.

"Can't you think of even one woman to add to that list?" I shot back. "Or perhaps a black person? Is that too much of a stretch for you?"

Jennifer met my glance, and waved her hand dismissively. "What's so horrible about requiring people to understand the foundation of Western civilization?" she asked. "Come on."

"She has a point, Nikki," Leo interjected.

"What's horrible is that it discounts the contributions of others who were out of the power structure, but who had a lot to offer," I snapped.

Ian was regarding us with some amusement, but remained silent. I knew what he would think about this. He was a great fan of the Great Books.

"I was interrupted before I could add that I believe Austen and Woolf and Ellison and Hurston *also* should be required reading," Dante retorted.

"Of course, the obligatory nod to the two black authors of whom you've actually heard. Thanks for throwing us a bone," I returned.

"You've got to be kidding," Jennifer interjected almost simultaneously. "I hardly think that Zora Neale Hurston is on the same level as Virgil."

The entire table was now listening to our conversation. I could already predict where the battle lines would be drawn.

"You're promoting a set of ideas that get passed on from one power elite to the next," I continued, "and you wonder why those of us who've been marginalized by these people resent not being considered 'educated' until we swallow their words and cough them back up on an exam blue book."

"So you don't believe that there is a set of transcendental values that are worthy of learning, even though the vessels that delivered them may be flawed?" Dante returned. This was old, familiar ground for us.

"Flawed?" I snorted. "In these works, women are treated like souvenirs of war, and people of color are barred from political life altogether. You call those transcendental values?"

"Be careful, Nikki. This has nothing to do with race." Suddenly, Leo seemed to be taking the conversation more seriously. "We're talking about whether these writers are noteworthy. Not whether they're noteworthy *black* writers, but whether they've earned their place in the canon based on the enduring value of their work."

There it was again. That irritating conservative streak of Leo's. How could he be so consistently supportive of my career, but so wavering in his support of diversity in the curriculum and the faculty? I was beginning to think that Maggie was right. His liberalism really *was* only skin deep.

McAllister cleared his throat. "I have to agree with Leo. This is no time for affirmative action. If there is any force holding Western society in check, it is our adherence to certain fundamental tenets that had their origin in the classics. Students must be taught that."

"Ian, I think it was Katie Roiphe who first wrote that teaching literature is, implicitly, teaching values," I said, trying to remain patient. "And if you do it carelessly, you perpetuate a damaging social order."

Bob Raines weighed in. "Whether we acknowledge it or not, it's not just teaching literature that teaches values. We're all keepers of that torch. Doesn't teaching introductory economics instill a fundamental faith in capitalism?"

No, because we changed the syllabus years ago to accommodate sections on socialism, managed capitalism, and communism, I thought, but didn't say. It was time I gracefully bowed out of this discussion. After snapping at Kenneth Irvin earlier that week, I couldn't afford the luxury of actually speaking my mind.

"I think these books are a catalyst for each of us to define his own values," Raines continued. "They are a beginning, but surely not the end, of what we as educated people should know and consider when we develop our moral compasses."

Unwilling to argue further at the risk of calling a tenured professor a pompous asshole, I lapsed into silence. Jennifer looked at Dante and rolled her eyes mockingly. I resisted the urge to fly at her throat and instead turned back to my plate.

"Are you all right, champ?" Ian whispered in a rare moment of solicitude.

I waved my hand dismissively. "I'm fine. Just thinking about how I'm going to prepare for that department seminar next week."

He nodded, unconvinced but unwilling to pry.

Meanwhile, Leo Barrett's attention was fixed across the table on Jennifer Blum. "So, you're a fan of the *Iliad*." I peevishly assured myself that it was her legs and not her ideology that he was hoping to explore further.

I was refilling my plastic cup with lemonade when I felt something warm settle around my shoulders. I turned to find Dante placing his sweater around me.

"Nice outfit, but you look a little chilly," he said.

"Thanks."

"Ouch! That tone is pretty chilly, too. Are we at war again, Nik?" His hand brushed my cheek as he tied the sleeves of his sweater around my neck.

"You know how I feel about the Great Books," I said, pulling away. "We've had this conversation more than once, as I recall."

He smiled down at me. "Do we get to end this one the way those used to end?" Which involved ferocious arguing right up to the moment when we'd call each other names and end up tangled on the floor, kissing wildly.

"No," I said, reaching for my lemonade. "I don't kiss Republicans anymore."

"Well, I'm an Independent now, so I'm in luck."

"Oh, the policy extends to Independents, too."

"Really?" he said, in mock disappointment.

"Yep. Can't stand a man who can't make a commitment." I took a sip from my cup, and turned away.

"Your eyes are particularly bright today," he said as he followed me back toward the terrace. "You must be having a good time."

"How could I not? The suspects are assembled, and the night is ripe for investigation."

"Great. I'll meet you in your room as soon as we shake off this entourage, and we can get started."

"I don't think so."

"Come on, I thought we had called a truce," he said impatiently.

"We had. But your new friend Jennifer seems stirred, and may resist being shaken."

The wind drove us into the brightly lit kitchen for dessert: cherry and blueberry pies and ice cream. Clearly annoyed with me, Dante seemed more fascinated than ever by Jennifer Blum, and I noticed the two of them slipping out to the terrace with coffee cups in hand. *Fine*. I quietly stepped out of the kitchen as the rest of the group began to disperse for the evening. The main house had an alarm system that might preclude my moving around during the night. This was my best chance to find out what its denizens might be hiding.

I had already decided that Ian's study would be my first stop. I had seen Christian duck in there while dessert was being served, and it would be a good warm-up for the pool house, where Leo and Victoria were staying. By the time I was finished, everyone would have gone out for the evening and I'd have the run of the place. I had left my room and was coming down the main hallway on the second floor when I ran into Ian with his dog, Maxwell Friend.

"Hello," I said cheerfully, noting that Maxwell was looking more menacing as the evening wore on. "What are you up to for the evening?"

"I'm going to take Max for his evening constitutional, and then I'm calling it a night. It's been a long day."

I yawned conspicuously. "I know, I'm beat. I'm just going to grab a cup of tea, and then hit the sack. It's pretty windy out there, better bring a sweater."

He shook his head. "I'm used to it. The night breeze is invigorating."

As we walked down the stairs together, Max stopped at every other step to look back at me. This wasn't shyness. That dog was just mean. I waved them out the door, then quickly ducked into the first-floor study, pulling the heavy wooden double doors shut behind me. I crossed the room in darkness and closed the blinds, sealing out the view of the front lawn. As I pulled the cord on the blinds, I realized that Dante's sweater was still tied around my neck.

My miniature pocket flashlight revealed that the room was nearly identical to Ian's office back in Cambridge: dark wood walls and furniture to match, deep maroon leather sofa and desk chair, and a richly patterned maroon carpet. I would have started with the desk drawers, but my flashlight illuminated a leather briefcase tucked into a cranny behind the sofa. I heaved it up to the top of the desk, and saw that it was engraved with the initials "C.C." That could only be Christian Chung.

It was the type of briefcase with a combination lock. All letters. And of course, it was locked.

If I were Christian Chung, what combination would I use? I tried different combinations of his first name. No go. His last name. No. Lowell House. Nothing. What was important to this guy? Expensive clothing. I tried Giorgio Armani, Hugo Boss, and Calvin Klein. Strike out. After ten minutes, I finally got lucky: HAR on one side, VAR on the other.

I snapped open the locks and found what you would expect: pens stacked neatly in the lid of the case, a sheaf of papers stacked neatly in the main well.

But underneath the stack of papers was something that at first seemed like a mirage. Was I dreaming? I rubbed it with my fingertips. Then I smelled it. No, it was real. It was stacks of cash, a suitcase full. Flat, neatly stacked bundles of hundred-dollar bills. Ben Franklin regarded me gravely from every turn. There must have been half a million dollars in that briefcase.

Half a million dollars.

This could be the proof that I needed to tie Christian Chung to the embezzlement scheme. A sound on the stairs outside stiffened my spine. Was Ian returning from his walk already? I had to get out of there. Ian and that nasty dog could be back any minute. I removed the top bill from each of five randomly selected stacks, and then quickly closed the case and slipped quietly out of the library. As I turned, I found myself face to face with Jennifer Blum.

"Hi," I said, quickly. "Just looking for a book to read myself to sleep with."

"No luck, I see," she said, regarding my empty hands.

"Nothing but textbooks and abstracts in there, and that will only keep me awake. And you?"

"Dante and the other boys are going to a bar in Oak Bluffs, and I'm going along for the ride. They didn't mention you," she added with a saccharine smile, "but I'm sure you'd be welcome to come along."

"No, thanks." I dramatically stifled a yawn to let her know that I couldn't be less interested. "I was up at six today, and I'll be crashing shortly." I waited impatiently as she disappeared out the door.

How quickly a man can ruin a friendship between women.

I had to get word to Rafe about the cash. But how could I use one of Ian's phones, when there were a half-dozen people who might pick up the extension and hear me? Back in Manhattan, I had never been without my trusty Motorola cellular phone, supplied for free by the bank. But no more. Academic poverty grated on my nerves some days.

Then I remembered the fax machine in the master bedroom suite. Ian had given us a tour of the main house, and had said in passing that he had recently moved his fax machine into their bedroom because he didn't use his study regularly enough, and incoming faxes had often sat there unnoticed for days. As long as I could get in and out before Ian came back, that was my best bet. I found a pad in the kitchen and scribbled a note to Rafe, and taped one of the bills to the bottom of the sheet. I nipped up the stairs, listening for voices on the second or third floors of the house, but everyone seemed to have gone out. Quietly, I opened the door to Ian's bedroom. The fax machine was sitting innocently on a small desk overlooking the shore. Relying on the moonlight streaming through the window, I dialed Cambridge and waited for the reassuring transmission beep. Instead, I got a busy signal and a redial message. Who could be faxing the Harvard cops at midnight on a Friday night?

I picked up the phone to dial Rafe directly while I waited. I tried his home number, knowing that I'd get yelled at for waking him up.

The phone rang and rang at the Griffin residence. And the paper lay still untransmitted in the fax machine. Nervous, I pulled a piece of Bazooka bubble gum out of my pocket and popped it into my mouth. It was a habit I had picked up when I was trying to cut back on the nicotine and caffeine I used to rely on in my investment banker days. The wind whistled outside, and I strained to listen for the sound of Ian returning from his walk.

A minute passed, and the machine redialed while I tried to reach police headquarters. I heard the fax line connect with the police station's just as a night sergeant picked up the phone.

"I'm trying to reach Griffin," I whispered.

"What?" barked a voice on the other end. "Speak up!"

"Get me Raphael Griffin. Now."

The sheet was disappearing through the machine, and I could swear that I heard voices on the stairs and footsteps coming toward the bedroom. I hung up and started opening the sliding glass door leading to the balcony outside the bedroom. As the paper disengaged from the machine, I grabbed it and stepped out onto the balcony just as the light came on in Ian's bedroom. The machine chirped cheerfully, ending the transmission. I prayed it wouldn't immediately print a journal report that would allow Ian to see where the fax had gone. Whatever it did, I had to get out of there.

I crept down the wooden spiral staircase attached to the balcony of Ian's bedroom and crouched at the foot of the stairs as Ian stepped out onto the balcony and looked out at the shore.

"I thought I had closed this," I heard him mutter as he slid the door shut.

I sat at the foot of the outdoor staircase while I considered my next move. Just then, I saw Christian quietly making his way across the lawn and into the back door of the main house. I made it around the corner in time to see him disappear up the stairs. Following him, I saw him quietly entering Ian's daughter's empty bedroom on the second floor. The lights were out, and it appeared to be deserted. Was he meeting someone?

"Yes, understood. You should have taken care of it sooner." That was Christian's voice. Was he talking on the phone? I crouched down on all fours outside of the door. No keyhole.

"I know the telephone seems unnecessary . . . have to take precautions . . . watching. Look, the important thing is . . . debugged it finally," Christian murmured. Was he talking on the phone with someone who was staying at the compound? What did he mean, *"the telephone seems unnecessary"*?

"He's young," he continued after a pause. "Should have done it the way I said . . . would've finished the shit weeks ago . . . brought the cash so you can head south."

I crawled closer to the door, closing my eyes and straining to pick up his voice. Suddenly, I felt a wet hand on my neck. I stiffened, but instinctively had a response ready.

"I know this looks crazy," I whispered, "but I dropped my contact lens, and I can't find it anywhere."

My interrogator removed his hand and made a deep gurgling sound.

"What the—" I muttered to myself. I swung away from the door, still on all fours, and found myself staring into the deep brown un-blinking eyes of Maxwell Friend, mastiff. From this vantage point, the dog was nearly twice my size, all massive head, huge red mouth, and muscular neck. Although I'd insisted only an hour ago that he was a dirty, mean-spirited animal, I was now willing to consider that Maxwell was everything Ian suggested: a shy and misunderstood pet. I told myself that though I couldn't see it from here, surely Maxwell was wagging his tail, that his heavy breathing and tightly clenched jaws suggested a toothless smile; that his face was wet not from per-spiration in anticipation of the kill, but only from dew drops from his delightful evening walk. That his refusal to move or do more than growl was merely a manifestation of his shyness.

After an eternity, Maxwell blinked. So I blinked. *See, we're all the same under the skin, doggie.* We regarded each other on all fours matching blink for blink. Then I saw his neck swell slowly.

"This is it," I thought. I have to scream now, or this dog will kill me. I opened my mouth, but no noise emerged. I closed my eyes, unwilling to witness my own blood being shed.

I heard nothing, and then a small whimper.

I opened my eyes and saw Maxwell reclining in front of me, chewing on something oval and pink. I checked to make sure it wasn't a piece of my tongue.

That was when I realized that my wad of Bazooka was gone. The dog was chewing my gum. It must have rolled out of my mouth and caught Max's fancy. He growled contentedly.

"Veronica, what are you doing?" Ian McAllister was towering over me. "Is there a problem?"

"No," I said calmly. "I was just playing with Maxwell."

"Well, have fun," he said, patting the dog's head, then mine for good measure. He disappeared down the hall and back into his bedroom. Apparently, he hadn't noticed that I was bathed in sweat.

I clambered to my feet and watched Maxwell amble down the hall chewing loudly on my Bazooka.

"Veronica! I thought I wouldn't have the pleasure of your company until tomorrow." Christian Chung emerged from the bedroom, smiling broadly. "I figured everyone would have gone into town by now."

"Well, everyone else has," I said, without thinking.

His eyes narrowed as he smiled salaciously at me. "Well, then, I guess that means I get you all to myself. And the night is young."

First a mad dog, now a snake. I could have pleaded a headache and escaped to my room, but it was clear this man was somehow involved in my investigation, and this seemed the perfect time to try to find out just how.

"Yes, it is," I smiled back. "Shall we go for a walk?"

"Absolutely," he said, taking my arm. "Let's go."

We walked down the stairs and I resisted the urge to back out. I could handle this, I reassured myself.

We stepped out the front door of the main house, and the wind immediately swirled around us. "This is wonderful," Christian said, inhaling deeply. "But it's as cold as a witch's left tit. Come here." He put his arm around me and I relaxed against him. Just get him talking, I told myself.

"You know," he said, looking down at me as we crossed the front lawn, "I think it's too cold for a walk. Let's go to my place instead."

"Your place?"

"You know, the guest house." His arrogance was astounding—using the phrase "my place" to describe a guest cottage that he had been invited to share with three other people for thirty-six hours.

"Great. Then I can return this sweater. One of the guys loaned it to me." Dropping the sweater off in Dante's room would buy me some time to figure out my strategy with Christian. After all, Dante was out somewhere with the scantily clad Jennifer. So he'd never know.

"That's fine, you won't be needing it anymore," Christian said assuredly.

We reached the porch of the guest house and he backed me up to the door and looked down at me.

"So, how happy are you to see me?"

"Thrilled," I said, feigning breathlessness and stifling a laugh. "But I am freezing!" I ducked under his arm and through the door. He followed me slowly, and I heard the click of the lock as he pulled the door shut behind him.

"Looks like we have the place to ourselves," he said. Suddenly, he wasn't smiling anymore. "So, Nikki. What were you doing in Ian's study earlier tonight, anyway?"

The expression on his face made my blood run cold. He had been watching me all along.

"I was looking for something to read myself to sleep," I said lightly. "But everything there just reminded me of work."

"Really? So then I guess eavesdropping outside Ian's door was just to help you sleep."

I smiled innocently. "I have no idea what you're talking about. I was playing with Ian's dog for a while, and I was just about to go to sleep when you came by." Maybe if I could keep him talking, he'd slip up and reveal something.

"If you say so." He crossed the floor and encircled my wrist in an iron grip. "But I'd be careful if I were you, Nikki. You know what they say. Curiosity killed the cat."

"Let go, Christian," I said calmly, ignoring my accelerating heart rate. "You're starting to hurt me." I realized with a sickening certainty that there was a familiar odor in the air. It was cloves. The scent of my attacker in Widener Library.

"Oh, come on, Nikki," he said evilly. "You like it rough, don't you?" His arm went around my waist, feeling like a steel bar, and I realized how physically powerless I was against him.

"Am I interrupting something?" a voice asked.

I sprang away from Christian as if I had been singed, and found Dante Rosario regarding us from the hallway.

"Yes, you are," Christian said smoothly. "I thought the lady and I were alone. Is there a problem?"

"The problem is that last time I checked, the lady was with me,"

Dante said, walking further into the room. "So why you have your hands on her requires some explanation."

The two of them regarded each other silently, and then Christian shrugged. "My mistake. Nikki, we'll talk again soon." Then he was gone.

"I. Am. Going. To. Kill you," I said, turning on Dante. My hands were trembling, but he didn't need to know that. "What the hell are you doing?"

"Let's see. Keeping you from getting attacked? Perhaps a thank-you is in order?"

"I had the situation under control, thank you very much. I could have talked my way out of it."

"He's a thug, Nik. You're in way over your head."

"And you're the big hero again. What a surprise."

"What the hell were you doing *alone* with him when you know he may be a killer? You know what you are?" he said, moving toward me.

"What?" I taunted from the safety of a good ten feet.

"Stubborn." The distance was closing between us. "Dangerously naive." I realized that I was quickly running out of space to back away from him. "And in need of a good spanking."

"You don't have it in you," I mocked, my back to the wall.

"Wanna bet?"

Just then, the door swung open again, and Michael Treger bounded through the door. The place was like Grand Central Station. "Hi, kids," he called as he passed through the living room. "Just getting a copy of my book. I met this guy at a bar who's a producer. He's on vacation from LA."

The spell was broken. I pulled away from Dante and shook myself. He stifled a groan as he watched me retreat.

"What's that in your pocket?" he asked, resignedly.

I looked down and saw the edge of the sheet I had faxed protruding from my shorts. I pulled it out, and sat down on the sofa. "You won't believe what I found tonight."

Michael Treger raced back through the living room and out the door, shouting goodnight as he went. I filled Dante in on the contents of Christian's briefcase.

"So where is the briefcase now?" he demanded.

"Right where I found it."

"I've got an idea," he said, standing up. "Come on."

Silently, we walked back to the main house, which seemed to be deserted, and slipped unnoticed back into Ian's study.

"What are we doing?" I whispered.

"Open the briefcase again, will you? But wipe it down for finger-prints afterward."

I complied while he rolled a sheet of paper into the typewriter that sat open on Ian's desk.

"What are you doing?" I hissed.

"Typing a ransom note."

He typed a few lines on the paper, and then pulled it out of the machine and handed it to me.

I've taken what is mine. Don't try to cross me again.

Reaching into the briefcase, he took out seven bundles of bills and left the note in their place.

"Now what?" I asked, as we slipped quietly out of the study and headed for the kitchen.

"We watch Chung like a hawk, starting tomorrow morning. Bet he checks the stash at least twice a day. After that, he'll be arrang-ing a meeting with someone. And when he does, we'll be there."

"Very clever, Rosario. I'm impressed."

"Just trying to keep up, Chase."

His intelligence was incredibly enticing, always had been.

"We're not done for the night," I said, forcing myself back to the task at hand. "Christian's got an accomplice; I heard him talking to the person tonight. We need to search the pool house, and the Bar-retts should be gone by now."

Indeed, the house appeared to be deserted as we let ourselves in the side door. Nice that all the doors in the compound were always unlocked. I pulled out my flashlight and shone it around. We were in a utility room that held a coat rack and assorted pairs of muddy shoes.

"Come on," I whispered to Dante. "Let's check out the living room."

A lamp gave off a soft glow, so I switched off my flashlight. As we moved into the room, which was filled with elaborate contemporary paintings and furnishings, I noticed a movie screen hanging from the ceiling near an aquarium filled with exotic fish.

"And they say that crime doesn't pay," Dante said, moving past a blue and white sofa and into the kitchen. "Where do you think Leo keeps *his* briefcase?"

"Probably not in the refrigerator," I teased. "What are you expecting to find in there?"

"This," he said, walking toward me holding up a small wooden box. "Torie once told me she keeps her jewels in the freezer in case of a robbery."

"Them WASPs, they sure is crazy," I muttered. I looked up to find his eyes on my face.

"So, how is Danielle?" I asked, apropos of nothing.

"She's history."

"Funny, I thought she was Biochem."

"Har-har." His eyes never left my face. "So the playing field is clear."

"That would explain your being up at bat with Jennifer, then," I said, turning away.

"A sports metaphor from you, Nik? I'm impressed."

"Yes, I'm obviously overdosing on testosterone tonight. Too much time with you and Christian."

"Then you should be able to interpret my attention to Jennifer as what it really is. A Hail Mary pass."

"Meaning?"

"A desperate, last-minute attempt to score before the game is over."

"With a teenaged, miniskirt-wearing cultural fascist?"

"No, Juliet. With *you*."

Oh.

"Let's look upstairs," I commanded, avoiding his amused expression.

There were three bedrooms on the second floor, and the Barretts had taken the largest for their own. It had a commanding king-sized bed, and two large windows overlooking the pool. I could see the faintest outline of the stone terrace from across the room.

"You take her bag, I'll take his," I said, not exactly sure what we were looking for. We rummaged in amiable silence for a few moments, and then Dante let out a low whistle.

"What?" I said excitedly.

"Torie must have some interesting hobbies." He held up what looked like a black leather whip, then a pair of chrome-plated handcuffs.

"Get out!" I breathed.

Just then, we heard hurried footsteps and shrieks of laughter downstairs.

"It's freezing out there!" Victoria Barrett was squealing.

"I've got the cure for that," said a deep male voice. It was the voice from the beauty parlor. And I realized now, it wasn't Leo's. "Come here, woman."

"You have to catch me first," Victoria taunted.

"Oh yeah?" the male voice countered. There was a rush of footsteps, and I realized that they had started up the stairs.

"Holy shit," I whispered to Dante. "That's *Ian!*"

The voices were rapidly getting louder.

"She must be crazy!" I hissed. "And where's Leo?"

Loud thumps echoed against the wall in the hallway. It was already too late to escape into another of the bedrooms.

"Stash that," Dante said hurriedly, motioning to Leo's bag. "We've gotta get out of here."

I stuffed Leo's possessions back in his bag, still dumbfounded.

"Okay, we've got two choices," Dante whispered urgently. "The closet or the window."

"Gotcha!" Ian cried. There was a loud slurpy scuffle on the landing outside the door.

"Slow down, darling," Victoria cooed. "What's the hurry?"

Suddenly, the window looked really good. "Let's go," I said.

"What do you have on under here?" Dante murmured. His hands ran along my back underneath my sweater.

"A T-shirt," I breathed.

"Perfect." In a smooth gesture, he lifted my sweater over my head. "Hold onto this," he said, then knelt quickly at my feet. I felt his hands slide along my legs to the laces of my boots. "When you hit the water, you'll be glad you're not wearing it. Or these boots. Kick them off as soon as we hit it."

"Oh!" squealed Victoria. I looked over my shoulder at the door.

"Sure you want to leave?" Dante whispered with a grin.

"Let's move it."

He took my hand, and we stepped out onto the window ledge. That pool looked a hell of a lot farther away now than it had from inside, and the wind was blowing ferociously.

"Ready?"

I shook my head. "Not really."

Then he pushed me.

I hit the pool hard, feeling the sting of the impact across my thighs and legs. The icy water closed in over my head, and I plummeted to the bottom. Frantically kicking off my boots in the darkness, I felt myself starting to rise. I surfaced with a mouthful of water, my sweater floating beside me and the chlorine stinging my eyes. It had probably taken all of fifteen seconds from start to finish.

A dark head emerged next to me, and I could just make out Dante from the light spilling through the pool house's upper windows.

"Sounded like someone fell in," Victoria's voice echoed down from the second-floor bedroom that we had recently vacated. She sounded worried. "Can you see anything?"

We treaded water quietly, hoping that we were out of their line of vision.

"Nothing. Too dark," Ian muttered.

"Maybe you should go down?" she asked tentatively.

"I'm sure it's nothing. And we don't have that much time."

We heard the sound of the window being pulled shut, and then nothing but the night sounds of crickets and singing insects and birds, and the insistent cries of the wind.

Silently, we swam to the shallow end of the pool. I climbed out shivering, my T-shirt clinging to me. Dante stood near the edge of the pool, his body silhouetted in the moonlight.

"We've got to get you warmed up," he said softly.

"I don't think that'll be necessary, *carino*."

I was already well past warm. My soggy sweater and boots slid from my hands.

A smile of recognition spread slowly across his face. "You haven't called me that for a very long time, Juliet."

And then he kissed me, finally, and it wasn't at all what I remembered. Eight years is plenty of time to forget how perfect a kiss can be: how simultaneously warm and cool, soft and hard, tempting and redeeming.

What followed was the inevitable result.

CAPITAL
OFFENSE

"Don't you agree, Veronica?"

Ian McAllister's voice abruptly snapped me out of my reverie. It was Saturday morning, and the Crimson Future Committee was arrayed around the dining room table of the main house of his Martha's Vineyard compound. We were trying to reach agreement on how Harvard should fill its projected funding gap over the next ten years. With the New Century press conference only ten days away, the group still couldn't agree on a set of recommendations.

"No, I don't," I said forcefully. "There are plenty of reasons for joint fund-raising among the different schools. For one thing, it would cut the costs of the development staff by over half."

I shot my comment in the direction of the bombastic Asif Zakaria to convince everyone that I had been paying attention. I had learned the hard way that the only way to gain respect with this crowd was never to let them see you equivocate or show mercy, even if you had no idea what you were talking about. Since Zakaria had been making the same comments about the impossibility of coordinating fund-raising efforts consistently for the past two hours, I was sure that he had been flogging the same dead horse again during my mental absence, and the look in Ian's eyes told me that I had hit the right target.

Zakaria frowned at me and launched into another lecture as the group expelled a silent collective sigh of frustration. Confident that Ian wouldn't cold-call me again, I returned to the solitude of my thoughts. My theory about Ella's having been murdered because she discovered an embezzlement scheme was looking good: Christian Chung was clearly up to something illegal, and now I just had to figure out who his accomplice was. *I know the telephone seems unnecessary, but we have to take precautions*, he had said last night. The remark had made it sound as if he were talking on the phone with someone whom he could have met just as easily in person. Which meant that his accomplice was at Ian's house right now. Which meant it could be Leo Barrett. Or Ian himself.

Having witnessed her midnight romp with Ian, I was now highly skeptical that Victoria Barrett had killed Ella in a fit of jealousy. It was perfectly conceivable that a flirtation with her husband's worst enemy was much sweeter revenge than killing his mistress could ever be. The repercussions were certainly less dire. The only possible penalty, other than losing Leo, was some diminution in her social standing amongst the Harvard elite. In her world, sleeping with the enemy was a capital offense.

The thing that had me really worried was the ominous absence of any package from *Partisan Review*. I'd called Maggie last night and that morning, but nothing had arrived, and all I'd gotten was voice mail when I called the archivist in New York.

None of my suspects had shown signs of having so many extracurricular activities under way when I saw them at breakfast earlier. Most of the group had drifted singly into the kitchen, and Ian had been among the first to arrive, glowing and ruddy from what he said was his morning run. Leo and Victoria came in a few minutes later, she as always leading the way. I watched her closely, but her demeanor revealed nothing except the spoiled petulance that was her trademark—no subdued silences, no furtive signs of guilt. Instead, in typical fashion, she imperiously ordered Leo to fetch her coffee and a croissant, and spent the rest of the meal gossiping with Bob Raines. Christian Chung hadn't shown up at all.

The sound of Dante's voice yanked me back into the conversation around the meeting table.

"When you're serious about balancing the budget, you should look into how fast costs are growing at some of the schools," he was saying.

What was he doing? I thought we had agreed to lie low until we figured out who Christian's accomplice was.

"What does that mean?" Ian McAllister said sharply. "The university has rigorous cost controls in place."

"It means that if you think about how many outside contractors and services we use when we already have a huge internal staff, it looks high," Dante said, leaning toward Ian. "At Stanford, they would never stand for this."

"I don't think that's fair, Dante," Leo interrupted firmly. His expression looked faintly ominous. Why was Dante pushing this so hard? It was as if he *wanted* the embezzler to know that he was on to them.

"That's right," Zakaria echoed close on Leo's heels. "We made a decision a few years ago to cut the permanent staff and outsource more. I believe our colleagues at the Business School told us that was the fiscally responsible thing to do."

"Sure," Dante said, shrugging, "it makes sense in theory. But if in practice the outsourcing costs keep rising, it becomes extremely inefficient."

"Are you really suggesting that this group focus on cost reduction instead of increasing our revenue stream?" Leo said abruptly, rubbing his temples. "Because I've already taken a number of steps to reduce costs, and I feel comfortable about where we are on that right now."

This wasn't good. If Leo was this defensive, he must have some reason for not wanting anyone digging any further into the expense categories.

"Help me out, Rona," Dante said, smiling at her in a way that got her to drop her notebook and rejoin the meeting. "Are these the expenses we should expect to see in an operation like ours?"

"Now that you mention it, they are a bit high," Rona said. "But not unreasonable," she quickly added, smiling at Leo.

Ian's mouth was settling into a grim line, and I felt him really noticing Dante for the first time. "Then unless anyone else feels strongly that we pursue it, I suggest we focus more on increasing alumni fund-raising, and less on dissecting minor expense items—notwithstanding what goes on in California. Don't you agree, Leo?" There was ice in his voice.

Barrett nodded firmly. "Yes. Shall we move on?"

Dante paused for a moment, his eyes locked with Leo's. Then he shrugged casually, surrendering the field. The meeting resumed with Zakaria repeating his line of argument, in case any of us had missed it the first five times. I felt my heart breaking. Could either Leo or Ian really be party to Christian's crimes? It seemed unthinkable. And since when did the two of them agree on *anything*?

At twelve-thirty, we stopped for a lunch break. Christian Chung made an appearance, and I shadowed him as well as I could, given that the entire group was swarming back and forth between the kitchen and the pool. Had he found our note yet? His face was impassive, but he moved rapidly through the group until he spotted Leo Barrett leaning against one of the kitchen counters. Just as I drew within eavesdropping distance, he took Leo's arm and turned him away. Christian began whispering into Leo's ear, and their expressions turned stormy. Then they retreated to a corner of the room, still talking furiously.

A few minutes later, Christian walked off toward the guest house alone, and Leo wandered off to the pool and sat at the foot of Victoria's chaise lounge. Meanwhile, Ian spent the first part of the break on the kitchen telephone, loudly discussing his quarterly tax return. Then he selected a plateful of sandwiches and struck up a conversation with Jennifer Blum by the pool. I surrendered the chase and retreated to the kitchen. I had no appetite whatsoever, but the kitchen window allowed me to watch the group by the pool unobserved.

I picked idly at a turkey sandwich, tearing off small bites. Maxwell Friend, my newfound canine pal, waited impatiently at my feet, hoping for leftovers.

"Come on, Veronica, don't be such a tease. He knows you'll give in to him in the end, so why prolong it?" The sound of Dante Rosario's voice sent the sandwich spiraling out of my fingers and into Max's waiting jaws.

"So then what's the rush?" I was trying to sound flippant, but the lump in my throat was making it nearly impossible.

"Because even a dog deserves to retain his dignity." He rapidly crossed the kitchen floor and reached for a coffee cup from one of the cabinets next to me.

"Look, I said I was sorry about last night."

"Just because you pulled away and ran off into the night in mid-kiss? Don't apologize. It's a woman's prerogative to change her mind."

He sounded completely indifferent, which of course incensed me.

"You think I did it just to even the score, don't you?"

"Probably. By the way, if your objective was to inflict maximum pain, you succeeded."

"Well, it wasn't. I just realized that we were both on an adrenaline high, too caught up in the moment to think straight."

"Funny, I recall a time when you enjoyed being swept away."

"Well, now I don't."

"Obviously." His tone couldn't have been more polite and distant.

"Look, how do I know that you're not just playing Gauguin here?" I baited, determined to get a reaction. "Alfresco sex with a black woman as an antidote to white middle-class ennui. Can it be pure coincidence that eight years after you walked out on me, we're once again kissing in some dark corner while you're flirting with a steady stream of white girls in public?"

He set his coffee cup down hard. "That's the second time in a week that you've accused me of being a bigot, Veronica."

"And you still haven't proved me wrong."

"*You* constantly bring up race, but *I'm* the bigot." He laughed mockingly. "Did it ever occur to you that you weren't exactly the girl I was dreaming about my whole life, and that maybe race had nothing to do with it?" He took my arm as I turned angrily away. "No. You've got to hear this, Nik. Being black is not the only thing that defines you, you know. You're also brilliant, and stubborn, and incredibly demanding and ambitious. And that's a hell of a lot to sign up for at age twenty-two."

"Fine. So I'm not Francesca," I snapped, pulling away from him. He looked at me quizzically. "That stupid painting on your wall! I'm not sitting in a dark corner in a castle somewhere, waiting for you to swim across the moat and save me. And you're right. It's not just race keeping us apart. Because if you *were* black, I'd *still* detest you!"

"Sure about that?"

"There must be—I don't know—at least fifty-nine reasons that I can't stand you, and the fact that you won't be seen in public with a black woman is just the primary one."

He regarded me sardonically. "Fifty-nine reasons, and you *still* can't stay away."

"That will be changing, effective immediately."

"I doubt it," his voice echoed after me as I headed for the door. "I was there for that kiss, remember?"

Before the lunch break ended, I called the hospital to check on Justin Simms, then phoned Maggie again. My package still hadn't arrived, but she had spoken with her sister, Patrice, in

246 • PAMELA THOMAS-GRAHAM

Philadelphia. Patrice had never heard of Rev. Stephen Barrett or of St. Thomas Episcopal, but she had promised to ask around. She ran a beauty shop, and Saturday would be the perfect day to gather information, since the shop would be full of folks who might know something. Next, I called Rafe to see what he made of my late-night fax. He picked up on the first ring, and I quickly filled him in on the prior night's adventures.

He listened without interrupting, then asked me one question. "You seem to be thinkin' that Leo Barrett is most likely the accomplice. Why him?"

"Rafe, he's been acting strangely ever since Ella died. His wife is obsessed with money and is about to leave him. And he's constantly whispering in Christian's ear."

"What about Ian McAllister?"

"I considered that for about two seconds, but—"

"Listen, child, how close were he and Ella Fisher?"

"Not very. Why?"

"That's what I thought."

"What's going on, Rafe?"

He lowered his voice. "I'm only telling you this so you'll watch your back out there. We've gotten the telephone records for all calls from Littauer Center made by a few folks. Just to check out their stories. That McAllister had told us he was not close to Miss Fisher, that he only spoke to her at the committee meetings. But the man called her home regularly in the past four weeks. He called her office three times the day she died."

Three times?

I was still convinced that Christian's accomplice was under Ian's roof. But perhaps it wasn't Leo after all.

O ver a buffet dinner beside the pool, Ian announced that the evening's entertainment was to be a game of paintball on the grounds of the compound.

"It should be an important team-building exercise," Ian said to a chorus of groans from the committee.

"What's paintball?" Asif Zakaria asked, looking dubious.

"We divide into two teams, each of which is assigned a territory to defend. And our weapons are guns that spray paint."

"Really, Ian, this is too much," Rona Seidman snapped. "You don't expect me to run around in the woods like a child for the next three hours, do you? Isn't that a good way to get Lyme disease?"

"A little exercise might do you some good," Ian muttered *sotto voce*. "You'll enjoy this, Rona," he said briskly, at normal volume. "In fact, I'm making you the leader of the Blue Team."

Jennifer Blum, who had previously been draped languorously over a chaise lounge, sat up and regarded her polished fingernails with some dismay. "You think they'll give us gloves?" she whispered to Tony.

"I think it's a fabulous idea," Victoria proclaimed from the buffet table. "It sounds so primitive, so invigorating."

"Well, sure," Jennifer muttered. "You've been laying around all day anyway."

I shared Rona's frustration. I had been planning to have a snoop in Ian's study and bedroom, then make another run at Christian Chung.

But Ian was announcing the teams and ordering us to pick up our gear outside the pool house. Rona's Blue Team would consist of Malcolm, Michael, Victoria, Dante, Jennifer, and Christian. Bob Raines would lead the Red Team of Leo, Ian, Tony, Roberta, David, and me. "The winning team gets the rest of the night off," Ian said jovially. "Losers have to meet for another two hours this evening."

We filed obediently past the pool house and were handed a bag of warrior gear, and then retreated to our rooms to change.

I opened my bag and grimaced. This was obviously someone's wartime fantasy: inside was a heavy cotton jumpsuit in camouflage green and brown; a pair of fingerless black leather gloves; black elastic kneepads; a red bandanna to signify my team affiliation; and a huge face mask with a tag proclaiming it the "Intruder System, with reinforced ear protector joints, a panoramic lens, and a 5-lug retention system providing full face protection." What the hell were we going to be doing out there anyway?

Slipping on the jumpsuit, I gingerly laced up my Timberlands. This little game was starting to give me the creeps. Leave it to a Republican to spend his leisure hours playing at war.

I tucked the helmet under my arm and started for the pool house, where we'd been told to pick up our guns. Victoria Barrett was already there, squealing loudly as a dark-haired young man, presumably someone from the company that was providing the gear, tried to show her how to shoot the wood-handled rifle in her hand.

"Oh, don't you worry," she said coquettishly, "I know my way around a gun." She hefted it to her shoulder and aimed it—almost like a professional—out across the lawn. In seconds, a brilliant stream of blue paint splattered out of her gun, accompanied by a series of sharp reports that sounded like real gunfire to my untrained ear.

"Using a gun like this is cheating," Victoria said, swinging the rifle back to her side. "How can you miss when it has a rapid-fire trigger?" The young man was looking at her in admiration. "Give me a good old-fashioned twelve-gauge any day. What's in this bottle, anyway?" Victoria gestured to a small green plastic bottle attached to the gun's stock.

"CO2," the man said. "It's what propels the paint out of the gun."

"Torie, you look like Annie Oakley," Dante drawled from behind us. She turned to him, eyes sparkling. "Where'd you learn to shoot like that?" he asked, advancing on her.

"Daddy and I used to shoot skeet at the club," she said, laying her hand on his arm. "But I'm sure a man like you knows how to handle a gun. Didn't you grow up in the city?"

I rolled my eyes but continued to watch as Dante took the rifle from Victoria and raised it easily to his shoulder. "City kids don't use shotguns like you blue-bloods," he said, taking aim at the lawn. "But we adapt pretty easily." He lowered the gun without firing.

"Jesus," Michael Treger muttered behind me, "is this what WASPs do for fun?" He tied his blue bandanna around his neck, and looked cheerfully at the red one tied through my belt loop. "Great, we're on opposite teams. What say we shoot each other as soon as possible and then hit a bar in Edgartown? You and the boyfriend must have better things than this to do."

I shook my head, laughing. "He's *not* my boyfriend. And please, don't shoot me. I want to see this little drama unfold. But I'll be happy to put you out of your misery as soon as possible." Giving me a thumbs-up, Treger went to pick up his rifle.

"*Oy vey*," Rona moaned as she and I were handed our weapons. "Why did he make me the captain? That means I have to schlepp this thing around all night!"

"Chin up," I murmured. "Maybe we'll all kill each other off early and then we can relax the rest of the evening."

Dante strode purposefully toward me and took my arm as I started to turn away.

"Listen," he said quietly. "I think we should arrange a rendezvous."

"Are you kidding? I already told you—"

"This has nothing to do with romance, Veronica," he cut me off sharply. "It's for your protection."

"Why do I need protection?" I hissed. "This is just a silly game."

"You're going off into a dark forest with a bunch of people carrying guns when you know there's been a murder, an attempted murder, and someone has stalked you and mugged you, and you're asking me why you might need protection?"

"All right, all right," I assented quickly. We were in the midst of the group, and I didn't want anyone to hear us arguing. "What's the plan?"

"You know the clearing on the right side of the road that leads up to the compound? The one right by the neighbor's driveway? Meet me there at nine o'clock."

"Gee, shall we synchronize our watches?"

"Just watch your back." He started to walk away, then briefly turned back. "Oh. One other thing."

Before I could stop him, he kissed me full on the lips for ten seconds longer than anyone would have considered appropriate for public consumption.

"One down, fifty-eight to go," he said with a grin.

The rest of the group observed this exchange with varying degrees of puzzlement, interest and alarm.

"Really, Dante!" Victoria took his arm as he turned away. "I see you've been busy since you returned. What happened to the one you brought to dinner last week? She had such beautiful blond hair."

A few moments later, the teams assembled in their respective corners of the driveway while Ian reviewed the rules of the game.

"The Blue Team takes the territory to the west of the road, and the Red Team takes the east. The objective is to capture the other side's flag"—he waved two white squares of fabric over his head—"and bring it out of enemy territory. But if you get hit by enemy fire, you're out of the game. Got it?"

Everyone nodded and began pulling on helmets and slinging on rifles. We definitely looked like a supply of fresh meat shipping out for Saigon. My sense of foreboding had been growing after Dante's warning, but the mood of the group caused mine to lighten. Rona needed help with her mask and then complained she couldn't breathe; Tony shot himself in the foot as we were marching out of the driveway; and Roberta had a brief but lively discussion with Ian about the political implications of adults shooting at each other, even in jest, given the state of crime in our inner cities.

We fanned out over the territory designated as the Red Team's, following Ian's orders. The more reluctant in the group had been given "defensive" positions: all they had to do was stand near the "border" and shoot at anything that came across. The more adventurous, which included Ian, Raines, Leo, and me, had been assigned offense. We were to sneak across the border and go after the flag, so the four of us peeled off into the quickly falling darkness.

I knew the basic rules of engagement from my Girl Scout days: stay low to the ground, move slowly but steadily, and fear nothing. To which Ian had added a fourth as he slipped away: keep your trigger cocked.

Leo and I had been assigned to travel as a pair, and despite my suspicions about him, I found his company soothing as we scouted the border for a crossing. We had known each other for a long time, and up close it seemed impossible that he could be anything other than the intelligent, engaging man I had always known.

"This reminds me of ROTC," he said softly as we waited in a clump of bushes near the road for darkness to fall. "See, look, there's someone in the brush right there."

I could make out a faint ray of light moving back and forth in a small patch of bushes across the road. "What is that?" I whispered.

"Cigarette," Leo whispered back. "Probably Treger, trying to get shot."

We moved a few feet down the road, and then decided to make a run for the border. "Remember," he cautioned. "Once you're out in the open, you have to *move*. I'll be right behind you." His enthusiasm was infectious. I actually wanted to win this game.

We burst out of the brush and into the open night air. I tried to run, but the bulky gun and helmet reduced me to a gawky lope. Still, we made it to the other side of the road, and disappeared behind a tree. Safe in enemy territory.

"Stay here," Leo murmured. "I'll be right back." He crept off through the woods, and I listened for noises. Unfortunately, the woods were full of them: chirping cicadas, frogs, the whine of mosquitoes. I waved insects away from my face, breathed in the green scent of the forest, and waited.

Suddenly, I heard the crack of gunfire and a loud shout, and a chill went down my spine. Had I already lost Leo?

I waited for a few moments, forcing myself to count to sixty. If he didn't return by then, I would press on alone. Just as I was about to start moving, I heard muffled rustling in the woods, and then heard a voice say "Massachusetts."

"Leo," I said happily. That was our code word. "What happened?"

"I fragged Treger," he said cheerfully. "The guy wanted out, so I shot him and sent him on his way."

"Did you torture him until he told you where the flag was?"

"Nikki, that wouldn't be sporting," Leo said. "Come on."

We clambered through the woods, sometimes hand in hand when the brush got thick. It was growing darker, and the forest was starting to feel like it was pressing in on us. We stopped to rest at a log beside a small dirt path. I had no idea where we were.

Leo sighed reflectively. "This brings back memories. Although the boys in ROTC weren't nearly as charming as you. Why don't we take off these ridiculous masks?"

I smiled as my face emerged from the heavy face mask. "You sound like you miss it."

"I miss having things be that simple," he said. Now that I could see his face, I saw how deeply weary he looked. "Climb the rope. Hike through a swamp. Home in time for dinner. Simple."

"You need a break, Leo," I said. "Why don't you take some time off?"

"What I need is someone to talk to," he said softly. "I had someone, but now she's gone." Ella's name remained unspoken between us. "God, the things I've done," he muttered abruptly. Anguish tinged his voice.

I squeezed his arm in sympathy.

"I still remember the first time I met you, Nikki," he whispered, almost to himself.

"Where were we? Your office in Langdell, right?" I said, encouraging him to go on.

"You came to me with a proposal that we write an article together. I didn't have the heart to tell you that it really wasn't my area of interest, because when you walked into my office you seemed so smart, and so cute"—he laughed to himself—"you looked exactly like—like someone I was close to a long time ago." He was talking to me, but not really. "Do you find it hard?" he asked abruptly.

"Do I find *what* hard?"

"Being black. At Harvard. I mean, Ella seemed to thrive on the controversy, but it must be unbearable sometimes."

"You get used to it," I said, a bit puzzled. "It's no worse than other places, and better than some. I mean, it's not like you have any choice, so you get used to it," I repeated.

"I just finished re-reading a book by Andrew Hacker. He asked his white students what he'd have to pay them to agree to be born black in this country, and you know what they said? A million dollars." He shook his head. "Please don't hate me, Nikki, if you hear later that I—"

"If I hear what, Leo?" I prompted gently as he fell silent.

"I just wanted to define my own existence, not have it defined for me. But I was a fool. It's not possible."

Just then, the wind bore a pair of voices toward us. It sounded like two people were making their way down the narrow path in our direction.

"Get down," Leo said quietly. We lay down in the grass a few feet away from our log, listening and waiting.

The voices turned out to be Ian McAllister and Victoria Barrett. They were walking slowly, helmets off, deep in conversation.

"I don't think it will work," Victoria was saying in a troubled voice. "You've got to get—"

"McAllister!" Leo sprang to his feet before I could react. "Fancy meeting you here with my wife."

"Hello, Leo," Victoria said, sounding faintly annoyed.

I heard the spray of paintgun fire and then Ian protesting loudly.

"How unsporting, Barrett! You didn't even give me time to aim!"

"Sorry. All's fair in love and war. But then, you knew that, didn't you, McAllister?"

I would've killed to see their expressions, to see if Leo actually knew that the two of them were lovers.

There was another round of splattering, then an eerie silence.

"So, Torie," Leo said quietly, "we seem to have killed each other."

"Well." Her brittle laugh broke the stillness. "Then we're all corpses. A fittingly tragic end, just like *Hamlet*." She paused. "Let's have a martini by the pool before Fortinbras arrives to claim the kingdom, shall we?"

That woman was one cold bitch. Her husband discovers her in a darkened forest cozying up to his archrival, and she wasn't the least bit fazed.

I looked at my watch, considering surrender so that I could join them. Eight-thirty. Might as well stick it out until it was time to meet Dante at nine. I crept forward slowly, missing Leo's companionship as the forest hemmed in on me. What had he been trying to say to me? The mask made it hard to breathe, and I finally pulled it off and tucked it under my arm.

Freed from that constraint, I moved more quickly. After what seemed like an eon, I broke out of the woods and onto the main road. In the distance, I could see the lights of a house. Ian's neighbors. The glow from the single streetlight on the road illuminated my path.

"Rosario!" I called. "Are you there?"

"Nik?" I couldn't see him, but his voice sounded nearby.

Just then I heard the crunch of tires on the road behind me, and the roar of an engine accelerating. A pair of bright lights swung around a bend in the road, and suddenly a large truck was racing toward me.

As I recalled it later, everything seemed to happen very slowly. The truck drew closer and closer, so close that I could feel the heat of the engine radiating across my back. Then something hurtled into me, and I felt myself flying through the air and landing hard on my side in the brush by the side of the road. Seconds later, a heavy object landed on me. The left side of my face felt as if it were on fire, I had no feeling in my right leg, and I was pinned beneath some heavy weight. Slowly, I opened my eyes and found Dante Rosario's face inches from mine. He was lying right on top of me.

"Jesus Christ," I breathed.

"Not yet, Juliet, it's only me," he said slowly. His voice sounded as if were coming from a long distance.

"What happened?" I sat up sluggishly, fighting the wave of dizziness that flooded over me.

"That truck was trying to run you over, and I—" Dante's voice trailed off. He seemed to be in as much shock as I was.

"You saved my life," I whispered. My head was finally clearing, and I was starting to make sense of it. That truck was heading straight for me. And Dante pushed me out of the way. "You just saved my life," I repeated slowly. "Are you all right?"

He was clearly as shocked as I was. He was staring at me as if he were really seeing me for the first time.

"This is serious," he said gravely. Both of us understood that he wasn't referring to the accident.

"What happened?" a voice called out. Ian McAllister was walking down the road from the main house, shining a flashlight. "It sounded like someone ran off the road."

"These damned teenagers!" he exclaimed after we explained what had happened. "They joyride around drunk, and almost kill someone."

Dante's eyes met mine briefly. Neither one of us believed that Edgartown teenagers were behind this incident. Clearly, we'd overplayed our hand by stealing that cash.

Because this smacked of payback.

CHAPTER TWENTY

THE
WRONG MAN

"Harvard! I knew you'd come. What took you so long?" Isaiah Fisher called out from the lower bunk of his cell.

He sounded damned happy, for an accused murderer.

He cheerfully waved a cigarette at me as I hobbled down the darkened hallway of the Cambridge Police Station. It was eleven o'clock Sunday morning and I'd been back from Martha's Vineyard for less than an hour. I hadn't even made it home yet; Fisher's call had intercepted me at Littauer, where the Crimson Future Committee van had dropped us all off.

"What's with the cane, Harvard?"

I looked down at my sprained ankle. "Let's just say I had a close encounter with a pickup truck last night. I hope I wasn't your one phone call."

"Naw, I've got some raggedy public defender who negotiated phone privileges for me. Listen," he said, moving closer to the bars, "you've got to talk to that pseudo-black cop that you run with. Griffin."

"Why? You havin' trouble bullshitting him yourself, Ike?" Alix Coyle's voice echoed behind me down the dark hallway.

"Damn, what'd you bring that cracker for?" Fisher snapped. To my surprise, he actually sounded frightened.

"I figured it was time to cut to the chase."

"That's right," Alix said with a smirk as she joined me in front of his cell. "Because the truth shall set you free, Ike."

"I've got nothing to say to you," he snapped, turning away. "Get the hell out of here."

"Fine. I got a room full of cops upstairs just waitin' to hear all about you," Alix replied coolly.

"You don't have the balls. And if I go down, you're coming with me."

"Come on, Fisher," I said sharply. "You called me down here. So spill it."

"I'll talk to you, Harvard. But Trailer Park's got to go."

"Fine." I shrugged. "Then we're outta here."

"Hold up," he muttered as we turned away. "Okay, okay."

I looked at him, then at Alix. I was bluffing like hell, unsure of what either one of them really knew about Ella's death. But it seemed to be working.

"These white cops have the wrong man. You know why they decided to frame me for Ella's murder, right? Because I'm some powerless black man. They think they can lock me in here for all eternity and no one's gonna notice. And that Uncle Tom cop friend of yours is worse than the rest of 'em."

"They've got proof that you were blackmailing Ella," I said. Rafe had filled me in on that much when I'd seen him upstairs at the jail.

"Yeah, they said they found an uncashed check from her in your underwear drawer. You're a real genius, Ike." Alix lit a Marlboro and glared at him.

"Look, Blondie, if I tell them what really happened, you'll be in a hell of a lot more trouble than me."

I held my tongue. That was the part the cops couldn't figure out. What did Fisher have on Ella that made her willing to pay him thousands of dollars to keep it buried?

"That's where you're wrong," Alix said calmly. " 'Cause I've decided to tell them myself. I figure no jury's gonna convict me." She took a drag on her cigarette, then looked straight at me. "You've been lookin' for a murderer all this time, Miss Detective? Well, you got her."

The cell fell as silent as a tomb while they both looked at me.

"What are you talking about, Alix?" I said quietly.

"You know old Bud?"

"Your ex-husband?"

"That's right. My ex. Except I'm not a divorcée. I'm a widow. Ella and I killed him."

"You heard that, right?" Fisher prodded. "You heard that. And I'm the one behind bars."

Alix's eyes never left my face as she talked. "When Bud and I were married, I used to walk into a lot of doors," she said matter-of-factly. "And fall down the stairs a lot. That's what we used to tell people."

"He beat you."

"Beat the shit out of me. Just for lookin' at him wrong. I took off from Muleshoe and came up here to get away from him. But the son of a bitch followed me." She dropped her cigarette butt on the floor and stubbed it out with her toe. "Ella and I were good friends by then, and she got one of her Law School buddies to get me a restraining order. But evidently old Bud couldn't read. Because he broke down the back door of my house one night. Ella and I came home together, because she had attended my performance that evening at the ART. She came inside with me to get a CD I'd borrowed from her. And Bud was waitin' in the dark. With a kitchen knife."

"Jesus Christ." I prompted her gently as she fell silent. "So you fought him."

"Yeah. But he damn near killed me. And he would have if Ella hadn't knocked him out dead, first. With an iron skillet across the back of his head."

"But that's self-defense."

"You could say that." She looked at the floor as though there was more to the story.

"You didn't take the rap for that?" I pressed. "It sounds like it was clearly self-defense."

"Not exactly," Fisher interjected. "Tell her, Saltine."

"Shut up, Ike," Alix flared. She turned to me. "There were no charges. Because nobody told the police."

"What?"

"Look. It *was* self-defense. She wasn't tryin' to kill him. She just grabbed the heaviest thing she saw and swung it at him. But how'd we know if the police would see it that way? We didn't know, and we couldn't risk it. We were scared shitless. How could we be sure that these Irish cops up here were going to take the word of two Southern folk, one of 'em black?"

"So what did you do?"

"Well, to begin with, we didn't think he was dead when she hit him. We figured he was just out cold, and we didn't want him wakin' up in my house with a lump on his head. So we put him in the backseat of Ella's car and drove over to South Boston. To the docks. And we dumped him there—we figured he'd wake up down there with the wharf rats, thinkin' that he'd just had another wild night. And maybe he'd just wander on out of town."

Her expression went cold. "But he never did."

"How do you know that?"

"Because a few days later we read about a dead John Doe found by the waterfront. Fittin' Bud's description. They finally ID'd him and then they called to inform me, as his next of kin."

"Did they ask you when you had last seen him?"

"Sure, sure they did. Police procedure and all."

"So what did you do?"

Alix looked down. "What *could* we do? We were scared to death, we hadn't thought he was dead. And it *was* self-defense. Ella really wanted to tell them. She said she wasn't afraid to take the consequences. But I was. I begged her to keep quiet. So we kept our mouths shut."

They kept their mouths shut.

Somehow, it seemed to me that justice had been done. A violent wife abuser had received his just deserts, and Alix looked as if she had been punishing herself all these years far worse than the police could ever do. Although I could see where they might not see it that way.

"Our mistake was taking Bud in Ella's car when we dumped him," she finished. "The genius over here figured something was up when he saw the bloodstains in the backseat before we cleaned it up."

"So you knew Fisher was blackmailing Ella over this when you showed me her checkbook that night at her house?"

"I didn't know for sure. But I knew you'd get the information to the right people. And here we are."

"Look, *I'm* not the one who killed her," Isaiah interjected.

"You've got no alibi, you've got a motive. Why should anyone believe you?" I challenged.

"And you sent that thug to attack me that night, didn't you, Ike?" Alix taunted. "To scare me into keepin' my mouth shut."

I remembered thinking that the mugger knew too much about Alix. He had called her "showgirl." Fisher's face confirmed that it was true.

"Look, I had no motive for killing old girl," he shouted. "She was paying me, wasn't she? And I'd have another five thousand bucks by now if she were alive. Come on, Harvard, you're smart enough to figure this out. Why would I cut off my own income?"

"Maybe she was about to report you to the police," I said sharply.

Alix shook her head imperceptibly.

Fisher certainly had the opportunity to kill Ella. His alibi had fallen apart after our visit to Finn McCoy's, and he could have snuck into Littauer that night and shoved her down the stairs. But he was right. His motive was to keep her alive and paying for all the betrayals he imagined he'd suffered at her hands. Besides, he couldn't have been the one who tried to run me over on Martha's Vineyard—he had spent the night in this cell.

"Fine," I concluded. "I'll talk to Rafe. I'll tell him he's got the wrong man."

"I knew you had my back, Harvard."

"Don't go getting all misty on me, Fisher," I snapped. I was still reeling from Alix's story. "Don't you have any shame?"

"What do I have to be ashamed of? Ella betrayed me, she betrayed the race, she had all this money and power from working for Mr. Charlie and I had nothing. A few ducats was the least she could give me in return for what she took."

I stared at him. "Not only are you a low-class crook, you're an intellectual hypocrite."

"Right. The Harvard Oreo is calling *me* a hypocrite."

"Hey, when a man who claims to be down with black folks blackmails his ex-wife for saving another woman's life, then uses the money to run around with a dim-witted blonde, I call that hypocrisy, brother man."

Fisher stared at me defiantly.

"Have a nice stay," I said coldly.

"So who really killed her?" Fisher called after us. Alix looked at me expectantly.

"I'm going to figure that out right now," I called over my shoulder.

"Then you better wait up, Angie Dickinson," he goaded.

"Why?" We kept walking.

"You ever wonder why Ella and Leo Barrett were so close?"

"Look." I turned to him, exasperated. "If you've got something to say, just say it."

"You're so damned smart, Harvard," he taunted. "I'm sure you'll figure it out."

ALL WRITE NOW

Isaiah Fisher's unexpected phone call had thrown me temporarily off schedule, but now the plans that I had made Saturday during a late-night phone call from the Vineyard were about to be set in motion. I was certain that I was finally on the verge of exposing Ella's murderer. I just needed a little help from Jess.

"Okay, it's ringing. You remember what to say, right?"

Jess nodded at me. "I've got it. Now, hush up."

A male voice answered the telephone. "Chung here."

"Hello, is this Christian Chung, the university comptroller?" Jess asked in her best brisk professional voice.

"Yes." He sounded impatient.

"I'm so sorry to call on a Sunday, but I see I've caught you in your office, anyway. I was hoping that we could discuss an urgent matter that has come to my attention."

"Who is this?"

"Forgive me, Mr. Chung. I'm quite upset, and I've forgotten my manners. This is Evelyn Harcourt. I'm the CEO of All Write Secretarial Services."

There was a long pause on the line. "How soon can you meet me, Ms. Harcourt?"

Ten minutes later, I was planted in the hallway outside Christian Chung's office in University Hall. From my vantage point, I could hear him striding around. It sounded as if he was cursing to himself.

"Hello, Mr. Chung?" Jess knocked lightly on his office door moments later, studiously avoiding looking over her shoulder at me. She was wearing the navy blue pinstriped suit and white blouse that she wore for department meetings at the hospital, and she looked every bit the confident businesswoman.

"Ms. Harcourt," Christian called. "Come in. How can I help you?"

262 • PAMELA THOMAS-GRAHAM

Jess disappeared through the door, and I crept closer.

"Well, I was hoping to get your help on these." I could hear the smart rap of her briefcase as she laid it down on what I assumed was his conference table. I moved closer to the door, unable to contain my curiosity. Through a crack in the hinges, I could see Jess open her briefcase and hand Christian a sheaf of papers.

As his eyes scanned the pages, his jaw tightened.

"I'm afraid I don't understand," he said coolly.

He was good.

The papers were a batch of invoices issued by the All Write Secretarial Service to the Harvard Economics Department. Invoices totaling $75,000 that Christian would never have seen or approved. What he didn't know was that Jess and I had created them on her laptop a half hour before she called him.

"These came to my attention because I got a telephone call from someone in your office saying that the payment on them would be slightly delayed. I believe he said his name was Mr. Gibbs."

Back when I started to suspect embezzlement, I had asked Rafe to get me the names of all of Christian's direct reports in the comptroller's office. Gibbs was responsible for cutting all checks over $25,000, and it was perfectly believable that if these were real invoices he would have seen them and needed to approve them.

"Yes, Gibbs works for me." I wished I were standing closer to Christian so I could be sure. But I could swear beads of sweat were forming on his forehead.

"I apologize for the delay," he continued, "but every now and then the university experiences cash flow constraints—"

"No, no, you don't understand," Jess interrupted impatiently. "My company never did any work for the university."

"You've lost me, Ms. Harcourt. If that's true, then why are there invoices on your company's letterhead in our accounts receivable?" Christian leaned casually on the edge of his desk, smiling quizzically.

"Well, apparently someone has been billing Harvard and using my company's name."

He watched her silently as she grew more animated.

"You see, once I received his call, I asked Mr. Gibbs to go back and see how many invoices had been paid to All Write Secretarial Services. And he said there were three years' worth, totaling almost two million dollars."

"That's not possible," Christian said in his most authoritative tone. "You must be confused. My office would catch an error like that. Maybe not right away. But certainly over the course of three years."

"See," she said, shaking her head, "that's what Mr. Gibbs said, too. He said I should talk to Professor McAllister, since the invoices came to his department, and then the professor said I really had to talk to you."

"Talk to *me*? Why?"

"The professor said I should ask you to explain why the records indicate that my company has been paid over two million dollars, yet we've never done any work with Harvard. He said it was impossible that you wouldn't know, since you perform all the audits. He's terribly upset that this has happened on his watch, but it's not as if he would have any reason to know the invoices issued were forgeries. He said I should call the police, too, but I wanted to speak with you first."

"That bastard," he muttered furiously, so softly that I could barely hear it.

"What did you say, Mr. Chung?" Jess said innocently.

It had taken me the better part of the night to piece it all together, and I still hadn't been sure until that moment whether it was Leo or Ian who was Christian's accomplice. Plenty of clues had pointed to Leo: there was the conversation that Dante and I had overheard in the men's room, where he had clearly acted as if he had something to hide. There was the fact that he had overheard at the President's Open House that I had Ella's disk, and then I was mugged three hours later. There was the fact that his wife was desperate for money. And also incriminating was the fact that he and Christian were together constantly—Leo was the first person Christian went to after he discovered the missing cash Dante and I had taken on Martha's Vineyard.

But somehow the case against Ian McAllister had seemed more compelling. He and Christian had both lied to me at the Fogg party about the outside services expenditures in FAS being reclassified into the comptroller's budget. And he had called Ella three times at her office the day she died. That was pretty damning evidence. But what sealed it was my gut instinct that embezzlement was a crime perfectly tailored to Ian McAllister's personal style: covert, cerebral, and incredibly lucrative.

264 • Pamela Thomas-Graham

"McAllister said you should talk to me?" Christian's voice was rising, and he sounded furious. "That's laughable, the son of a bitch."

He was starting to sound out of control. Time to send him over the edge.

"Christian, I need to talk to you," I said, hobbling through the door. "I just spoke with Ian McAllister and he told me the most incredible story about you. Oh, I'm sorry, am I interrupting something? Hi, I'm Nikki Chase." I extended my hand to Jess.

"What are you doing here?" he snapped. "What did McAllister say to you?" Jess determinedly maintained an air of bemusement.

"Well, we were working on the final Crimson Future report, and I told him that as I was analyzing on the university financials last week, I came across a discrepancy of about two million dollars in the FAS budget."

Christian's eyes narrowed.

"Anyway, he's awfully upset. I think you'd better call him. I'm really sorry to have interrupted your meeting." I glanced over at Jess.

"Mr. Chung, it sounds like you may be in a bit of trouble," she said regretfully.

We were definitely getting to him. His eyes were glittering with rage.

"What did McAllister say?" he said, his voice shaking.

"As I said, he was pretty upset by the time we got to the police station," I replied.

"What?" Christian exploded.

"Well, he insisted on going there, after I showed him the discrepancy I found between Ella Fisher's spreadsheets and the ones you gave him. How your set disguised the fact that there's been an embezzlement going on within FAS for over three years. And how Ella figured it out."

"You don't know what you're talking about."

"He said you created a fake temporary secretarial agency and then charged Harvard for phantom services performed, using false names and Social Security numbers. That you've been storing the cash until you can fly it out of the country. And that you killed Ella Fisher once she figured it out."

"Killed?" Jess interjected. "What's going on here, Mr. Chung?"

"Hey! *I* didn't kill her," he shouted. "That son of a bitch isn't pinning *that* on me."

I had suspected it for two days. But hearing him say it still jolted me. Ian McAllister had killed Ella. All the time he was smiling in my face, playing the Harvard power game, he had murdered her. I swallowed hard and kept talking.

"But he's right about the rest of it, isn't he?"

"Yes and no," he said coldly. He seemed to have regained his preternatural composure. "I could tell you the whole story. But then I'd have to kill you." He wasn't smiling.

"Mr. Chung!" Jess exclaimed. She knew what he was capable of. That's why there were two of us for this gig.

Christian's eyes locked with mine, and I watched the truth sink in. *Game over, baby.*

He shrugged slightly, and reached for the phone.

"Get out of my office. I'm calling my lawyer," he said calmly. "And I suppose you have another stop to make."

The third Monday of the semester is always the day that Ian McAllister serves as a guest lecturer to all nine hundred Ec. 10 students. He always speaks in Memorial Hall, a cavernous red stone building at the edge of Harvard Yard, and I knew that he'd be there Sunday afternoon, rehearsing. So an hour after we left Christian Chung in his office, I went there—a police escort trailing discreetly behind me—to bring the walls down around him. The ancient gray stone gargoyles that ringed the building's tower scowled down on me as I vanished into the dim, dusty interior.

I found Ian behind the podium in deserted Sanders Theater, the ancient crescent-shaped auditorium at the rear of the building. The afternoon sun streamed through its stained glass windows, glinting off his silver hair. At the sound of my footsteps echoing down the center aisle, he slowly raised his head.

"Veronica," he pronounced slowly. "Somehow I knew I would be seeing you soon. Come to watch the denouement?" Christian Chung must have called him as soon as I left.

"Ian, I—" His voice had stopped me in my tracks at the foot of the stage, and I craned my neck to look up at him. I felt bereft and furious and the combination nearly choked me.

"Don't say you're sorry, Veronica." His voice echoed throughout the room. "Don't insult me."

It was crazy, but for just one moment, I really *was* sorry.

"There's something exhilarating about patricide, isn't there, Veronica?" His voice rolled down from on high. "The righteously indignant children overthrowing the old regime. You must feel quite omnipotent."

"And you, like Lear, must be royally pissed," I said sharply. I stepped back so that I could see him more clearly.

Ian snorted and moved from behind the podium. "When I think of all the things that I've done for you and your career," he said with disturbing equanimity, "it's disappointing to think how little regard you've shown me. You, a nothing. An absolute *nobody*. Searching my home. Stealing my money. That sophomoric note. After all I've done for you. I thought better of you, Veronica."

"You think I should have spoken to you before going to the police," I said flatly.

"I could have explained it, Veronica. I could have spared us the indignity."

"Or you could have had Christian run me down with your handyman's truck to shut me up for good."

Ian shook his head sorrowfully. "Veronica, I took you under my wing when you were a sophomore in college, up from some ghetto in Detroit, too timid to call me by my first name. I allowed you to take up hours of my time, discussing all of your silliest and most irrelevant theories. I arranged for you to return here after your foolish jaunt to Wall Street—against which I warned you in the first place. And this is my reward?"

"The one has nothing to do with the other, Ian. And you know it."

He looked down at me, refusing to speak. I thought I saw a flicker of sorrow in his eyes.

"I know you won't believe it," I said quietly. "I can hardly believe it myself. But I'm really sorry that it came to this. I remember every kind gesture you ever made to me. But what could I do? Did you expect me to look the other way when I discovered you committing murder? Is that what I signed on for?"

"If you are seeking absolution from me, you won't get it," he said flatly. "Betrayal is unforgivable, Veronica. You should be ashamed of yourself."

"Ashamed? You stand behind your towering lectern year after year, in a building that symbolizes the honor and integrity this university stands for, preaching at a roomful of students about the morality of capitalism. Then you steal enough money to build a million-dollar monument to your cleverness in Edgartown. And you kill anybody who gets in your way. And you say *I* should be ashamed?"

He glared down as I continued. "You called Ella three times to make sure that she'd be at the committee meeting that night. Then you sent her upstairs to your office, while you cut the fuses in Littauer to cause the blackout. You surprised her on the staircase, hit her over the head, and pushed her down the stairs in the darkness. Then hung around long enough to make sure she was dead."

"That's a lie!"

"It was the act of a coward. You didn't even have the balls to look her in the face when you killed her."

"That's enough," he commanded.

"Then you set about covering it all up. You sent Christian to mug me in Widener and steal Ella's disk. And you kept loading me down with work so I wouldn't have time to piece it all together until you could get the last bit of cash out of the country. You even got Kenneth Irvin to criticize my lecture style and threaten me. You'd utterly destroy me if that's what it took to cover your ass."

"Damn it, you've got no proof, other than your word and that lying little bastard Chung. And who's going to believe some nigger and her Chink boyfriend over me?"

I absorbed the shock of his words, and then a coldness settled over me. It really was over. "For an innocent man, you're very agitated," I said icily.

"You thought you could bring me down with your little tirade," Ian declared contemptuously. "Well, think again, Veronica."

"She may not be able to," came a voice from the back of the auditorium. "But I can."

I turned to find Victoria Barrett standing in the aisle behind me, smiling triumphantly up at Ian.

"Torie, what are you doing here?" he said slowly.

"I'm here for the denouement. Isn't that what you called it, darling?"

She sauntered down the aisle toward us, every bit the aging former debutante. She wore a wide-brimmed hat and a black Chanel suit; her left hand held a Kelly bag and a pair of black leather gloves. "You thought that I was helping you to incriminate Leo. Setting him up to look like the embezzler. What was it you said? 'We'll send him packing, and then Harvard will be back in the right hands?' Well, I hate to break it to you, lover, but you're the one who's going down. I've got all the details about your little crime. The printing press you used to create the invoices, the stolen Social Security numbers. I even have the passbooks for the bank accounts where you were storing the cash. And I'm going to sing like a canary."

I heard footsteps behind Victoria. Rafe and the other cops had started toward Ian.

"You meretricious bitch," he whispered in disbelief.

Victoria stopped in the aisle beside me and delivered the final shock as she put her arm around my shoulder. "Nice work, girlfriend."

The truth about Ian McAllister was fully revealed by two-thirty Sunday afternoon. The truth about Leo Barrett remained hidden for twenty minutes longer. Just time enough for me to take a cab home, where Maggie was anxiously waiting for me.

"Where have you been?" she cried. "I've been tryin' to reach you all day. Dante said to try your office, but the phone just rang and rang."

"Well, I'm here now. What's going on?" I laid my cane against the kitchen counter and gingerly sat down in one of the kitchen chairs.

"That package from New York finally showed up here early this morning. They had delivered it to Mrs. Freoli across the street by mistake. And my sister found somebody who knows the Rev. Stephen Barrett."

"And? Tell me what she said!" Maggie's face looked grave, and I felt as if I was going to jump out of my skin.

"Why don't you open that package first?" She gestured to a manila envelope on the kitchen table.

My fingers were trembling as I tore it open and pulled out a photocopy of Leo's article, "Why Negroes Should Support Bobby Kennedy." I looked at the bottom of the first page, where the contributor's note lay intact, and then looked up blindly at Maggie.

The note read *"Leonard Barrett is a Negro student studying political science at City College in New York City. He was born in Philadelpia."*

"It says he was a *Negro* student," I said dumbly. "But how can that be?"

"I asked Patrice to ask her folks at the beauty shop if they knew a Rev. Stephen Barrett. Leo Barrett's father. And it turned out one of her ladies used to know him. He died four years ago. He was the minister for over forty years at a church called St. *Timothy's* Episcopal, on Fitzwater Street. It's just a little church in South Philadelphia. A little black church."

She sat down heavily in her chair to finish the story. "The Rev. Stephen Barrett was a fair-skinned black man, very handsome and charming. Loved to tell jokes. His wife, Anna, who died almost fifteen years ago, was a fair-skinned black woman; she taught at an elementary school for almost thirty years. The worst day of their lives was the day they lost their youngest son, Leonard. He left home in 1965; he moved to New York and no one in Philadelpia ever heard from him again. About five years after he left, the folks in the congregation were told that Leonard had died up in New York; he'd been taken suddenly ill and had passed quickly. They all mourned him, because he had been so handsome, and so smart, and so ambitious. The apple of his father's eye. Everyone said Rev. Barrett was never the same afterward. So imagine their surprise when the three or four old folks who had known Leonard Barrett when he was a boy saw his picture on the front page of the *New York Times* last fall. He was being inaugurated as the new President of Harvard University. The new *white* President."

A DARKER SHADE OF CRIMSON

"I told you from the get-go that man was no good."

It was four o'clock Sunday afternoon, and Maggie, Rafe, and I were sitting at the kitchen table, soberly drinking tea and mulling over the events of the day. After Ian McAllister was led from Memorial Hall in handcuffs, Rafe had spent the next hour waiting at the Cambridge police station while Christian Chung cut a deal with the D.A. He claimed that he had discovered Ian's embezzlement during a routine audit, but had allowed McAllister to buy his silence. The whole thing seemed to have started soon after Ian was told by the Board of Overseers that he was unlikely to ever be named the Harvard President.

Maggie had just filled Rafe in on Leo Barrett's history. "I knew there was something wrong with him. Didn't I tell you that, right from the start?"

"Now, Magnolia, you don't know what the man was thinkin'," Rafe said quietly. "Things were different back then."

"I know *exactly* what things were like back then, and I know what he was thinking. He was thinking that this was his ticket to all the white girls and all the white privileges, and the hell with the rest of us, that's what."

"So when did he start passing?" I asked.

"As near as my sister's client can tell, he got the idea while he was in college. So when he turned up at Harvard Law School in 1969, it was as a white student. That's around the same time his family told everyone in Philadelphia that he had died."

"He must have broken his parents' hearts," I said softly. I knew my heart felt that way.

272 • PAMELA THOMAS-GRAHAM

"The boy was only twenty-two. Maybe it seemed like a good idea at the time, and then later he realized his mistake, but by then it had gone too far." Rafe seemed to feel more pity than anger.

"Why are you defending him?" I said impatiently. "He had the opportunity to show what a black person can do—how brilliant and talented one of us can be—and he abdicated it. He denied his very being, and he implicitly accepted the view that if he were black, he could never have made it that far."

"Don't be naive, child. He *wouldn't* have made it that far if folks had known he was black," Rafe said quietly. "Can you blame him for wanting to have all the opportunities that the white boys had? Are you so sure you wouldn't do the same thing if you had the chance?"

"Yes. And yes," I said adamantly. "I just can't believe he got away with it this long. Why didn't some journalist figure this out when he was named President?"

"Girl, look at how much it took for *us* to figure it out," Maggie interjected. "And we knew there was something to look for. He's so slick, how would some journalist know he had something to hide?"

"I'm amazed that one of those old folks in Philadelphia who recognized him didn't go to a tabloid," I said, sipping my tea. "That story would have been worth at least ten grand."

"Girl, we would *never* air our dirty laundry in front of white people that way," Maggie replied. "Those folks knew better than that."

"So what should we do?" I asked.

Maggie and Rafe exchanged glances.

"From what you've told us, it's clear that guilt is kicking his butt," Maggie pronounced. "So let's let him stew in it for a while, and see if he does the right thing."

"I bet the mon will come forward," Rafe responded quietly. "We should give him a little more time."

"I think he should resign if he has any remaining shred of integrity," Maggie declared. "What kind of message would he be sending to the black students if he didn't?"

The jangling of the phone interrupted us. It was Vivian Simms calling from Mass General Hospital. My throat tightened, but she quickly told me the good news: Justin was finally conscious, and he was asking for me.

When I arrived at the hospital, I was greeted by an incredible sight: Lindsey Wentworth was chattering with a nurse outside Justin's room.

"No, I always use an orange stick to push them back. You should never, never trim your cuticles. You're a nurse, Liz, you should know that!"

Lindsey turned to me, breathless and glowing. "Nikki! So you heard the news! Liz, you've *got* to let us in now—who'd want to be with his parents when there are *two* women outside waiting to fuss over him?"

"I'll check on it, Miss Wentworth," the nurse said, rolling her eyes in relief as she escaped into Justin's room.

"You must be surprised to see me here," Lindsey said, prattling on. "I was at the hospital because our butler, Gaston, slipped on the pavement this afternoon while he was bringing cocktails out to the terrace, and Daddy asked me to come with him and make sure he's all right." Her voice dropped a bit. "You know, he's really getting too old to continue on, but Daddy doesn't have the heart to let him go."

Who needed Social Security with such noblesse oblige running rampant amongst the gentry? "So how is he?" I asked dryly.

"Gaston? Oh, he'll be fine. He's staying overnight. And I figured that while I was here, I might as well stop in on Justin Simms, to see how he was doing. One can never have too many visitors when one is sick, can one? And can you believe it, he was just coming to when I stopped by? It was so exciting. But of course, his parents have been the only people to see him so far. What happened to your ankle?"

The nurse stuck her head out of Justin's room and beckoned to us.

"I'm giving you five minutes," she whispered. "And only two at a time."

As we entered, Mr. and Mrs. Simms were sitting beside Justin's bed, murmuring and laughing. It felt heartless to break them up, even for a few minutes, but Lindsey was already halfway across the room.

"Hey," I greeted them softly. "How is he?"

"He's awake. He's still pretty weak, but he's awake." Vivian Simms looked as if she might never let go of her son's hand.

"We won't take long," I said. She nodded, and the nurse ushered them out.

I leaned over Justin. "Hey, kiddo," I murmured. "Whatever happened to leaving the party with the one that brung you?"

He smiled and beckoned me closer.

"You owe me a date," he whispered.

"Mr. Simms, it's so unusual to see you with nothing to say," Lindsey said brightly. "Ella would never recognize you!"

Justin smiled weakly, and I could swear he rolled his eyes at me. "What have I missed?" he whispered, looking down at my ankle.

"A lot has happened while you were sleeping," I teased. "But you may not be ready to hear it yet."

"What, are you married?"

"Of course not!" Lindsey interjected. "But do tell us." She settled into the chair closest to Justin's head and looked up at me expectantly. "I haven't even heard what happened to your ankle."

Perched on the edge of his bed, I filled them in on the high points of my investigation, my mishap in Martha's Vineyard, Fisher's and Ian's arrests and Christian's plea bargain. About Leo Barrett I said nothing. I was too disheartened to discuss it with someone like Lindsey. But I admit to bragging a little. No one else on campus knew anything about my role in the investigation, and this audience was particularly appreciative. By the end of my story, Lindsey's mouth was hanging open, and Justin was wide awake.

"So you've been investigating Ella's murder all this time? And Ian McAllister is the murderer?" she repeated. "I know this sounds crazy, but you know he's in the Social Register!" About Isaiah Fisher, she was strangely silent. Apparently, their romance wouldn't transcend prison bars. "President Barrett will be so happy to have this resolved. I know it's really been worrying him. Maybe it will put all of those horrid rumors about him and Ella having an affair to rest."

"He'll have plenty of new worries shortly," I muttered before I could stop myself.

"What do you mean?" Lindsey's eyes were searching my face.

"Nothing." I shook my head. "Forget I said it."

The nurse came barreling through the door, her expression sober. "Girls, time's up. His heart rate is getting a bit too high, and we don't want to overtax him now."

Justin's face *did* look troubled. We were wearing him out. I shouldn't have told him so much about the investigation.

"Nikki—" He was struggling to speak.

"Shhh," I said gently. "You can tell me next time."

"Of course his heart rate is high! Mine is, too, after a story like that!" Lindsey exclaimed as she rose and stood beside me. "We'll go. But we'll come back and see you again soon. Okay?"

Justin still looked distressed as I kissed him good-bye.

"So, what are you up to tonight?" Lindsey turned to me in the corridor. "There's never much of anything to do Sunday nights. We usually have a late supper—wow." She paused. "Do you realize it's been exactly two weeks since Ella died?"

Two weeks.

Blame it on the excitement of the day, but I was halfway out of the hospital before I realized that I was missing a huge piece of the puzzle.

I was certain that Ian McAllister had killed Ella to keep her quiet about his embezzlement scheme.

But if that was true, then why on earth had he tried to kill Justin Simms?

Twenty minutes later, I was on the roof of the Science Center, looking out over the Yard. Legend had it that the building, donated by the creators of the Polaroid, was designed to capture the shape of a 1970s pop-up instant camera. When I was a freshman in college, a friend had taught me the secret route to get access to the roof of the building. Since then, whenever I want uninterrupted thought time, I escape to one of its seven recessed roof terraces.

By the time I arrived, dusk was just unfolding, the gaslights in the Yard beginning to glow in the soft ocher air. I could see groups of students walking by far below me, some stopping to sit near the misting fountain in front of the building. I laid my cane on the cement floor of the terrace and leaned against its waist-high balcony.

So why would Ian McAllister try to kill Justin? Not just once, at the Fogg party, but again at the hospital? I was positive that Justin hadn't known anything about the embezzlement before he slipped into the coma. I hadn't even suspected it until I realized that Ella's disk had been stolen, and that was on Monday evening, two days *after* Justin's collapse. And I'd never mentioned the discrepancy in the financials to him.

So if Ian had no motive to kill Justin, who did?

I thought back to the Fogg party. Justin had started acting strangely after about two hours. The last thing we had discussed was sapphires. Sapphires—which led me back to Torie Barrett. I never *had* figured out how her earring had turned up at Littauer that Sunday night. What if Justin had seen something at the party that linked her to Ella's murder? And then she had slipped him a tranquilizer to keep him quiet? Torie seemed like the type that would keep Zanax close at hand.

But why would she want to hurt Ella? Unless Dante had been right all along and she was trying to bring a violent end to Ella's love affair with Leo. In the hair salon, Torie had said that Leo had been having an affair, and that he had promised it would end. But given that Ella had been dead for a week at that point, her comment didn't make any sense.

Unless it wasn't Ella that Leo was having the affair with.

Amy Collins had said that her source for the *Crimson* article had told her that Leo was definitely having an affair, but that he was being very discreet. He must have incredible discipline, because in two weeks I hadn't seen him talk for more than two minutes with any woman other than Torie. Except Lindsey Wentworth, of course.

Lindsey Wentworth. Of course.

A series of images flashed through my mind: Leo with his arm around Lindsey's shoulders at his Open House. Lindsey arguing with Leo in the shadows of the Fogg Museum. Lindsey calmly suggesting that Victoria was terribly jealous of Ella and Leo's affair. Why hadn't I seen it before? It was *Lindsey* and Leo who were lovers, not Ella and Leo. Her dates with Isaiah Fisher must have been a complete ruse to distract everyone's attention.

"You know, don't you?" said a breathy voice.

Lindsey Wentworth stood at the doorway to the terrace. Her expression was dead cold, and it sent a chill straight through me. She closed the door quietly but firmly behind her, and I heard it lock. She was holding a gray object that glinted in the fading light as she walked toward me.

"I was sure that you would let this go once they arrested Ian McAllister," she said. "But you're so damned persistent!"

As she moved closer, I saw her hands close around the gray object. She seemed a little shaky. As she came toward me, I finally figured out what was going on.

She was holding a small revolver.

"Look, Lindsey, why don't we go somewhere and talk about this calmly," I said. This had to be an illusion. She couldn't possibly be pointing a gun at me.

"No, I think you should stay where you are. It's a little too late, now, for talking, don't you think?"

"I really don't understand what's going on," I said slowly.

"Nice try, Nikki."

I considered lunging at her, but thought better of it. I was in no hurry to die. Students were passing by in a steady stream below the terrace. But would they hear me if I screamed? And would I be dead before they could send help?

"What's this all about, Lindsey?" I asked, stalling for time.

She smiled icily and nodded. "Yes, you'd like me to think that you have no idea, wouldn't you?" She calmly crossed the terrace to the railing where I stood and kicked my cane across the floor.

"You killed her, didn't you?" I said slowly. My chest was tightening as the truth finally penetrated. Ian hadn't been lying. He *hadn't* murdered Ella.

Lindsey shrugged nonchalantly. "Yes. I had to, once she figured it out."

I shook my head, genuinely confused. "What are you talking about? You killed her because she knew you were sleeping with Leo?"

Lindsey laughed. "I thought you were so smart! But you're not getting it, are you? No, I had to kill her because she was threatening to *expose* Leo. She was planning to tell people that he was black."

"*What?*"

"Don't look so shocked. I know you finally figured out that he was passing. You've been sneaking around ever since Ella died, asking all these questions. I knew it was just a matter of time, and I could tell by the expression on your face when you said his name tonight that you finally knew. She figured it out, too. That's why she had to die."

This was absolute insanity, but I had to keep her talking to buy myself some time. "How did you know that Ella knew?"

"Because when I told her that Leo and I were having an affair, she said 'You don't know *what* you're sleeping with, child.'"

"And that's how you found out?"

"Of course, I didn't know what she was talking about at first. So I confronted Leo and he finally admitted it. He told me that no one but Ella knew he was passing. But since no one but he and Ella knew, why should I care? It didn't have to be true if we didn't want it to be true."

"And so you killed her."

"What else could I do? She gave me no choice. She would have publicly humiliated Leo and me. And made it impossible for me to marry him. I mean, it's not like I could marry a—"

I stopped looking at the revolver and stared straight at her. "A what? A black man?"

Lindsey raised her eyebrow. "Well, he wouldn't have been President once people found out."

"So Leo told you to kill her?"

"No, no, no. Leo started to get all stupid and sanctimonious. He started listening to Ella. Believing all her speeches about Martin Luther King and the content of our character and all that nonsense. He actually told me that he was thinking of confessing to the Board of Overseers and the press now that Ella was forcing him to deal with it. Can you imagine that? As if they'd ever accept a black President!"

She turned to me. "So you see, she gave me no choice. She was going to expose him! She had worked with him all those years and never figured it out. Then she goes on vacation over the Fourth of July to some black resort in the Catskills, and someone tells her something that gets her thinking. And she puts it together. So she comes back and gives him an ultimatum: either he goes public by the start of the fall semester, or she'll do it herself. 'He's an important role model,' she said. 'People need to know that a black man could have gotten to where he got to,' she said. She didn't care that it was going to ruin his career!"

"So you killed her. To save his career. You killed one black person and damn near killed another, you—" I started toward her.

"Stay right there." Lindsey pointed the gun squarely at my chest. "And don't even think about moving. It wasn't about something so superficial as *race*, Nikki. It was about love. I had to protect Leo. You can understand that."

We glared at each other for an eternity, and then I swallowed hard. I'd get this tiny little bitch if it was the last thing I did. But I had to stay cool. Lindsey sighed and brushed her hair back from her face. She was tired. Maybe if I could keep her talking, she'd drop her guard.

"Now the bastard wants to drop me," she muttered. "I did it all for him; his career would be ruined if it came out. He's worked so hard to make it this far, why should he be made to suffer because of other people's bigotry? But he thinks I was wrong."

"So he knows all about it?"

"Well, he didn't know until almost a week after it happened, because he wouldn't return my phone calls. He kept saying that he was going back to Torie, that we were over, but I knew he didn't mean it. I mean, she doesn't love him like I do."

"You told him about it at the President's Open House, didn't you?"

Lindsey laughed mirthlessly. "Yes. He just about died when I told him."

"So you planned it all out yourself. You knew Ella's schedule. You knew she'd be at the Crimson Future Committee meeting that Sunday night. So you waited in the lobby, milling around in the crowd, watched her go up the stairs, and then cut the fuse. Then you surprised her on the stairs in the darkness and pushed her down."

"I was very clever to do it at Littauer, wasn't I?" She was actually preening. "I had heard her talking about Ian McAllister and the Crimson Future Committee financial analysis for weeks. I figured if it happened there, they'd either think she fell, or that one of the committee members pushed her. Little did I know that Ian McAllister wanted her dead, anyway. And now he'll go to prison for her murder." She snorted derisively. "He deserves it, after the way he kept trying to take Leo's job."

"Funny. I figured you wouldn't stop until they arrested Victoria for the murder. I mean, you went to the trouble of stealing her earring and leaving it at the scene of the crime to try to frame her."

"So you *did* find it!" she said delightedly. "I was hoping that someone would, but I never heard anything more. I kept hinting to you that she was a likely suspect, but you were very dense about that."

"That's what Justin Simms saw at the Fogg party, wasn't it? You had access to her belongings, thanks to your affair with Leo. So you took two of her earrings, but realized later that if you planted one at the murder scene, you needed to have the other one found on her. So you were slipping it into her handbag when Justin saw you."

"Yes." Lindsey shook her hair back in exasperation. "That man is nothing but trouble! Twice I came so close to getting him out of the way—"

"Sleeping pills in the champagne, and pulling the plug at the hospital. You're nothing if not thorough."

"Well, yes. And once I'm done with you, I'll have to finish the job with him. Can't have him telling that earring story, can I?" She sounded almost happy now. Clearly, it was cathartic for her to be telling me this. But it was just as clear that she would never be doing it unless she intended to kill me.

I had to keep her talking.

"So what about your great romance with Isaiah Fisher?"

"I needed something to distract people from Leo. And I knew I could pin Ella's murder on Isaiah if worse came to worst. It was so easy to get people to believe he was unstable. I mean, even you believed that he was the most likely suspect, and you're black yourself."

I guess I deserved that. "I'm surprised that Alix Coyle didn't smoke you out."

Lindsey shrugged. "Like the rest of you, she'd written me off as some stupid little secretary. I knew she'd never figure it out. But you were a problem right from the start. I kept sending you off chasing Christian Chung and Isaiah Fisher and Ian McAllister and even Victoria, but you just kept coming back." She regarded the gun in her hand. "I should have killed you the night I got Justin Simms at that party. That was my only mistake."

"Lindsey, it's gone far enough," I said slowly. I swallowed to keep my voice from trembling, keeping my eyes away from the barrel of her gun. "Get your father to hire a good lawyer and then cop an insanity plea. You'll do a little time in a nice, peaceful, environment; afterward you can get on with your life."

"No, I don't think so," she said dreamily. "But it is over, Nikki. You're going to have a little accident. Or better yet, you're going to commit suicide. Because of your grief at having betrayed your mentor, Ian McAllister. You're going right over that ledge."

She smiled sweetly at me, and I realized that she really was crazy, with guilt and fear and perhaps with fascination at the power she had over other people's lives. I debated trying to list the fifteen reasons that her plan wouldn't work, but realized that it was going to sap what little energy I had left. Enough already. I had to get out of here.

"Rafe, thank God you're here," I said breathlessly. Lindsey turned to face the doorway and I lunged at her.

She screeched in surprise as we crashed to the floor of the terrace. I tried to pin her down and wrestle the gun away from her, but she was surprisingly strong. I scratched at her face and arms as we struggled, drawing blood on her forearm. A shot rang out as we rolled across the floor. The bullet struck the wall of the Science Center, but it seemed to renew her strength.

She broke out of my grip and tried to sit up, the pistol firing again as we wrestled for control.

"Bitch!" she screamed.

That was when I bit her arm.

Her grip on the gun loosened just enough for me to get my hand around hers, and I bent her thumb back as she struggled to point the barrel toward my head.

"Damn!" she shouted as the gun clattered to the floor. I kicked it away, then scrambled to reach my cane, which was lying just out of reach on the terrace floor.

As Lindsey lunged for me, I stood straight up and swung the cane with all the force I could muster.

It connected with her face as if it were a tennis ball, and the force of the blow hurled her across the terrace. She lay motionless as I stood over her, and I was gratified to see that her nose was bloodied and swollen. With any luck, I had broken it. That was the least Ella deserved. I turned away and leaned against the railing, feeling as though I was going to throw up. My ankle was aching and I leaned on my other foot to relieve the pressure.

That was my mistake.

With one savage motion, Lindsey grabbed the end of my cane and swung it straight at my good ankle. As I fell to the ground, she scrambled to retrieve her gun. Through a red haze of pain, I saw her hands lock around the grips.

She stood over me, laughing, drenched in sweat with blood streaming down her face. Her pistol was pointed straight at my head. "I hope you enjoyed your little game. Now get up."

I slowly got to my feet, leaning on the ledge for support, and she gave me a twisted grin.

"You're going over that ledge," she said. "Face first."

It seemed high time to get spiritual, so I took my eyes off of Lindsey's contorted face and looked down to pray. And that's when I saw salvation. There was a small square drain in the floor of the stone terrace. Our scuffle had kicked its iron grate cover aside, and there was now a hole about a foot across, of indeterminate depth, just behind Lindsey's left foot. If I could get her to back up a couple of steps, she'd go straight down.

"This is never going to work, you stupid little bimbo," I taunted evilly, shuffling slowly toward her. "You're too dumb to pull it off. How are you going to explain all this blood and those gun-shots?"

"Get up on the ledge," she snarled, instinctively stepping backward. "And stop looking over my shoulder. We both know there's nothing there."

She shrieked as she stepped squarely into the open drain and started to fall backward. I stayed low and hurled myself at her at full force. The pistol fired once before it flew out of her hand and came to rest a hundred feet away.

I pinned her to the ground beneath me, grinding her wrists into the stone terrace floor. Our eyes met for a long second, and then she began laughing hysterically.

By the time someone heard me calling for help and phoned the police, her laughter had changed to high-pitched sobs.

It was well past midnight by the time I finally got home, and I found myself gripping the knob tightly as I opened my apartment door, stroking the nubby texture of the sofa as I hobbled by on the way to the kitchen, practically caressing the glass as I poured Keynes and myself some milk. Yes, my fingers told me, I was still in this world. Yes, I was still alive. And Ella's murder was finally solved. I had left a message with Amy Collins, intrepid *Crimson* reporter, telling her I'd meet her for breakfast to give her the whole story. With her tips about Leo Barrett, she'd more than earned her exclusive.

A saxophone moaned somewhere in the night, and the lilt of it lured me to the front of my apartment. I opened the window and nestled into the window seat, letting the wailing sound wash over me, erasing Leo and Victoria and Isaiah. Erasing Ian and Christian and Alix and Lindsey. Erasing everything, finally, except the thought of Dante Rosario.

It wasn't going to work out between us. Again. That was clear from the fact that he hadn't spoken a word to me since he'd rescued me the night before. Not one word. Not that I was surprised; it was typical Dante. The game had taken a serious turn, so it had to stop. My respect for Ian was dead. And my affection for Leo was shattered. But somehow this felt like the greatest loss I had suffered all day.

The saxophone wailed on, speaking about yearning and desire. And slowly it dawned on me that the music was coming from Dante's apartment.

It wasn't Italian opera, and it wasn't hard rock. Therefore, it wasn't Dante music. Or Ted music. It was the sort of thing that I usually listened to.

Which meant that perhaps it was intended for me.

Bewitched, I crept slowly down the stairs.

And that was when I saw her.

The portrait of Francesca, the dream girl who had presided over Dante's mantel ever since I had known him, had been stuffed unceremoniously into a trash can outside their door.

I knocked softly, and then he was standing before me.

I know that there are certain rules in life that should always be obeyed, based as they are on centuries of accumulated human experience: Always pay parking tickets on time. Never borrow a friend's favorite sweater, no matter how good it looks on you. And never let a man know that you find him utterly irresistible, especially when he hasn't spoken one word about the future. Or made one mention of love.

But I was way beyond rules, and well past reason. Wordlessly, he beckoned. Silently, I acquiesced.

WHAT REMAINED

I sat in my office on a Monday evening in late October grading midterm exams as rain and stray autumn leaves lashed against my window. I sighed impatiently, thinking that it was work like this that had led to the unionization of most of the manufacturing industries in this country: mind-numbing, repetitive tasks that paid less than subsistence wages.

I jumped as I heard a noise outside in the hall, and then saw a slip of white paper pushed under my door. Wondering if I would live to regret it, I opened the note. There was no message, just a Library of Congress code for a book. I looked at the citation in my hand, then at the pile of unread blue books. No contest. I grabbed my backpack and headed for Widener Library.

The rain was slacking off as I climbed the steps, and I wondered what awaited me in the stacks this time. I found the location of the cite easily enough, and at the end of a row of fiction, I found the book: *100 Love Sonnets* by Pablo Neruda. A slip of white paper marked one of the pages. I quickly turned to it and read the first line of the poem that appeared there:

> *Amor, cuantos caminos hasta llegar a un beso;*
> Love, what a long way to arrive at a kiss.

The slip of paper contained a hand-written note.

> *Meet me at Algiers tonight. I'll be waiting at a table in the back.*
>
> —*Dante*

> P.S. *If you're really nice to me, I'll chase you around the stacks afterward.*

What a difference a month makes.

I stood at the top of the magisterial staircase leading down from Widener into the Yard, considering whether I would've raced headlong into investigating Ella Fisher's murder a month ago if I had known then what I knew now. Two weeks had passed since Lindsey Wentworth had confessed, and in the end, no part of Harvard had remained untouched by Ella's death. Lindsey was being held without bail in a jail in Cambridge, charged with first-degree murder, attempted murder, assault and battery. Having resigned his chair in the Economics Department, Ian McAllister had been charged with embezzlement and was awaiting trial with no bail set. Christian Chung would face no jail time, having plea-bargained his way down to a misdemeanor charge by turning state's evidence, but he had lost his job in the Treasurer's Office. Isaiah Fisher had copped a plea as well, and would serve two and a half years for blackmail. Leo Barrett had simultaneously announced his true racial background and his resignation as the President of Harvard at the New Century press conference two weeks ago. To my surprise, Victoria was by his side for the announcement, and rumor was that she intended to stand by him. Justin Simms was released from the hospital a week ago and has called me every day since. We went dancing last weekend, and I can vouch for the fact that he's as good as new. Alix Coyle is back on stage at the ART, talking tough and breaking hearts five nights a week and twice on Saturdays. Maggie and Rafe are an item now, even though they find it impossible to watch any talk show together without almost coming to blows, and Ted is trailing around after Jess, much to her delight.

I started down the library's broad stone stairs for the Yard, which was hushed and shimmering in the aftermath of the rain. Of course I would do it all again. What was a university for, if not to foster the discovery of the truth? And what more could I aspire to than to play a part in its discovery?

In the end, I was still optimistic.

After all, what remained at the bottom of Pandora's box, once all the evils of the world had escaped, was hope.

PAMELA THOMAS-GRAHAM is a Phi Beta Kappa graduate of Harvard-Radcliffe College, where she received a degree in Economics *magna cum laude* and was awarded the Captain Jonathan Fay prize—the highest annual award bestowed by Radcliffe—as the student "showing the greatest promise" in her graduating class. A graduate of Harvard Business School and Harvard Law School, Pamela was an editor of the *Harvard Law Review*. At age thirty-two, she became one of the most influential women in American business when she was named the first black woman partner at McKinsey & Company, the world's largest management consulting firm. A leader of the firm's Media and Entertainment Practice, she advises Fortune 500 companies on a wide variety of strategic issues. Pamela serves on the boards of directors of the New York City Opera, the American Red Cross of Greater New York, and Girls Incorporated (formerly the Girls Clubs of America). She has been profiled in several leading publications, including *Fortune* and *Ebony*, and was named to the prestigious "40 Under 40" list of fast-track executives in *Crain's New York Business*. Originally from Detroit, she divides her time between Manhattan and Westchester County with her husband, Lawrence Otis Graham, a writer and attorney. *A Darker Shade of Crimson* is her first novel, and marks the beginning of her Ivy League mystery series.